2

ANOTHER THINK COMING

Copyright © Todd Nelson 2005. All rights reserved.

The right of Todd Nelson to be identified as the Author of the Work has been asserted by him in accordance with the Copyright, Designs and Patents Act 1988

CONTENTS

1.	6
2.	8
3.	10
4.	19
5.	37
6.	40
7.	48
8.	51
9.	59
10.	66
11.	72
12.	74
13.	80
14.	85
15.	93
16.	97
17.	104
18.	108
19.	112
20.	115
21.	123
22.	127
23.	143
24.	145
25.	152
26.	156
27.	164
28.	167
29.	173
30.	180
31.	183
32.	187
33.	194
34.	196
35.	200
36.	204
37.	207
38.	210
39.	214
40.	217
41.	220
42.	222
43.	225
44.	235
45.	240
46.	252
47.	257
48.	259
49.	266
50.	273
51.	276
52.	278
53.	281
54.	292
55.	294
56.	300
57.	305

1.

My first recollection of a malevolent world was my junior school examination record. I was quite sure of my true position at the Top of the Class, yet the official examination results midway through Miss Nicholas's class in the first year showed me to be third. An injustice, if I say it myself, I accepted easily despite having to endure a new seating arrangement based on the exam results until the end of term. In the second year there was an improvement to second in a much publicised result. Then in the following year I was given official second again, this time to Iain Hedges to whom I finished three marks shy. Each stage of the marking process in that year had produced a publication of the league table to date. I had lead through four of five announcements, slipping to second at the last. After the event I was given my exam papers and in particular a set of five graphs for which I received 0 out of 5 in the final maths stage. For the life of me I could not see why they weren't right and I asked Miss Thomas for an explanation. All she could do was point to the fact that the graphs did not start at zero on the y-axis (she didn't explain it like this but I knew what she meant). I started the graphs at 10 or some such other unit that wasn't gone below. Miss Thomas was not one for accepting a reasoned argument and justice was not done. I had done enough for my first first but the record books would never show it.

In the fourth and final year of Junior School the end of term results produced a first. The exam results were not announced. Mr Cameron merely said that he was "pleased and surprised, very surprised, by Hector's exam results." He didn't rate me. I knew that I finished first because two independent and reliable sources Robin Beard and Robert Martin had looked into Mr Cameron's register left inadvertently open on his desk. They had looked because there was a desire to know by the class deprived of the usual end of term announcement. Under the heading Exam Position, there was a 1 by Hector Somes, 2 by Ronald Carson and 3 by Iain Hedges.

I hated not to be given the credit I knew I merited but that was all. Then it happened again at my next school and that's when I started to think of myself as someone who was in some way marked out to be different.

My first year of senior school satisfied the desire for the excitement of open competition beyond all expectations. Each subject, being given by a different Master produced its own set of results. Progress was keenly tracked between us all, even the no hopers, we craved the exam results as much as we craved to know the Top 10. A third in History, a fifth in Geography and a second in Maths were averaged into seconds or firsts overall in our hopeful minds. At the end of term the Form Master would put us all out of our misery by announcing the official "over-alls", the result that was written into the end of term report. I was third in the first year. It struck me then for the first time that I was capable of being not quite good enough in whatever company I found myself.

The second year followed the same formula and I hit form. Picking up plenty of firsts and seconds in all the proper subjects, I took a clean sweep in all the lesser ones, that is to say music, art and woodwork, which counted with the same weight to the over-all results. That year too the results weren't announced. Michael Morris asked why we weren't to be given our end of term positions and Mr Corrie, simply said that there weren't to be over-all results that year. An effort was made to find out the winner and I had won, but it was never official. Ringo Devlin received the Form Prize as usual.

I didn't think about it until I was much older really but I sort of sensed I wasn't everybody's cup of tea. It wasn't that I was unpopular. At the time I was one of those types that was in all the teams and I was always voted captain of the form and that sort of thing. If anything that seemed to put Mr Corrie off me a little bit more. Not that I was a creep either. But whereas there seemed to be something acceptable about being a gallant third it didn't seem to be right if I was Top. It wasn't that there was a coincidence in achieving my best results under people that didn't rate me either, it was more as if the world, if not malicious, was at least capricious towards me.

2.

There were other parts of my life like this that didn't leave me - that I can recall in the smallest detail. Unlike the junior school exam story which is best classified as an injustice, most of my memories like this were of personal errors and failings and bad decisions and embarrassing moments. A sort of living purgatory where I was forced to confront all the worst moments of my life until I was cured of them.

In truth I didn't really think about these things at the time they happened. But as I grew older I found that they more and more occupied my thoughts and I began to recall more and more previously forgotten episodes. In fact now that I've reached my mid-thirties they tend to dominate my conscious hours, they stop me from falling asleep at night, wake me up from comfortable, deep sleeps and take me off into reverie when my mind should be on other matters. In some ways too it's a progressive condition. For example, it is now perfectly normal to talk to myself and I am sure that it didn't used to be. I try not to get caught at it but it's got to be accepted that it's something I do. More worryingly these days is that I have begun to develop a physical reaction to my daydreams. Say for example I was dreaming away about something that had now come to embarrass me or maybe an episode I had just remembered and was re-running for the first time, I might end my daydream by crying out "Oh no!" in shame and put my hands up to protect my face. I shouted out like that the other day on the bus and I was forced to turn it into a song when it brought me into consciousness. It was a humming song since I didn't know anything with the lyrics "Oh no!" but I felt obliged to keep on going until I got to the "Oh no!" chorus again. I hadn't got away with it either because the girl opposite looked up when I first said it. I felt discovered but I knew that I would be able to talk myself out of it having been so obvious when I got home – all I needed to do was reconstruct the event enough times to make it support a version of what happened that I was comfortable with. That was difficult with the hand movements but I was well practised at deceiving myself.

It was worse when the shouting was accompanied by big arm movements, which came simultaneously with an "Oh no," if say I really couldn't face the ending of my daydream, an ending that has already happened. Worse still was stopping altogether in the street with my head in my hands. That hasn't happened too much yet but I've done it enough to know that I am going to have to get used to it. It's only a little malady and it feels like I am just as likely to stop it as continue, except that I seem to talk out loud and wave my hands about more than I ever used to.

I had spent a long time talking to myself. Starting as a teenager, there was me on the one hand and a panel of Oxford Admission tutors on the other. They would ask me a question about some routine element of my life and I would have to answer with the best academic sounding response I could come up with. One day they might have asked, "tell me Hector why do you put brown sauce on a meat and potato pie whilst you opt for red with your fish and chips?" whereas on another they would say,

"Hector, why do you take this route to school, surely it would be more direct to cut across the park than walk round it?"

I know now that I did this over and over for the smallest things and the desire to explain my every action has stayed with me. That is why I can be found on the street today shouting, "I didn't mean it, I didn't mean it, I didn't mean it," over and over. When you learn to explain everything at an early age, it makes you weak. And when you're weak you do things that make you ashamed. I didn't know it then but I do now that the roads of Hell are circular and incidents like the one on the bus would become my new nightmares that I would have to re-run countless times.

3.

It was Saturday morning in early November and I woke up alone in my Islington flat, well apartment, not quite loft but not far off. It was 9.30 and later than I had hoped, not to worry I could cut out the trip to the Magic Shop. I would also swap strolling up to the Italian Deli to buy an ad hoc breakfast and instead I would have my breakfast out. Just as well because I was useless at going to the Deli and coming back with an interesting collection of things to eat and drink. I was more likely to buy some warm or sour or thick or otherwise unpalatable milk, hard bread, olives, yoghurt, Parma ham, eggs, salami, Italian sausages sort of mixing up the themes of about four recognised national breakfasts without actually managing to buy enough for one complete one. "I won't do that but I like Italian Cooking," I said to myself as I walked round the flat preparing to get ready. I said Italian as "eye-talian," and I said cooking as "cooooh – king," as my father would. I said it over and over, getting faster, working out of the initial rap style into something closer to a camp version of Russell Harty. In the end I found myself saying it intently to my own image close up in the bathroom mirror with very exaggerated lip movements. I probably did this for about five full minutes until in the end I looked at myself in silence in the mirror. Eventually I said "you cunt," shook my head and turned back to the bedroom.

I laid back on the bed. Getting up was always an ordeal for me. Sometimes I had to toss off before getting up even though I wasn't really in the mood. This could put getting up off by two or three hours on bad days. No real desire to wank, no strong sexual urge but nevertheless a wanting that stopped me doing anything else until it was satisfied. Just a perfunctory evacuation like a good trip to the toilet or a well timed squeeze of a pussy spot.

I went to work on the project but with no real success. I was drifting in and out of sleep and I couldn't really hold a good image in my head. And as much as I tried for something else the only consistent image I could get was of my grandmother. Even I drew the line at that. I wasn't averse to taking on her friends every now and again but me own flesh and blood?

And while I strove for a good image and I was falling in and out of sleep I also started to ponder the greater burden of just getting up. The key to my inertia as always was that I didn't know what to wear. If there were a set of clothes ready for me to put on I knew I could just bounce out of bed in the morning. When there wasn't (always) I would lie there not knowing whether I would be going for the intermediate, i.e. going out to the Deli shop first outfit, then changing after a leisurely breakfast with the Racing Post, or whether I would go for the day time outfit. If the latter, as it was probably going to be, it would mean showering and preparing and maybe ironing and well, that created an inertia that I couldn't overcome. Particularly showering, which involved getting totally wet, much more thoroughly and comprehensively wet than a bath, although a bath was no better as an idea being too much palaver altogether. I'd been put off the idea of the thorough, stand-up, wash having met a woman in a Camden laundrette one day in summer many years ago who'd just had one. She described it as a strip-wash which she had taken on account of the extreme heat. Ever since I'd never been able to disassociate the stand-up wash from rancid urban squalor. I went to work on weaving her into the wank but the woman had become such an icon of filth for me in the intervening years that it was a non-starter.

After a while I was making a little bit of progress with Aunty Frances when I heard the front door slam. There was no-one it could have been mid Saturday morning, "Jesus," I wished, "please don't let it be Caroline home a week early to ruin my liberty," then, considering my vulnerable position I started to panic a little bit.

"Who is it? Who's there?" I was shouting, trying to sound all authoritative.

"Alright Mush keep yer hair on,"

I was relieved to see the diminutive form of Irene silhouetted in the door frame, not that I was too pleased with what it was doing to uphold our master and servant relationship. Besides I was convinced that the maternal instinct in women meant that they knew when you were mid-wank. I was never very sure whether that extended as far as having a special sense of knowing that they had been the subject of a recent wank but I'd decided to be flagrant with Irene's sensibilities as soon as she'd left me alone.

"What's the matter with you, shit the bed or something?"

"Jesus Irene I thought I was going to be attacked in my bed," it was an open enough remark to let her respond positively. I wouldn't have refused a blow job from her gnarled little fifty year old body, it was an improvement on what I was about to do to Aunty Frances.

'A big lad like you, you could look after yourself."

"Was that a positive response?" I wasn't sure. "What if I just said, "get in here you dirty little gypsy?"

"What's that?" She said.

I didn't think I'd said anything so I said, "it's probably time to be up," it was only when she said, "have it your way, I'll be back in here in fifteen minutes anyhow," that I thought perhaps I'd blown it all on my own, with no help from her.

"I'll put the kettle on Mush," she shouted from the hall.

"Bollocks," I sighed as I laid back in the bed. I'd never been able to think of Irene as a sex object before and I couldn't help wondering. I told myself that she had upset my plans because I was about to get up and get showered but now I couldn't because it meant wandering around semi-naked in front of her. So perhaps I would skip the washing part and deal with that later. Yes that was right, a cursory brush of teeth and a swill (that was a family term), then proceed to dressing. But that only put on hold a bigger problem. On a day like that, a fresh, Autumn, metropolitan day I could have dressed accordingly, jeans and sweater or cotton shirt and chinos even a tweed or corduroy suit, all of them being appropriate to season and weather, giving me the option to have lunch, breakfast or whatever wherever I wanted, with a further option to go to the races and not to be out of place if I stayed out for the evening without coming home in between. My outside clothes were particularly carefully selected and each of them individually was expensively acquired but despite that I never quite had the right coat to go with the right outfit. If the style was ever right the colour would never be. That meant that I often ended up wearing an ensemble that was basically off white throughout, or when I had the wherewithal to buy something contrasting for a change I could equally easily end up in all red. I always inadvertently drew attention to myself like that.

Eventually I just got up. That is to say that I rolled over slowly and allowed one of my feet to touch the rough wooden planks of the bedroom floor. Once there I accepted the inevitable and came to assume a sitting position. I held my head in my hands for a few moments and then said, "Oh Jesus," really slowly, which for me was habitude, a sort of reverse praise for still being alive.

I was making my mind up and putting clothes on and off I started chanting, "outerwear, innerwear, underwear." In the end I stopped doing anything else so that I could just chant. I had a scarf stretched tight above my head held in each hand and I was swaying to and fro chanting the underwear song as a terraces song to the tune of "Here we go."

I had just about decided to wear a suit, although that meant risking getting it wet, or wear a coat and getting myself too hot, or a raincoat, that should have been to the dry cleaners, and although charming in its way just looked plain scruffy against a suit; or a sort of half length Mac-style jacket ideal for Autumn days, warm, waterproof and mushroom coloured. The only problem was that where that jacket was sort of young-middle aged cool the rest of the outfit as planned was young fogey. Then I became enraged. I had a stupid round, fat, young, hairless, red face and in classic clothes I was as close as you could be to Billy Bunter. I really craved the taste, mannerisms and figure for cool expensive clothes. I went through a couple of options as I worked myself out of the Master Bunter look and in doing so I left some expensive and hardly worn items in crumpled heaps on the floor as I flung them off in fury. I didn't quite work the appearance up into something I liked, just a little better than it had been with the first effort. Whilst not chic I managed to reach the stage where I didn't need to take a hamper as an accessory. But when it came to it all I'd managed to do was mix up two styles in one, part Little Lord Fauntleroy, part some twat from a Marks & Spencer advert. I started to fling the clothes on the floor again but before I'd got very far I was overwhelmed by the need to crap. Not an usual occurrence for me. The problem was I couldn't. Not in the flat with Irene in it. It was something to do with inflicting the noise of ablutions on her and something to do with the after effects she'd have to suffer when she went to clean the bathroom and a lot to do with my morbid fear of anyone else sharing that level of intimacy with me. But whatever it was I knew from previous patterns that I had very little time to spare and that I had to do it somewhere elsewhere.

As I re-dressed I knew that elsewhere would have to be the bookies. I'd sworn myself to abstinence but they were the only places I knew that served as a reasonably public toilet facility, anywhere else you were too easily homed in on as a customer and I didn't like to have to say, "I'm not buying thanks I'm just here for a pooh," especially at the speed at which I would have to enter the establishment, and particularly so in the outfit I found myself leaving in, worse in every way and twenty times more incongruous than any of the previous incantations.

I knew that from the first warning signal I had about three minutes dead before I shat my pants. Despite knowing this I didn't have it in me to turn round and go home or go into the first shop I saw. I had to hope that the bookmakers had something reasonable. The shop I was going to was well known to me, the sort of bookies you find occasionally in the middle of London that has a slightly clubbish feeling. That was encouraging.

I immediately regretted the choice of suede shoes. I'd first chosen them because they were expensive, not that anyone would know by looking at them. If I had the gift of insouciant style the suede shoes would have looked brilliant and expensive and I need only have worn jeans or similar to set them off. Instead, mixing up the casual, metropolitan-country look I managed instead to make myself feel like a physics teacher. But worse, because as soon as I left the flat I stood in a sort of milky, cement, puddle.

Fortunately for me I lived in the Brighter Borough of Islington so it could have been worse. Within fifteen feet of where I stood I saw a pile of bin bags, maybe about twenty-five, that looked as if they had been left for ever, I was overcome by the stench of sewage in the site cleared for building between my apartment block and the main road, I saw the contents of an old office clearance that lay where they'd been left about six months ago, general detritus was liberally strewn about the street before me and the abandoned car that had been left half on the street, half on the pavement three weeks ago was still there.

There was an alarm ringing which I suddenly tuned into and in doing so I noticed that I'd been living with it since I woke up. I nearly started crying but unhappiness and despair overtook me. It was hot and I hated all the woollen wintry get up I'd put on. Why I couldn't be one of those people with a classic, casual wardrobe? I was angry, frustrated, hot and uncomfortable and dying for a shit and it was a feeling I knew very well.

It was a much better way to face the tramps that lived at the bottom of Exmouth Market. I walked past the tramps once or twice a week. They sat on the public benches in the little pavemented triangle where Rosebery Avenue meets Farringdon Road. They were proper, classic drunk tramps, preferring cider, sherry and strong larger. I recognised a hard-core of flattened faces of a gang that was never less than six and could be up to about fifteen on Saturday afternoons. I was thinking about them as I approached knowing that for the most part they were benign drunks but that they could be aggressive and frightening. As I started to turn into the bend of Exmouth Market the tramps came into sight, about eight of them, three sitting and five standing around one bench. There clearly wasn't much doing as the only activity was one tramp doing that tip-toey vaudeville dance that only tramps do. I was practised at noting where they were sitting, plotting a course to avoid them, keeping my head down til they were behind me and avoiding eye contact at any stage. Somehow though today they locked onto me. It was as if it was because it was the last thing I wanted to deal with I felt that I had sort of drawn them towards me. A savage, ginger, Scottish tramp wheeled towards me. Looking at me sideways from below chin height, he pointed his finger and looked along his arm towards it, then up to my face. "Ma mate wants to fight ye, ye wee poof." Normally that would have made me at least frightened, not to say thrown me into a panic. Today I had fallen into a poor mood and didn't care about anything, so I said, "Fuck off you cunt," as close to the Scottish tramp's face as I could. I carried on walking without looking back.

Then a feeling of comfort came over me, I was relaxed and felt as if I could walk at a normal speed and arrive there in plenty of time. Experience had taught me that these moments of relative comfort were false dawns. I knew that the feeling of desperation would be back soon and when it did I would be a stage further advanced in my predicament. Despite knowing all this I still couldn't stop myself from going into the newsagents looking for a Racing Post. I looked for a long time before eventually giving up and asking.

"Last one just sold," the shopkeeper said. I was tired of getting this response from places like this for any non-mainstream request.

"When?"

"When Sir? When is what?"

"When did you sell your last copy?"

"Last copy Sir?"

"When did you sell your last copy of the Racing Post?"

"Don't know. Hard to be exact Sir, not long."

"How many did you have in total at the beginning of the day?"

"Oh many."

"You mean not many, I think," I said turning to go, putting back the two other dailies that were going to be part of the order.

"It's not my fault if the wholesalers don't send more. Innit?" he shouted at my back.

I vowed not to go back to a useless shop like that again. In fact I vowed that the last time I was there about four weeks ago but I had got it mixed up with the one over the road. The tramps and the shitting had upset my equilibrium. But I wouldn't go back, except to buy cheap pornography out of a lack of respect.

Then I got another reminder. At this point I tightened up below. My stride shortened and I quickened up a little bit for the first time. The bookies wasn't in sight and I started to think that I had passed it and not noticed. No pubs were open and I was so desperate then I considered running back home. I convinced myself it was ahead so I kept going but when I crossed the next road I became truly desperate. I drew my breath in and held it, I tightened my buttocks as tight as they'd go, I started to walk in very short fast strides, and I began to talk to myself in a rushed stage whisper. "Keep going son, keep going son, keep on going." I said that as a three line verse over and over. "Please don't let me see anyone I know," I wished. "Please God I will do anything, do not let me see a friendly face now, please no, no friends, please no."

Then I promised God I would do anything for him if he got me out of my scrape. It came outside the Pie & Mash shop just as I clapped eyes on the bookmakers sign. It was about 300 yards further and even then I couldn't be sure whether it was an old Mecca Bookmakers sign that hadn't been changed for years or whether it wasn't the bookies I thought at all. As I walked towards it I became more certain but every now and again I doubted my judgment. I was hot, sweating in fact, but every so often a cold shiver swept through my body. Within 100 yards of salvation I received the final warning. It was that point where the sphincter was officially breached but it hadn't come out from the buttocks. At this point all that was left to do was to try to pull off the finest of balancing acts between letting go with the last wall of resistance and finishing the journey with the least most delay. I hobbled and minced faster than I'd ever done before and by sheer force of will I arrived at the door of the bookies intact and unsoiled. It wasn't over yet and I still had to negotiate the step in and find the bog once in there. The step alone was bound to make me fill my pants, there was no way of stepping up without parting my buttocks sufficiently to breech that last, fragile barrier. In the end I opted for hopping up keeping my legs and feet parallel as a skier might so that the same muscle tension could be maintained. It meant that I took on a forty-five degree angle while executing the jump and the man who was standing in front of me coming out as I landed on the way in looked at me like he pitied me for whatever it was I was suffering from. Normally this would have bothered me but not today, there was but one goal.

I was sweating heavily. Once in I didn't see it straight away and panicked again but I forced myself to concentrate rather than run round in desperate circles. Then I fixed on it, the internationally recognisable sign for a male toilet. I made for it and made one final wish that it wouldn't be occupied. In that bookies it could easily have been occupied by a builder who was carving up half gramme cocaine deals to sell later, a tramp who had made it his home, a couple of Islington professionals having sex. I hated all divergent types at that moment. I was there, I could nearly relax, not quite, I turned the handle. Locked. I looked down and saw that it needed a key, which they often did. My heart quickened again. I would have shit myself if only I could. It meant good news and bad. On the one hand the toilet was likely to be clean, intact, dry and equipped with paper on the other it meant going and asking the cashier for the key and that normally would have been devastating, it was like saying "I am going for a shit and I wanted you to be the first to know." Then though, at that moment, it couldn't embarrass me.

"Can I have the key please?"

What key?

"The key to the fucking toilet."

"OK, OK, it's supposed to be for clients you know."

"I'll be a client soon just get on with it please."

"Have you seen the key Eric?"

"No it's usually over there."

"I'm sorry I don't know where it is."

"Please can you look it must be close by?"

It was close by for me. I was already in the fifth minute of injury time.

The cashier shuffled around for a moment brushing his floppy mop of student hair back with his right hand while he half heartedly picked up miscellaneous piles of paper with his other. He shrugged as if to say "search me."

"What would you do if you wanted to go to the toilet?" I said.

The cashier looked puzzled. In the end he said; "I'd just go."

"No what I mean is .."

"It's here," said the manager tossing it to the cashier.

He dropped it. The fucking, feckless, good for nothing, cunt dropped it. He scratched his head as if to say "how am I going to find it now," then consented to bend down slowly, keeping his hair from falling into his eyes with his right arm. He took an age to descend and rise again but eventually he gave me the key and I went away listing heavily to the left, walking on my heels at top speed.

I turned the key in the lock, stepped in and locked the door and by doing that a certain safe haven had been reached. I pulled apart the button up fly and lost a button in the process, took off my pants and underpants in one movement while still keeping my knees locked and buttocks clenched then threw myself backwards onto the seat.

A quick exit would only have brought more unwanted attention so I sat for a moment. I drew breath and let the sweat dry. And I shouldn't have done really because the first thing I did was notice my new smell, a cheesy, stale smell of poverty that I would carry round with me for the rest of the day. And then I moved on to my predicament, "a grown man soiling his pants," I thought, the sort of thing that babies do, that I would have been ashamed to do from the age of four onwards and now it was part of my life and I accepted it. What a fall from grace, what a reduction from what I was supposed to be. I thought of my contemporaries, with proper lives and proper jobs who would have been having proper weekends. They had families and leisure pursuits and an infrastructure in their lives. Me, I was so loose I could be blown away on a strong wind. I knew where I was going with these thoughts because I'd been there so often before but nothing could stop me. The next stage was to analyse all the steps that lead me to where I was. Each considered on its own with twenty-twenty hindsight. I had heard that you could control these thoughts and unwanted recollections just by chanting "no, no, no," to forbid yourself to continue and to start the braking process of the enormous juggernaut of the depression. I knew that doing that could work and I can't say whether I really tried or not. In truth I couldn't resist the compulsion to punish myself again. I went cold as I went deeper into my own personal history as if I was hearing the sad tale for the first time and realising only now that I had fucked up. Like I'd just received my exam results for a failed life through the post.

It was a familiar journey and took me through all the old highways and byways and backwaters and disused stations. Bad choices at school, wasted time at university, failure to get off the mark and get a proper job, failure to catch up since realisation dawned, bad advice, bad decisions, the light but disastrous touch of my father, the claustrophobia of my upbringing and the limited horizons of my youth. All lined up like old friends to check off in the list of missed opportunities and wrong turns.

As I reached the final stages of my re-read odyssey, I would stop and think about what I called collateral damage. Being happily and securely employed from my early twenties meant that I would have been relatively prosperous from then rather than scratch around like a student until my early thirties. With the wisdom of age and despair I knew that it didn't really matter what I did, at the age of 35 I'd be an experienced and established whatever it was. Instead I was stuck. I could have taken holidays, I could have had a richer social life, I'd have done things. I could have afforded to have had a life and I would have worked alongside people who would have provided the stimulation and inspiration to have had a life. But me, on my own, I had committed the only sin that's worth talking about. The only commandment. I had wasted my life.

I reached the end and I was saying "Oh God please," out loud and put my hands over my head as if to protect myself from an attack. I had stopped breathing properly. I had to be normal. I had to make myself normal. I had to get up and go forward. I was nearly through but not quite, I still had to reprimanded myself that in my late twenties all I did was reflect on my past failures instead of making something of the time I had left. I knew at the time that I would come to regret my lack of action and acceptance of depression later in life. And here I was still doing it even though I knew that one day my mid-thirties would seem young. No lessons learned.

On certain terms I was considered a success and I decided to make a determined effort to concentrate on those things to get myself up and going again. At the age of thirty-five I had made more money than most people of my age, although not an excessive amount and the awful truth I had to face was that I had to make my current deal work or else find something new equally well paid. I often wondered whether the money I had made could be seen as the reward for the time lost but I never managed to convince myself.

"Oh please stop," I said, I'm sure it was under my breath but I was never sure. People had looked at me like I was weird a long time before I knew I talked out loud. "Get up and get going, there are opportunities round the corner," I told myself. I believed it too.

I emerged from the toilet. And there was business to do.

"I've done me business and there's business to do," I sang to myself as an olden day ballad. I continued the extempory lyrics until I became embarrassed by the song descending into simplicity to achieve a contrived rhyme. I thought it was the sort of song that certain arseholes in the office would find hilarious for its comic inventiveness. I imagined singing it openly, absolutely earnestly in a loud voice in the office on Monday morning and started laughing to myself. I couldn't help breaking out into a large smile, half a laugh.

"You enjoy that?" said the Manager holding his hand out for the key. He had come out from behind his plastic partition. I felt embarrassed and couldn't think of anything to say that reflected the light-hearted, mickey-taking banter of the Manager.

"Just relieved," I said. But the Manager didn't laugh. He just carried on with pinning up pages of the Racing Post.

4.

It was a great day for the national hunt enthusiast. An unusually rich fayre of high grade jumping racing when proper jumping horses were finally on the go and there was high quality racing giving proper clues for Cheltenham and the other big races later in the year. Better than we'd been used to. I found myself in a usual dilemma: I had too much choice and I didn't know what to do.

I had a real pang to be what I called a proper person, with an easy routine to fall into. If I'd achieved as I should in life I would have been playing golf with international businessmen not hanging around betting shop toilets in Islington. "I should go to Sandown," I decided, better still, I would buy myself a small radio on the way so that I didn't miss out on anything else. Yes that was it. Clear, committed, decisive.

"What's that son?" the Manager said passing me on his way back behind the counter. I realised that I was stood still in the middle of the shop in a world of my own. I'd probably said something out loud.

"Err nothing, just thinking out loud." The manager looked at me like he didn't exactly trust me. He gave me a sort of "I've got my eye on you look."

I went over to where the Sandown form was pinned up and deposited myself and my belongings on the low plastic stool and thin counter. I felt like a bagman. I hated taking up a position like that in a betting shop, because I knew what I thought of other people who did that. Losers. As far as I was concerned they were a fucking nuisance, people that were always in the way of the form when you needed to read it.

"Before you go anywhere Hector old son, work out the logistics," I said to myself.

I decided it would take about twenty minutes to get to Waterloo, anywhere between immediately and a thirty minute wait for a train to Sandown and a thirty minute train journey after that. Then there was the small matter of crossing the course from the railway station which was not to be underestimated. I thought I should gamble on a total journey time of one hour forty minutes minimum. It was 11.15 a.m.. I looked at the card and saw that the first race was off at 12.40. It could easily have been 1.15 as I'd sort of assumed but it wasn't.

"No chance, you disorganised twat," I said. That was Plan A down the toilet.

Plan B was staying in the bookies and watching the racing.

I'd already had a football bet worked out. I'd done it the night before in the bath. Five homes, £200 accumulator, higher stakes if I was up approaching 3 o'clock. I felt very confident about the bet, it had a winning look about it. Although I was nothing of a football fan gambling on football appealed to me, much more than my stated first love of horse racing. I loved the fact that there were only three outcomes, win, lose or draw, an unconsidered outsider from the front three in the betting could not happen. I loved the feeling of certainty and I loved the fact that there were about fifty matches every weekend and that it was possible to feel pretty confident about predicting the results of five to ten of them. I loved the fact that five correct results ran up into big accumulators.

There was horse racing before that and I hadn't done my homework on that last night. Reading the form was an unsatisfactory experience. I tended to dip in and out of the all the different meetings and never really got to the bottom of any race. It was in truth too early in the season for me to know the form with any authority. I berated myself for not taking a closer interest before now. I had to acknowledge that I was no more than a dilettante horse racing punter and that I couldn't justify betting with my knowledge of the form as it was. I knew that I was only interested in betting because it had reached the time of the year when I wanted to take up an interest in jumping racing and that I wouldn't take any notice of it unless I "was on". I wandered around the shop from card to card, trying to pull my ideas together. I had been in there nearly an hour without having a bet and it felt like I was being scrutinised by the staff. I was sure I overheard one say to the other "what's that weird cunt doing now?" But I stuck to my guns and eventually I created a shortlist of betting opportunities.

The list read like this: Bindaree, 12.30 Chepstow, novice hurdle over a distance in soft ground, six runners, all of the opposition looked poor, forecast at evens. That was a knocking bet, a gimme; Country Store or Edmond, 1.00 Chepstow, a five runner steeplechase and although it was a handicap only Edmond or Country Store could win, forecast at 6/4 and 2/1, a decision between the two was deferred; Lord York, 1.15 Sandown, in a three runner novice chase. Three runner races were often not to be bet on but it was really between two of the three and the favourite, Skycab, looked like a dog. 2/1 was a good price to beat one horse with an attitude problem; Breeze Girl, 1.45 Sandown, a six runner three year old novice hurdle, at 6/4 she had good consistent form in the book and those that had run looked poor, I was frightened of the unraceds because they may be good horses waiting for a better race to make their debuts, but I trusted Martin Pipe to have the right horse to win it, especially one with a lot of experience.

That was half, or nearly half the work done pending the Edmond, Country Store decision, next I had to structure a bet out of it. I had long since learned of the stupidity of expecting too much from a multiple bet and I knew not to go shit or bust on a five timer. That said I was into betting to win decent amounts of money and I wasn't interested in winning a few hundred quid by betting them all one at a time, level stakes. Also there was a certain confluence in terms of time of the first four which lent themselves to a bet. I thought I could set off a decent accumulator and if it went wrong still have the opportunity to get it going again. I looked again at the Edmond/Country Store dilemma and suddenly saw the situation clearly, that Country

Store was a 10 year old, going nowhere, made to look good in the early season by Martin Pipe and that Edmond was a proper horse in the making. It was clear.

It was nearly time for the off, they were coming into line at Chepstow, I hadn't even started to write a bet out. Suddenly, having been in the betting shop for about an hour and half I had to rush into a decision. I started to write out a bet on a slip near to hand then after writing Edmond I realised that I was using one of those slips with writing underneath which some fucking dosser had leaned on when writing his own bet out. I said "Oh fucking hell why is everyone so fucking useless?" out loud, screwed up the slip and looked around for others. They were just about off. I ran over to a betting slip holder and reached over the shoulder of a fellow punter who was working out how to turn the handle to produce a single slip. You didn't do that, instead you just grabbed the first half a dozen or so from the open top of the dispenser, although you didn't lean on the waste slips when you wrote your bet out, you put them to one side. I had annoyed the man I barged in front of but I felt sufficiently at ease with my knowledge of betting shop etiquette to tut at the novice.

They were off. I wrote all four names as quickly as possible and wrote "£150 acc" on the bottom, I hadn't timed any of the selections and the names I wrote were barely legible. They were about to jump the first flight as my slip went face down in front of the cashier. I did this just as another punter was picking up his change and moving away. I knew that they were entitled to refuse the bet but would normally take it up to about that point. The trick was to act like you'd been queuing a little while, that was why placing it face down was important, you would only place it face up or worse still, thrust it into the hand of the cashier if you knew that you were late with the bet. Acting like it was normal would have allowed me to invoke righteous indignation at "being here for ages." It was accepted, albeit with an audible intake of breath and a little double take at the hieroglyphics. I handed over the money and it was on.

"I didn't have time to time all the races."

"It'll be alright."

"Can you read them OK?" I didn't want an argument afterwards about unclear instructions and was pleased that I'd remembered to address the issue straight away.

"Yep, yep," said the cashier nodding.

"Do you want to say what they are?" I said, realising that I had to take him to the point.

"Err Bindaree, Elfland, Lord York, Breeze Block."

"No it's Edmond and Breeze Girl."

"That's only two."

"What's wrong with you two fannies?" said a new voice behind me.

The Manager noticed and came down from his settler's rostrum all pissed off to take the other bets. I hated the cashier, because he was thick and took far too long to do something simple. He had also turned the other punter aggressive towards me and he had made the Manager hate me even more. He was still looking at the slip unaware of being a pain in the arse to anybody.

"Give me the slip," I said, poking my hand between the bottom of the partition and the counter.

"Why don't you give us the slip?" said the Manager, sharing a joke with his new friend he was serving.

I felt embarrassed but I decided to stick with the point I was making.

"That says Bindaree, that says Edmond, that says Lord York and that says Breeze Girl," I said.

"Do us all a favour mate and write the time's on the slip," said the Manager in a world weary way.

That was what I had wanted to do from the beginning but I thought it would cause too much difficulty to ask because the top slip was separated when the bet was put on.

"Yes that's what I..... but I ...." I realised half way through that the Manager meant that I should write the times on to my copy, which wasn't exactly right but at least it represented my record of what I thought I had bet, ".....oh right on my copy yes, yes I will. Thanks."

I wanted to say that I had been in hundreds of bookmakers, I wanted to tell him how much I had lost over the years, I wanted to let him know that I was at least semi-pro, at least in my betting comportment. I felt ashamed that I had given the Manager the impression I was a rank amateur, novice gambler. I thought that in other circumstances the Manager would really take to me, find me interesting and informed. I hated the injustice of situations like that. I wanted to tell him. Meanwhile Bindaree was winning by a large margin, "*Pissing-up* is the expression," I told myself. I was immediately in a better mood.

I thought about going for a pint between races but there wasn't a real half hour, racing half hours were really only twenty minutes. I passed the time by having a couple of dog forecasts, always 4 and 3 reversed, or if it had won twice 1&2, then 3&2, then 1&5, then 5&6: it never got that far but I was prepared.

I knew the bet wouldn't win. The reason being, it had received too much publicity. I knew that bets like that, that become the centre of attention like mine had done have no chance. I knew that the smallest element of good luck was paid for by the tiniest element of bad luck. I knew the balance of fate. I thought for a moment that because I felt humiliated in public by the Manager that would bless the bet but I knew in my heart of hearts that I had ill intent towards the cashier and I had let my bad temper show. That on its own would equal out the Manager's nastiness towards me and I hadn't built up enough other minus points to make my bet a winner.

Before I knew it, it was one o'clock and time for Edmond. Three miles in soft going at Chepstow takes somewhere between half an hour and a week to run. Edmond looked a class apart throughout the race but then they reached the last fence and he still didn't have the race won, he hadn't shaken off Country Store and all of a sudden all that Country Store had to do was galvanise himself on the run in, take advantage of his extra fitness and Edmond's sterling effort counted for nothing. I started urging him privately, I hoped, "Go on Edmond, Hector for Edmond, go on Edmond," over and over willing him on. He was resolute and won. "Two in," I said to myself. The next race was off five minutes later at Sandown, the three runner novice. That would put the bet bang on target.

I stood still, for a moment, then walked towards the door and had a look outside, walked back in, stood in the middle of the shop looking up at the screens, tried to look nonchalant and inconspicuous. It wasn't working, I thought I'd sit down and wait. I sat down and realised I could get my football coupon filled in. I got up again and went to look for the football section. I lapped the shop twice and gave up, thinking it was one of those shops where they kept them behind the counter. I didn't want to ask before the next race "to spoil the ying and yang of it" I thought. I sat down again. "Why am I here?" I suddenly thought to myself. I could be doing this at home.

They went off to time. Lord York lobbed along in front and Skycab lobbed along behind him, as far as I was concerned Guilder was beaten straight away. They just went steady, not a false pace as you often get with three runners but well within themselves. Lord York pecked at one down the back and I nearly jumped out of my skin. I think I shouted "No," out loud but I wasn't sure. It's funny when you are watching a jumping race or a football match you spend the entire time terrified that something's going to go wrong for you and it really is impossible to enjoy the experience but then when the thing you least want to happen happens, well it's not that bad. It's easy to accept because it has to be accepted. It was never worth the worrying. Yorkie was going well but so was Skycab. They put the railway fences behind them and started on the long curve, on the way to the straight, still all was well and I was telling myself Skycab didn't like a fight, they straightened up and coming to the second fence from home Lord York was ridden into it. "It's gone," I thought. Skycab was still on the bridle, I thought he could take Lord York as he pleased. But he didn't, Lord York kept going for pressure, Skycab wouldn't pass him.

"I knew he was a dog," I said to myself,

"Go on Yorkie," I allowed myself to externalise quietly. I may have said it a bit too loud but it was at that stage where people began to externalise. We had one of those shameless old men amongst us that just started shouting out. "Go on my baba," was his phrase. He started as soon as they came into the straight in every race. Once he'd started he legitimised our more specific urgings to begin. I would end up like him one day. Even with a general cacophony, the bloke I had pushed past to get the betting slips turned round and looked at me, I didn't have the deep authoritative voice I gave myself in my imagination and I suddenly realised that I looked and sounded like a faggot. He knew I had a chance and he hated me for it. There is no such thing as betting shop camaraderie or the gamblers union. Punters hate seeing others win. There is such a gulf of emotion between desolation and the warm confidence of winning and it shows. However much you try to be a decent winner it shows, something in your gait as you walk to the pay out counter, some look of peaceful relief you wear on your face, some expression of being released from torture. Whatever it is the other gamblers recognise it and hate you for it. All winners are bad winners if it is not you. Once, on the final day of Cheltenham I had done my bollocks, officially, and I was stood on the lawn watching the County Hurdle next to a bloke who wore the confident cloak of a winner, against my threadbare suit of the persecuted gambler. As the leaders reached the final hurdle he shouted out "Go on Peanuts make my day," referring to Peanuts Pet, the eventual winner. He said that all the way up the straight, "make my day," i.e. give me an unexpected additional winner to the several I've already backed. I felt like smashing my elbow somewhere between his trilby and his upturned sheepskin collar.

They came to the last and suddenly Skycab was hard ridden, much more so than Lord York. "I've got it," I said to myself. Skycab responded to the urging, he took it up at the last, Lord York landed a stride behind but anyone would have given it to him at that stage. Skycab's jockey was desperate and the hill at Sandown killed horses like that, Lord York was bound to overhaul him on the run in. His jockey got him going, just a matter of time, Skycab was all out, "here comes Lord York, here he is just now, here he comes to win, there's the post, can he do it, he's bound to do it, he's going to do it, there's the post, he's not done it. Has he? No." It was close and I finished watching the race with my head at right angles to my body as I tried to squeeze the horse past the post, as I tried to make the angle work to make Lord York the winner. It didn't work, he'd lost. My friend turned round and shrugged his shoulders as if to say "hard luck you deserved it."

The bet was down, I'd backed two winners and yet I was down on the transaction. "I am a fucking arsehole," I told myself. The next race was half an hour later at Sandown. I didn't want to wait another half an hour, to have a large bet on an 11/8 shot to get my money back. I'd let my winners go. I was at a loss to know what to do. I decided to put first things first and to put the football bet on. As I believed in that more than I believed in my horse racing selections I decided to increase stakes. £300 accumulator, I felt very confident about the bet. It was getting on for two o'clock and the sensible thing to do was to go home. I hated the fact that I had backed winners and I would be leaving them behind. I had to get something out of the work I'd put in. I couldn't accept having to leave on a loss when in a way I was on form, two winners and a head second. I had to be careful, my grandfather died of seconditis. I would stick to my shortlist. I had £50 double Breeze Girl and Lady Cricket and left it behind unwatched to bring me more luck.

I thought I should set off for home but they were on the course for the next race at Chepstow a decent handicap hurdle. I decided to have a quick look at the form, I didn't have to set off until about quarter past to be sure of getting there in time. I thought I might as well have a little each way interest on something to pass the time. I did and he suffered the fate of all great each way bets he finished a gallant running on fourth.

"I am useless," I told myself. I was £600 lighter plus the odd and I'd left two good winners behind but I had two unsettled slips in my pocket and that kept my hopes alive and my head off the pavement. I had to get home as fast as I could. I would have to walk, it would be quicker than a taxi or a bus on Saturday afternoon.

I set off retracing the steps of the morning's journey and I'd been walking less than five minutes and was about to cross the road where I remembered receiving a final warning less than three hours before when I saw Danny Palma. He was a poof that worked with my wife who like many people who worked with my wife had always liked me. I rationalised this as me being a bit of a novelty and the fact that I came from outside the PR media world they all lived in. I was perceived as a switched on business man by those people, which was as ridiculous as it was hilarious. I had a go at not recognising him and sliding past unnoticed but it didn't work. Just as I reached the opposite kerb Danny arrived, I'd tried so hard to time my crossing to be syncopated with his but I was so far off form that I couldn't have contrived a perfectly coincidental meeting any better. I wasn't sure whether Danny was also trying to avoid me, he seemed to have a genuinely surprised look when we came face to face but I wasn't sure. But he also looked a little delighted and I knew really that Danny wasn't intellectually capable of such a level of deceit. I could have given him the swerve but fucked it up.

"How are you?" he said stressing the you.

That had never been a straightforward question for me, a simple matter of form, a conversational more that everybody on the earth complied with. For me it was always a real question demanding a real answer. I knew it wasn't but I simply couldn't reply "I'm fine thanks, how are you?" I always seemed to pause a crucial fraction of a second longer than I should which made saying "I'm fine thanks how are you?" sort of bad form. Well it felt like that to me, as if the delay in responding in the standard way required that I give a more interesting answer to justify the delay. The trouble was the more interesting answer didn't always come, it was just a boring, factual, far too personal answer to the question. In this regard I reminded myself of my father, too open, too personal, too prepared to say things that should not be shared with other people. Unlike my father I had a very acute sense of being embarrassed, but nevertheless I still had what I considered to be a destructive honesty, at least a personally destructive openness. I hated myself for being like that. I detested my father for being like that. I thought of him then answering the question. He'd look down, turn his head a little bit, turn his palms upwards and start by saying "Well ..." It was not unknown for him to give the short form of his life story in such circumstances. Often it would end by him saying "If I had stayed I'd be drawing twice the pension AND I would have banked the redundancy payment." God help you if you happened to ask him what he did for a living.

I said "I'm err ... OK fine, sort of terrible really."

"Really? Why's that sweetheart?"

"Oh you know I'm still in that terrible job and you know, life is sort of on hold while I am."

"How long have you got left?"

"I am supposed to stay til a year next February." I was embarrassed at the way I had let so many people know about my deal. I had set off with the intention of keeping my own counsel several months ago when I first made it but I had managed to make it the central plank of any conversation with anyone who might remotely be considered a friend since. So much so that all of my wife's friends had now started to refer to it as "the deal".

"And you can't think of anything to make them let you out earlier? Can't you get out early for good behaviour or whatever you lawyers say?"

"I might be able to get out early for bad behaviour."

"Well if anyone can you can sweetheart."

I felt guilty to be hogging the conversation about my boring life.

"What are you up to?"

"It's Paddy's cat's birthday, I've got to get him something, he adores that fucking cat."

"Is there a special cat shop here?"

"No but there's a great gay card shop."

"Is the cat gay too?"

"No sweetheart. Well, we're all biddable," he said winking. "There's a bloke in there and, you know, any excuse for a visit."

"I hope he's got lots of cat cards."

"I hope there's a few in the basement," he winked again.

"I thought you were supposed to be in Berlin?"

"Not when there's cat birthday's parties to go to."

"I don't blame you, it sounds like the same old story."

"Yeah right, I'm always going to cat parties."

"No I mean Berlin."

"Beirut with sequins darling, Beirut with sequins. Has Caroline called you?"

"Yes about every half an hour, although I tend to leave my mobile behind more often than not."

"How is she coping?"

"Well they all sound so unhappy all the time. I don't know how they are persuaded to do these festivals, they never seem to remember how bad the last one was."

"Never underestimate the power of the media," all deep he was. Prick.

It was an awkward staccato conversation and I was struggling with my end of it. For some reason with people like Danny I could never get going with them. I didn't feel nervous but I acted nervously. After a silence during which either of us could easily have signed off and carried on our way I eventually came up with:

"How's the new flat?"

I knew that I knew a recent fact about Danny that I had been striving to recover throughout the conversation. I had eventually found it and despite being desperate to get away I felt obliged to ask once I'd remembered. Well except that I didn't really feel obliged, it was more that as soon as I remembered something about him I just blurted out.

I suppose I felt that I had not offered much in terms of conversation up to this point and was pleased that I could indulge Danny with a couple of home questions. I had no interest in hearing the answers and once I found the question I switched off again. Not exactly that but I was now into the Danny file in my mind and I was on autopilot.

The supplementary was already prepared when he came to an end of his current answer. That was why I struggled so much to make conversation with people like him, I never concentrated when they were speaking, I spent the entire time trying to remember something about our last conversation.

"I love it, it's darling, it's so This Life. And of course right in the heart of the People's Republic of Islington."

"Oh yes of course you're one of us now." I was disappointed that I hadn't remembered that Danny had moved recently at the beginning of the conversation. I could have got the conversation over quickly, politely and with an interesting subject (for Danny) to talk about. Instead it had been awkward and only now was the conversation getting going.

"I just love the life here, bars and café's and all that."

"Didn't you like Kew better. Wasn't it more civilised?"

"Darling it was Holby City - a waiting room for death."

"Don't you think it's filthy and disgusting?"

"The more filthy and disgusting the better. Look what are you up to now?"

I thought he was going to invite me to a bath house. "Err nothing much I'm just on my way home."

"Let's go and have a coffee."

"Err yeah, I, err I, I can yes go on." I hadn't been able to find the words straight away to say no. I couldn't say "I am going home to listen to the radio," and because I wasn't compelled to be on my way for a better a reason I just couldn't come up with any convincing words at all to get away. The last thing in the world I wanted to do was to have a cup of coffee with Danny Palma, even if I didn't have bets to coax home.

"Where do you go?"

"The Dome, the .. "

"Great, I love the Dome."

I meant to say "not the Dome," because I'd been there during the week and felt that I had slightly embarrassed myself. Instead I said "the Dome." That was because I was a prick, I couldn't think on my feet and I couldn't remember the name of any other café in Islington. I despaired of myself. They already thought I was weird and now I was going back with someone all camp and gay, it wasn't the way I wanted to be thought of.

"I'll meet you there in five minutes. Just popping to the bank."

It was one of those doors that you couldn't tell whether to push or pull it. It seemed like you should push it but then you would have had no room to stand once you got in, and it would be especially difficult if someone else was coming the other way getting out. I delayed only a moment considering the options but while I did I caught the eye of the waitress inside who signalled to me as if to say "yes we are open, come in." In that moment I felt stupid. I always allowed people to see me as an incompetent, no more than a boy. I went in by pushing the door and struggled to close it behind me. I was wearing too many clothes and I didn't know whether to take my coat off before being given a seat or wait until after I was installed. I had to take it and hang it up because the flimsy chairs in the Dome weren't sufficiently large or robust to hang a jacket and a coat and I needed to take both off. The form for sitting in the Dome wasn't clear, whereas on some days you would just walk up to a free table on others it was obvious you would have to wait to be given one. As far as I could see nearly every table seemed taken without it looking too busy. I was unsure whether if I waited until I was given my seat before hanging my coat up, someone would walk in behind me and take my table while I was away. On the other hand if I went to put my coat up straight away I might miss my chance to get the next table. I compromised and started to take my coat off. Then a young woman with a pram came in. She held a small child under one arm and the pram aloft in the hand of the other. She pushed into my waiting area without any regard for the too small space we shared and then in a business like way slid past me sideways and towards a vacant table. She smiled one of those pleasant but "I'm coming through," smiles and left me standing mute as if I was on some other business. Hers was getting a table and eating. I started to say "I think that we're supposed to wait here," but being struck by how stupid that would sound to a together sort of babe like that I muffled my words and let them tail off. In the end I said something like, "I think we are yes sorry," and when she looked back having passed me I pretended I had been talking to someone else, sort of swinging my coat in front of my head as part of the disrobing routine so that we wouldn't meet eyes. I was sure that she rolled her eyes up slightly as she continued on her way but I couldn't be sure about that. While I waited I started to think about shouting at the tramp on my way and I began to wonder if I was observed while I did it and perhaps, if so, whether anyone that saw me then was in there looking at me now. What had I looked like? Mad and out of control. At least not normal. Not like them. Perhaps I hadn't looked too mad when I shouted at the tramp. All I had said was one sentence, delivered quickly, although there had been a certain level of venom and I had been very close to his face. I tried to recreate the scene to reassure myself that it hadn't looked too bad by saying it to my reflection close up while I waited. I was on about the fourth go when I realised the waitress was looking at me on the other side of the glass.

"On your own?" she said coldly, I wasn't sure whether she thought I'd been saying "fuck off you cunt," to her.

"Err yes, I was just practising." I didn't really mean that but it was the only thing I could say quickly. But I think she was ignoring me by then.

Then Danny returned and marched in through the front doors and took a window seat.

"So you're not on your own now?"

"No, not now, no. But I was when I ..." I decided to let it tail off again.

I followed him but I found the journey far more obstacle strewn than he did. Whereas he walked straight to the table I found that I had to turn sideways and brush past people to follow him. I was only a little bit wider than him but it made a massive difference. He didn't have to say "excuse me" once whereas I must have said it to half a dozen people. I really felt bad about brushing past people at the level of my groin to their head. Had I been on my own I would have taken a more circuitous route but because I was with Danny I felt compelled to follow him. I was particularly embarrassed when I finally slumped down into my seat and got a waft of a musty body smell from my trousers, almost yeasty you would have called it.

It reminded me of the day I was sitting in Chemistry next to Keith Morrison, at the time my best friend. A propos of nothing he said "you stink of urine," and he was right I did. Basically I didn't change my underpants often enough. I thought of sitting next to my piano teacher stinking of urine and trying to snog girls stinking of urine. I just hadn't realised, but my parents were far more culpable, they hadn't done anything to prepare me, they hadn't insisted on regular baths and showers and changing of underwear, it wasn't that we were socially dysfunctional it was just that they lacked discipline, they were useless at bringing people up properly. They shamed me.

I laid the coat on the chair then took off my jacket. I saw in the mirror in front of me that my shirt was creased and in addition to the great rounds of sweat under the arms I also had parallel lines of sweat in the crack of each crease circling my arms. As I put the jacket on the back of the chair it fell over backwards and for a moment blocked access to the cash register. I picked it up rebalancing the chair and took my car-coat round the other side of the horse-shoe bar to find a place to hang it. Whilst there it meant I could pick up a daily paper from the table. That wasn't too nice to Danny but reading and talking to him a the same time wasn't exactly Challenge Aneka.

None of the broadsheets had any sports sections left, there was one copy of The Sun so I was forced to take that against my better instincts. I walked back round to my table excusing myself again as I slid in between and around all the other diners. I was reminded of the time in Miss Nicholas's class as I walked through cramped together desks and between other pupils I would raise my hands high and make myself slim like I'd seen the Fijian rugby team doing. Once when I did it, I glanced sideways and saw Miss Nicholas laughing at me. As that thought came to me then it hit me like a dagger of pure concentrated embarrassment right in the chest. What a prick I was. It made me breathe in deeply and deliberately and audibly. I realised that I had made a noise and tried not to meet eyes with anyone else. I felt embarrassed to have chosen The Sun to read, then as I straightened up for my seat I saw myself fully in reflection, sweaty, fat, red, creased, hair too long, and I also noticed that the bottom button of my shirt just above the trousers was undone and some flesh was showing. And this was me making an effort. And I stooped. I'd always stooped. I'd had a chronic pain in the lower part of my back since I was about twenty. Since then I'd been to every witch doctor, chiropractor, osteopath, reflexologist, aromatherapist, physiostherapist, trainee physiotherapist, every head shrinking, manipulating bastard that I could find but none of them had a clue how to make it any better. I probably got the bad back through stooping too much (slouching actually) and now I stooped too much because I had a bad back. I just didn't realised how absurd I looked when I walked until moments like that when I caught myself in reflection. You could only describe my gait as apologetic. It made me make an immediate conscious effort to straighten up, but then it always did. And that made me feel more absurd. Shoulders back, stomach in was all very well but no-one ever said what to do with your chin. Mine stuck out like a caricature of a sergeant major or like I was about to do a chicken impression. I got back to my seat and made a big effort not to make any clucking noises. I was thinking to myself about chickens and eggs and my big ungainly shape and I think I started to say, "big bird will take a boiled egg please," in the same way that a bookmaker would shout out, "9 to 4 the field. 3 to 1 bar one," and then I added, "bring him a sesame bap now," I know I said that.

"What's that?" said Danny

"Oh nothing, just thinking of having something to eat. Are you?"

"No, coffee's fine for me."

That meant that I would now have to order something eat and drag the whole event out even longer when I was desperate to get away. The clock was about ten degrees to the left of Danny's shoulder and I was so obsessed with getting home on time that I looked more at the clock than I looked at him. Just off centre with my gaze, which to me was rude, as if I was taking more interest in the strangers around us than I did with my chosen company. But there were plenty of people that behaved like that and Danny wouldn't have thought anything of it, if he even noticed. The waitress arrived at our table re-filing the cardboard flap of her order book, she leaned her left hand on the table and blew out deeply as if it was the first time she had paused since she started working.

"Yes boys?" she said semi-concealing a little amused laugh.

"latte," said Danny, immediately and confidently.

"How did he know to order that?" I thought. The waitress just noted the name and looked at me. I thought to myself that if I had gone blind on the name of a drink without looking at the menu she would have just looked back at me blankly and said "what?" or she would have said, "we don't do that but you can have a mocha-milk," or something equally implausible where I would have had to risk saying the name of a terrible made up modern product.

I sort of shrugged trying to impart that it didn't really matter what I had, as if to say, "bring me anything." No words came out though. To the waitress I just didn't say anything for a long time.

In the end I said "a coffee." I almost said "a filter coffee," meaning the most ordinary coffee that they had that they would serve to anyone who made a non-specific order but I had once made that assumption in a similar place, Café Rouge or Chez Gerard or one of those and the waiter had said to me "we don't do filter coffee would you like an espresso?"

She made a gesture to me to say "go on, elucidate."

"Just a normal coffee."

"A filter coffee," she said out loud whilst writing it down, "that comes black."

"With milk please."

"A filter coffee with milk please," she said, adding the milk bit to the order and adding an obvious full stop after the please as if she had written it as that.

"Anything else?"

Then I made the mistake of saying, "can I have a little snack." I suppose I hoped that she would respond like my mum and just nip off and rustle something up without any further questions. I wasn't banking on everything having a proper name and being part of a formal order.

"Toast, bread or rolls?"

The toast option was listed on the menu under "lite bites" but I couldn't call things by their brand names. It occupied that ground between pretentious and areshole-boring that I considered not to be my territory. I couldn't possibly conceive of ordering something called a Full Monty, or for that matter a Full English or a Great British, however much I wanted a fried breakfast. Had I had the time and inclination I would have said to the waitress, "a fried breakfast please," to which she would have replied "the Full Monty?" then I would only have to affirm the order without saying the name.

"Err toast."

"Brown or white?"

"White," then I added "please," to try and draw some civility out of her.

"Jam, marmalade or honey?" It must have been my lucky day.

"Whatever you've got left," I didn't know. I would only know when it was in front of me. Upfront I had no idea.

"You can have any," it really was my lucky day.

"Honey, honey," a little non-joke might make her a bit less wary of me I thought.

She sighed and wrote down the order. I'd probably been a bit too familiar too soon. I felt a little bit sorry for her having to go through that charade dozens of times every day on behalf of the pricks that ran her business. I couldn't think of a single person I knew who would feel that they were being given a better service for being inundated with inane questions like that. Who wouldn't rather have less choice? What waitress would not want to not have to say those lines over and over every day? What kitchen manager would not prefer to have one option for toast and marmalade for every customer? Well perhaps I could think of one or two people but nobody that counted.

"I wonder how much extra I'll be charged for the milk?" I said to Danny as she left. I felt embarrassed to have made such a twat out of myself over something as simple as ordering a cup of coffee but I knew that if I had said "filter coffee" it wouldn't have been right.

"we live in a complicated world," said Danny.

I had never attributed such grand expressions to him, to me Danny was one of those lucky people that breezed through life not knowing what there was to be unhappy about. I felt slightly embarrassed over the trouble I had caused in making my simple order but it didn't really matter with Danny. He felt no shame or guilt or sense of embarrassment like me, to him it was forgotten as soon as it was said.

"Ah here's Boudicca now," he said when she arrived back with the drinks. He just said things whether they made sense or not.

"Can you pay now, I'm going off shift," she asked.

"I'll pay now as I'm going on shift," I replied, God knows why. Perhaps it was because I was with Danny, it didn't matter what I said.

She looked at me blankly and Danny laughed and shook his head as he stooped to sip from his latte.

I pealed a twenty of my wedge and noticed how thin it felt in my hand. I reflected that it was £600 lighter and my stomach did a little somersault.

"Thanks a lot," said the waitress, smiling like she meant it, perhaps noticing the implied large tip or perhaps just warming to me a little bit. I hadn't been so bad or as weird as she had first thought.

"Look at her," he said after she'd gone, "standing there like Mother Mary."

What the fuck did that mean? I simply couldn't think of a single thing to say in response.

So we said nothing, we just sipped our drinks. In holiday programmes what we were doing would be described as people-watching to me it was an excruciating silence which the longer it went on the more difficult I found it to break.

I tried a sneaky little look at The Sun and realised straight away that the racing section on Saturdays came in a pull-out section in the middle that was missing. I looked around to see if there were any discarded sports sections near to hand. There weren't.

"Why the fuck hadn't I bought a daily paper while I was in the newsagents this morning? But more why, why did newspapers come in two parts on certain days? In the name of the holy god of providing a customer focussed product? What could be more focussed than giving a traditional product in the way it had always been given, with a beginning, middle and end that everyone understood?"

"I like your desert boots," Danny said.

Great. My carefully selected and expensively acquired shoes were classified at a sub-hush puppy level.

"They're brothel creepers actually," I replied in a falsely haughty voice but he didn't laugh.

Another silence established itself, then eventually Danny, who had looked genuinely shocked when he saw the size of my bundle of cash, said:

"What are you doing with that bundle of money, going to meet a contract killer?"

"Oh no, I was going to go to the races."

"I would be terrified to carry that amount of money around with me."

I couldn't understand why, I considered people like Danny to be reckless with money, to be obsessed with worthless ephemera. People like him ordered lattes because they were current and vogue, they bought smart stereo systems and DVDs, things that I considered excessive and unaffordable. All I did was carry a bundle of about £1,000, all other material trappings of the latter day yuppie were denied. I couldn't think of an interesting reply.

"Oh you have to really if you're interested in gambling."

"Not with my fiver each way on the Grand National you wouldn't. What do you put on exactly?"

"Well it depends, you know, £50 or a £100 normally, depending on the occasion."

"Do you win?"

I had heard this question from outsiders hundreds of times but still didn't have a very good answer prepared. If he knew what he was talking about he would have said, "how much do you lose?" which meant that I could tell him anything I wanted and he wouldn't know any better. But as usual I felt compelled to tell the truth.

"I suppose not, well it's difficult to say, sometimes, but perhaps as a whole over the years, no. I suppose it's because from time to time I win a lot and it feels like a lot when I win."

"So you're really just in it for the buzz?"

·"I suppose I like it because it's terribly dashing."

"Well you are terribly dashing."

"I wouldn't go that far."

Then I thought that Danny said "we all think so," but I couldn't be sure.

He could have said "if you think so," or "I don't think so," but he definitely ended with "you should keep at it."

As I didn't know whether it was an aggressive, honest or complementary remark I couldn't reply as I preferred, which was to say "that's very kind thank you," from where I could have proceeded to a wrapping up remark, instead I said "I think I'm destined to be a loser."

Danny didn't reply quickly so I felt obliged to ask if he wanted another drink. It was the last thing I wanted but I felt that I should say something and as I had forsaken the chance to wrap everything up and as I had managed to make an open and embarrassing remark I couldn't leave it at that. Instead of going as I desperately wanted to I had to keep the meeting open. Although I had at least offered Danny the chance to close things off which I hoped he would take in a way that I never could.

"I've got to go darling cats and all that."

I preferred it when it wasn't me that had to make the closing remark. That way I hadn't stood in judgment on Danny, it wasn't me that had rejected Danny's company. I was absolutely delighted to be given the opportunity to set off home and I wasn't in the mood to let the opportunity go once offered. I knew from many times practice that the right rounding off comment now would get the meeting over in a pleasant way, one that would send Danny on his way thinking what a lovely chap I was and not that it was a short and pointless interlude into an otherwise, structured and focussed excursion.

"That was nice. Thanks Danny."

It made no difference that I didn't mean it.

"Thanks to you."

"See you very soon I hope," I said taking Danny's left hand with my right, closing my four fingers flat against Danny's. I knew that someone like Danny would be very touched by a gesture like that and that he would carry away tender thoughts of me.

Danny gave me a final double eyed wink and then we both turned and went in opposite directions.

"Go and fuck yourself," I said out loud as soon as I was sure he was out of earshot.

5.

I was in such a rush to leave that I didn't check the clock as I got up to go. I thought that it had to be getting on for three o'clock and another great plan and a free afternoon wasted.

Eventually I came to the top of Rosebery Avenue. I reckoned on having taken at least ten minutes to get that far. I plodded on, trying to work out the most efficient route as I went. Unusually for me I retraced my steps entirely rather than swing round on the target from the right like I nearly always did, until, that is, I reached the tramps when I decided that the best course for the fastest route back was to nip down the last left before their encampment. As I went through the front doors of my apartment block I felt a sense of relief, I was home and I immediately peeled off my jacket. I knew that I should check the post boxes, it was only a turn of a key but I told myself that I was missing valuable commentary and the post could be picked up any time. I hated the flat I lived in but I loved the new smell each time I walked through the lobby. That meant something to me. I had a haven.

Inside the flat my instinct was to throw my coat and jacket on the floor as soon as I walked in but I fought against it and I was pleased to note my self-discipline in laying all the unwanted garments on the bed. It was a step too far to go and hang them all up. I felt I should have changed my trousers too but I couldn't be bothered.

The preferred radio was in the main living space, that is to say the only living space, which opened on to a kitchenette. I had ruined the ambience of the space. It started when I persuaded Caroline to dispense with normal furniture and to replace it with what I called "day beds". I had seen something like it in a house and home magazine in the dentists and I was so taken with the idea that I ripped the page out when nobody was looking and brought it home to show her. Essentially it was two single beds that were passed off as sofas. Ours had never looked like anything other than single beds, they were impossible to sit on, you either lay on them or left them alone. I had sold the idea to Caroline on the basis that it was a practical measure that would provide extra sleeping if we ever needed it. Other than the day beds there was virtually nothing in the room: a shelf which was really a shoe rack with some videos and a CD player; a portable television stand with an old TV and video on it; a wooden CD rack on top of which I kept my favourite plant who's condition I monitored as the only true barometer of the state of my life; a dining table and chairs in front of the kitchenette and the final item was the hated coffee table that matched the dining furniture. I had never been persuaded that a coffee table did anything useful. They always seemed to me too far away from each bit of seating to serve any purpose. I saw them as big ugly pieces of furniture that took up valuable space.

It was about as uncomfortable as a room could be. What made that worse was that I had spent countless hours pacing up and down in it, wondering how to organise it better, feeling uncomfortable, ill at ease with myself, growing in frustration. I knew very well what I liked, what I thought might make the room work but somehow I never quite pulled it off. It wasn't for want of searching, or for buying, usually expensive, items but whereas I admired the houses of my friends and acquaintances and rooms I saw in magazines I saw my own creation as no more than a collection of objects.

I turned on the radio and went to the fridge to find a beer and I could only find eight tins of very strong lager that Caroline had bought when she last went to the supermarket. I had berated her for doing that at the time though it was obvious that she had bought it innocently. She didn't know that "only tramps and alcoholics drank stuff like that," and had been quite indignant when I told her so. As a point of honour though I had to leave the eight tins un-drunk so she would understand, which was no great challenge really since I hated the syrupy sweetness of strong drinks like that, despite there being no alternatives in the fridge. I also knew the cloudy nausea that followed drinking a couple tins and I could sense it when I looked at the brand name. It was enough to look at the tins to make me feel annoyed. I shook my head and said "stupid bitch," and slammed the door shut. Those tins would be in the fridge on the day I left the flat.

I put the kettle on and decided to make do with a cup of tea and perhaps a few custard creams for company, maybe a cheese sandwich first, as the sort of main course, in which case, cheese snacks prior to that as starter and perhaps a beer after all? No a glass of wine, better all round, not half as fattening. Good idea, a general grazing feast to coax the results in with. I'd address the question of snack pudding later. Then it all needs to be assembled around one of the day beds, all within reaching distance, some on floor, some on day bed itself, the rest on an upside down fruit bowl from Egypt.

I switched the tele on to warm up so that I could get the back up service from Ceefax to support the radio commentaries, re-tuned the kitchen radio to 5 Live and finally settled into a proper Saturday afternoon. Useless, true, but correct enough and safe, warm and comfortable and the prospect of a large bet land to make it even sweeter.

I'd somehow gone too early on the tele warming up procedure so I went out to the bedroom and put that one on for back-up. On the way back I found myself outside the front door counting to fifty as fast as I could. I had my foot wedged in the door so I wouldn't lock myself out. I only realised how stupid that was when I switched from counting to days of the week. I'd been through the week about six times when I finally persuaded myself to go back in

I settled down, closed my eyes and waited for a good hour's entertainment. The disappointing part of the incident was that this was the one afternoon per year when rugby internationals took precedence over football. I sat through the next hour and ten minutes of Argentina versus Tonga, including twelve minutes of injury time, wondering if I'd been singled out for a wretched life because I had been inadvertently wicked when I was younger. I had a proper debate with myself but in the end I decided that you could only be deliberately wicked you couldn't even be recklessly wicked. That's the advantage of an education you see, having the tools to work through issues like that. The rugby match ended and the commentary switched to bringing in the full-time football results from around the country. The first thing I heard was, "Middlesborough 1, Spurs 1," which meant that I had got less than one second's entertainment out of my bet.

I hated the cool objectivity with which information about results was given. Middlesborough had drawn with Spurs. There was nothing, when they gave the results, about the fact that Middlesborough had totally dominated, that they should have been five up at half time, that what little chance Spurs had of getting something from the match completely evaporated when they went down to ten men shortly into the second half, like the commentator had said when they came to him. Nor did they speak of the injustice of the late missed penalty. They simply said Middlesborough 1 Spurs 1, like it was a fact that everyone had known for ages. It had gone through that flimsiest of gossamer barriers that turn live, emotional, passionate, subjective, partisan occasions into a piece of accepted history. I hated the indecent haste with which it became an item of history.

You need a convalescing period between taking part, albeit vicariously, in a live act before it became a reported fact. Live events should be forced to go through a qualifying process before historians or journalists were allowed to report them as having happened. You needed a period to lie down, to digest reality before being forced to face it.

The reporters spoke as if they belonged to an exclusive club that always joined on the side that won or supported the result that happened. In their after match reports and interviews they seemed to enjoy the fact that the correct result had happened, it had to be correct because it was what had happened. They celebrated the last minute come back goals with the goal scorers, they enjoyed the fact that such a team deserved to get something out of the match. They loved seeing justice being done. They would have equally enjoyed the result had it not, in which case they would have celebrated the winners hanging on to gain a deserved result. Whatever way it turned they accepted it without question and just reported it.

And there it was, it had happened all too fast and it had to be accepted. Squint eyed hope and anticipation had turned into another losing bet. It didn't seem right that it was suddenly the evening, an hour or so earlier it had been lunchtime, it had been before anything had happened. Now it was after. One and a half hours had turned the end of a bright morning into the start of a dark evening. It was winter, there were no late kick-offs, no evening horse racing, summer was over and the end of the day came quickly at this time of year.

6.

I left the radio on to listen to the post match phone-in programme. It was my way of coming to terms with the unjust results that had been inflicted upon me. All gamblers need to speak to someone about it as soon as they have suffered a losing bet. Ideally to someone who understands. The need to get it off your chest to someone with genuine sympathy, who can really appreciate how close it came, who can tell you how right the bet was in theory, is crucial in the process of moving on. You have to be told that what you did was correct. That was the key to losing.

The phone-in programme was not quite that but it was the best I had. To hear the fans talk about the bias of the referee, revealing the terrible atrocities inflicted and let go unpunished how much the result did not reflect the run of play, did me good.

For a time. After half an hour I couldn't stand it any longer. The trouble with phone-in programmes was that they failed for the massive ego of the presenter and the inarticulate stupidity of the people that phoned in. They were all basically unbearable and the panacaeic qualities of this one couldn't make up for the fact that it was still a phone-in programme. The main think that I couldn't deal with was this: the point the caller was making was obvious yet the host would not see it or could not see it and had an argument with the caller on a different basis to that which was proposed; that and the appeasing, subservient, bridge-building, humility of the poor people who called in - it reminded me too much of the young me.

I also spent the duration of most phone programmes doubled up in excruciated embarrassment at the things people said. How come people were so flawed at arguing? I rarely met a single person who could construct and stay loyal to the terms of an argument, who understood the protocol of arguing. And phone-in programmes were sublime examples of the low status of the art. In the end I shouted "shut up you fucking cretin," at the top of my voice. Too loud really because I strained a bit at the 'cretin' end and I immediately regretted the excess. Were the neighbours in? Did they know I was unhinged yet?

Witnessing a badly organised argument between two strangers was bad enough but it could never be as bad as being the one rational party in an argument that didn't follow the rules. I reserved different rules for that on the basis that it made a lump of molten fury form in my chest. An apoplectic impotent rage could descend on me at the injustice of suffering an unfair argument. I simply could not understand why adversaries couldn't respond within the terms of the argument. All three names at the top of my 'People I Hate' list, which I kept on the fridge door, had distinguished themselves as having no arguing technique. And come to think of it, that was probably the real reason they were there.

Its not good to have petty obsessions, I know that, I knew I had to take the heat out of my hating. It was much better to treat people with absolute disdain rather than going to the bother of hating them. The hating part cost the hater too. But at the end of the day, wrong is wrong and if you can see it you have to say it.

I kept my own almanac of flawed arguing styles. The first was the one preferred by my father and other faux intellectuals. Franck Gilligan was one: I called it the self-declared-objectivity style. In its simplest form the perpetrator would reach an acknowledged divergence of views and would then declare himself (this was a male only technique in my experience) to be reasonable. In my father's case this would be unashamed, unabashed and express, "I am a reasonable man," or, "it is what any reasonable person would think," with more intellectually capable adversaries their assertion of holding the reasonable view would be more subtle. Sometimes my father's assertion of his right to be rational over others was that he was a scientist. He seemed to regard that career choice, however low the level that he operated, that he absolutely possessed the rational, objective judgment of the subject under discussion. Franck was the same by virtue of his computer training. He thought that by dint of that he cornered the market in logic. Only someone who had been through the rigours of a programming course knew in an academic sense the rules of logic. Which, by flawed logic on his part, lead him to the sure knowledge that he possessed all the tools of judging what was right and what was not. Neither Franck nor my father understood that theirs was a subjective view. They were incapable of understanding the simple truth that assertion of one's view was subjective. Incapable. That made me hate them more than I did to begin with.

Once established with them the argument would proceed on the basis that they were being attacked for holding an evidently reasonable view by someone recognised by the argument to hold an unreasonable one. Confronted by this I would become exasperated and although it could send me into an apoplexy of rage it could equally render me baffled and mute, depending on the level of undefendable idiocy of the perpetrator.

The *non-sequitor* was a style preferred by women and psychopaths. It was more correctly classified as two sub-styles: there was the straight non-sequitor which involved making a quantum leap from the established basis of the argument, without explanation or acknowledgement, and then to carry on nevertheless with the argument as if it had followed a continuous thread; the second was to use a line of the argument or a fact established within it as a justification for moving to an unrelated fact. To be a true species of the non-sequitor the argument must then continue as if nothing abnormal had happened, however if I was involved myself it would descend into discussing the terms of the argument, the original subject matter being dropped. I would often pull out of these arguments on the basis that the other person was not sufficiently capable of observing the terms of an argument.

The *doesn't-know-how-thick-she-is*, was not so much a style, more a reflection on the stupidity of the adversary. It cropped up often enough for it to get its own classification. It described those differences of opinion where it was impossible to reason with the other person on account of their profound stupidity. Strictly their were two sub-classes here too. One was represented by Franck's wife, who talked to her conversational partner as if they were as stupid as her. She just didn't have the intellectual capability to give other people credit for having more brains than her. The other was more a triumph of ego over brains. Aude Hardley who worked for us was like that. She was a graduate, in fact she was qualified as a solicitor, but that didn't stop her being dense. She was like thousands of people you came across that devalued the education system. In the old days people like her would have been forced to leave school and get a job, whereas today they are encouraged to become graduates and professionals. I wasn't so much against the thousands of halfwits who wanted to do office jobs, what I hated was the sense of empowerment it delivered to them. Employing them was a matter of continuous negotiation just to reach a basic level of co-operation. It being but one of a number of weaknesses I had but I found it hard to deal with people who held an unmerited view of their talents. Aude had that moral certainty about her views that only idiots can have.

When we'd been giving Aude her annual review, we'd ridden the rough seas of her ignorance for about an hour or so and finally reached the new salary bit. We wanted to give her £36,000 from her current £33,000. The budget was tight and that was what we could afford. We'd been honest with everyone and said to them what their maximums were. We had a go at trying to get her to accept £35,000 and flexing her bonus scheme but Aude was a cash-in-the-pocket type of girl. She preferred not to do that but hold out for the maximum salary. "OK," we said, "we can pay you £36,000." "Is it negotiable?" asked Aude. "Well," said I, "that's what we can pay you. In so far as anything is negotiable it is negotiable but really there's no more money available."

"Is it negotiable?" she said.

"Well like we were trying to explain, if you can adapt to changes in your bonus structure and other benefits, everything is negotiable." It was left at that. When Aude came back for annual review part II a week later, she said "I want £43,000."

"We told you that the maximum we could go to was £36,000," I said.

"But you said it was negotiable," she said.

It turned out that she wanted £40,000 and to arrive at that she asked for £43,000, on the basis that it would produce a counter bid of £37,000, she would come to £42,000, followed by a response of £38,000, then our £39,000 would be matched by her £41,000, from which the only place to go for both sides was £40,000. She believed that because she'd established it was negotiable all she had to do was negotiate. She had been taught how to negotiate on her professional skills course when she learnt to be a solicitor.

Aude took umbrage for the two or three weeks following. After a couple of days I had a quiet word to ask if she was satisfied with how things worked out.

"I can't believe I was told something was negotiable that wasn't," was all that she would say.

Her unwordliness confounded me - she was just too thick to have to deal with.

There were other argument styles that I formally recognised: the last word; the false common ground; the unable to agree premise and often the most disagreeable of all, and that favoured by Franck Gilligan, the unreasonable reliance on a third party view as fact, but those three were top of the pops. Once established I couldn't get Aude out of my mind. "Where was she when I needed a wank this morning?"

The phone was ringing. I woke up from my reverie and realised that I was gripping the table tightly and speaking out loud. "Stop obsessing you twat," I shouted. "Why do I let a brace of cunts like Franck and Aude bring me down? They're nothing." I went into a crescendo with "they're nothing," took a deep breath and ruffled the hair on the back of my head and let the phone ring off as usual.

"Oh fucking Jesus God release me," I said as I walked towards the phone. I didn't ring back straight away, for one thing I didn't have the temporary office number near to hand and I would have to go and look for it, but mainly I wasn't in the mood for holding up my end in a nice phone call. I also felt bilious and needed to let the feeling pass. I had added another four custard creams, an orange, a packet of bacon flavoured snacks, a bowl of cornflakes and a lump of cheese to the original day bed picnic. I had also thrown in a pot of tea and two more glasses of red wine and I needed to rest. I set my face in a disapproving grimace and shook my head slowly from side to side for several minutes until I broke the spell with a vomit-belch.

I shouted, "God save the King," as loud as I possibly could then went to find the number in Berlin.

"Hello darling it's me."

"Oh hi, I've just phoned you."

"I haven't been in long."

"What have you been doing?"

"Oh not a lot, I was going to go to Sandown, but I didn't really want to go on my own."

"Oh do you miss me?"

"And I ran into Danny Palma, so I had to go and have a coffee with him."

"Oh how nice for you, you know he fancies you, you should be careful."

"He's still here now."

"What?"

"Yes I am making him dinner, it seemed like a good idea as we're both alone."

"You're joking aren't you? Tell me you're joking."

"Danny you better go, Caroline's not very happy about it ...... she says you're a dirty old queen or something like that .... Did you come here under false pretences? .... Get out you dog ..... go and fuck off to your cat party ...... and see yourself out .... And put your pants on before you go, what'll the neighbours say? And don't come back for at least half an hour."

"Oh shut Hector you fool."

"I'm not a fool I'm an arsehole."

"Oh god just shut up and listen."

"Not until you call me by my proper name."

"I did, what are you talking about? Just listen."

"No you didn't."

"OK what is your proper name?"

"Hector Arsehole."

"Jesus Hector."

"No, nearly, it's Hector Arsehole."

"Have you been drinking?"

"Yes I've just had a lovely pot of tea thanks pet," I thought that sounded best in Geordie.

"Hector will you just calm down and listen?"

"Proper name first."

"What?"

"Come on I shan't tell you again. Say it."

"I can't say that on the phone I am in the office."

"Well it's your choice. If I were you I'd just get it over with and say it."

"Jesus what do you want me to say?"

"I want to be called my proper name."

"What Hector …. Arsehole?" she whispered.

"Yes now a little louder so I can hear you."

" ……..Hector Arsehole."

"Yes what is it darling?"

"Jesus you're mad. Now has that letter arrived from the bank?"

"Not it ain't ma'am."

"Where the fuck is it? It should be there by now."

"I'm afraid I can't help you there miss."

"Hector, it happens to be very important. I mean ….."

"I can't write it for you."

"No but it's important. Ring me when you get it."

"Yes I did."

"Now what else has happened?"

"Besides fucking Danny and hiding the letter from the bank hardly anything."

"No really be serious Hec. Are you prepared for your meeting on Monday?"

"I've set aside the whole of tomorrow to prepare."

"Well make sure you do. If you get sacked we need that money."

"Don't worry I won't do anything stupid. Trust me. I'm a lawyer."

"Well just see you don't."

"What is it like there?"

"It's so boring it's nothing like Cannes, just boring, we've got absolutely nothing to do."

She had too much to do and no time to do it two days ago.

"Ah well you'll be home next weekend."

"Friday."

"Yes next weekend."

"You should look forward to seeing me."

"I am."

"OK darling big kiss."

"Oh by the way Craig off Big Brother's dead."

"What the one that won it?"

"Apparently."

"Oh God, when did it happen?"

"During the night I think."

"Oh God what a shock."

"Yes. OK darling take care see you next Friday. What time are you here?"

"God Hector I land at 3 o'clock, you better not be late home. In fact you promised to get home early."

"I will I promise."

I hung up and although I regretted the Craig remark I didn't regret it that much. Not a nice thing to say about Craig but he was a public figure and he'd be used to it. I loved the idea of telling an outrageous lie to publicity consultants who I knew never read a newspaper between them. I loved the idea of being the genesis of an untrue story and longed for the day a casual lie I told to Caroline made it back via the newspapers and tele. I loved it for no more reason than Caroline telling everyone in the office and making a fool of herself. I could only hope for poor Craig from Big Brother.

I walked back slowly to the living room and switched the radio off on the way to the furthest day bed from the television. All of a sudden the flat was dark and I contented myself with a period en repose with some lowest common denominator television. I tried to watch Ant and Dec for a little while but I just didn't have the stomach for it, I simply couldn't stand a moment of the Generation Game, there was nothing more I needed to know about the life of mammals, back editions of Brookside were just plain unwatchable and I didn't like the Six Million Dollar Man first time round. I started to circle through the channels then realised on the third time through Ant and Dec I was achieving nothing.

"Fuck it I'm going to bed," I declared to nobody in particular.

In the bedroom Ceefax Page 303 was shining brightly and took me back to the disappointment of a little while ago. I switched it off quickly and left Five Live running to go to sleep by, not that it was exactly my cup of tea at that time of day, I just couldn't be bothered to re-tune it to something better. Just as I couldn't be bothered to hang up the clothes still laying on the bed. I chose instead to move them over a little bit hoping that that would stop them from getting creased. I switched the light off and felt at peace. At 8 o'clock I was fast asleep.

7.

Monday morning came a little more quickly than I had hoped. For one thing I hadn't prepared for the big meeting scheduled at one o'clock that afternoon. It was a big meeting and should have been prepared for. I had known about it for over a week. It was a week last Friday that Julian Barrow had taken me out for a cup of tea to tell me to attend. Any other meeting would have been arranged by email or a telephone call. That it had been set up in that way added significance to it. Julian had not said anything in particular that had bothered me, in fact, having expected worse, it came over as pretty routine, albeit that there was something in his manner, some element of gravitas that he brought to those very brief moments together that told me that I should be concerned. It had not been long enough to smoke a full cigarette and Barrow was never like that, there was always a little bit of small talk.

My attitude to the meeting had unfortunately been like my attitude to many other things in my life, full of good intentions. I went away from the cup of tea with the arsehole Barrow thinking to myself that I wouldn't just prepare for the meeting, that what I'd do was completely over prepare and give such a compelling account of how great I was and what a complete mess they were making of our integration that I'd have them eating out of my hand. What actually happened was that I lost the impetus of my initial enthusiasm quite quickly and then the preparation turned into a chore that I couldn't face each evening. After a while it became crucial to prepare and I simply couldn't be bothered despite the damage it might do to my own interests.

It always puzzled me the way that it was always presumed that one fights to protect one's interests. Nothing could be father from the truth. There are thousands of us who can't be bothered however crucial it is. I remember the night before my maths A' Level, there was this sort of core subject that came up all the time and was in a way the essence of lots of others that would be important in the exam: it was something like: the tangent of x equals the sine divided by the cosine and loads of variations on that theme. I should have learnt it during the year but didn't get round to it. Then on the night before the exam it was absolutely crucial that I at least committed those few simple equations to memory. I even turned to the page in the text book but I couldn't be bothered. I simply couldn't be bothered to make the tiny effort to bother to learn them. I think I watched Brideshead Revisited that night.

That the subject of the meeting was going to be me and my performance was beyond doubt, I accepted that and it held no real fears for me, although it was obviously going to be a little bit more serious than usual. I, and with me Franck, feared most for the hidden agenda. We had learned not to trust Barrow, he was the Finance Director of Martins Fleet the company that had bought our company and he was the one we dealt with during the sale and since on any matter of importance. Barrow had a big intellect, he knew how companies worked, talked business speak and was utterly unscrupulous. Me and Franck, you couldn't say that we were thick exactly but we just never held the same ambitions in business as Julian Barrow and he could run rings round us. Just like the maths A' Level, neither of us got round to taking any real interest in the detail of the sale of our company. Not in the way that we might if we were out to impress anybody over something inconsequential. The sale took 9 months to negotiate and it would have appalled Barrow to know how little detail we knew about the deal. All we knew is that we'd get quite a lot of money for something that neither of us truly valued and we just hoped that we'd stay in business long enough to get away with it. I remember on the day we signed, and picked up a big cheque each, and the first thing we did was go to the bookmakers. It mattered far more to us the fate of £100 each way on a horse at Sedgefield than it had done to make a life securing deal.

Our joint view was that Barrow realised he had paid too much for our crummy little company and was set on a course to unravel as much of the deal as he could during the three years we were to spend together. Me in particular and Franck to a lesser extent, regretted having thrown our lot in with Martins Fleet, particularly with Julian Barrow but we were forced to stay to collect the rest of our payments which were spread over three years. Leaving, or worse being sacked for breach of contract, meant that we became so called "bad-leavers" in the language of the contract we had signed and it meant that all future payments were lost. There was also a bonus deal tied up with our contract based on our financial performance at Martins Fleet which Franck and I considered to be of no value whatsoever since Barrow had made it virtually unobtainable from the outset. The small glimmer of optimism that we had held when we arrived at Martins Fleet had evaporated as soon as we encountered the unyielding administration that was that company. But it was for this that Barrow was always on our case to re-write our deal and re-structure the company that he had bought from us. Franck and I knew that we didn't really have the stomach for a fight with him and that if we did we would lose and with it lose what advantages we currently had. Those advantages were simple to understand: if we stayed for three years we got paid. If Martins Fleet decided that that the deal wasn't working they could sack us but for the privilege they would have to pay up the three years money. We were six months in and we were determined to see it through however much we hated the experience.

This was why when a seminal meeting came up it was a matter for both of us. Particularly so because the hated Barrow had made us sign a clause that said if either of us was made a bad-leaver the other one would become a bad-leaver too. We had been signed as a pair. Such things were apparently normal when owner-managed businesses were acquired. We just accepted without checking whether that was true or not. The meeting was all about me and just me but Franck had worried more than me about it during the week.

Franck Gilligan had been my partner, Franck Blockel was his real name, his father came from Czechoslovakia or somewhere in the centre of Europe. Gilligan had been his mother's name and he had adopted that as something more commercially acceptable than his original Eastern Block surname, "quite lidderally Eastern Block," as we used to say to each other. To everyone at work we were known as the owners of Gilligan Somes not that most people there readily knew one of us from the other by name, bar the fifteen or so staff we brought with us. It didn't bother me when I was called Franck or when someone said to me "I've just been talking to Hector and he said …". It drove Franck mad and he took it as a personal slur always. He also corrected anyone every time they had the audacity to misspell Franck without its central European "c" whether they had previously met him or not. Better still was when people who didn't know him well enough to take a liberty referred to him as "Fran", then Franck's ego which was not up to letting a European "c" slip could not abide being referred to casually by a girl's name. I never did that but neither did I correct people on his behalf, it amused me to see him get worked up over something as stupid as that and I loved seeing the latent fury in email discussions to which we were both party.

I had not made any effort to prepare for the meeting on Sunday as I had promised Caroline, promised Franck and promised myself. True I had set out with good intentions and at one stage I even got some papers out of my bag and opened my notebook but it didn't happen. Instead I pored over the Sunday Papers all morning, that is to say that I looked at the football results for about half an hour, then cooked and ate Italian sausages and eggs, then spent about an hour studying the football tables and prepared a bet for the following Saturday. I had intended to call a couple of friends to have a lunchtime drink but before I got round to it, it was 3 o'clock, so instead I arranged an early evening drink. That was all very well but, as I knew it would, it ended when the pub shut not at 9 o'clock as I had told myself when I set off. Drunk and determined at half past eleven I settled down with a cup of tea and a sausage sandwich to do my preparation but gave it up within about ten minutes deciding a good night's sleep would be a better contribution to the preparation. I talked myself into thinking the best course of action was to devote all of Monday morning to preparing for the meeting. It was after all a work related activity and they had called the meeting not me.

8.

I rang Franck as soon as I arrived in the office and asked whether he fancied taking the morning off to help me prepare. Franck never needed asking twice to skive off particularly if there was a semi-justified excuse to pin on it. We headed off to our old stomping ground up the road at Hoxton Square and installed ourselves in a bar.

Franck and I hated each other. Well I knew I hated him and I was pretty sure he hated me back. In fact I knew because he had a nasty streak and sometimes he let it show. We were good enough not to talk about it. We had been in business together one way or another for about 10 years and before that we were, if not best friends, extremely close friends at university. I thought about him nearly all the time: how to get round his intransigence; how to anticipate his non-cooperation in things we needed to do for our business and how to get round that; how to counter his sheer bloody minded hypocrisy about nearly everything. He sapped my energy and I wished I'd had the courage to fall out with him sometime long ago but I found myself tied into this project for life with him and I always felt that I had invested too much of myself to give it up so simply. Neither of us ever confronted the fact that we hated each other. We were slightly gentlemanly about it I suppose although that could more accurately be described as an unwillingness in both of us to confront hard subjects. And the interesting part of the story was that together we never failed but to get on like a house on fire. We laughed at the same things, we despaired of the same things and we recognised all too readily our own weaknesses and we laughed at them too. When we were together we spent our whole time laughing and enjoying ourselves.

In our business I represented the law – if I was prepared to talk business speak I would have called it our vertical market, and he represented computers – which, mutatis mutandis, that not being business speak, would have been called the business solution. The world of computers was his world that I was not allowed to go into. I wasn't supposed to hold any opinions about computing either specifically or as a general subject because I didn't have any valid opinions about it and therefore I didn't have the right.

It was a pity then that I looked at computer people as the Twenty First Century car mechanics, not because I had anything against Franck, well not particularly because I had anything against Franck, it was self evident to me. However, if I ever dared to make such an utterance in front of him he would sulk for days. To him it was an utterly personal slur. Once when I said that the new computerised system at some public body wouldn't work because that was what always happened and then they'd start again and pay twice as much – which is what did happen - he said to me that I was "worse than Chambers," which was a pretty bad insult at the time. In fact abnormally direct for him.

To get his own back he would insult the noble profession of the law. Like I gave a fuck. To my mind the law was no more than the commercialisation of pedantry which normally was right up his street. The petty fuck. If he'd had put as much effort into running our business as he did in trying to get the better of me we wouldn't have ended up at Martins Fleet.

You realise in business that there are certain universal truths that simply have to be observed but at Gilligan Somes we weren't allowed to adopt any of them until Franck completely understood them too, working from first principles, i.e. starting from a position of total ignorance. We had a mail shot list but we weren't allowed to us it because it was his kept in one of his databases.

Our company generally expanded at the rate that Franck got through his 'to-do' list. If he thought he was working too hard he didn't bother coming in for a few days, or sometimes he only worked at night for weeks at a time. If we thought of a new idea while he was off, when he next came in he would say "my role in this is ...." and then it went on his to-do list and we all waited.

"How did the betting go?"

It was the first conversation we had with each other every Monday.

"I did my bollocks on Saturday but I left a double behind that came in, so I got a bit back."

"What was it?"

"Breeze Girl in the three year old at Sandown and Lady Cricket did you see it?"

"Yeah she was impressive wasn't she?"

"Well I didn't see the Lady Cricket race, I squeezed it in the newspaper the next day."

I, like Franck and for that matter any gambler I've ever met, couldn't stand the idea of being presented directly with a result. If we missed the result some form of vicarious re-run of the race must be found. Ideally it was to watch a video replay from the beginning "as live" but in the want of that it was to receive a clue about the result without being told it, a newspaper headline that inferred that the result may have happened, a radio report that said that a particular trainer had had a good day, something that hinted at your horse without giving the result directly. Waiting for the newspaper was not ideal but when it happened that way the result had to be squeezed. That meant covering the result with another page of the newspaper and slowly moving it up the page revealing the third, the second and finally the winner.

"Oh great I haven't squeezed one for ages," he said laughing.

"Actually I had bad luck I backed four out of five winners and I got done on that three runner at Sandown."

"What Skycab and Lord York? Were you on York?"

"Yeah."

"God, tough shit I was on Skycab."

"You cunt. I thought it was a dog." We were allowed to call each other a cunt but only occasionally and it had to be said quickly and only then if it wasn't really being used harshly.

"Yeah I was sure you'd do me on the run in."

"I know it looked certain didn't it?"

"Another Dancing Brave, it could only win."

"But failed. Did you win much?"

"No I was about a grand up but I put it on the football."

"Constructing an exit strategy bet?"

"No I just really fancied it."

"What let you down?"

"Middlesborough"

"Me too. Did you hear the commentary?"

"No it was rugby internationals."

"I know, I mean the reports."

"It was on Match of the Day, it looked like they should have won." I only wanted to know if he knew what happened in the match not the precise media through which he was informed. He couldn't help but correct me on what were for me, small irrelevant details. It was important for him to establish that out of the two of us he spoke more accurately.

"They fucking murdered them Franck but I guess our bets put a stop to them winning", I sighed, "It's one more week at Martins Fleet I'm afraid ….. or perhaps not if I get lucky this afternoon."

"Aah this afternoon, are you prepared?" He picked up on the subject at the first opportunity. And he didn't like me saying that our betting on something stopped it happening, he was far too scientific for that. He saw my references to fate and mystical subjects like that as a weakness. Me I knew that I could influence events by betting on them. I was an old spirit and he was a new one. He just didn't know stuff.

"Not really, I did a bit of work last night but it's difficult to prepare not knowing what it's about – I've been denied natural justice innit? I've been trying to think about what it could be and I haven't got a clue .... perhaps I should aks Aude to go in with me, she's a very good human rights lawyer isn't she?"

"Fucking hell could you imagine it? Mind you she doesn't let us get away with anything. By the way, what have you done to upset her lately?"

"Lately, when didn't she have a valid grudge? When didn't I stand in the way of her career?" I was in the mood to go on but Franck brought it back to the point again, "what did Barrow actually say to you again?" He'd got me onto his subject at last.

"Something like, "I can't say too much in advance of the meeting but we want to take stock of where we are in light of the changes to our current management team and whether it can deliver to our objectives," something like that."

"What do you think that means?" Well I'd already told him that I didn't know what it meant last week when he asked. My "don't know," that time obviously wasn't good enough for him who'd been thinking about it since. So I decided to say "don't know," again on the basis that he needed to learn that my judgments weren't to be questioned all the time.

He was leaning towards the unreasonable-reliance-on-third-party-view-as-fact style, for which I particularly detested him.

"I don't know, I don't think it means anything, it was more the earnestness with which he said it that struck me, it was like he was putting me on notice that I was going to get slaughtered."

"It doesn't make sense after my meeting with him on Friday, he was getting right into the deal and trying to pull it apart. You'd think it had to be about Gilligan Somes not you." he said, trying to undermine me. He did this when he wanted to let me know that he thought that I was mistaken in my reporting of a conversation.

"Well I'm not bothered about being criticised and I think the meeting is about me because Declan Barry is in it too – and he is my new boss, you know, you've got to respect the relative positions – ain't you read this week's organigram yet?

"I just worry about getting caught out on the record for the bigger issue," I continued, "what was the main gist with you on Friday?"

"Oh Jesus he had a right go. He basically said that the old deal had no relevance, that they were haemorrhaging money to support the old Gilligan Somes …." and with that we started on a familiar conversation where we batted back and forth the obvious complaints about us and what our responses would be. We were both rather less good at giving those responses when it mattered than in these little mock-ups we staged for each other.

Our conversation took all the usual twists and turns, starting with doubting that we were of any interest to the Martins Fleet executive at all, to realising that whole swathes of board meetings must have been given over to discuss the disappointment of our acquisition.

We always mused on the rise and rise of Tim Hartley, our Chief Executive, who just seemed to us to be incapable of holding his concentration to the end of a sentence and Declan Barry, my new boss, who ran the part of Martins Fleet that accounted for about 80% of the income but represented the office equivalent of working sixteen years on night shift in a salt mine..

Declan we had long since agreed had no quality whatsoever and was the patsy on Hartley's climb to prominence. We knew they had played rugby together once upon a time and Declan just seemed to have fallen in love with Tim Hartley as a dashing square jawed hero. That was the only man that we could see he held any sort of relationship with. Everyone else that worked for him in any position of prominence seemed to be a woman, short of me. Basically he was in charge of a massive personnel department.

We always reserved most time for Barrow. The thing that he had that Barry and Hartley would never have was brains. And that made us frightened of him. He was also completely untrustworthy. And so our meandering and pondering and role play ended in a familiar place.

"Yeah he's a cunt isn't he?" I said coming round to Franck's view.

"What are we doing here?"

"We sold our souls my son."

"To a fucking cunt like Barrow. I rue the day I met him."

"Me too. How much would you take to go?"

"Don't know. I haven't really thought about it lately. Have you?"

55

"Yeah, I think about it all the time. Don't forget I tried to resign, without prejudice, last month."

We both started laughing madly, one of those laughs that builds on itself, that wasn't about anything funny to begin with but doesn't end. We laughed at how pathetic we were or at least how pathetic I was and we couldn't stop. Eventually Franck said:

"What would you have gone for?"

"Jesus Franck, listen if it gets to it I'd go for a oner now."

"God I'm sure it was two hundred last time you told me. I love the way your price is falling," and he started laughing madly again.

"Ask me at five to one, I'll be going cheap."

There was a long reflective silence and eventually Franck spoke:

"I suppose it's time to go back."

"I'm not."

"What are you going to do?"

"I'm going to stay here all morning then I am going to the Greasy for a bit of lunch, then I am going to go and gird me loins in Despatch, have a fag, get tooled up, then I am going to scrag the fucking neck off Declan. Are you in?"

"Let's see, I've got a meeting but it's only with Carmichael, I've got to go to Schraders at two, bit of preparation for that. I'll ring Carmichael and put him off, where will you be?"

"I'll wait in the Square for you like a proper tramp."

Franck joined me after what seemed like an age and we passed the rest of the morning talking about gambling opportunities and falling back onto the subject of Martins Fleet and Julian Barrow. I indulged him by rehearsing with him standard responses to standard criticisms Barrow was likely to raise against us, our old company and its failings. By midday when we adjourned for lasagne and chips at the Nelson Café we had persuaded each other that we were victims in the affair of Martins Fleet and we had nothing to explain to anybody.

The Nelson was alternatively known as Daisy's because of the fat old bird that owned it. But all she did was sit on a large bar stool by the till and smoke fags. Because she owned it and was unfriendly and occasionally said, "be lucky darling," all the cab drivers that went there too declared her to have a great personality. That accolade belonged to her assistant as far as Franck and I were concerned. He was between forty and fifty and looked like Elvis. He was the one who welcomed you in and showed you to a seat. On the way there he ran through all the specials on that day including puddings. He never talked about anything other than what was on the menu or eating related matters, not because Daisy had told him to act in a certain way, simply because he loved food. He absolutely loved the idea of eating every dish he set before you. He was proud to be associated with Daisy's because it was proper food served hot in large quantities. To him it was self-evidently obvious that you would love working in a gaff like that. When he put our lasagne and chips down in front of us he said, "check that out," and made a little assertive thrust of his head.

We parted at the door of the Nelson at five to one, Franck heading off for the betting shop and I, head down, towards the office had a desperate longing to remain at liberty with my comrade.

"I'll come and find you afterwards," I called out after him.

"I'll have my mobile on," Franck shouted back.

Suddenly the gravity of the situation hit me. I was on the carpet, I had some explaining to do, of what I didn't know, and I hadn't prepared in any way, except to fine tune my already well trained attitude. My mouth went dry, my stomach performed a little somersault, I was alone.

Outside Despatch my old friend the Evening Standard vendor was there:

"Hya mate," I said.

"How do you go on?"

"On Saturday? Alright, I got let down for a decent bet by Lord York."

"Who's is that?"

"Williams. You know that three runner at Sandown?"

"Oh yeah that's right I didn't bother wivvit. I had a few quid on that Lady wattsit of Pipes,"

"She won well didn't she?"

"Fucking shit home mate. She's a decent horse. You see that thing won?"

"What's that?"

"You know that thing I'm always betting Had it off or something,"

"Oh Haditovski."

"Yeah that's it, it went in at eights."

"Were you on it?"

"Naah I'm a cunt me. I put it in a yankee and had that thing at evens with it but I wouldn't back it on its own. How many times have I told you about it? I must have backed that cunt the last five times it run."

"Jesus."

"I've got one today for you."

"Oh yeah what's that?"

"Lord Esker. It's no price but it'll shit home. Go and have a look at it."

"Yeah I will, thanks. I've got to have a meeting with a wanker now, I'll go out after and have a look at it. What time's it off?"

"Dunno, later on, you'll have time."

"See ya mate."

I left my last friendly face.

9.

I went into Despatch and took the forbidden goods lift up to the fifth floor. Then I took the long walk from the back of the building to the front, through the Sales Department, through the secretarial area which served the Directors and up to Julian Barrow's office which was open. Barrow and Declan Barry were already there and I knocked on the open door to see if they were ready for me. They were and I was beckoned in.

Meetings in Barrow's office, although serious, usually had a bit of banter and I was struck by the froider which greeted me. His desk was connected to a round table which meant that Barrow could sit in his normal chair whilst hosting a meeting around the desk. Usually all the participants in a meeting with Barrow just sat at a chair facing him around the round table, today Declan had already drawn a chair back away from the table and put it against the far wall so that his gaze was straight into the middle of the room. I took the tip and pulled my chair back a similar distance but angled mine slightly so that I could face Barrow or Barry as required.

I looked at Barrow and nodded my head slightly to show I was ready. Like that moment just before they put the hood and the noose on. As usual Barrow began:

"I'll come straight to the point. We've got a situation here that doesn't seem to be working. I want to use today to get it resolved one way or the other. It would be correct to say that we had expected a lot more of the restructuring that we have been through with you and we want to take a view on that now. But this is more about Declan's view of the success of the new arrangement so I am going to ask him to do most of the talking."

Declan Barry was something like my age if anything perhaps a little younger but he was large and slightly going on top and took himself very seriously which all added up to him coming over as being much older than me. I delighted in the fact that Declan's appearance was worse than my own. Like me he tried to carry off a sharp executive look but his frame was bigger than mine and his suits, which were not expensive enough, didn't hang right on him, he wore shirts that buttoned up, not cuff-link fastenings, and despite his round fat head his shirts still looked baggy at the neck. He was at least one size bigger than me in every department.

Declan started, virtually spitting out the words, I would tell Franck afterwards:

"I want to know what Hector thinks, what is his view of the current situation?"

"What?" I was pleased to note that there was a tone of indignation in my voice. I knew from past experience that it was very important to get off and running in the right mood in meetings like that but so often for me it depended on something beyond my control. I just had to start talking and see what came out. I could equally have started in a high pitched squeal, talking far too fast and that would have been self fulfilling in making me more nervous. Fortunately today I set off alright and unusually for me, I was conscious of being annoyed by Declan when normally I would have just fallen straight onto the defensive. Once off and running the rest was a little easier, it was as if I was acting and I need only keep up the pretence. It was only one word but it was important. I sensed that I really didn't have any respect for Barry at all and I warmed to the task slightly.

"I want to know what you think of how it's going since you started working for me?"

"I want to know what this meeting's about."

"It's about trying to ….."

I interrupted him, "But since you ask, not well, it's very hard to get anything done, my so called assistant manager is off on a completely different agenda to me. Nobody seems to have told Chamberpot that I am in charge of Legal."

Chamberpot was Bryan Pottinger, up until recently he'd been in charge of sales for the legal division for about five years. Chamberpot was mine and Franck's name for him. I liked to use his joke name in a serious meeting with Barrow so that I could deliver a bit of unchallengeable insolence.

"Alright, I want to know why you think it's right to shout down your managers in the office, I want to know why they complain about you, I want to know why you don't show some leadership and inspiration and initiative?"

"What?"

"I think we're waiting for you to reply."

"I've never shouted at anyone in my life. When was this? Who did I do it to?"

I was trying not to shout.

"You shouted at Sophie."

"No I didn't."

"How come Sophie, Sarah and Kirsty came to see me afterwards and told me about it?"

"I don't fucking know. You should have made a better effort to get your story right because it didn't happen. And as for that other stuff you couldn't have anyone with more initiative or leadership than me, it's what I do, that's my thing. I admit I'm not your classic Martins Fleet manager I'm not good on budgets and things like that but don't criticise me for the things I'm good at."

"Well you haven't made a good job of inspiring the people around you."

"Haven't I?"

"No."

"Look this isn't very constructive," interrupted Barrow, "Hector you appreciate that it is a very serious matter to us if you do are not supported by your management team?"

"Management team? You mean Sophie Chawdray?"

"Well yes, you seem not to have hit it off as a team. Why do you think that is?"

"It is because she is fundamentally dense."

"You can't talk about one of our senior managers like that, it's outrageous," he screamed it.

"But they can say anything they want about me whether it's true or not? If you think that she's better than that that's your decision, I happen to think she's fundamentally dense and our relationship will always be compromised by that," I couldn't resist the chance to repeat the offending words.

Barrow gave me a look of absolute contempt.

Declan Barry, who had become a dark red colour during the conversation, decided to take back the initiative:

"Whatever your opinion of her that's no reason to deny her a review and to treat her with contempt. You might not be one our standard managers we don't expect you to be, we are trying to build a new legal division and we have to take a different approach to it but I don't see anything in what you do taking us there, I don't see you doing anything at all. It's not like we haven't had plenty of meetings before now during the last two or three months and it's still like we are at the beginning."

"I didn't deny her a review."

"She seems not to have had one and James was available to do it with you."

"I had a meeting when they wanted to do it, what's wrong with that?"

"Not letting her know until five minutes before, not arranging a new date with her, not showing an interest," well he had me there, to be fair.

"Well maybe, she should have been constructive with me about finding another date instead of using it as something to complain about."

My last comment tailed off and a silence fell over the meeting. Barrow started to speak to draw out concluding remarks, then I remembered there was an open point against me to be responded to but I had forgotten the detail of it, I couldn't get the false accusation of shouting out of my head and I had been thinking about that and lost track a little bit. I was a little put off my stride when I realised that there was more than just Sophie and Declan against me. I started to construct a reply but I stuttered and stammered and fell over my words and it didn't come out very convincingly.

They probably couldn't recall there was an unanswered point to be dealt with either and they'd have thought that my stuttering was further evidence of how ill equipped I was to stand the cut and thrust of business life. Then I hit my stride a little bit.

"....... you've had me supposedly working with you here for three months but I haven't been allowed to say so or to get on with it, in case somebody 'mis-managed the message', I put my fingers into that quotation mark shape that wankers do and I said, 'mis-managed the message' as if I was retarded. Then Tim re-drafted the announcement 10 or 15 times or something and we're still waiting for it. Meanwhile Chawdrey and Chamberpot just get on things on their own and do whatever they want but unlike me they don't seem to attract your attention.

All I hear is "Hector you are charged with building us a £50 million Legal Division and I'm sat amongst all your other managers with established £50 million businesses and I am prey to every HR bird and every two bit accountant that takes a fancy to me. I've got no-one working for me..."

And Barrow interrupted to say, "alright, alright, point taken, we're not used to seeing such passion from you. You always seem to keep it for meetings like this," which made me respond by saying, "it's a pity that it takes meetings like this for you to take any interest in me," which I shouldn't because it made me look far more interested and hurt than I had any intention of showing. Also it raised the stakes with Barrow,

"what exactly is it that we haven't taken an interest in?"

"take your pick. I submitted a business plan to order about a month ago and I haven't heard a single word of reaction to that, good, bad or indifferent."

But Barrow said "that was not a proper business plan," so I started getting all tongue tied and waffley all over again. My moment had gone.

"I know but as a draft document it was the precursor to a business plan, I need to know whether that approach is backed or not. Nobody has given me any idea about that. I don't mind being told it's rubbish and to start again but it's sort of gone through without any critical analysis and I know myself that it is open to challenge, it needs to be challenged critically. I am out there in the wilderness and I don't know whether you are with me or against me. I submitted a new staffing structure for the new business, including people I brought with me from Gilligan Somes but I am still waiting for a response on that, my staff have been in the same vacuum as me for two months and I am the one who has to bullshit them and egg them on every day not knowing what is really going to happen," I hated my lack of lucidity in the heat of debate but was happy that I'd got on a bit of a roll and dumped a few things on them. Especially as most of the things I talked about were things which I had been lacking in too but I was pleased that I took the opportunity to lay it all at their door.

It was a particular weakness of mine that at that stage when I had made a couple of direct hits I would start to be constructive and begin looking for common ground. That day luckily because it was so easy to dislike Declan, I just shut up and left them with it.

"What I am seeing here, is a lack of connexion between you two," said Barrow.

Declan just rolled his eyes and sighed. I bowed my head in injured pride. I felt entitled to sulk.

"As for the matter between you and Sophie," he continued, "we really are going to have to rely on you to pick that one up and make a job of it. The accusations of shouting, you might consider unjust but I suspect there is no smoke without fire and it needs sorting out before it begins to fester. But I think that the important thing to come out of this is that we need to get behind a legal business plan as an executive team quickly and publicly. I want you and Declan to work together on something that we can take to Tim but it needs doing soon. We have got to get this thing going by Christmas, that is a pretty crucial time for the business in general and I can't stress enough the importance of getting something running properly by then."

With that the meeting was over, I still had my head slightly bowed and was determined to say nothing more. Declan looked, if anything, slightly chastened by the experience. An awkward silence fell over the three of us, there being nothing left to say, but nobody had formally brought the meeting to an end. Finally Barrow said "OK then," which meant that the meeting was over. I simply got up and walked out without saying anything, trying to leave the meeting with a sense of being wronged. I wasn't sure whether it worked or not but I was pleased to leave Barrow and Barry together to reflect on what had happened.

In truth I was still slightly crestfallen at being falsely accused of shouting and was finding it difficult to attribute any exchange or any sort of date or time to the event. I walked back down the main stairs to my desk three floors below and I was still thinking about my accusers. Sophie I could understand, I imagined her in Declan's office saying, "I've got no respect for him as my manager or as a person, no respect for his methods and my career will suffer by having to report to him." Sarah Walsh was just a nasty South African bitch who had taken against me the first time she had met me. I had acquitted myself well with her. She was just plain ignorant and antagonistic and she had tried to bully me into doing various things when I first arrived. I wasn't having any of it but instead of telling her to fuck off like any normal person would have done, my desire to have the last word, 100% inherited from my father, meant that I had indulged her far more than I should have done. That meant that we had some sort of relationship when in fact we should have had none. She was thick, aggressive and personal and spiteful and I was incapable of giving her the cold shoulder like I set out too and couldn't resist being sarcastic when the opportunity was given. That added up to me having my first known enemy at Martins Fleet. She would have probably put Chawdray up to making a mountain out of a mole hill. But Kirsty? I couldn't come to terms with Kirsty. Kirsty was the sort of person that loved everyone, a gentle, intelligent girl. She was an accountant and that made her about the only person on my floor that had a proper job. How could she have given evidence against me? For a fictional event? I simply did not recall the event or anything that it could be it and it puzzled me and saddened me that I had to explain it. I had always thought that people that alleged false accusations were generally losers and that it didn't really happen. Now that it had happened to me I was at a loss to know how to deal with it.

I had just finished saying, "fucking bitches," out loud as I arrived at the second floor door. The same time as Sharon Copeland coming up the stairs from the floor below. She was Head of Human Resources, or personnel as I preferred to refer to it, "something upset you dear?" she said.

"Nothing especially," I replied and let her walk through the door in front of me so that I could make it clear I considered it a two statement conversation.

Back at my desk I resisted the temptation to call Franck straightaway sure in the knowledge that there would be an immediate follow up from Declan. He was just too thick and lacking in class to do anything other than cobble something together quickly off the cuff that seemed right at the time without thinking about it properly.

In the meantime I contented myself with wading through my emails which, although they were most likely to contain bad news or rubbish, I always relished looking through them in the way that you enjoyed picking up a Chance or Community Chest at Monopoly. There was always just enough good news or funny messages sprinkled in with the rest to make the looking at them worthwhile. I had eighteen new messages, the entire day's inventory since that was the first time I had sat at my desk properly all day. Seven of them were from Stacey Arnold, "my" human resources coordinator. The first two were normal messages but the following five were tagged to show that they were urgent.

"Bad idea Stace," I said before I had read any of them. Only the first one had a real message, the subsequent ones were various forms of chasing messages. Although she could have been forgiven slightly for the message that said she was leaving for lunch and the one that said she had come back, I was not in a forgiving mood and preferred to take my inspiration from the last message. It simply said RING ME NOW! In red capitals and had been tagged at the highest priority level. It seemed to scream. Before I did anything else I decided to reply while the blood was still high. I wrote:

"To date I have not responded to your oppressive and bullying tactics. Guess what? I wasn't here to respond you fucking ignoramus. Do you get it? I only come to work at this shit company to make some money for myself and you are standing in my way. I couldn't give a flying fuck about you and your fucked up idea of a career. I am giving you one more chance to leave me alone after that I will fall back on the traditional method of a toe end up the fanny."

Then at the bottom I wrote:

"PISS OFF NOW!" in red capitals.

I looked at it for a few seconds before I let it go. It was only a matter of pressing the send button then I would have about fifteen seconds to get out of the building before the whole putrid mass of personnel fell in on me. I nearly sent it. Then I thought that I might put myself in more trouble than I already was and perhaps I was in trouble. In the end I wrote to Declan and said:

"This is her seventh message of the day. Any chance of calling her off?"

Good as gold Declan didn't let me down. As soon as I'd forwarded my message to him his name appeared at the bottom of my in-tray. The message was titled "Seven Point Action Plan"

Inside the message read:

"Following our meeting today 8th November I propose the following action plan:

1. agree legal division business plan – HS DB 26/11
2. agree legal division marketing strategy document HS DB 26/11
3. agree job description SC – HS DB SC asap
4. agree management team legal division – HS DB 26/11
5. agree personnel structure legal division – HS DB SA 19/11
6. present legal division business plan to Tim Hartley 10/12
7. create client presentation to illustrate new legal proposition HS DB 17/12
8. Agree programme of presentations for New Year HS DB MM 17/12

Declan"

So the plan had eight points not seven but the poor lad was in a rush I thought. I turned off my computer and walked out of the office.

65

10.

I went straight to the King's Arms which was the nearest proper pub no more than 100 yards away. It's main attraction was that it was back into the hinterland of old warehouses and printing workshops behind the office and once you were there out of sight of the office there was virtually no chance of anyone that mattered or anyone that would be indiscrete finding you there.

Once there I phoned Franck on his mobile who was with me within five minutes.

"You'll be disappointed," I said over my shoulder from the bar.

"What's happened, have you been short-listed for a Talk About It! Award?"

I waited for Franck's "aah" after his first long draught.

"I got a sort of massive bollocking. It was all about Declan having a go at me really."

"What sort of things?"

"Well get this for their main complaint, I was supposed to have shouted at Sophie in the office."

"What? Did you?"

"No, as if I could be bothered. I can't even think what it might have been confused with. I am totally at a loss."

"She probably just exaggerated some conversation or other."

"But there were witnesses."

"Who?"

"That fucking bitch Sarah Walsh who doesn't count because she'd do anything to be nasty, especially to me, but the worrying one is Kirsty."

"Who's that?"

"She's that pleasant Scottish accountant bird who sits along from me."

"Why would she make anything up?"

"I don't know. The only thing I can come up with is that they want to start building up a file against me so that next time I get a verbal warning, then a written then all of a sudden I'm a bad leaver."

"Do you think they'd bother to do all that?"

"It seems stupid but I can't think of any other good reason and of course it's on the record now. The only other explanation is that in his haste to condemn me Declan has mixed up two different stories."

"But you're right, even if it's only a convenient by-product they might be starting to turn you into a bad leaver."

"And that would be a disaster."

"For both of us."

We fell silent and it felt like the silence was to consider Franck as the unfortunate victim of my predicament.

Franck broke the silence by saying "fuck" into his glass.

"Look Barrow has always been quite genuine about not stitching us up like that and as he has always said it has to be a gross misconduct type of offence. A normal sacking can't make us bad leavers."

"Yeah so he says."

We fell silent again.

"Look Franck I'm going to have to put it on the record tomorrow morning that I object to the accusation and that I don't know anything about it, just to play safe, if it's an undefended remark it will have a different status to something in dispute and if for any reason they were thinking of pursuing it, that will make it not worth the while."

"Are you going to ask Sophie about it?"

"No I'd rather she didn't know that I know and I don't think I'd get a straight answer out of her anyway…….. I suppose I could beat it out of her."

Franck laughed and I felt relieved that he was my friend again.

"It's been over a week since I gave her a good dressing down," I said, warming to the task.

"So what else have you been doing?"

"Well apparently I've not done anything at all really, which is about right. I think that I was slagged off to Declan by Sarah and Sophie and probably one or two others like the personnel birds and he took what they said at face value and decided I was no good. It's really obvious that he judges people on gossip and hearsay - the result of spending his working life surrounded by birds. He said all sorts of stuff like I didn't show any leadership or inspiration, basically that I'd been a massive disappointment. You should have heard him though he was virtually spitting the words at me."

"Jesus what did you say?"

"Well, it's not that what he said isn't justified but I tried to turn it on them and say that all the delays were down to them, that the delay in making the restructuring announcement was out of my control and costly, that I wasn't given any support by the executive team all that sort of bullshit."

"It sounds like a proper fight."

"No, I mean I was alright, well I am usually useless at meetings like that but I gave a reasonable account of myself I suppose. Declan was just plain aggressive and Barrow was just the usual haughty cunt and I tried to take them on point for point. I wasn't great because I was a bit shocked by the low-brow nature of the accusations and I wasn't really ready for them …….. but I guess the measure of success if you could call it that was that within ten minutes of the end of meeting Declan sent me a seven point action plan to take us forward."

"So really you won the encounter?"

"No, my view is that Barrow was rightly embarrassed by Barry and he forced him into doing something constructive after I left."

"But they obviously expected to give you a good hiding and didn't manage it."

"Perhaps, … maybe, but Franck I'm so bad at thinking on my feet, I've lost a brilliant opportunity to get out."

"Do you think so?"

"Definitely. Look when I went into that meeting they must have considered that the worst might happen – if say I didn't have any answers – that I would have had to have gone. Instead of trying to beat them point for point in their arguments and coming up with answers I should have turned it into an issue of confidence. I should have said "if you think that you've clearly got not confidence in me, it's time to go." I'm just so fucking useless at seeing the opportunity in meetings like that."

"I think it sounds like you gave a good account of yourself."

"Oh Jesus I really upset Barrow you would have loved it."

"What happened?"

"Well they were going on about Chawdray and the fact that we didn't have a good relationship and I said her problem was that she was fundamentally dense."

"What did he say?"

"He went fucking ape and said that people like me shouldn't talk about other senior people in such terms."

"Fucking great," we loved winning our minor moral battles that counted for nothing.

"It was hilarious, I wish you'd been there."

"What are you doing now?"

"Going home."

"Fancy a pint in Best Pub?"

"Yeah but I thought you were going to Schraders this afternoon?"

"It's all off, in fact it turned out to never be on, you know Lynda Briar?"

"Do I? She's dreadful."

"I'll tell you on the way, get your coat."

We set off to the Victory about 500 yards further away from the office, which we had fallen into the habit of calling Best Pub, an almost forgotten recollection of a football tour joke when we were at college. Many afternoons were ended there and it was always where we headed if we wanted to keep our conversations absolutely confidential. The pub could be guaranteed to have the match on if there was one and not be crowded. It also had a sympathetic landlord who was not against putting up Ceefax so that we could get a little squeeze out of bets on unbroadcasted events. It was also a pub that we knew as a place where adventures started. Countless times in the past that had been where we had gone for a quick pint on the way home at nine or ten o'clock after working late and discovered the next morning that it had actually been the starting point on a colossal night out. We were in too early for that. All I would manage to do that night was stagger home down Old Street at midnight after ten pints of Young's Ordinary.

All the way home the false accusation of shouting dominated my thoughts, I knew I was drunk but felt a sense of clarity brought on by beer euphoria. By the time I reached the kebab shop I had made up my mind to take Kirsty aside first thing the next morning to ask her what exactly it was that she had witnessed. That was a bit naff and very Martins Fleetish behaviour and it would also make me look like I cared more than I did but I simply had to get to the bottom of it and to know what it was I was supposed to have done.

There were two women in the kebab shop and it took me a while to realise that they weren't buying. They were all dressed up but I couldn't work out where they might be going. After my order was taken they started to take an interest in me. They were made up and, well, they were all sexy looking and I was gratified by the attention.

"Are you going somewhere interesting gorgeous?" the slightly uglier one said. Then I realised I was really pissed. I tried to say that I was going home to my really smart apartment alone which was just round the corner in an alluring and interesting way, instead I said roughly all those words but not in the right order.

"Is that a proposition love?" she said and threw her head backwards and laughed like a demented hag.

Then she just dropped me and went back to talking to her friend. I heard the nicer one say, "do you think he's interested?" and I didn't know whether she meant me or not.

I was sort of coming to the idea that they were prostitutes but I couldn't be sure. Being pissed I wasn't exactly against the idea of spending the rest of the night with them and I started to try and work out how much money I had left on me.

Kebabs take ages. If it wasn't for the fact that 95% of kebab customers were pissed there'd be no end of complaints. There doesn't seem to be anything to wait for. That triangular piece of meat doesn't seem to start cooking or change colour or texture during the process but the server just stands there waiting for something. Perhaps it's something to do with health and safety. I always classed kebab shop owners with barbers in that I could never work out how they managed to serve enough people per hour to make it pay. They had their own businesses with costs to meet and staff to pay and I never worked out how the sums all added up. Perhaps they're fronts for brothels.

I reckoned on a long wait and I had plenty of time to reflect on my decision to come in in the first place. I knew that I shouldn't have at the time and I knew that I would regret coming in afterwards but at that time, despite knowing these things, I threw myself in quickly when my mind was on something else. A quick in and out. The old in and out. Quick in long out. I had been staring at the prostitutes.

"You after something love?"

I felt a wave of confidence, well bravado, so I said "yes," I didn't know what it was I was after.

"Oh yeah what's that then?"

"Whatever you've got."

Then I did a sort of semi-vomit belch but I was pleased with the way I contained it and kept it discrete. Unfortunately it made my stomach contract a little bit and with that I had a three minute warning.

Any normal person would have asked to go to the toilet in the kebab shop but I couldn't. I didn't want to because it would have contradicted the dashing image that I was putting over to the prostitutes, not that I would ever see them again if I ran home, but had I gone to the establishment toilet and had they showed any interest when I came out I would have stayed. Besides I couldn't imagine the toilet was anything but unacceptably filthy so I said to the shopkeeper to stop the kebab, left him a fiver on the counter and ran out of the shop.

The nicer prostitute called out after me:

"Come back soon," and so, despite being terrified of cacking my pants in public I stopped and re-opened the door and shouted back:

"I'll be here tomorrow."

The sad thing was I meant it.

I semi-trotted home, nearly a mile, and I got my final warning in Clerkenwell Green, which still left a good two hundred yards to go. I thought about going in the churchyard but I didn't like the sacrilegious connotations of that. I thought that defecate and desecrate were too conveniently close for a tabloid writer should I have been caught in the act. And most of all I didn't want to be taken for soliciting a rude act involving my bare arse so I pressed on. Sparing the worst of the details I made it, but only just, it was very tangential, very dy by dx. I implored myself to take greater care of toilet management.

By the time I emerged from the toilet I had also decided to make a call to the lawyers to check the bad leaver point. I had a two point action plan to take into the next day. Just to make sure I switched on the computer and wrote down the two points and why they were important, I was still alert enough to think that my notes were likely to look ridiculous the following morning but I reasoned that being drunk there was a chance I would have forgotten all my bright ideas by the next morning and I didn't want to take that risk. My suit from Saturday was still on the bed. I reprimanded myself for being a shambles, hung up my underpants to dry in the en suite shower, took off my jacket and trousers, and went to sleep with the rest of my clothes on.

11.

I needn't have worried about the aide-memoire, I woke up thinking of the action plan for the day. I remembered the note and went to get it from the back of the front door where I had blu-tacked it the previous evening. I expected to be embarrassed by my drunken thoughts but found that they were far more coherent and reasoned than I expected. So much so that I folded up the page and slipped it into the inside pocket of my suit jacket. It was still early so I decided to set out to work and have a decent stop on the way for breakfast in the restaurant at the gym, better still, as this might be the false dawn before an enormous hangover I would go and take a sauna then have breakfast.

The on-paper simplicity of wearing gym kit and packing suit, shirt, shoes and tie was never that for me. Even where it didn't involve ironing a shirt, choosing between different suits on the basis of differing degrees of greasiness and smelliness, forgetting various items of underwear, cufflinks and tie, it always took a disproportionate amount of time. I would have spells of going to the gym and going to work on my bike where I would fall into a reasonably efficient routine with my preparation and getting dressed and undressed but when the regime was recommenced it took me an age to get organised. As a result I left my flat at twenty past eight and had I proceeded directly to work I would have only just arrived on time, albeit that my colleagues sitting around me would have been there for at least an hour before that. However I had set my course on sauna and breakfast and so that was what it would be, I could play the early meeting card when I arrived late.

I went to the gym with a spring in my step, I felt positive. I had gone through the stage of making a bad job of a job I didn't like and I had entered a period where my sole objective was to get through or get out of my deal on reasonable terms. Now I saw my job as exclusively that and felt invigorated by having something to focus on. As I walked to the gym I rehearsed the conversation I would have with Kirsty. I cast myself as the quietly spoken falsely accused, not quite pathetic but not far off. A figure to evoke sympathy from the decent and gentle Kirsty. I considered skipping the gym altogether because a certain desired atmosphere of incisiveness would have been lost by turning up at something to ten. That would not send the right message to Kirsty. But I talked myself out of it on the basis that I would send a very polite email to ask her to spare five minutes with me so that she was not steamrollered into an unwanted meeting. That decided once in the sauna I turned my attention to rehearsing my brief conversation with the lawyers. There were three goals for the telephone conversation: to get a clear understanding of what sort of dismissal was a bad-leaver dismissal; not to let the request develop into a fee-paying scenario; not to be seen to be ignorant of matters that were well established. I worked on a conversation that I might have with the lawyer, grateful for the solitude in the sauna. Most proper people would have already long since been at their desks.

The more I thought of it, the more I knew that I couldn't lose my deal for an orthodox sacking. Bad-leaver was essentially to cover me packing it in, it worked a little bit in the other direction for gross misconduct, not for run of the mill sackings. I was sure it was a well established fact in our negotiations. It had to be that. I berated myself for not taking enough care and attention to know matters like that properly, matters of such crucial importance for me. The more I thought about it the more convinced I became. I couldn't lose my deal for being sacked for being useless, or uncooperative or thick or ignorant. Just like all the people that I had had to put up with working for me.

In fact, I could be much better at being all those things than the people who had worked for me over the years.

"Eureka," I experienced the warm glow of a good idea. I paused and thought again. But I was sure I was onto something. I was. I could make myself dispensable.

They obviously didn't rate me very much on the basis of the previous day's meeting and had perhaps already faced the prospect of dismissing me. Why not? I recalled the words of some industry figure I had talked to at some party or other, he had described a friend of his as a "serial business seller," he never stayed long after the sale, he made it his business to get out. He made himself unbearable. That's what I would do. It was a legitimate business activity. I had a career at last. It was decided.

"Get in there you bastard," I cried out, raising myself up giving an abdomen punch to the air, when I noticed I wasn't alone. A bald, naked, fat man was stood on the lower bunk of the sauna and I, rendered mute by my sudden discovery, stood naked, legs akimbo in front of him. Neither of us said a word, we just looked at each other. Him: pink and grey, covered in wiry hair, button mushroom cock, loose, low-hanging, ball sac, flat triangle shaped, very small arse, sausage fingers, sky blue flip-flops; me: smooth, hairless, heavy torso on small frame which suddenly stopped just before my legs started making it look like I could fall over forwards at any time, mini-trunk style foreskin, with compact ball sac to rear, little feet and hands. Most people that looked at me like this were struck by the same injustice that I was: that I was too young and too skinny to have a fat body stuck on me. It was like I was the victim of a terrible conspiracy. Eventually the man left without either of us ever having spoken. I thought he shook his head slightly before leaving as if he was puzzled. Then, I think I may have imposed these words on the situation when I thought about it afterwards but he could have said "poor fucker," or something like that. Definitely "poor".

Nevertheless I wasn't going to let that embarrassing interlude hold me back, I was bubbling with excitement and couldn't wait to get to the office to get the ball rolling. I just had to get the balance right between being sacked and being dismissed for gross misconduct, the lawyers would put me right on that and I still had to put my objections to my wrongful accusation on the record. In fact I could make the objection the start of things to come.

12.

The meeting with Kirsty could not have been scripted better. She had no idea what I was talking about. She "certainly hadn't reported such a thing to Declan." I felt like kissing her but that would have destroyed the injured innocence I had conjured up. I played it a little bit too pathetic for my liking but I heard what I wanted to and that was all that mattered. I hurried back to my desk and composed my email to Julian Barrow and Declan Barry.

It was my declaration of war, not that they would know that. As I wrote it I was saying "I have in my hand a piece of email," like Neville Chamberlain. It read:

"Regarding yesterday's meeting I was distressed at a couple of matters that were raised - not to say at the meeting as a whole – and I want to deal with them straight away. I was extremely upset by the false allegation of "shouting down" Sophie in the office. I have no recollection of any such incident and this morning on checking with Kirsty, who was supposed to be one of the witnesses, I find that she also has no idea what you're talking about. Were you taking the piss? I have got to say that I found the accusation disturbing and I have spent a sleepless night thinking about what it might have been. I particularly do not agree with Julian's remark that "there is no smoke without fire," and I don't know what you are getting at when you say this. Do you mean that you think I am liar? I resent above all that you saw fit to accuse me on the basis of unsubstantiated hearsay. I know that you wouldn't let me deal with a photocopying clerk in the same way."

As I cc'd it to Franck and let it go I suddenly realised that I would sound like a wanker, particularly to Franck. "Aah what the fuck," I said and deciding to get positive I congratulated myself on using clerk instead of operator or whatever fucked up description they used. That sounded like a decent insult. As a declaration of righteous non-cooperation went it wasn't a bad start.

I gave the lawyers a ring and got a reasonable confirmation of my interpretation within about 30 seconds. In fact I sorted of regretted ringing since there could only have been one reasonable interpretation and indeed the lawyer confirmed it was so whilst seeming to yawn for the entire duration of the call. I felt small, he was probably the same age as me. It was eleven o'clock and under the new regime I had created for myself that counted as lunch. I decided that my disobedience needing plotting properly so I took myself off for a proper lunch.

The Home and Colonial didn't have a lot going for it. First it was about 30 seconds walk from the office and by dint of our pathetic office conditions it doubled up as on overflow office. Second it was one of those modern phenomena, a mini-chain that was neither café nor bar, nor was it a restaurant but it did food. It was one of those places that was sophisticated only in marketing material and its owners' imaginations.

In fact the stripped wood floors and modern furniture served only to rob it of any atmosphere at all, making it a poor version of a pub and the dominating presence was of a railway station waiting room. It wouldn't have been so bad but the next nearest place was just the same, that was called Bar Sol or something like that and tried to evoke the Mexican Cantina.

Anyway I was happy to take my lunch there since it was only just after eleven and it would be at least two hours before any of the plebs from Martins Fleet turned up and given that it was only Tuesday, there was very little chance of very many of them going out to lunch. Even if they did I'd be in the bookmakers by then. It was winter and it was the days of the lunchtime yankee. That is to say that you were pretty much guaranteed at least four races during the period that most of the population called lunchtime.

The girl that ran the bar was little, Welsh, young and fat and she had one of those early eighties, flock of seagulls haircuts, a first whiff of independence. Hers was died black. She was friendly or at least trained to be superficially so and because I had got into the habit of going in there at odd hours, say for a meeting at 4 p.m., and taking a glass of wine, she had latched on to me as a "fellow businessman".

"Good weekend?" she said. That meant that she had done something interesting or sophisticated and wanted to tell me about it. I reflected that I had nearly shat myself twice in the last three days but decided against telling her.

"A grown man, poo-ing his pants," I thought.

"I nearly shat myself on Saturday," I said.

"Sounds interesting," she said slowly and warily.

"when Wales looked like they were going beat Romania."

"Very funny, we'll still give you lot a good game next time."

Then I felt I owed her it so I said "what did you do?"

It turned out she'd been somewhere with Quad Bikes. Fortunately I had only to spend a few moments listening to her desperate search for life before she left me alone, having to change a barrel herself because she had been let down for staff. I found myself a corner and broke out a fresh page of my notebook.

Before I wrote anything I drifted off into re-running the previous day's meeting with Barrow. I remembered how it had been my original intention to blow them away by over preparing and being able to dominate the meeting and I started to think about the part of the meeting where I lost the thread and couldn't remember what question I was answering. It shamed me now as it might have done to have gone to the meeting

75

naked, and the realisation of my awful, inadequate, mumbling response made me go cold, suck in my breath and freeze. It made me think about something I did when I was younger which made me feel the same way as I felt then.

It was no more than a long forgotten memory of a secret wank, which I thought was secret but I realised some years later my sister and my best friend witnessed together.

I don't know what brought it on, probably just an idle moment thinking about things that I hadn't got away with that I thought I had. But when I recalled it I thought for the first time of them watching my little white skinny arse pumping up and down on the brown velour settee, him and my sister together. What did they say to each other? It made me weak with shame. I sort of semi hyper-ventilated if you can do that, as I had done the first time I remembered the story. But there and then I was convulsed with shame and embarrassment. I held clumps of hair with both hands at the side of my head and rocked on my chair like I was riding a horse, suddenly I became very hot and felt myself going red. I started crying out "oh no, oh no, oh my god, please stop, why, no." Suddenly I realised I was doing it in public in a bar. I sort of shuddered and stopped and then started to panic about what sort of exhibition I had made of myself.

The little Welsh manager was back and shouted over:

"everything OK?"

"Oh Jesus what a fucked up cunt I was. How much had she seen?" My only hope was in the way that she said "everything OK." She said it in the way that sounded as if she had just come back and wondered if I was being seen to, not in a way that she had just witnessed a previously respected young businessman in the course of having a breakdown. I hoped.

I scanned the bar for other witnesses but I was alone. Then I noticed someone looking at me through the far window, they were on their way away from me which indicated that they had walked past me recently and may have seen me through the window adjacent to my seat. They were vaguely recognisable as someone from the office and they were definitely looking at me. They were laughing in fact. They must have seen and they were sending me a look of recognition. They were probably some junior bod for whom I was something of a minor office celebrity. They were still looking so I had to do something back. I found myself giving him a big wide, silly grin, acting like I'd been rocking and pulling my hair out as a little visual gag for him. In fact I found myself sort of re-doing it for him so that he could be sure it was a crazy gag for him. Pretending like I was cracking up.

I took my usual steak sandwich that allowed me to get out quickly and more importantly deliver the order quickly so that there was less chance of having to have a conversation. I had decided to sort of shout it out when I saw her on the way over from behind the bar so that she couldn't get within five yards of me.

While I waited I started to work on my non-cooperation lists as I had started to refer to them. They ended up like this:

Go to gym each morning. I had put a dash and then wrote sauna and swim, to reassure myself that I wouldn't have to actually go the real gym. It was more a lifestyle list I was trying to create.

Then I wrote *eat breakfast each morning*. Just in case I forgot. Why I wrote each morning I can't recall. Then it went:

Arrive work 9.30 ish. Fair enough.

Take lunch (pretend client) everyday.

Spend one – two hours each day at lunchtime in bookmakers. Easy.

In the afternoons I decided that I would spend the entire time on the Racing Post website or Betfair or something like that and listen to sports radio. The next four months would be devoted mostly to getting my knowledge of form up to date.

I thought that I would give them two and half hours to three hours work each day from 9.30 until lunch. That was probably far more than I had to do to impress them I reasoned, not that I exactly wanted to impress them, but it would allow me to keep one step ahead in my new game.

Then I wrote: leave each day not later than 5.30. I also wrote: leave Fridays 3.30 and arrive Mondays 11. Then I wrote *invent lots of meetings*. The important thing about this last point was that all our diaries had to be kept on our PCs so that anyone could look at them. It also meant that anyone could look to see if you were free at a given time and impose a meeting on you. I was lucky because nobody knew anything about the legal market where I was supposed to have lots of contacts. I didn't but they didn't know that. So I decided to fill up my diary with back to back fictitious meetings. It would keep me out of the office and they would soon get used to that. It would be the way I worked.

I also decided to take not less than one afternoon off per week to actually go to the races, Ludlow, Folkestone, Towcester all the interesting gaffs that I didn't normally get round to going to and where I let the form go unnoticed. I had four months to go until Cheltenham and I decided to make it my single focus from then on. If the idea went to plan I would be out of work by early Spring with a big pay off and I would need something to do. I loved the idea of turning myself into at least a semi-pro by then and with a wedge coming on stream to back it up. Secondly and by way of contingency I thought that if I could land a decent bet at the same time as getting paid off that coincidence could change my life favourably for ever. Thirdly if there were to be any difficulties with Martins Fleet, a winning Cheltenham would allow me to be sacked with impunity.

My penultimate line was "Get a job." By virtue of my ill gotten gains I could for the first time in my life try and look for a job that might interest me. As soon as I had a firm offer I would either have to go the final step to getting dismissed or I would go to Barrow and cut a deal to leave. A firm offer in the bag would make the rest easy. I had underlined it and put a large asterisk to the right of it as if I realised that this was the only really important point on the page.

The final point I wrote was "don't cooperate with wankers."

By 11.45 I was in the bookies.

I spent over an hour reading the Racing Post, which, despite it being the Racing Post, was sheer bliss. And I picked up Saturday's double to refresh the wedge. The only low point was reading the results and seeing that Lord Esker had duly shit home as predicted by my Evening Standard friend. I hadn't backed it because I had been getting pissed in the middle of the afternoon instead. Never mind, I was entering a new era of professionalism.

There were a couple of novice hurdles and a seller for openers and by the time they were off I had banked the form. I had formed a view but decided against a bet. If I was going to watch a lot of racing I needed to break the habit of betting on every race. I needed to read the form as assiduously as I would if I was betting, without betting, so that I could get the most out of just watching the race. Pipe's horse was a walk over for the seller, it was 6/1 on. At Huntingdon only Doigts D'Or could win really and 15/8 looked a bit generous to me and the Sedgefield equivalent was so bad only (even) King's Hussar had to win. They all did. A 5/1 treble. I just watched.

Franck came into the shop then and it stopped me taking the approach I wanted to while he was there. I felt embarrassed to let him see my little notebook in which I wrote the names of running-ons and those that went round the wide way and finished full of running. I brought him up to date with my good news phone call with the lawyers and my meeting with Kirsty. The cheeky fucker said, "what exactly did he [the lawyer] say?" Like he didn't trust my interpretation of the conversation, and like a fucking arsehole I tried to recall a word for word version for him. He backed a couple of winners and went off to buy his cheese foccacia, green apple and can of diet coke. He was nothing if not predictable.

I just had time to squeeze the two o'clock before going back. It was always much easier when taking the piss to take it at the front end not the back. I decided to have a tenner interest on the basis that standard stakes were not less than £50. It was a staying handicap with eight runners, which put it up there as one of my favoured mediums. I took agin the favourite and liked the look and price of Our Carol down the field. With 8 runners and decent price I had £10 each way. I'd had a short list of

3 none of which was the favourite so I had a little combination forecast with them. Then I thought that it would pain me for ever if I got the tricast and didn't back it so I went back and covered that too. I noticed the feeling immediately, it was entirely better watching the race being on. I was engaged. As the leaders got to the top of the hill I was out of it. Then I realised that my little interest as I had called it added up to £40 something. That could constitute a proper bet for me and I had had it on a no hoper for a bit of fun. I had stood and selected winners without betting them and if I had been betting anything like normally I would have had £50 or £100 on them. Instead I didn't bet them then threw a load of money away on a dog. I felt disgusted and sad for myself. Then I decided that I'd get my money back and put the temporary set back behind me, at least my analysis was on form I told myself. The next race was a four runner with a big odds on favourite so I gave it a swerve and got stuck into the next at Newbury, the 2.20. That had an even money favourite and at first I really liked the look of £50 at evens to get my money back but when I looked into it it wasn't worthy, although amongst the four other runners there wasn't much in the way of a worthy challenger. I decided that the race wouldn't take much winning at all and so I had £50 on Brown Melody, he had not raced much recently but he looked like he was a class apart from the rest. He came second.

Suddenly I felt very low. I felt the blood drain from my cheeks. I walked out of the shop with my head hung low. It was a feeling I knew very well. It made me feel very alone, as a drowning man might. There was nothing, not the flimsiest of straws to reach for, I had to accept my fate. On auto-pilot I did what I always did when I felt like this, I went to the corner shop and bought three or four packets of sweets which I ate one after the other until they had gone. I always associated this desire with losing, like the need to bring up the blood sugar after a night on the beer. It wasn't so much the losing of £100, I had done far worse than that many, many times. It was the manner of losing. The fact that a casual habit like that could add up to £600 a week without noticing. It was my uselessness, my indiscipline. At times like that I felt that I would never recover. I recognised a gambling illness and it frightened me.

13.

It was hot as I walked back and all proper people would already have been back at their desks. I felt like a bum to be hanging around outside. When I got back to my desk I was in such a slough of despair that I couldn't get going, not even on my fictional diary. I thought that the best use of the afternoon was to tidy up a few personal things that had been hanging around for a while. For a kick off there was the calamity of our bank account.

We had decided to marry our bank accounts together so that we would be a proper married couple. Caroline set it all up, all I had to do was close mine and transfer it to the new one which by any other name was hers. I had rung up the bank a few months earlier, told them the story and a very helpful young man, assured me that it would be simplicity itself, since I was moving my account from one part of his great institution to another. It hadn't been. At first he had done no more than transfer the balance, £7.00 on the due date but hadn't done anything else. That meant that all the standing orders and direct debits had lapsed, which meant that all the things they paid for had stopped or gone into default. I only found out about them one at a time as they came into default, first my mobile phone, then my pension and so on. It took me a while to realise the cause of the problem and when eventually I did it was a long way from straightforward to reactivate them again. It was one of those sagas that didn't have an end. I had been assured about six or seven separate times by different people that it had all finally been put right once and for all, then a new disaster would happen. It was like the plot of a horror film since each time I found a new champion of my cause I put my trust in them and they turned out to be more dastardly than the previous.

Currently my plight was: my wages weren't turning up in the new account; my previous account hadn't been closed and one or two standing orders had gone through on it and they had been writing to me to clear my unapproved overdraft, especially since my wages weren't going into the account; and I had got totally out of sync with my bank cards, as each one eventually arrived it had already been cancelled. It would be delivered home when I specifically arranged it to be sent to work or vice versa and other calamities on the same theme. The last one I received was Issue 9 and that said Mrs Hector Soames with an "a" and a Mrs. Trying to make any progress on the matter was like pure torture for me. I just didn't have the appetite to tell the whole story over again to a new person. However I had promised Caroline that I would get to the bottom of it while she was away. I had to get a cash card, get my last three salaries credited to the account and generally deal with all the un-dealt with stuff and I also had to make sure they had written to us with a complete list of previous standing orders and direct debits and a comparative list with all the new ones. We had taken on a massive, for us, new mortgage and Caroline had a paranoid fear that we would go straight into default and become non-people.

I had no desire whatsoever to do any of it but I was so utterly morose I thought that I might be in the right mood to plod through it slowly. I picked up the phone.

"Hello how can I help you?"

"Can I speak to someone who deals with problems with accounts?"

"What branch are you?"

"But I'm ringing you at it."

"No sir you are calling the service centre for all our North London branches. If I could start with your Branch."

"I don't really have one err know what it is, I mean what it's called."

"do you have an account with us?"

"Well yes, in a way. I don't really know who you are."

"Do you want to open an account?"

"Not really."

"So you have an account?"

"Yes, I do."

"And you don't know the branch?"

"No I can't remember the name."

"Well can I take the account number?"

"No I don't have any cards."

"Do you know what you are ringing about?"

"Yes I do. I want to complain about something."

"But you don't know your branch or bank account number?"

"Correct."

"What is the nature of the complaint?"

"It's about lots of things, I don't really want to say it all twice."

"I'll put you through to my line manager to see if she can get any sense out of you."

"Fuck off,"

I don't know why I said that exactly, I just wanted to slip it in casually as she passed me over, so that she wouldn't be sure whether I had really said it or not. I wanted to punish her for being so incapable of living outside her world of standard answers to pro-forma questions.

A new voice came on the line.

"Hello who am I talking to?"

"Mr. Somes."

"Well Mr. Somes before we go any further I must say that we don't enjoy being abused and I want you to know that we are under no obligation to continue to provide a service to you when you use abusive language to our staff."

"I didn't think you'd started," it was a bit of a professional misunderstanding to pick up on the bit of her sentence about "providing a service," to respond to. If I was truthful I was trying to draw her into committing an unintentional non-sequitor.

"Mr. Somes, is there something specific we can help you with or have you simply called to cause trouble?"

"I am calling to discuss how your useless service has ruined my life and to see what you intend to do to get yourself out of the predicament."

"Mr. Somes I have warned you already about your language."

"What language?"

"To tone down your language."

"Like what exactly?"

"You know very well what I mean."

"Know I don't actually. I don't understand what's so offensive about the words I used."

"Your manner is not conducive to providing you with a service."

"My manner? I thought it was the words. What exactly is it that you object to?"

"I really don't think we are achieving anything here. You are wasting my valuable time."

"I only asked you to tell me what it is you objected to and you haven't been able to do that yet."

"I am not here to play silly games with you."

"Well you started it."

"Don't be absurd."

"Why can't you tell me what it is you object to about what I said."

She just sighed loudly.

"Unless you mean useless. Is that what you didn't like, my saying useless?"

"Well it is one of them."

"I thought you'd have been used to words like that by now. What were the others?"

"What others?"

"You said it was one of them. What are the others?"

"I'm not exactly taking notes."

"No you're not are you. You're taking offence instead."

"I am in no mood to carry on with this conversation."

"Well why don't you stop and get on with your job."

"If we can keep it civil, very well."

"If you can keep to the point I will."

"Why don't you start?"

"Are you the most senior person there?"

"I am the Line Manager for this section."

"Are you or not?"

"I can assure you that I am the most senior person you can speak to at this time."

"I bet you're not."

Silence

"This is a very long and complicated and unhappy story and I am not prepared to say it twice. That means that I don't want to be passed on when you realise that you are out of your depth. Is that clear?"

"Yes."

"It's only fair to tell you that this problem has been going on for a long time and this is probably the twentieth call I have made and I am sure that you will not be able to deal with it. And I reserve my right to be abusive when that happens. Do you understand?"

She was merely a doesn't-know-how-thick-she-is at the end of the day.

"Please hold the line."

Then a terrible thing happened, I got put on to someone who was kind and cooperative. She was thick, sure and her bedside manner was kind of overbearing, she was just too sympathetic really, but I got the story out and she promised to deal with it personally and promised that I would get a call back off her personally at the beginning of next week. She even gave me her direct line. And she assured me that the letter had been sent. I made a note to empty the letter box when I got home so that I could go through the letter before Caroline got home.

I had probably just met another champion in my horror story but it felt like I'd got somewhere. So much so that I nearly rang John Lewis about the washing machine that had never worked since we bought it six weeks ago. That could wait until the next afternoon I had nothing to do. There'd be one soon I was sure.

I checked my emails and noticed that I'd been invited to a couple of decent quality meetings for some grander projects that were going on. Declan must have been under instructions to get me involved. Just when I had decided to take a low profile. That was always the way with me. I confirmed the review for the truculent Sophie for 9.30 on Friday morning, responded to say I would go to the meetings, ignored the messages from Stacey Arnold, switched off and went home for the day.

14.

I was down and I knew from past experience how long it would take me to come back round again. It couldn't be rushed, nature must be allowed to take its own course.

Wednesday was out of the question for a recovery, in fact I went into a deeper slough of despair as the day wore on. I woke up with a semi-determination to crack on but the mood was deep and the shroud was heavy and everything that confronted me from waking only served to convince me more that I was entitled to be morose and without hope. I tried to brush my hair but I had nothing like a proper haircut, the idiot I went to last time didn't even follow the standard rules of haircutting, she didn't know that you could start with the clippers loosely without having to select a number. My back hurt, it would always hurt, there was no cure, I woke up with it hurting but apart from taking aspirin there was nothing to do other than accept it. I needed to get my teeth fixed but a visit to the dentists on spec was far too much of gamble, a morning spent ringing round trying to find somewhere was plain unpalatable, the idea of getting out of the dentists for anything less than a few hundred quid given about two years of delay filled me with dread. Even if I did I had no means of paying for anything that cost more than petty cash. I had to sort out my bank account so that I could do things in general, just the normal things that everyone did, but it remained an insurmountable hill of bureaucracy that had no chance of being resolved in anything like the foreseeable future. I had the sort of job where it didn't matter whether I arrived at work at 7.00 a.m. or 11.00 a.m., and I longed for a job where it did. I was too heavy, not fat, just heavy - why hadn't I been programmed by my parents to get up at 6.00 a.m. every morning? With that came purpose, even without a goal purpose came by just doing it. Discipline; with discipline came purpose, with purpose came desire, with desire came essence, the need to carry on living was a given. I shuffled off to work.

I tried to create some purpose for myself but no inspiration came, I reflected on my non-cooperation lists and they felt like another excuse to re-start my life all over again. I virtually staggered to work only stopping to say "oh God no," as the shame of my thoughts and recent actions recurred to me. I knew there was no fighting it. I plodded on and contented myself with the idea of feeling justifiably sorry for what had become of me.

I knew that just as easily as it came it would go. I would find myself thinking of something I should deal with and with that would come a collateral idea and before I knew it I would be planning. Little time would be lost before I would be feeling positive about the plans and then, a short time after that, I would feel ridiculous and self indulgent for ever having entered the slough in the first place. Then out of a plan would emerge a little purpose and from that some hope.

Wednesday was lost. Friday was already spoken for by 'in the book' Martin's Fleet based appointments, that left Thursday to try and do something. Just a little thing was all that was required, some tiny element of constructive behaviour that got the juices flowing again. That was the one thing I gave some attention to on Wednesday. In the end I realised that I had to clear my outstanding Gilligan Somes matters, to allow me to get on with not cooperating and pretending to be a renascent Martin's Fleet person. When that thought lodged I eventually managed to rationalise it into an action.

There really wasn't very much to do to clear my desk of Gilligan Somes matters, only those small things that went round and round in my head that were no where near being on the public record with Martins Fleet. It really only boiled down to having one action of any importance to deal with and that was to wrap up the outstanding issue with Aude. Well that and the sacking of Daniel but the Martins Fleet machine had already absorbed Daniel and his issue all their own without my help. Aude on the other hand was an HR gift; thick, useless, ideas above her station, soft-left sympathies and an inviolable sense of being right. She was just the sort of thing that would come back and haunt me, even if everything else went perfectly to plan so I decided to be brave, confront it and get it behind me.

The issue was her new bonus scheme which she had assured me she had understood when I took her through it about six weeks previously but events had transpired to show that we were at cross purposes.

Well not cross purposes, Aude had taken a view of our conversation that was untenable. Nevertheless during recent weeks it came to light that Aude's expectations were running at an entirely different level to those that I'd given her. No-one, especially Aude had told me so, I'd just picked up on the mood, as you do in offices. I got the impression that my former colleagues had been concurring about 'how typical it was of Hector to make such a simple matter so confusing'.

I knew that I had been clear and fair with her when I first took her through it but I knew that there was little chance of her understanding properly. In fact the first time that I presented the idea to her, so simple and childlike was my approach that I was worried that she would find me patronising and condescending and I would get in trouble for that instead. I had indulged her in her ignorance throughout my explanation and I had talked to her in the way that you would teach a six year old their 6 times table. I had prepared spreadsheets and double checked them for compatibility against our own budgets. I had prepared derivative spreadsheets for Aude to explain to her just the bit that was relevant to her. The offer I made had been a pure bred offspring of the deal I was working under myself. It took a good week of my time, including working at home, to produce it and when finally it was done I spent another day drafting a document to explain in idiot's terms what it meant.

I had spoken to Franck at the time about the need to motivate Aude with a deal on similar terms to us and he had said, "she's refused a bonus hasn't she?" but I managed to convince him that she was uncooperative without what she perceived as 'fair terms as the rest of them.'

In the end he just said, "I'll do something about it when I have to," which actually meant he would do something just after it was too late. So come the day I decided that it was about time he should take his share of the deal and I called him to the meeting I set up with Aude on that Thursday.

He'd said, "is it really necessary for me to be there I've got a lot on?" to which I should have said, "you're in it as much as me, take responsibility for once and just be there," but instead I said, "well not really, but it really goes to the heart of all the bonus schemes, including ours and it will go on and on if it's not addressed now."

So he said, "I can come between 12.15 and 12.45 on Thursday."

At about 12.45 on the Thursday after Aude and I had looked at each other for forty minutes, he arrived.

"What's been decided?" he said.

"Nothing," I replied and when he said, "oh I see," it was as if we had deliberately set out to make him feel like a victim of his lateness. He said,

"I don't know anything about this so perhaps you can both tell me the story so far so that I have each of your perspectives," as if Aude and I were to present our cases to him and he would decide which of us had been correct - and in doing so leaning far too close to the 'relying on third party opinion as fact' style of arguing for my liking.

Rather than bring him to order, I just started speaking and I said something like, "there's been a little bit of confusion about Aude's bonus scheme," which was a little generous to Aude but Franck interrupted to say, "that was supposed to be sorted out at review time," and Aude just raised her eyebrows and tutted.

I continued, "whereas a certain percentage of income would be counted towards her bonus scheme after reaching a qualifying level, Aude believes that all income counts towards it. That can't be, it is unaffordable and I have the spreadsheets which prove my point. It was what I had presented to her and her assistants a few weeks ago," or something like that – I wasn't good in the spotlight.

Franck said, "I didn't realise it was a strategy meeting, I thought you said it was management? I've only brought my day book. I'll go and get my strategy book." Then he went out of the meeting for about 15 minutes while he went back to his desk to get his other book.

He came back and set his book down on the table while he took out and changed a cartridge on his fountain pen. Then he opened his book and turned it to find the next new page, ruled a margin, checked the date on his Palm Pilot and wrote that in the top right corner of the page. Then he wrote 'Bonus Strategy and Policy' and underneath that, the word 'present'. Under 'present' he listed our three names and he put an asterisk next to mine. Then he wrote a couple of lines of notes, then looked up and said, "OK I've got that."

That meant that both of them were looking at me so I said, "do we have a problem Aude?" which drew a response of, "everyone's unhappy it's not just me."

That was just plain non-sequitor so I'd said, "look, it couldn't be afforded if we did it on any other basis," which I immediately knew was not a clear enough way to speak to Aude.

Then Franck's mobile phone rang and he said, "excuse me," and went out of the room to take the call which lasted for about ten minutes or so. When he came back he didn't say anything, he just nodded for us to continue.

For some reason I said, 'well do you agree Aude?" Which only prompted her to come straight back in with, "I wouldn't have agreed to it if I knew it worked like that."

I nearly started to explain to him what it was that she didn't agree to but for once I managed to stop myself. It wasn't something for her to agree to, I'd given her a free offer that I had made up all on my own to motivate the miserable bitch. She, herself, she'd actually refused a bonus to squeeze the most out of us as a salary. She should have been delighted with any gratuitous offer. Instead, even though I'd fallen all over myself and more, all I'd managed to do was to confuse and alienate her even further.

"Well actually you did," I said and whilst I did I drew a small graph in the corner of my notebook and drew a parallel line with the figure 10 against it, to indicate £10,000. The drawing took up about a square inch in total and whilst talking I pointed to the drawing. I felt embarrassed and ashamed that the drawing, no more than a doodle really, became the focus for the discussion that followed and was pointed to and looked at by each speaker in turn as they had their go. It wasn't the crisp professional open and shut case that I had in mind to present. Instead, in the end it disintegrated into a row between Aude and me each in turn spinning the notebook round and pointing to the doodle while we made our point.

"No that wasn't the basis on which I understood it," Aude said finally. It was aggressive and it raised the stakes.

She needed rough handling and I was close to telling her, 'that she had refused a fucking bonus, what exactly were her expectations based on?' But I thought that might turn the whole thing into a dogfight so I was working on a different way of saying the same thing – I don't know why, she wouldn't have spared me if roles were reversed - when Franck piped up, "I don't think we are going to achieve anything by going back over it now. Lets agree to do something we can all go forward from now."

It was sort of the right thing to say but it didn't please me. Franck knew that Aude was stupid and aggressive and he should have realised what torture I had been through with her already and given me some support. He had just assumed that I would have presented my ideas in a confused way to Aude. He had put no effort into trying to structure and present a deal to Aude at the time it mattered, i.e. six weeks earlier, when I had bothered to do it. He just came along at the last minute and said something grand. He should have said "I have been through your deal with Hector and it is perfectly clear to me," as I would have done for him in the same circumstances. Instead he cast a light judgment on me for my bodged handling of the matter and he implied that with his calm wisdom the problem was now over. Not that he would put any effort into re-structuring and re-presenting the deal nor would he assist in the re-education of the truculent Aude, as usual I would try to do that later on for no praise and a lot of grief. Franck would wait until I was next implicated in a misunderstood deal and come and put his cool hand on fevered brows.

I hated the arsehole Franck who only ever acted to promote his own interests and own image, I detested Aude for her refusal to be reasoned with. I hated myself for letting it happen to me, for losing control when I was the only one who knew what I was talking about, who had right on my side and still came off last out of the confrontation, who let things like this torture me.

"But you do understand Aude that the qualifying level has to be reached each month? It is not a matter of reaching it once and that is it for the year?" I was making a fool of myself by that stage.

She didn't say anything.

My instinct was to put her right, to try to understand how she could have arrived at a different understanding. I had taken such an enormous amount of time and trouble to explain it to her in the first place.

At about 1.30 I had to accept that the meeting had been inconclusive and that it was time to wrap up, despite the fact that we had only had about ten minutes of actual 'meeting' at that stage.

Against all my best interests I heard myself saying "I'll talk to Stacey and we'll try and get it sorted out next week," as Aude walked out.

I sat and stared at the floor for a few moments before Franck broke the spell by saying, "I don't know how you deal with these people."

I should have said, "what's your secret?" but I couldn't believe his audacity so I said nothing.

Eventually he got up to leave and as he reached the door he said, "fancy a pint?"

I should have said I had too much on like he would have done to me. Instead I thought I would forgive him his ignorant behaviour and act like it hadn't happened.

On the way to best pub he was a different person. As we left the office he said, "she's a fucking ignorant arsehole isn't she?"

Why didn't he think like that in the meeting?

"Sometimes I think that we should put her right," he continued.

I just said, "I wouldn't dignify her with the effort," to which he said, "yeah, I suppose you're right."

In the pub I went to the bar and got the drinks. I always went first, not for the desire to always pay first but for the wanting to take the pain of queuing off the other person. Franck was having a pint of 'Technical Directors' which was his funny non-joke and I had a pint of Legal Eagle which was my non-funny non-joke.

When I returned with the drinks the meeting was well and truly behind us and we were into being mates. "You'll never guess what happened to me last night," he said.

"No I probably won't, can I have odds?"

"You know the Phoenix?" Well I did actually, it was a lap dancing club on the Farringdon Road, £30 in, £10 a dance, and £20 a drink, which all added up to being about £300 down by the time you were kicked out.

"I was going home last night out of there about 3.00 a.m. and this bloke asks me if I wanted a taxi."

"You should have come round to my place," I said, becoming all decent and non-sequitor.

He, rightly, ignored me and carried on.

"I was saying to him how much to Hithcin? But he just kept saying, 'just get in the cab, don't bother about the fare,' as if something bigger was going on."

"Yeah go on," I said suddenly warming to the story.

"I got in the back of his cab and there was this bird there lying on the back seat stretching like she'd just woken up," "yeah ...."

"then she goes, 'oh how nice to see you' and she started kissing me."

"what was she," I said, "a whore or just a girl or what?"

"No, listen, she starts snogging me all seriously and the cab driver just acts like nothing unusual's going on,"

"what sort of car was it?"

"oh a Mondeo or something like that, there was no partition for the driver or anything. Anyway she's snogging me and rubbing my cock and everything. Then when we get out of town a bit she starts to get her kit off, doing a strip and saying that she'll do anything to please me. She gets down to her knickers and stops stripping then she starts to give me this massive blow job,"

"go on, go on," I said getting far more excited than I should have done really.

"I could have done anything to her but I was pissed and I didn't know what was going on and I was really confused and frightened,"

"so what did you do?"

"well I didn't do anything for ages because it was all so great, so I just let it happen. Anyway by Junction 11 I hadn't come so I just shouted out to the driver to carry on for a couple of more junctions or so."

"Weren't you frightened that you'd end up in a land fill somewhere?"

"A bit but I didn't really think of it and the driver was just laughing all the time, so I just went with it. I didn't know what to do but I daren't shag her unless she asked me to."

"Did she?"

"No, not really, then after we'd been round Junction 11 and 12 a few times it was starting to get light so I told him to head towards Hitchin, then just turning into my street I gave her one up the knicker leg. It was fucking brilliant."

"So what was it, whore and pimp or what?"

"Oh yeah, definitely,"

"So how did you deal with it?"

"I don't know really. I think I made him go round the block and I just got out and gave him loads of cash, probably about £250 or so I can't really remember."

I didn't know what to say, there wasn't a good rounding off comment so in the end I said, "I'm just so really pleased for you, when can I come?" and he said, "tonight if you want."

I had to admire Franck. For all intents and purposes he was like me but he didn't stew on the difficulties of a horrible job, he accepted it and made it pay for his fun.

Suddenly I was full of the desire to play it cool like that so I stayed out all afternoon, drank ten pints and dropped two hundred quid in the bookies on the way home.

15.

All I knew when I went to bed on Thursday night was that I had to be up early the next day. First there was the matter of giving the arsehole Sophie a review, for which I hadn't prepared; I had to attend a meeting/seminar, as it had come to be known, about the Nexus system, whatever the fuck that was; I had finally been caught up with by Human Resources and agreed to attend "an absolutely urgent and overdue meeting" straight after the Nexus meeting, in fact slightly before it ended; then I had come to owe Declan a progress meeting on account of not being in the office at 9.00 p.m. on Wednesday night when he decided he needed to see me and as the next day was Friday when I received it, there weren't many options available; and finally I had promised Caroline to be home when she arrived home, that being a barely acceptable second to picking her up from the airport. I also had to be prepared with the bank crap stuff that meant so much to her and I hadn't actually read any of it yet, more to the point, I hadn't opened the letter box, even though it was about 30 seconds away in the lobby. It only came to me about every hour or so that I should have dealt with it but I was always doing something else more important at the time. When I last remembered I was trying to sleep. All of this meant that I had to be up extra early and to get my act together right from the off, then fitting all the meetings and other obligations before leaving at 2.00 to be home for 2.30. And all of that meant that I didn't sleep during the night for fear of being asleep when the alarm clock went at 6.00.

I finally relaxed at 6.00 a.m. and got a good hour's sleep in. That meant that I didn't get to do the thorough tidying up as planned, I had to make do with doing a week's worth of washing up before setting off. I was still on target so I allowed myself to stop off for a Racing Post. I couldn't find one straight away so I took my place in the long queue behind all the proper people with their Guardians and cartons of orange juice, with the exception of the fat fuck in front of me who chose that moment to bring in several reams of lottery tickets to see if he had a winner. About half of the tickets went through first time, all of the rest had to be de-creased by the newsagent and put through the machine about forty times, until eventually he declared that he'd won £36.00, which for some reason, mainly the shopkeepers reluctance pay, I thought, became impossible to find in the till. Meanwhile all the regulars were leaning over me to leave the right money next to the till for their regular purchases. I had a question to ask so I just waited. Eventually it was me and I realised as soon as I asked that I should have left straight away.

"I can't find the Racing Post."

"Last one just sold sir."

"You fucking cunt," I don't know whether I thought this loudly or whispered it.

That was a good five minutes wasted but having waited I had to have one. I went past the next newsagents who were guaranteed not to have one and decided to go the long way to work through the back of Smithfield to take in a good newsagent.

There was only one person in front of me, a painter or plasterer by the look of him, about 50 or so. He was rolling a fag and looked like he'd decided to hang around to kill a few a minutes. When he spoke I realised he was pissed - at half past seven in the morning. I was waiting behind him and it took me a little while to realise that he wasn't actively buying anything and that it was sort of my turn. He was generally unaware of me and I couldn't get to the counter to ask. I tuned into their conversation and I was sure he said:

"you fucking pakkis are all the same," or something like that. But it was sort of said and accepted with no malice.

The shopkeeper said,

"don't insult me."

"What?"

"Don't insult me, calling me that."

"well you are in't yer?" the pissed plasterer said.

"I'm no fucking pakki," the shopkeeper said, "I fucking hate pakkis innit."

Then he started to say he was a Ugandan Asian, which I thought was ambitious with his current audience, but the plasterer was already speaking over him so, even if he could have understood, he never heard what he said. The painter could hardly speak for laughing.

"What are you then? A fucking innki-pinninki?" Which made him start laughing his head off.

"No I'm a Ugan…." He couldn't get through to him.

"£1.30 sir," he said to me.

I paid and left them to it.

I was so far behind schedule I gave it up. Instead of being well prepared for Arsehole's review I would play it by ear out of disrespect for her, I wouldn't go through all my emails and get on top of the day so that I would be clear to attend all the meetings on time and prepared and I wouldn't call in on Declan at 8.00 a.m. to say that I would be going a bit earlier today to pick my wife up from the airport, making it obvious that I was in early making up the lost time. What I would do is go and have a cup of coffee and read the Racing Post. Fucking right.

I was concentrating on the feature race at Cheltenham, not the cross-country -a load of fucking bollocks designed to enlarge the appeal of racing to the masses (yeah right) - the two mile handicap chase. It was a handicap but with only five runners it was my sort of thing. Races like that were often weird, in that by rights, only Dines could win and he should have been odds on, but because of the small number of runners a couple of the others had to be marked up at the sort of price as if they had a chance, and for some reason Dines was 6/4, 6/5 ish. That made him a knocking bet in my book. I decided to have a decent punt on him. Then I realised that I wouldn't have any opportunity to get to the bank to get some money out. That put me on a chain of thought, because it meant ringing through a bet and I couldn't do that to any great scale now that I had a joint bank account with Caroline, I couldn't let her know the scale at which I did it. Then I started to reflect on the evidence that was there to see on my old bank account, if only she could see, not only were there regular large amounts going out all the time but there was a long term standing order to cover a debt on a serious error I made when I was into spread betting.

"Oh Jesus,"

I hadn't emptied the post box for the entire time that Caroline had been away and I had promised that I had dealt with the problems on our bank account when I hadn't even seen their most recent letter. That letter was supposed to be the final statement of every standing order and direct debit and was to be the defining document in getting our lives back in order. And then I started panicking about the standing order to SpreadBet.com showing up. No that had finished, I was sure, but what if they, in their misplaced thoroughness showed a list of all standing orders, including those recently finished? I really did start to panic a lot then. I knew that she would have my guts for garters just for being lazy, so I rushed back to the flat took the entire week's mail planning to deal with it somehow during the morning.

So much for my fucking plans. I trudged into work, late to normal hours, reflecting on my great losses. That spread bet had been £3,000 nearly two years ago, "it has been paid off hasn't it?", as I never looked at my statements I couldn't be certain, but I was pretty sure it had to be finished.

In the last 100 yards to work I became desperate for the toilet and I rushed in, which at least made it look like I cared about being late. I had to run past Sophie's desk and I didn't exactly get a warm reception.

"I'll be two seconds," I shouted to her on the way to the bog.

"What room have you booked?" she says. Well I hadn't booked one obviously, so I said;

"I'll tell you in a minute," so that I could think up a lie.

16.

There is a smell which is a mixture of shit and toothpaste that can only be made by a woman. I noticed it that day in the shared, one cubicle, second floor toilet. It was quite luxurious for a work toilet because once in you essentially had quite a nice bathroom to yourself. But it was terrible for me because it was always occupied when I needed it most and I didn't like the way the next person in always knew your business. I had followed Amanda Phipps the other day and she had left that smell. It turned my stomach and I reflected that Amanda had not learnt the social etiquette tip that my father had given to me - to waft a lighted match after you've had a particularly smelly shit. The odious vapours are burnt off and leave no lingering smell. Simple.

I was sat on the toilet and the tip became an idea. The idea was this: Social-Lites, a new brand of match for the bathroom. They would come in a big plastic wipe-clean box and contain about 20 or so enormous matches. They would be big soft matches giving a generous flame and their long stalks would be made of wound cardboard, as tampon cases were, that would burn well but would flush away easily too. It was a hum dinger of an idea and would proliferate like Evian and Perrier. All I wanted was a tiny percentage royalty for ever.

The idea was simple but like all works of genius it was simple, so simple in fact that it was remarkable no-one had thought about it before. It was a "solution," as we business people referred to such things, for a mundane, albeit slightly tasteless, human function. I was at first slightly embarrassed by it. But I loved it too. My idea was to give an ordinary boring household product a new lease of life, like had been given to Lucozade, and Polos and all those other things that you always thought there'd only be one of for ever. I would be the man that revamped matches.

All I had to do was find the Marketing Directors of all the major match companies and set up some presentations. In fact I could pretend to Martins Fleet that I had turned up an opportunity in a Match Company through a personal contact and I could attend the meeting and prepare for it in their time. I could even get New Media to do the drawings for me.

I came out of the toilet and resolved to work on my idea as soon as possible. I would set about documenting Social-Lites. I didn't know whether my new idea could be protected in any way, like a copyright or something like that so I decided to draft a letter to my lawyers, reasoning that at least that was some proof of the idea being mine. I realised that I'd have to have a confidentiality agreement with whoever I presented the idea to but I could create one. I also had to create a portfolio of sketches to illustrate the image of Social-Lites, I had to create a pitch letter to get people interested without telling them too much about my secret idea. But it was fantastic I was engaged, happy, purposeful and I didn't mind having to do all the shit things at Martins Fleet all day, not even arsehole's review.

This was a fantastic revelation. It made me realise that I wasn't limited to having to find a new career. If I got my full money out of Martins Fleet it would buy breathing space and would give me the opportunity to take an alternative approach to a career. I loved the idea of dabbling a bit in various schemes, having some independent income. It would allow me to take a more considered approach to my job seeking and it would give me three solid schemes to get on with at work: getting sacked, getting a new job and working on my new idea. That could be the first of a portfolio of ideas that would take me into the next stage of my life.

If nothing else it meant I was a little less sour for the Arsehole's review.

"We're in Room Six," she snapped at me when I came out. She'd been all business like and got it organised while I was in the bog. Or rather she'd rang reception while I was in the bog and presented the securing of a meeting room to me as evidence of her great organisational skills and of my shambolic organisation. I could ring reception too.

We went to Room Six together in silence.

Once in she made a point of standing until I asked her to sit down, like she suddenly respected me as her boss. On sitting she span an envelope of documents towards me.

"You're supposed to start with them."

Supposed to? Like that is what reviews were, some prescriptive formula in case you couldn't manage to do it on your own. Or just in case some low ranking idiotic wanker with ambition got treated slightly differently from the next.

"Right well let's go through it then," like I fucking cared.

After we'd filled in all the shit about what her name was and how much she earned, I had to go through the charade of giving her marks out of 5 for her current performance and marks out of 5 for her potential in such matters as skills index management. You might as well have asked whether a monkey could pick a banana when a green light flashed and put its finger up its arse when it saw a red one.

What was wrong with talking to these fucking dickheads about their sad jobs? Sophie's problem was that she was extremely ignorant and thought that everything she had learned at Asda or WH Smith or wherever the fuck it was, was the bible of management. What she really needed was to be told that she was relatively thick and that if she bothered to read a few decent books she might come to learn a little modesty, balance, even gain a tiny little bit of wisdom. If I gave a fuck about the nasty little bitch I might have diverted from the text of the Appraisal anyway. As it was I didn't.

I gave her 3 for her current ability to manage the skills index and 3 for her potential. My reasoning was that she had very little control of the skills index. It was one of those things that some business guru somewhere had dreamt up and all the idiot sheep running Martins Fleet were happy to adopt without question. This is what it meant: a given business needed a certain level of particular skills to continue to exist as a business; each of those skills was given a value and such skills that the workforce had were added up and divided by the number of workers. Our skills index minimum was 55.7, our current score was 63.2 and our target for the year to end next September was 67.

Things like this were just accepted, by Management and staff alike, no-one ever questioned why someone who could work a photocopier could get a maximum score of 2.8 whereas the world champion faxer and emailer could only get 2.4. They just decided that at the beginning and accepted it as an inviolable truth thereafter. But they were absolutely painstaking about whether a member of staff had achieved a 2.4 or a 2.3. The whole practice, if it ever had any validity to begin with had become an utterly faux science.

The other problem with Martins Fleet was that there was no real skills base to speak of. All they did was photocopy bits of paper and deliver the mail. For this reason they had to stretch the meaning of skills to breaking point. They tried for example to put a value on written and spoken communication skills. They didn't just satisfy themselves with considering whether someone was thick or not, or whether if they weren't thick whether they were lazy.

I was the only person that didn't believe it. So when I gave Arsehole a 3 for her potential she said to me,

"you don't have any faith in me do you?"

to which I said , "I don't know what you mean," I didn't.

"Well it isn't my fault that Perry Maclean was taken to Nat West."

"I'm sure it wasn't, that's my point really."

"Well why should I be marked down by you for something out of my control?"

"Yes, but with all due respect, how can you ever have any control over things like that?"

"I can assure you I know how to manage."

"Yes I know."

"And I don't need to be told by you that I don't."

"Well perhaps but …."

"I've managed massive contracts and I don't see why my career should be held up by someone like you that hasn't."

"The point I'm trying to make is that the situation is beyond your control."

To which she just tutted.

"Isn't it all just down to luck, who gets recruited for you or who happens to leave or gets moved to another client?"

I don't know why I persisted in trying to be constructive with someone so intent on falling out with me whatever I said. I think it was because she just wouldn't or couldn't accept the logic of my argument that kept me interested.

"Yeah sure, it's all down to luck, my whole career is down to a bit of luck now, nothing to do with me. Thanks."

"OK I'll put you down as a 4 but what happens next year when someone like Perry gets taken away from you?"

"You may not believe in me but I do."

You can't beat people like that by talking to them so I wrote down 4 in the potential box.

And so it went. She was intent on using the meeting to criticise me and as it went on I could tell that she had one or two well rehearsed pieces that she wanted to deliver. She set off on them a couple of times but as they were essentially non-sequitors they sort of faded out. Hence the rest of the review became a competition between us for her to find an opening to deliver her tirade and me heading her off at the bridge. From that point of view I started to enjoy it for a while. Until in the end because I was weak, or because it was the only thing I didn't want to do and couldn't get it off my mind, I said:

"This is your review is there anything you want to say," a proper person would have put the cunt to the sword. Me I just said, "I can see your dying to walk all over me and you haven't had a chance to do it yet, so please go ahead now."

"Well yes, there is actually, rather a lot," Oh fuck.

She went on about how she loved her job, how she'd always been brilliant and well thought of in any job she had done, how she loved working at Martins Fleet. By omission she meant that the only thing that was wrong with her career was me. At least I was not weak enough to say to her, "it's me, isn't it?" instead I just it let hang there and hoped she'd be satisfied that she'd got it all off her chest. When the diatribe ended I greeted it with silence, I didn't say thanks, or have you finished, or I will make a note of that, just a long silence.

The last part of the form was where I had to give some specific pointers to her. I couldn't think of anything relevant to her job so I said, "you must learn to be able to take part in a discussion with someone who holds a different point of view to you without taking offence."

She just said, "alright," shrugging.

So I said, "I am going to write that on your form,"

"You can't," she said.

"What?"

"You're not allowed to write things like that on appraisal forms,"

"Like what?"

"Like what you just said."

"But what in particular?"

"Long sentences like that one you just said."

"What because it's long?"

"No."

"Well what then?"

"That type of thing. It's supposed to be things about your job."

"And you don't think that what I said had anything to do with your job?"

"No it's not that, you know what I mean."

"Actually I don't but if it means that much to you I won't write anything."

"I'm not saying that."

"Well would you mind telling me what you are saying?"

"Forget it, it's not worth arguing with you, you don't listen."

"God that's the very point I am trying to make."

"What that you don't listen? I know that already."

"No that you need to accept that other people have a different point of view to you."

"Oh you're just trying to tie me up in knots."

"I'm not, I'm trying to say something very simple."

"Well it didn't sound simple to me."

"Since you can't tell me what it is you object to perhaps we should stop going round in circles."

"Oh that's right, just give up. It's my career we're talking about."

"Jesus, Sophie, can't you understand that you haven't been able to tell me what it is that I have said that you don't like," I said the last part of the sentence slowly word by word.

"I've told you over and over, you're just being awkward on purpose,"

"Sophie," I was sort of weeping as I spoke, "I don't know what you don't like about what I said."

Silence

"Do you not like it because it was negative?"

Silence

"Do you not like it because it's not the sort of thing you would write on an appraisal form?"

"Oh thank God, he gets it."

"Right, what sort of thing would you write?"

"It depends on what's relevant."

"Obviously, I know that, give me an example."

"Well that I should increase my click rate or something like that. Not that I should."

"Yes, well I didn't want to say that. I consider that your major problem is understanding the protocol of an adult conversation."

"If you write that I'll complain."

"Sophie Chawdray thank you very much for letting us hear your desert island discs."

"What?"

"That's the review over. Thanks."

Pure 100% non-sequitor. Despite being thick as fucking pig shit.

17.

At 10 o'clock when I got back to my desk I could not be but officially late for the Nexus meeting but despite this. The pressure was building and I wanted, as best I could to keep on top of the day. Declan, Caroline, letters, meetings, getting a bet on Dines all before 2.30 p.m. So instead of toddling off to the meeting without delay I got out three weeks post and tried to put it into some sort of order on my desk, so that I would be able to go through them discretely during the meeting. I also took the opportunity to leave a message for Declan, I could see he wasn't at his desk and a nice polite sensible message now would get me out of the obligation to see him and get the meeting put off as a whole til Monday. I cradled the phone between shoulder and neck and continued to sort the mail. Rather than the cheap clean solution of voicemail I fell on Scrubber's Haircut.

"Hello Declan's phone."

"Yes it's Hector I was hoping to leave a message for Declan."

Silence.

"Is anyone there?"

"Yeah I'm looking at yer, yer bloody idiot." She was on the other side of the office to me.

"Well can I leave a message for him?"

"What yer doing there? Have you started to work for George now?"

"No just sorting out a few weeks post in one day."

"There could be cheques and contracts in that lot."

"No personal stuff."

"Aah, I see."

And again I had given away far more than I need of done for nothing. Just like my father.

"Anyway the message."

"Yeah go on I'm waiting. God what are you like?"

"No I mean on his voicemail."

That was taken by Scrubber's as a bit of an insult, which I suppose was right really. She would just say to Declan, "Hector isn't coming," and not give the detailed and more acceptable declination that I intended to give.

"He's meeting you at two o'clock you can tell him then."

"It's about that," I leaked by mistake "but if I could leave a voicemail it would be better."

"I'll transfer you."

At which point the phone went dead and there was no ansaphone message from Declan. I looked up and saw Scrubber's on the phone to someone else.

I rang again thinking that her being on the phone would send me straight to his voicemail, and instead I got the engaged tone. A last throw of the dice and I rang reception to ask them to put me through to Declan's voicemail. They obliged, the phone rang and Scrubber's picked up the phone again.

"Not you again. Can't you do nuffink for yourself?"

I had to act like I was a bumbling idiot rather than the victim of useless technology, "sorry Liz, but can you help me out again I can't get through to his voicemail."

"As you ask so nice alright," she said, then the line went dead again. I gave up.

I was also drawing too many curious glances for all the letters on my desk so I decided it was time to go to the meeting.

There are meetings and meetings. To be invited to the Nexus meeting was privilege indeed. All you needed to know about its importance was that Giles Fulton-Warke was there, a member of the executive as they called themselves, Fullsome-Wank as me and Franck called him. There must have been twenty of us there and a good two thirds of them were like dogs with two dicks, just delighted to be there, to be part of something. Me, Franck and Fullsome couldn't give a flying fuck. Fullsome was actually half decent for the esteemed executive, he had been there long enough to be utterly cynical about big new developments. He knew well enough that if the idea was worth doing that Martins Fleet was not capable of coming up with the idea all on its own and that it could not afford to pay a proper company to develop the idea on its behalf. Not that he would let it show. In companies like Martins Fleet the lower ranks needed to find reasons to be excited all the time. Fullsome like me was wishing his time away on a big salary and a share options deal and was hoping for the end to come before anything exciting of note happened. That said he was very good at giving lip service to these brave new ideas. Much more so than me, my mock enthusiasms were received as just that. I was a bullshitter, Fullsome-Wank was a good communicator.

The rest who were mostly from IT, or as we were supposed to say, Systems, were in some way responsible for the design and implementation of Nexus. And these people, who expected to spend a career behind the scenes working in a factory, now found themselves as sort of semi-celebrities, someone part of a big new idea before it came public knowledge, sharers of a big important private secret. And just being part of it conferred celebrity and status. None of them were actually capable of either designing, developing or implementing any sort of idea so that was why the meeting was chaired by a Microsoft Business Partner, whose company would be doing all the work. Not that that was anything to get carried away with. A Microsoft Business Partner was usually just a two bit company with hardly any employees that were prepared to fill in forms. Alan Barlow's lack of class was immediately apparent.

My arrival brought the pre-meeting small talk to an end and looking up at me and thereby thrusting me into the limelight when I was set on taking an anonymous role, Alan Barlow announced: "now that we are ad quorum perhaps we can all be seated and be upstanding," then he laughed. Then he said, "have a good meeting one and all."

He spent the first half an hour of his opening address bringing us up to date with the progress made on the project to date. This could more reasonably have been achieved in five minutes since nothing of what he said made any sense to me and was clearly superfluous to the boneheads who sat with arms folded wearing broad grins of deep satisfaction borne of already being in the know. What I knew before I went into the meeting was that Nexus was the system that was going to "coordinate all client printing demands through a central hub accessed from a dedicated client intranet," it was something of a solution to beat all solutions and to revolutionise our approach to this work. After an hour of the meeting all I could discern was that we had inherited a disused printing works from a client that had gone bust and that Nexus was no more than one person sending an email to another asking them to print a document that they attached to the message. For the life of me I couldn't see anything more complicated than that but I was sure that I had missed the point so I said nothing. One hour later I was no wiser but considerably more bored and one and a half hours later I started to panic that the rest of my day was beginning to concertina. I spent the half hour after that in a real state of agitation alternating between problems with Declan, my wife, all the routine jobs I hadn't done, the need to get some money from somewhere for the weekend and on top of all this I had Human Resources on my tail. More than any of that, even all that in aggregate meant nothing compared with getting a bet on Dines. If I was denied getting on by this prick the horse would go in, that was for sure.

At one o'clock Alan said, "now gentleman, if you'd be so good as to turn round and walk acrost the presentation room to the demonstration models we have set up behind you … and by all means bring your orifices with you," by which I think he meant

106

cups of tea. When he said this I think I groaned audibly in fact I was sure I did but as I looked up to see how far my voice had travelled I thought I detected a glance of sympathy on the faces of Fullsome and Franck. This must have encouraged me a little bit too much because fifteen minutes later when Alan asked for questions, whether it was out of desperation or whether it was because I had detected kindred spirits amongst us or whether it was because I thought it was about time that I started to do something positive towards getting sacked and being perceived as anti-social, I said "why isn't cunt in the Microsoft dictionary?"

It wasn't so much that you could have heard a pin drop, nor that my remark lacked timing and had failed to make an impact, it was more that everyone suddenly looked at me like I was irretrievably stupid, that whatever motivation I had to say something like that could never be explained to normal people. When the meeting finally ended a few minutes afterwards - Fullsome had intervened with a sensible sounding none-question to fill the silence - I was left on my own in the presentation room to ponder my idiocy. Not even Franck stayed.

18.

Head in hands rendered immobile by regret and despair I was finally hunted down by Stacey Arnold. I was just reflecting on the additional stupidity of having eaten 39 sugared almonds during the meeting when she arrived. The bitch had smelled the blood of a wounded animal and tracked me down in the open prairie of the presentation room. I quite genuinely did not have the time to spare her, it must have been heading towards two o'clock by then and an exit by two was imperative but there seemed to be an unsaid acknowledgement between us that I owed her a meeting and I couldn't find the words to tell her to get out of my fucking sight. Apparently she had passed by my desk and used her human resources training to find out that I would still be in the presentation room. It seemed she had liaised in a positive non intrusive way with my colleagues, she had found an appropriate moment to ask a non-core question and from that she had been able to deduce where I might be. Wonderful training at British Telecomm.

Had she approached me at any other point in the week I would have given her short shrift yet of all the times to track me down she found me then when I was at a low ebb and with too many other things on my mind. I found myself saying anything to please her to get her away from me. It wasn't so much that the crucial issue on her agenda had to be dealt with, that was bad enough, but now, because she had found me feeling sorry for myself, I had opened myself up to pastoral care.

I had just said, "be buggered with sugared almonds," and I think I'd vocalised, when she said,

"All a bit too much for you today?" Trying to be all soft and full of bedside manner but really just probing trying to find a bit of dirt, trying to find some weakness that she could turn into a raison d'etre for her pathetic non-job. The last person that talked to me in that deliberately useless soppy voice in the name of sympathising was a nurse when I had been in hospital with Caroline when all her feminine tubes got fucked up. She assumed, wrongly, that I was overcome with grief, and, presumably because her training programme had told her to, she tried to involve me in the process of preparing my wife for theatre. She got me to fill in a label that was to be tied to her toe. I did it as best as I could with the information to hand, then a few minutes later a big black nurse came in and looked at my label and shouted out,

"who the fuck did that? Do you want her to die in the fucking theatre?"

"who the fuck did what Hector?"

"What?"

"Who the fuck did what?"

That time I had been speaking out loud and now she could reasonably conclude that I was going mad. She would be able to say to her team leader that Hector was not coping with the stress of his new position and needed to be watched, he was obviously suffering at the moment and had shown clear signs of not coping. I knew that it was important to give a robust response that put the matter to bed once and for all but being unable to think on my feet I could only say the absolutely truth. That was:

"I am sorry I was day dreaming, I've got a lot on my mind at the moment I am not thinking very clearly, don't worry about me, there's nothing to worry about."

Then I said, "I'll bounce back don't worry." Not that I had anything to bounce back from nor that I had a weakness that needed to be owned up to, it's just that I found myself saying it. And with it, with that inability to present myself properly to the outside world I had given the fucking thick bitch licence to intervene in my personal well being and state of mind. On behalf of the company you know, doing her job.

"OK lets park that for now," park it, park it? PARK FUCKING IT? Like it was a serious issue that we would come back to in time. Like that was a legitimate way of speaking, to park things. It was bad enough if a wanker like Barrow said something like that but a fucking amoeba like her? It was as if she really did think that what she did mattered.

Then she did that thing, that women in offices do, she paused, acted like she was reflecting on the serious matter to come, bowed her head slightly and swallowed a little, then she moved a quarter turn with her head to look at me in the eyes. In this way she had communicated the gravity of what she was about to say next and she had made it clear that she fully understood the consequences of what she was about to say. She said:

"Patrick."

I knew full well what she meant but I chose to not understand all the body language and based my response on just the words that I heard.

"I don't know what you are talking about."

"You do Hector, I know for a fact that Moiraigh has already spoken to you about this, nearly a month has slipped by and this needs actioning now. Apparently Moiraigh is still waiting for your report."

Patrick was the poor cunt who ended up being our accountant at Gilligan Soames. He was crap but so what? Martins Fleet was full of useless people. Unfortunately at a management meeting about a month ago I had found myself agreeing with Moiraigh that Patrick was crap and since then it had been a burning issue to sack him. I hated my weakness in opening myself up in things like this so easily. Franck had been in the same meeting and was equally Patrick's boss as I was yet no-one had dreamed that Franck would have anything to do with working with Moiraigh to prepare the case to get him sacked. He had this way of just ignoring it without consequence.

It wasn't as if Patrick was that crap actually. If someone like Barrow had said that some useless accountant or clerk from a client needed to be accommodated it would just be done, easily. He would have been given a seat next to a load of other wasters. Yet because this poor fucker had slightly different antecedents and because accidentally someone like Barrow hadn't told someone else to find a place for him, suddenly he was a massive issue and he had to be sacked.

"Jesus why don't you just leave him alone?" I shouldn't have let my frustration show.

"Perhaps Hector because you're not satisfied with him and he is causing a great deal of damage to your prospects."

"Well just make him redundant or something, what's wrong with that?"

"We have been through this, it is not a case for redundancy."

"Well presumably someone else is going to do our accounts?"

"That would be Moiraigh's decision."

"Well actually its mine and yes we will have an accountant, one that was already here at Martins Fleet, so he has been made redundant."

"It is not a case of redundancy and you know that the decision has already been taken."

"But nobody has told me why."

When I said this I had a slightly pleading, nearly tearful tone, it was borne of frustration but she took it the other way.

"Hector, you're clearly under a lot of pressure, and we are going to have to have a look at that, for the moment can I ask you to liaise with Moiraigh without delay?"

"Yes I did."

"I take it that that's a yes?"

"Yes Ma'am."

"Actually I know your record we will do it a different way. You got your diary on you?"

"What?"

"It's a simple question Hector."

"I thought we were supposed to keep our diaries on our PCs?"

"Well that doesn't prevent you from carrying a diary does it?" And she smiled a condescending school teacher smile. I didn't bother explaining to her the idiocy of keeping two separate diaries in separate places and how people like her would be the first to come down on me like a ton of bricks for any diary inconsistencies.

As if to reinforce the point she changed tack and said, "leave it to me Hector, I will liaise with Moiraigh directly myself and I will put a meeting into your diary. How does that sound?"

"That sounds great thanks," and with that I had allowed one more person to treat me like an idiot child. Other people just didn't allow their colleagues to speak to them like that.

"Good. Perhaps we will find five minutes to settle Aude's bonus scheme too?"

"But it's done, it's decided. It's … our business isn't it?"

"Not according to Aude it isn't sorted out and she should know really shouldn't she? Anyway we're all in the same side aren't we?" and she stroked the back of my hand as she got up to go.

And by way of parting shot she shouted out:

"Oh and by the way I want you in my employment law seminar next Tuesday, you've missed the last two month's. I'll put that in your diary too."

111

19.

Then I had no choice, the bitch left me alone at 2.15 which just about gave me time to run to my desk, turn off the PC, gather my letters and rush to the bookies for 2.25. Fuck Declan I'd call him later from the safe haven of home and as for Caroline that would all fall into place by going straight home after the race, I just needed about half an hour to myself to get all the letters in order and do a general tidy up before she got in. She had mentioned 3.30 and that would do for me now.

That decided, the only pressing thing on my mind was how to raise the money for a bet. I didn't have a current bank card, it was too late for last minute arrangements with the bank and even too late to borrow a few quid from Franck. I decided to have a shot at the title with my old bank account. If as it seemed it wasn't closed down properly I might as well use the facility. I rang William Hill and being of the view that it would either work or not I had a £400 rather than the oner I would have had for cash. She said "I'll just get that confirmed for you," and immediately responded "with that's fine sir," and read the bet back and I knew I hadn't backed a winner.

I left the office with indecent haste. Just the opposite to how anyone else I knew would have left. They would have left without being noticed. I might as well have shouted, "I am leaving early," out loud to everyone as I raced across the office. Most people were actually laughing as I ran out.

I ran to the bookies and I was delighted to find myself there before the off. As usual for Fridays it was packed and I struggled to get a view of a screen for a while. When I did I wished I hadn't. Dines was a bad starter, everyone knew that, but the fucking useless ex-Army twat starting the race managed to be half way up the steps when everyone was ready to go. Thanks to that Arsehole, one of the other horses broke the tape. After about four centuries someone tied the tape together and when eventually they were ready to let them go again Dines had had enough and stayed at the start.

It was perfectly obvious to me that had I not had the bet they would have jumped off first time and Dines would have beaten them. My involvement seemed to induce a massive, unforeseen and unusual outbreak of unprecedented incompetence. He had a five horse race to start the fucking cunt. I didn't know whether I would cry or whether the veins in my neck would burst out of pure undiluted hatred and anger. I didn't even get the chance to see whether my reading of form was right or not. That is the most basic and reasonable request of the gambler.

I found myself saying, "I will not let you beat me however much you hate me." I was talking to God at the time. One of the old boy regulars looked up but he could see in my face that I needed to be left alone and he was good enough to do that.

My phone was ringing as I left the bookmakers and a quick glance showed that it was Declan. I was in no mood for dealing with a loser like that, acting all corporate but behaving like a secretary. The confluence of two losers of our scale on the same call may have caused the telecomm network to implode.

I continued head down, hands in pockets on the slow plod home. I'd had the wind taken out of my sails and I had the twenty minutes of the walk home to pull myself together to present an acceptable front to Caroline, who was entitled to think that she was the only thing that mattered to me after three weeks absence. I wished that was right. I found myself saying, "you stupid fucking cunt," out loud, then, as I reflected on the stupidity of having had a large bet on my non existent bank account I stopped and took my head in my hands and drew deep, frightened breaths. I was saying "Oh God, Oh God, Oh no" as I exhaled.

Then someone said to me, "Are you alright?" and it snapped me out of my trance and made me feel ashamed again but this time just for being ridiculous. It was Declan.

"I've been calling you," he said.

"Oh was that you, I didn't get to it in time,"

"I just wanted to know if you wanted me to get you a sandwich so we could eat during the meeting."

"Oh, err, err no thanks. I mean I can't," suddenly having had it all worked out and having tried to present my case properly and in plenty of time, now I had to stutter and stammer my way out of the meeting at the last moment. And having to do it like that made me look like an absolute flake, someone who was unable to face up to what needed to be done, someone who tried to slide out of his obligations at the last moment. Never mind that I had tried to do it all properly but got let down by Scrubber's Haircut, all that counted for nothing now. Who else, having made all that effort would accidentally bump into the last person he wanted to see on the way home? It just didn't happen to other people. They managed to make themselves look all professional and grown up. Me I felt like a little truant. A dishonest little schoolboy. I reminded myself of the sort of people I considered ridiculous when I was at school. I couldn't help feeling like I was being dishonest, even though I wasn't. When I heard myself start to explain why I couldn't make the meeting I didn't even believe it myself and I knew I was telling the truth.

My parents had taught me that I was dishonest a long time ago. I never thought that I was, in fact of all my faults I couldn't admit to that. But somehow I manage to sound dishonest when I'm explaining myself or when I'm saying no to someone. And people relate to me like I'm not telling the truth. And I sort of live up to it. When I was in the first year of secondary school, those of us that had been picked to play for the school soccer team were called to a lunchtime meeting with the games master. It was in those days when all schools had absolutely no money and we were told that we had to buy our own shorts that were supplied as the school kit. They were 80p. That way we could have new ones. From the outset my parents convinced themselves that I had made it up to make 80p out of them. I wish I was capable of being that shrewd. They reminded me about it throughout the rest of my teenage years and in the end it became the reference point for all complaints that went to my integrity. It even came up the other day, about 24 years later. And as per usual there was no doubt about their not having understood at the outset. It was an established fact that I had committed this heinous act of dishonesty when I was younger. We all knew I was dishonest. Now Declan did too.

As we went our separate ways Declan colombo'd me that I was not to forget the Monday meeting at eight o'clock with which he started the week. I was one of his team now and I needed to integrate, apparently,

20..

Any success I achieved in beating Caroline home by five minutes was lost within the hour when I couldn't think of a good reason why my underpants were hanging on the handle of the en suite bathroom. Then I had to confront the fact that I had two full sets of clothes on the unmade bed, one of which was a suit shirt tie and shoes. And after a while all the little things that I thought I would get away with on their own, became just one more piece of evidence in the case against me as an absolute shambles.

I was happy in the circumstances, that I'd confronted the backlog of post at the very beginning, before she started to lose real faith in me as it were. In truth I didn't quite have enough time to get organised and get my story right on everything but, if I say it myself, I gave a consummate performance. I'd even managed to triage out all the bookmakers statements and got as far as binning all the circulars so that gambling and losing was taken right out of the equation from the start. True I was forced to tell a white lie about the state of our bank account, well not so much a white lie in that I repeated the assurances I had been given earlier in the week by the operative I talked to, more that in doing that I gave her the impression that I'd been thorough with the correspondence I handed over. All I had done was skim read it for dangers and put each letter into a general classification. I hadn't bargained for the letters that weren't there, that she was expecting to see, and the first disappointment that I had to own up to was that I hadn't made any progress in getting the washing machine and CD player that hadn't worked since the day we bought them, changed or repaired. Later on in the evening when I did the decent thing and strolled out with her for the evening I also had to own up to not having made any interim arrangements for getting cash. That really wasn't my fault but I didn't sound very convincing when my explanation for not having done so was that I hadn't had the time to do it.

I felt bad when we had to spend her end of tour bonus on our night out. That was supposed to be for her to buy herself an indulgent present for all the crap that she put with. I told her I felt bad about it and she said never mind, she would buy something when the bank finally got round to putting all our money in one place. I didn't tell her that I had managed to get a £400 bet out of our non-existent bank account. Enough money to go out on the town and show her a good time. Instead we struggled to have a few drinks and a pizza on Islington High Street.

I managed, during the course of our painting the town red, to bring her up to date with my plans. I told her about the absolute need that I got myself a new job and with that I bought myself Sunday afternoon to re-write my CV, write an application letter and get my change of life on the road. I didn't tell her that my exit plan from the old job involved getting sacked, only that the money I was owed would be safe and that I would be able to negotiate my way out. She was quite supportive, which I suppose was indicative of how miserable I made her life in the current circumstances. I was pleased to a certain extent that I now had some backing and focus for my plans although that was tinged with a great deal of regret that here I was mid thirties starting out again and looking to start a career that I might actually like, when all along I wanted to be someone in the fifteenth year of a great career and to be whisking my lucky wife off to Milan for the weekend. People I went to college with actually lived like that. People that I dismissed as useless at the time. They had lives now.

I was pleased that I turned Sunday into an outing. It wasn't glamorous and it was much less than she deserved but our picnic at Windsor Great Park felt so wholesome it kind of out scored any more sophisticated alternatives. Sure, I had set aside Sunday to start my job applications and if I didn't do it on Sunday as planned, then it wouldn't be looked at until the next Sunday or the one after or perhaps never, but a day together, just me and her, it was so close to what I called real life and so far from the misery of my actual real life that it made me feel the life I yearned was tangible.

The only longing I was left with was the desire to work days like that into such a regular occurrence that they became part of the fabric of our lives rather than one-offs, where the infrastructure of life and home and job worked was so well settled that outings like that knew their place within it.

The only negative was getting stuck on a log in the car park for an hour. I drove over it instead of reversing but I was pleased with the fortitude I showed in adversity. I didn't say "why me?" once while we waited for the tractor to pull us off even though the logs were there to define car parking spaces and were there but couldn't be seen from the driver's seat.

I did say that the car felt all stiff and awkward as we drove off but that was it. Caroline just said, "don't let it spoil a good day, just go and get it serviced, I'm sure its due one," so I didn't, for her sake.

We arrived home and she declared herself ready for an early night. I kissed her goodnight and set about the task I'd set myself for the day. One hour after I'd switched on the computer I was still looking for my CV. It was the one I prepared for the Martins Fleet sale so I knew that it was semi-professional and business looking and that meant that I had to have it. The creative energy in making a new one was more than I had to spare and the shame in confronting the paucity of achievements on my CV meant that doctoring an old one was a far less unhappy process than starting from the beginning again. But it couldn't be found.

In the end I realised that there were hardly any Word documents on the PC at all and then I remembered that we deleted them all after we got that virus that sent random parts of them to anyone in your email address book. On the basis that some fucking geeky service orientated wanker decided that anyone to whom you sent an email was automatically added to your address book, I ended up sending a fucking email to my aunty, telling her that I knew that she was responsible for the persecution of farmers and that it cut no ice with me blaming all her faults on them. She hadn't sent me a book token since. As a consequence I deleted all the Word documents and as a consequence I had to re-write my CV from scratch, and as a consequence I had to take myself line by line through the shame of my education and career all over again.

I groaned the deep groan of despair of a missed opportunity as soon as I wrote the name of my Grammar School. I still had the world at my feet then. But as I was once told in one of my less spectacular job interviews each successive year showed a progressive falling in standards. The cock sure American twat that some how thought he had the moral authority to say that to me on the basis that he had a job and I didn't, had in some small way done me a favour that day. He told me that when I was still young and I had the chance to arrest the decline. That I didn't wasn't exactly because I didn't want to, I did, but to a certain extent the die was cast. It seems ridiculous to look back on it like that now but you soon become stuck in the bubble of your past that is hard to burst. What that superior cunt did to me on the damage side was far worse. He made me start to realise how other people see me. He made me realise that I was average and that I had already been going downhill for a couple of years and that the damage had already been done. I suddenly knew that I couldn't just go and do anything I wanted on the assumption that I was smart and everyone knew it. It became clear that the doors weren't open for me anymore. He taught me that day that I shouldn't believe in myself anymore and that I'd already blown the best of the chance I had to start with. He's probably very happy with his career choice now. He probably takes his wife to Milan for the weekend.

Of all the things I hated about my CV was the flawed choices in my education. I saw that as the root cause of everything. How had I allowed myself to be talked into taking science subjects? If I had just known one thing then. If I had just known how important it was to always do what you are best at. If I had just known that there was no point in working at things that had no appeal. If I had just had the self belief to assert my own choices. Instead my father had pushed me into studying sciences. At that age his simple stupid self declared logic was very convincing to me. I firmly believed that people that studied music, history, art and English, the most they could hope for was to become teachers. Me I was going to be something. I was going to make a fortune. He never ever impressed on me the importance of liking something. To be fulfilled. To search for joy.

Science. Jesus. I just wasn't scientific. I could see how there had to be a science to the body, it's just that biology was indescribably boring, it put me off in the same way that installing a central heating system would now. And chemistry I suppose I could see why two different chemicals might have a certain reaction with each other but I couldn't see why it was any business of mine. I suppose my real grouch was with physics. As far as I was concerned it was just made up. Perfectly normal things that were easy to explain were given ridiculously faux scientific explanations. Physics was that branch of science that needed to explain how the outside world worked but mostly we already knew, just by looking at it. And the shame for physics was that whereas one of its theories might have some plausibility the rules of science meant that by extension a variation of the rule had to be applied to some other way the world worked that just didn't have any validity at all. For example what is a hammer but a heavy object on the end of a stick? It's got absolutely nothing to do with angles and leverage and forces. It works the same way as it would if you took your shoe off and hit something with that. I suppose I hate physics so much because it's wise after the event. The person who first made a hammer didn't use physics to work out how to make an efficient tool, he just put something heavy on the end of a stick and started. It's obvious that that's the best way to do it. Same with a wheelbarrow, all you do is put all the weight on a wheel and push it instead of carrying the same stuff, which would be much harder.

None of the theories we tested in the classroom laboratory ever worked. In our homework we always had to include a little bit about how human error had meant that we didn't arrive at the true figure given in the text book. Bollocks, how about what we saw was real life and the theory was flawed? The worst of all for me though was all the theories about the transfer of energy. Get this for an explanation of your life: as you walk along you gain kinetic energy, if you go up a hill you transfer kinetic into potential energy. Like how much energy did we have to start with? And if you went up the hill by walking you had as much potential energy as if you went to the same height by hot air balloon? If all of that stuff wasn't just made up as they went along, well Malcolm Hislop wasn't a cunt. They even had an explanation for gravity.

In two hours I had a CV that could have been written in ten minutes. It probably had less than one hundred words on it. I'd managed to convince myself that at my stage in life I only needed headlines the rest could be talked about. With headlines the holes were less obvious too.

Into the third hour and I was into an application letter too.

The number of those I had written in my life. If only I had written one of them before I left university it would have saved the thousands I've written since.

I was re-inventing myself again but this time I couldn't go anywhere on the basis of potential and brains and get myself trained and work my way up. At my age I had to go in with a track record and a capability. The only trouble was I didn't know how to do anything. I was fit for nothing. I had but one guise to adopt. I had to call myself a businessman and had to be brave enough to try and go in at a high level. Not that I was any sort of businessman but I had nowhere else to turn and I had to be prepared to play it.

I had always had a hankering to work in an American bank, not that it wouldn't be full of detestable wankers but I knew I could pull my weight on the trading desk and I fancied myself at it. I also loved the idea of working with a few people like me and having a craic on the job. It was the sort of environment I belonged in. If anything that was the only place I could make my businessman profile fit. Anywhere else I had nothing to offer. I could play up the Marketing Director bit and go somewhere with that perhaps but that would have to be my reserve option.

I re-read my first draft and I sounded like an excuse for a human being. I just didn't feel that I had the right to be assertive. Somehow I had to make consistent being wholly committed and a great success at what I'd been doing with a complete change of heart to do something completely different. I remember very well new people coming to work in various places I'd been in the past and when they were presented as someone who had been running their own business they always sounded really impressive to me. Now it was me and I was an apologist. Just like my father.

The phone was ringing and I felt so low I picked it up, nothing could be worse than what I was doing.

"Alright Hec." It was my father, "Hya love." My mum was on the extension.

"Did you have a bet?"

"Yeah I did that fucking thing of Reveley's." I hated myself for saying fucking in my mum's hearing, especially so early in the conversation but there wasn't another appropriate word.

"She can't win big races son I've told you."

"What did you do?"

"Oh god I had really hard luck." It turned out he had backed a first, a second and two thirds as he seemed to do each Saturday and ended up with about what he started with.

"Have you been watching the match?"

"They'll win nothing this year, they've gone awful, even me old little favourite Scholesy is playing bad."

"Yeah what do you think's gone wrong."

"It's obvious, buying big names, it's ruined the team, it's the same mistake they all make."

"You ever heard me talk about my mate Charlie? From Ireland?"

"Maybe, what's he say?"

"Well you know he's a massive Man Utd fan?"

"Well I am."

"Yes I know but you know he's like a proper fan."

"There's no more proper fan than me, is there Beth?"

"No what I mean is he's properly into it, he's in fan clubs and he knows all the transfer stuff before it happens and he knows all the statistics and that sort of stuff."

"I'm not interested in that, that's for anoraks all that."

"That's what I'm saying he's a bigger fan than you he's really devoted to it."

"That doesn't make him a big fan, sitting at home looking at figures."

"No I am just trying to establish ….."

"Alright alright keep your shirt on."

"What are you talking about?"

"There's no need to turn it onto an argument. It's only a simple conversation."

"Jesus, " I said, "lets talk about something else." I was seething, his ignorance stood in the way of the most simple conversations. I was trying to help him out with some information. If he wasn't so obsessed with being right, he might have learned something.

"What else have you been doing love?" said my mum.

"I'm applying for jobs."

"Oh," he said, meaning I was supposed to explain. I didn't.

"Aren't you happy there?" says my mum.

"No mum, it's terrible, I'm going mad."

"Oh dear," she said with a big sigh.

"I thought you'd made it there?" he said.

"No it's about the worst job I could imagine."

"What is it? What exactly is it that you're looking for? No jobs are good son I can tell you that."

"Yes but dad, since I have entered the world of work I haven't enjoyed one single waking second that I have spent at work. I haven't had any form of fulfilment from work at all. I am not being melodramatic but I haven't ever got anything from a job."

"Neither do any of us son."

"Yes but I want to before I stop working. I really want to enjoy going to work. God it's the thing you spend most of your life doing."

The main problem was that they had always been obsessed with being rich. They judged everything in terms of being rich. Young people didn't take up careers because they might be fulfilling, form a fabric for your life, make you happy. People chose jobs on the same basis that they tried to win the National Lottery or get the Pools in, as they would have said. The other day when they were last on the phone they were telling me about a Manchester United player's party, apparently Ryan Giggs had had a fight with the reserve team goalie. My mum's take on the incident was, "Imagine that Hec, two multi millionaires fighting," although speaking her version of posh she didn't pronounce the H of Hec the t of multi nor the t of fighting. She thought it was bizarre that they were fighting because they were very rich, she didn't think that the interesting part of the story was that they were team mates and they should have been sublimely happy because they played sport in a team for a living. She thought they were mad because you couldn't reach a higher station in life than being a millionaire(multi).

I would have pitied her were it not for the fact that this pathetically limited outlook was responsible for ruining my own life. Instead of keeping a level head and letting it go as I should, I let it infuriate me. I hated her for being so limited. The only way in which I sympathised with her was that her views were formed in blind allegiance to him. She would say things like "Come on Hec, two multi millionaires fighting, come on," said with incredulity to back up some idiotic point my myopic father was trying to make.

I remember when I was younger I was a member of the golf club and my father used to harangue me to go more often. He'd say to my mother, "who they going pick Beth," referring to Oxford admissions tutors, "three lads with 9 O'levels, one's a swat, one's a musician and one's a scratch golfer." My mum used to go "derrr" like it was absolutely obvious to see, on no more than what he had said, what the answer was. "Come on Hec a multi millionaire scratch golfer, come on." Then he would look at me and say, "am I right or am I right?"

The real reason I didn't go to golf more often was that I was embarrassed and I didn't fit in. Whereas the other boys there had real Wranglers and Levis I had Marks & Spencer's jeans with an aeroplane embroidered on the pocket, one pair, whereas they had Slazenger wool sweaters I had nylon ones that made my hair stand on end. Worst of all was that I had women's golf shoes, everyone knew they were women's shoes but were good enough not to say, I used to try my best to hide them out of general view in the locker room where we hung around and played cards, I would only put them on at the very last minute so that they wouldn't be noticed and I took them off at the door on the way in so that I could carry them in behind my back and put them back in their hiding place. I realise how obvious this must have been now and makes me wince more now than it could have ever done then.

One day I got a new outfit, made entirely of nylon, which was ostensibly smart from a distance, close up it was cheap and horrible, not that anyone could get that close, they would have been repelled by the static electric force field that enveloped me.

"What did they say Hec, the other lads?" my dad said when I got in after its first airing, all proud. I felt embarrassed and played dumb. But he tried to coax something out of me, "you know Des and the rest of the lads did they think you were smart?" I felt truly embarrassed to the balls of my feet. He didn't stop to reflect for a moment that they were bought new rig-outs, as he called them, all the time and that when they were bought proper things they were made of wool and cotton. He didn't realise that he had only highlighted what a cheapskate I was by turning me out in a Z-Brothers outfit, not even Marks & Spencer let alone the Pro's shop and that when I wore it the next time and the next time it would kind of diminish the "classy" look that he was so proud of that day.

"You're not going to lose any money by leaving early are you."

That was another of his things, the self-interested, rhetorical question.

"No dad, don't worry."

"Well we do worry about you son."

"Too fucking late," I thought.

"There's no need dad. I'll keep you informed. Goodnight." His self-declared-objectivity was becoming too much for me.

21.

By Monday morning I was already in breach of my non-cooperation list. There I was in the office waiting for Declan's 8 a.m. meeting. It was absolutely par for the course that just as I decided on quiet disobedience and anonymity here I was becoming a major personality. The meeting was particularly bad from that point of view since it firmly put me in the limelight within the engine room. Declan was last to arrive and I presumed from the way everybody assembled themselves round the table that he would be sitting at the head. To the left of that was Sharon Copeland, Head of Human Resources and essentially Declan's right hand. She was no more than a gossip and loved knowing a bit of information prior to everyone else that she wasn't allowed to divulge. When the news eventually came out it was always something like two girls in the print room at Nat West Bank had had a fight during the nightshift or something like that. She was one of those lucky people that you come across more and more today in that she was as thick as shit but had a penchant for filing and blindly following stupid rules, and those skills combined with her love of gossiping had got her the job of Head of Human Resources at a rubbish company. She would probably pick up about £55k for doing that. She was the sort of person that advertising was aimed at, that massive tranche of middle England that were useless and once upon a time would have been lucky to hold down a job as a junior ranking secretary in a proper company but nowadays had spending power and choices and lifestyle and were made to feel important by their unmerited salaries and job descriptions and the attention given to them by advertisers and consumer profilers.

The meeting also included the four (although I was one of them) Divisional Directors, the Head of Recruitment, albeit that she was referred to as Head of Resourcing for some reason, Kirsty, the Accountant for Declan's division and Davina to take notes. They were all women, apart from Steve, one of the Divisional Directors and me, and Steve was almost officially a dwarf. That meant that Declan could bully and boss them as much as he wanted and in return they sucked the arse off him. I was the only one in the room that didn't have any respect for him.

Pre-meeting time is always interesting especially before the most senior person arrives. Usually everybody uses it as a time to find out a little bit about their colleagues' lives, especially on Monday mornings. But the sad middle management fucks at Martins Fleet were more inclined to use it as a time to make little boasts about how sophisticated their outside lives were. Or more precisely to show how closely they resembled advertising stereotypes. Unfortunately, because I was a new face and because I wanted to stay anonymous all their attention was turned on me.

"What had I done this weekend?" Sharon wanted to know, for her secret files I thought. So I lied to make myself sound more dashing.

"I went to Cheltenham for the races."

"Oh are you into that?" she replied, all innocent sounding but secretly hoping to find some juice for her files. Recidivist gambler, if she knew what that meant.

"I love horse racing," piped up Amanda but that was only an excuse to give her the opportunity to say that she had been horse riding at the weekend. She needed to present herself as someone of a certain standing, commensurate with her important management position. She had all the largest banking clients and as such she saw herself a cut above the rest of the Divisional Directors. She was one of those people that tried to evoke an air of intellectual sophistication in their conversation by saying things like perturbed. Apparently she had been very perturbed when she had been. given a lively horse to ride at the weekend.

Nobody dare have the nerve to say that they had done nothing and I regretted that I hadn't said something like that to buck the trend. Not that everyone got to say something, they were queuing up to get their bit in to tell everyone how exciting their lives were but the conversation was dominated by only a few of the bitches.

"I went for Sunday lunch at the Cambridge Arms, you know that new place on the riv…"

"Oh it's fantastic I was there last Sun….."

"That place with the wooden floors and the open french windows and the veranda looking out to …"

"Yes with the rattan furniture and the old colonial style and ….."

"What did you have, I had the …"

And so it went, each trying to establish that they were just as sophisticated as the other. It was something to do with the age we lived in I suppose that everybody saw themselves as some grade of celebrity. These people were like the shit on your shoe but within Martins Fleet they held high rank and were some form of minor celebrities for the desperate fucks below them on the ladder. Just like celebrities from Coronation Street would love to find themselves at the same event as proper film stars so the Divisional Directors loved to frequent the same bars and restaurants as people with proper careers.

Declan came in and although he tried to pick up on the mood of semi-levity we had established he lacked the finesse to find the mot juste and the human moment was over. We were back to being automatons and I suppose I should have been pleased that the others fell into the mood more readily than me. But instead I felt a pang of longing for the same sense of purpose in my career that they had.

The format for the meeting was that each person had to give a rundown of what had happened in their division during the last week and what new matters needed flagging up, to use their language. As such I had nothing to contribute nevertheless Declan came to me and said: "Hector," and nodded his head slightly and raised his eyebrows above his Alfie glasses.

I should have said, "it's obviously irrelevant to me because I started doing the job last Tuesday," instead I just started talking. I based my talk on the bullshit business plan I had written for Legal Solutions that I knew hadn't been read by anyone. Suddenly rather than the business plan being something that I had put my heart and soul into which nobody had even given me the courtesy of reading, let alone have a serious discussion with me about it, it was now something that I had publicly announced as the way we were going ahead. Declan didn't have the quality or know-how to contradict me and so, as I spoke, I set out my stall as it were, as if we'd all sat down and thrashed out the subject and come up with this fantastic new policy for Legal Solutions. I knew I'd regret it later but at that moment in time it filled a gap.

I said, "We acknowledge that we cannot sell classic Martins Fleet contracts to the largest law firms. The reason being the Print Room is the one of the most profitable areas of law firm activity and they are not about to outsource it."

I didn't actually know this, I just made it up – and it saved me from becoming a salesman for photocopying contracts. Then I said, "that is why our endeavours will be based on presenting a new model of the Print Room to law firms, something we have decided to call an Imaging Centre." God knows why I used the word "we" or for that matter why I elevated a little idea that I'd had into company policy. Nevertheless I did. One thing was for sure, I was on certain ground when I talked technology to that audience. I knew fuck all about it myself but I knew ten times more than anyone else in the room so I kept on talking. In the end I said "our target firms are," and I randomly named three of the largest ten law firms.

When I finished there was a small ripple of applause. Instead of bringing me up for talking unendorsed bullshit, Declan beamed with delight. I had turned them on, and he wanted to be part of it. By the time I was off centre stage I had agreed to give presentations to the key managers of each of the other divisions.

The meeting went on and before Declan's summing up, which I gathered was a traditional epilogue to Monday mornings we had to endure the lesser trades. The last, Human Resources, was like watching paint dry and made all the worse by the way Sharon relished her position and next to her Declan who delighted in the ups and downs of personnel. He wanted to know the ins and outs of all the minor squabbles, in my view exposing his too recent past amongst the rabble. It also became absolutely obvious that he worked all day on Sunday and telephoned clients all day ironing out all the small matters he didn't get on to during the week. For a photocopying company. And for every phone call he made there was some other useless fuck with an excuse for a job and a life that was prepared to take it. The denouement this week when Sharon finally spat it out after alternating between schoolgirl giggles and straight-faced professionalism, was that someone called Leroy Williams had been caught sleeping on the night shift at one of the larger accountancy practices. It wasn't just sleeping, with Leroy, he had got into the habit of bringing a camp bed to work and going straight to bed as soon as he clocked in. She went on and on about it. About how the news wasn't to get out "throughout the business," and how they were going to deal with it.

The more I heard the worse it was. I couldn't fucking stand listening to the bitch. I thought about the fucking hoops of fire that me and my staff had to jump through to be part of Martins Fleet when we were all honest and diligent and the hypocrisy of the way they followed procedure to protect the interests of people like Leroy who asked to get sacked, and probably wouldn't have minded if they were. In the end, I said:

"why don't you sack him?"

And everyone laughed.

She didn't even answer me and just carried on explaining the same old bullshit. The total lack of respect in the fucking bitch made my blood boil. She went on and on and in the end she started on about needing to be careful about the "R" word.

I said, "It's not racist to sack him you fucking pussy," well I hadn't done anything towards getting sacked since last Friday.

There was a collective intake of breath which I thought was unnecessary and then they started preaching to me about the need not just to not be racist but to be seen to not be racist, talking to me like I was 10 years old. I should have let it lie but instead I said, "the only thing racist here is you."

Sharon countered with, "I take great exception to that," and some witless fuck said, "Martins Fleet is an equal opportunities employer."

I said, "anyone else would just sack him and you won't because he's black,"

To which she just said, "yeah."

So I said, "don't you think that's racist?"

And she said, "I've told you before I am not a racist."

If anything she erred towards self-declared objectivity.

"But…" I started but Declan headed me off and said that the rest would be dealt with outside the meeting and with that the meeting was over.

126

22.

A silence hung over us as we left and I felt like the arsehole that had just spoiled the party. Long term it had probably done me good but I felt like I'd just let the ball go between my legs.

Back at my desk I was on my own in a shroud of misery. I was all big shot one moment and a pain in the arse the next. Why wasn't I consistent? Why didn't I play it cool? Why didn't I stick to my plan? Since I'd drawn it up, I'd become higher profile than ever, I hadn't been to any race meetings and I had been in more office meetings than ever before. And because I'd opened myself up I was expected to attend many more meetings. I was suddenly part of the infrastructure, the last thing I set out to be.

I decided to get my non-cooperation plan back on track and launched myself headfirst into Social-Lites.

A quick bit of market research on the world match market using the world wide web reveals that there are few players worth pitching. It really it starts and ends with The European Match Company. It is one of those companies that sounds pathetic but is in fact enormous. When the Web Site invites you to "meet the Directors" you see a board of twelve or so proper heavy weight businessmen. I was delighted and I got stuck in. One thing was immediately obvious, they were desperate to have a wider range of products to sell that was in some way related to a match. They went on and on about their commitment to product development and they showed loads of pictures of barbecue lighters and artificial logs and stuff like that. Well you would if you sold matches wouldn't you? So that was encouraging. Now all that I needed to do was find who was responsible for bringing new products into the company.

Web-sites I concluded are useful until you want to use them. Under the job description of about half of the Board Members, you could reasonably imply that they were responsible for some form of product development. And of them you had no idea of knowing who was who's boss nor for that matter who worked where around the globe. Was the man who looked like the product development director but was called North American Commercial Director just product development director for North America? Wasn't the man called Group Commercial Director at Head Office responsible for product development despite the fact that it didn't say anything about it on his job description? When I looked at all the other job descriptions of the Head Office Board they were all Accountants and Lawyers and Operations and Tree Growing and were definitely not about product development. Perhaps it was the level below. In which case was it the UK Marketing Director, as I was in the UK? Or the Marketing Director based at Head Office? But did that necessarily mean that they were Group Marketing Director and therefore boss of the UK based one or were they just responsible for the home region? Anyhow it seemed that the North American part of the company was to all intents and purposes a separate company. So I decided to take a blind stab at the Head Office Marketing Director, no the UK one, no fuck it I'd go straight to the Commercial Director but he wouldn't be interested. No I'd start with the Information Officer. They could tell me who I should contact. But I couldn't tell them what my idea was. I could be brave. Yes, I decided, I would start there.

Sending an email through a Web Site was not going to serve me well. I would just look like one of those nerdy wankers that did things like that and I would be dealt with in some unthinking processed way. I wanted to speak to the person and impress upon them what a winner of an idea I had and get them to tell me whether to send a letter or not or whether to talk to someone else.

For some reason the arseholes that design Web Pages think that they have taken you and your clients to a new world and a new way of doing things. That is why they don't do things like make the telephone number of the company available. After half an hour I gave up and opted for Directory Enquiries. There was a block on the phones at work ringing numbers like that, that cost money so I had to use my mobile. Only it wasn't there. I'd left it charging on the other side of the office because there weren't any spare plug sockets by my desk. I found the phone under a pile of documents and it had been unplugged and a laptop computer plugged in its place. I tried the phone but it had no power it must have been unplugged almost immediately. I was getting frustrated but I was trying not to let it get to me. I hated having to ask Amanda for favours but she was my only option.

"Can I borrow your phone to ring directory enquiries?"

"I'm busy now can you wait?"

"Please Amanda, I am nearly going mad with frustration, please."

"Oh Jesus OK I'll just stop what I'm doing – why don't you use the Web to find it?"

"Look I did, it doesn't work."

"What the connection isn't down again is it?"

"No it just isn't that easy to find international numbers."

"Have you tried Yellow Pages?" I hadn't actually thought of that.

"Why?"

"On the Web, it's very good."

"Oh Jesus Amanda please don't make me, just lend me your phone."

She gave it to me from somewhere at the bottom of her handbag.

"See – fully charged Hector, organisation, you should try it."

"Yes very good five candles."

"What?"

"Fully charged, you've got five candles."

"Whatever."

I phoned Directory Enquiries and got the number of the UK office figuring that it would be quicker to ask them the number of the Norwegian Head Office. While I was ringing them her phone, which I was still holding, started bleeping so I passed it back to her.

"European Match Company?" she screeched out loud. She must have received a text message confirming the number. An unasked for and unnecessary over servicing. It hadn't done me any good at all, in fact the opposite. There was no choice about whether I received this extra level of service. There was no "would you like that confirmed by text sir?" It was simply assumed that it would be good for me, that I needed it, some fucking IT business man, some American arsehole with the brief to deliver more service to the client base. Someone who knew better than me had decided for me.

I was still on the phone to the UK office so I couldn't explain myself. The bitch at European Match UK seemed to resent that I phoned her up to ask her the number in Norway. A fucking telephone operator. She was probably a telephonist/receptionist if she were given the correct title but whatever she was it was beneath her to deal with such menial matters.

I thought I should explain to Amanda.

"I have got a lead into European Match, through a friend of mine."

"Does Dick know about it?"

"What, no, why?"

"All leads are supposed to go through him."

"Oh fucking hell Amanda he's an absolute twat."

"Anyway I thought you were Legal?"

"Yeah. I'm street legal baby."

"Well European Match will be corporate it should be one of Steve's."

"Look Amanda, I'm the only one that has a contact there, it has to be me."

"That's not how it's supposed to work but what should I care, I'm banking."

"Please Amanda, please don't say anything to anyone, please just let me get on with it on, my own, please."

"What's it worth?" and she winked.

"I'll plate you."

"You should not have said that Hector."

"Sorry."

And with that I had given the maximum publicity to my little private idea before I had done anything to promote it.

I thought it best if I didn't let Amanda witness my call to Norway so I went to find a meeting room. In all I think I did I did three laps of the office, all five floors. Starting on the second floor, where my desk was, there was one meeting room in the far corner. Not that you'd immediately recognise it as a meeting room. It was one of those things that you often found in offices, a hastily erected partition room made mainly of glass that had never been taken down again after its initial purpose had long since expired. In the average office of 150 to 300 people my experience has been to expect about 2 major and 3 to 5 minor office rearrangements per year and with every move new meeting rooms like that pop up out of nowhere.

When I first arrived at Martins Fleet we were put in the back part of the Second Floor next to the excuse for a meeting room. In those early days I spent about 75% of my week in that room with various shades of arseholes, people that thought they had proper careers and had no shame in imposing their contrary notions on people like me. We had too many meetings ourselves the fifteen or so of us at Gilligan Somes. It is a weakness of all educated people with an ego. Truly great people just get on with it and let others follow. On the other hand people who were very average with delusions of greatness didn't cooperate with meetings either, people like Franck who laboured under a false appreciation of his own iconoclastic brilliance. The rest of us knew him to be a contrary wanker and something of a hypocrite, since he was perfectly happy to spend all day in meetings pursuing his own agenda. The majority of the rest of us went to meetings all the time. I spent most of my time in meetings with people like Aude Hardley and Stacey Arnold.

The floor I worked on was divided in two parts and that room was in the other part by the back stairs. That was where the Site Managers and the Divisional Managers had desks. They were put there at the time of the last office rearrangement when the Client Services Directors and the Human Resources department was put in the bit I sat in. That rearrangement had seen Declan promoted to be in charge of that new department from Client Services Director which he was previously. He had been the only Client Services Director then. On his promotion four new Client Services Directors were created beneath him. That suited everyone, the new Client Services Directors felt great about their new job with a smart name, Declan felt like a dog with one dick, or at least acted like it, and the Company felt great because companies like Martins Fleet love gratifying their staff with job titles rather than cash. Handing out names has always been easy. There was only one person that wasn't pissing his pants with excitement. Me. Since I was the fourth Client Services Director and it was the first time in my life I had ever been referred to as something as ridiculous as that. They made me a CSD because there was no better way of fitting me into their absurd company structure. Rather than just leaving me without a title and trying to work with me to build a new aspect of their business for them I was forced to be something that didn't quite fit the existing structure.

It was taken. It always was. The Site Managers and Divisional Managers made sure of that. However because they were proper managers who knew how to behave in businesses they had made a Word Table with Monday to Friday on the x-axis and the day broken into half hour slots starting at 7.00 a.m. going to 9.00 p.m. on the y axis. They had also made a notice which read: "To reserve this meeting room please sign the availability chart below 24 hours before you need it. Please try to restrict yourself to meetings of no more than half an hour. If you require the meeting room for a client meeting please coordinate through Davina Askey." That's what they must have been teaching on the Management Trainee courses at Asda and Burtons. The net result was that the table was always entirely filled in and the room was always occupied. Whereas attendance at meetings was the bane of my life it was the essence of the cut and thrust of business for the Divisional Managers on the way up.

There may have been a meeting room on the First Floor but I was prepared to miss the opportunity. The First Floor was referred to as Systems which meant I.T., which in turn meant paedophiles and anoraks in equal measure. I just never went there. The Ground Floor was Recruitment, I mean Martins Fleet Resourcing. It had tons of meeting rooms for the purpose of interviewing hapless recruits to Martins Fleet. Most people that applied to Martins Fleet were sold on the idea of having a career in "Management" but what they didn't realise was that they had to have learned all their management skills at Marks and Spencer or the Army or some such place before they came to Martins Fleet. We didn't do training. We were a management organisation. It was either that or their Parole Officer had told them that it was about time that they got a job. What it came to mean was that legions and legions of Managers came through Martins Fleet every day of the week, day in day out. From 7.30 a.m. for a sneaky interview before going to their current job until 9.00 p.m. at night for sneaky interviews on the way home. Thousands of them. There was probably a day when there wasn't more than 1,000 managers in the whole of England. There must be about 1,000 per every 10,000 square feet of office space now.

Because they couldn't provide any management training at Martins Fleet they had to be sure that they had got the right person. That meant that each management recruit should expect not less than half a dozen interviews even for a shit job. Shit by Martins Fleet standards that is. Unbearable by normal human standards. I was once asked to "sit in" on an interview for a deputy to Chamberpot when I first arrived. She had been interviewed so many times that it had reached the stage where she had to be taken out for a drink afterwards to get to know us better. She was evidently brainless, so I said so and they all looked a bit crestfallen at my judgment. The reason being I had sat in on her eighth interview. To work at Martins Fleet. As an assistant to Chamberpot. Fuck me.

The problem with taking a room in recruitment was that they had absolute priority and you could be thrown out without notice without a right of appeal. And none of them were sound-proofed. The worst thing by far was that the birds that worked in recruitment were starved of human attention for months on end. They interviewed back to back social misfits, worked long hours, lived at the back of reception in splendid isolation, talked only to each other and when a normal person passed through their midst they were loath to let them go without at least an interrogation, often it required at least a promise of a drink after work. I was quite gratified by the attention of girls aged 20 to 40 but there was something about this lot. They were like the girls at school that I thought I would never have to meet again after I escaped to University. There was something unacceptably regressive about keeping their company. I put my head around the corridor for a few moments but there were sufficient signs of life and I was bound to be spotted so I decided to give it up.

The Third Floor was given over to a Board Room and a smaller meeting room that was used as a dining room, a kitchen and The Presentation Room. This floor was the pride and joy of the senior people in the business. And it was the most civilised and business looking part of the whole Company. The difficulty was that it was almost entirely block booked by Organisation Learning. That was because the careers offered by Martins Fleet were so utterly undilutedly awful that they had to recruit hundreds of new people all the time. They were recruited to a) photocopy, b) deliver said photocopies or mail c) manage people doing a) and b) and Organisational Learning's task above all others was to *induce* new people into the business. This process took at least a day and involved the training of such complicated matters as picking up the phone and answering like a normal human being, learning how to write a letter, learning management structures and such other things that would have been more easily taught by one of the several managers that they would eventually work for. The real reason they did things like that was not for the good of training the recruit, it was so that they could say to their clients that they would provide trained staff with no assimilation period when somebody left. Somebody left all the time. It was something that had to be reported to clients, it was called the churn rate. Martins Fleet had a churn rate of about 30%. You work it out. Their clients were easily

132

convinced about the faux training programmes since they were just the same breed on the other side of the fence. That is why the stupid management classes have proliferated. No-one says, 'No.'

Once you had an Organisational Learning Department it didn't stop at inducing semi-retards. It meant that you had created a department with ambition. At Martins Fleet the bird in charge, it always was a bird and she was changed every six months or so, would come to people like me and try to force me into some stupid scheme to transfer my skills "out through the business." What that meant was to attend meetings on the third floor and talk to people who had left school as soon as they could and took a job at Martins Fleet to pay the rent, about what it was like to be a lawyer, of which by the way I knew virtually nothing, i.e. a fucking massive waste of time. I always refused. However the current Head of Organisational Learning was Ex-WPC Knockers Mahoney so I took a different tact with her. I said I would do it and just went missing as far as she was concerned thereafter. That was why I rarely went to the Third Floor. And one of the other reasons why I never answered my phone.

From there it was the Fourth Floor which was exclusively New Media. That meant Creative and Design to people of my age. It meant drawing to people a little bit older. It was sort of always embargoed to foreigners and I never went without an invitation.

The Fifth Floor was board members' offices to the front and the Sales Department to the rear with the secretarial support to the board sandwiched in between, as it were, Mrs. Each Board Member had his own office which could occasionally be hijacked if they were out but were generally out of bounds. The Sales Department boasted three meeting rooms. They were all as crap as the temporary structure on the Second Floor but nevertheless three.

I was always a little bit nervous about going to the Fifth Floor mainly because as you came and went you were in plain view of the executive offices. I knew that when I was there I was generally skiving and I couldn't help but think that all the Directors that I nodded and waved to on my way through knew that too. That was why when I was there I generally walked through with an apologetic slouch like a fat ape.

It was always a relief to reach the gap between the two parts and put the executives behind me and enter the wonderful world of sales, although it was actually called Business Development. As I did I could see that my favoured meeting room, the one nearest the back door and furthest from the gaze of anyone important, was taken by Chamberpot and Chawdray. The fucking pair of bastards were having a meeting about the so called Legal Department without me, without even telling me. They were talking together about the thing I was in charge of, deciding between themselves how to do it and what was to be done.

Even though I didn't give a fuck and in fact if I had been able to stand back and look at it properly I would have been able to see that Chamberpot's usurping of my

133

function played perfectly into my hands, the sight of them together made me furious. Instead of enjoying the moment I let his underhand manoeuvring infuriate me.

He was clearly embarrassed and stopped the meeting to come out to see me.

"Hector, come and join us," the fucking wanker,

"Thanks, but I'm in the middle of something."

"Oh what's that?"

"I'm about to make a sales call – just looking for a room to do it really."

"Do it in our room."

"No it's alright thanks Bryan I just want to find a bit of space on my own to do it."

"Do it at my desk if you like."

"No I just want to do it privately really," I felt ridiculous saying that.

"Sounds interesting, is it anything we should be excited about?"

"I don't know yet, a mate of mine has come up with a decent lead and I'm about to give him a ring."

"Oh really, who is it?"

"Jesus," I thought, I didn't know what sort of lie to come up with. I knew that Chamberpot was totally disingenuous and that he wanted to know who my lead was so that he could either muscle in on it if it was any good, or use it to put me down if it wasn't. He was the sort of person who would put "my lead" on the record just to bring me under pressure if he thought that there was nothing in it for him. If I told him about European Match he would have me slaughtered.

"Slaughter & May," I lied.

"Great, who is it?"

"He's called Graham Bradley, Head of Business Development."

That was sufficiently vague to be unchallengeable. I banked on it being more than likely that there wasn't a Business Development Department at Slaughter & May or at least nothing called that. That way Chamberpot wouldn't be able to verify it and if the subject came up again I could play the I'm-better-connected card.

134

"Oh isn't it Roderick Bedgar any more?"

Jesus. Of all the made up names of departments I could have come up with I managed to pick one that existed where he knew the name of the person actually in the job.

"I don't know, I only know Graham Bradley."

"Oh well keep me informed. I wonder where old Roderick's gone off to now? I'll have to find out."

I knew he didn't believe me.

One of the other two offices was free, the worst office in the building. Quite lidderally not enough room to swing a cat. Last time I was there I'd snagged my trousers on the back of a chair as I tried to squeeze between it and the partition wall on the way to my seat at the far end of the room.

"I'd better take my chance," I said to Chamberpot nodding towards the emptying office.

"That one doesn't have a phone."

"I think I'll give up and try again another time," I was dying to get away from him.

I went back to re-run the circuit of meeting rooms by the back stairs, lest I met anyone. I was furious with the way I had let Chamberpot treat me. I was in charge of the Legal Department, I should have interrogated him. He should have felt chastised for not letting me in on whatever it was he was up to. Instead I allowed him to do it to me. Not only that but I had put myself under pressure I didn't need by having to live up to a false lead. And what is more I had told an easily verifiable lie. All he had to was ring up Roderick whatsisname and that was me exposed as being up to no good. All of that and all I need have done is say, "what are you two up to?" when he first came out of the office. I just didn't have the composure and authority to impose myself on situations like that. I allowed myself be dominated. He knew everything about what I was up to, albeit that I had lied, and I knew nothing about his nefarious business. I just lacked what it took to be sufficiently confrontational with people like him. I did not have it in me to say what I wanted to, to put people like Chamberpot in their place.

I should have been pleased. That they got on without me and that they usurped my function played straight to my game plan. In fact I could reasonably allege that they had implied executive backing to behave like that. In fact I would. Nevertheless, what I couldn't come to terms with was that I let things happen to me instead of my controlling the agenda. If I was managing my way to a sacking it should be to a master plan dictated by me. Not because I allowed cunts like Chamberpot to get the better of me.

The second floor meeting room was taken by Lynda Briar. I could see that she gave me a little wave and I acted like I didn't see it. As I walked away from the office I turned round to mouth "fuck off you cunt," to her, and as I did I could see she was still looking so I did it anyway.

I couldn't go back to the fifth floor, I would have looked too ridiculous, so I came back to my desk and waited until Amanda Phipps went to lunch so that I would have relative privacy around my desk space. Only she didn't. I waited and waited. At first I made a play of working by reading through already read emails, deleting those I didn't fancy replying to that had been hanging around a while with no chasing messages. I loved the way that emails which seemed to compel an immediate response when they arrived, could be let go unanswered after a couple of days without grave consequences. Often times, in the days that lapsed before answering, circumstances would change so that there became a sort of implied wisdom in the responder by having taken his time. I had adopted this rationale to deal with all complaints about delays.

At first Amanda accepted an unsolicited at desk meeting from one of her Divisional Managers, Helen Smith, in a way that would not have been tolerated had I asked. Helen sidled up softly and all coquettishly dipped her head and looked at dikey Amanda through her fringe:

"would you mind if I picked your brain for a moment?" all soft and shitty and sycophantic.

"of course," said Amanda all magnanimous, "pull up a chair," like she had a fucking brain to pick.

"It's a little problem at DKB."

"When is there never a little problem at DKB?"

Both sets of eyes raised skyward and they giggled, all knowingly.

"It needn't be a problem but err ....." and she took a deep sigh,

"I see it's a Terry problem."

"Very much so."

And they both laughed again. Jesus I hated the way women talked to each other.

Helen explained, that whilst following internal policies she had arrived at an increase to £15,325 salary from £14,875 for her photocopy clerks for their annual review, which was imminent, she had cleared her intentions with the client, Terry, who had

OK'd the rises for all of them bar one. One of the poor fuckers was unfortunate enough not to have just a photocopying job, he delivered the packages of photocopying too. That made him on certain terms a messenger as well as a photocopying clerk. Terry's messengers were on £15,100 and as a consequence he couldn't countenance a salary of £15,325 for the Martins Fleet person because of "the ructions that would cause." That was what the fucking conversation was about. They made it last about twenty minutes and in the end Amanda said:

"thanks very much for bringing it to me. I'll call Terry myself today, we don't want this to fester."

That was what they did for a living. And no doubt Helen and Terry had been back and forth over the issue many times more before Helen had sought to "pick Amanda's brains."

Worse from my point of view was that they were having one of those conversations that wouldn't come to an end. It should have been a two line conversation and it hadn't been. In the name of pretending to have proper jobs they had managed to drag out the stuff of secondary school role playing for over fifteen minutes. Then as they were winding up Helen got up from her sitting position while still talking:

"so then I'll get on to the team and ..."

"Yes get on to the team and try to reassure them ….."

"Yes."

"Well we can't actually reassure them because we don't know how Terry's going to react."

"No, so perhaps ..."

"No maybe not ..."

"What I could do is call Paul and tell him the whole story and get him to handle it for us."

"Can you trust him to do that?"

"Oh yeah, he's really stepped up to the plate since we promoted him, he'll know how to handle it. It was him that brought home the paper contract."

"Oh yeah that's right. He's a good sort isn't he? He was round here talking to Declan the other day. That's the one that the client really loves isn't it?"

"And the team too. He's a really nice bloke."

Then she sat down again. And the conversation rekindled.

"Have you thought about putting him up for a Talk About It! Award?"

The Talk About It! awards were new that year at Martins Fleet and they were designed by Organisational Learning "to deliver recognition to employees that have made an outstanding contribution to Martins Fleet during the year." The real reason Martins Fleet invented the Talk About It! awards was to make their staff feel appreciated otherwise than by paying proper wages. Why the staff allowed themselves to be bought off in such a cheap way was beyond me but the fact was, as patronising and excruciatingly embarrassing as they were, the staff loved them and coveted a nomination.

"I've been trying but he doesn't really fit any of the categories."

"What about most outstanding individual contribution?"

"Not a hope, Gordon's going to win that."

"Oh yes, of course."

Gordon had distinguished himself by going to a landfill site and finding every one of a bundle of documents that one of his clients had accidentally thrown away. He was a shoe in for the main prize.

And so it went, Helen rose to her feet several times and sat down again as the conversation petered out and re-started over and over. It was well past one o'clock when it finally ended, long since past the time when an organised person would have gone to lunch.

"Please Amanda, please," I was silently praying.

Eventually Helen went and Amanda wrapped up and it was all over. My liberty was close at hand. She picked up phone.

"Oh please, for fuck's sake go."

"What Hector?"

"Nothing."

"I'm making an important client call. Is there any chance of not grunting while I do it?"

I didn't reply. I just felt a form of pure undiluted venomous hatred towards her, which was always best communicated in silence.

She talked about the number of photocopies that they had done that month, which she referred to as clicks and how she needed a new DC 10 or something on the fourth floor. But she managed to make it last for a very long time. Eventually she hung up and I plucked up the courage to say:

"Amanda, do you go out for lunch?"

"I've been."

"What?"

"To Ponti's earlier."

"When earlier?"

"11 ish."

She did what loads of Martins Fleet managers did, they went to the nearby sandwich shop before 12 so that there would be no queue, came straight back to her desk, continued to work whilst they ate their sandwich and called that going to lunch.

"Are you trying to get rid of me?"

"I would pay money to have you removed. Are you going to be here all afternoon?"

"Yes."

That meant that I couldn't make my private phone call at my desk so I went on the rounds of meeting rooms again. This time I went straight to the fifth floor, there being a much better chance because most of the Sales Department had gone to lunch and this time I would give Chamberpot short shrift if I met him.

It was like the Marie Celeste. I walked straight into the preferred room previously occupied by Chamberpot and shut the door behind me. Relief.

I dialled the European Match Company headquarters in Stockholm. No ringing tone, no nothing. I did it again and again. Nothing. Then I realised that the phone was blocked for making foreign calls.

"Oh Jesus my fucking life."

I went back to my desk and tried the number from there and got the same result.

"Amanda, how do you make an overseas call from this shit office?"

"Hector, you may not want to work. I do, would you mind letting me get on with it?"

"Oh for fuck's sake Amanda, just tell me – it will take you less time than it does to slag me off."

"7982."

"7 what. What's that supposed to be?"

"7 9 8 2 now leave me alone."

It meant nothing to me. It would have taken her no time at all to have told me exactly what to do, as I would have done if our roles were reversed.

I went back to the meeting room and dialled the number with 7982 on the front. It didn't work. I did it with #7982, I did #7982 *, I did *7982*, I did #7982# and so on in every combination that modern phone systems demanded. In the end I gave up. I rang reception and asked why it wasn't working and they said that the phone was probably barred and didn't I know that I could do it from my desk. Apparently all you had to do was dial 7982 before the real number.

As meeting rooms were embargoed against calling abroad and my desk wasn't the place to do it, I decided to go home to do it and pretend I was having a late lunch.

I wish I hadn't.

I rang the office in Norway:

"I am very sorry I don't speak Norwegian, would you mind if I spoke to you English?"

"Go ahead."

"I'd like to speak to your Information Officer, I think she's called, Ingrid Svensson."

"Ah yes Ingrid, she is not in the office, today."

"Could you tell me please is she the right person to speak to with a product development idea?"

"No."

"Could you perhaps tell me who that might be?"

"Who? What might they be?"

"The person, the correct person to contact regarding a product development idea."

"What is the idea?"

"I'd rather not say."

"Ah then it will be difficult. You need to call Ingrid."

"When will she be back?"

"At the end of next week."

"Are you sure you couldn't suggest someone else to talk to?"

"Perhaps you should try the Marketing Director."

"Yes please, are they there?"

"No there is one in the UK office, do you have the number?"

"Yes."

And then she put the phone down. I had her down more as Norwegian than non-sequitor but I made a mental note to be prepared to change my view about that. At least I learned that there was such a person in England, that was more than the Web Site told me. Not that I knew whether the one in England was the only one or the one in charge or one of several. "Nevertheless," I thought.

Whereas I didn't mind talking through the idea and approach with someone called the Information Officer, I didn't like the idea of going straight to someone called a Marketing Director. I wanted to keep my ammo dry but I needed his name so I gave them a ring in Birmingham.

"Hello, I have some information to send to the Marketing Director, can I have his name please?"

A snotty middle class woman said:

"We do not give out such information over the telephone."

"Don't you?" I sighed and put the phone down.

"We do not give." We? What is a fucking receptionist doing saying things like: "we don't do this." What the fuck did it have to do with her? A £5 an hour tart that

141

answered the phone, telling me she didn't want to deal with me. Her judging me. Jesus Christ. The fucking lie of businesses. The Company has the audacity to say that it "prioritises innovation and is wholly committed to continuous product development," goes and employs a fucking dog who entirely contradicts the idea.

I gave up and went back to work. I would find his name out later.

23.

A month later we were in the last proper week before Christmas and some progress had been made. True I had not done well in other areas, for example, looking back now I had become so used to shitting in the open air that I averaged about twice a week by then and in certain circumstances it had become my preferred method.

I had rationalised Declan's seven point business plan down to one point which was to achieve executive backing for a Legal Solutions business plan, which was to be done by producing a presentation to illustrate it. The same presentation would be taken to my three short listed targets as soon as it was signed off. At this stage I sort of had Declan with me on the basis that I explained my thinking to him and he bought into it. Twat. We were just hanging on a meeting with Tim Hartley really, which kept on being postponed and was now a certainty to not take place until the New Year. This was down to Tim's general unavailability while he went to lunch and because he was currently considering a re-branding exercise to which our Legal Solution would have to be compliant. That added up to a general delay which suited me, although it did force me to take more of a hands on interest in day to day matters in the existing Legal Division and to have more of a relationship with Sophie Chawdray, which didn't. I dealt with that by doing fuck all. Apart that is from making a concerted effort to poison Declan's view of her to take the heat off me a little bit. I did what I could but fortunately for me one day she took one of our best clients out, got pissed, rang up her boyfriend in China on the company mobile and found out he was shagging someone else, then went fucking apeshit and got put in a taxi and sent home. Then her only decent manager resigned and said she did so because Sophie was a cunt, so by that stage I was home and hosed.

I had received dozens of rejections from my job applications. They had all thanked me for applying and some even sounded quite genuine when they said that they'd keep my letter on file if the situation should change. I wondered how they did that. How sophisticated their filing systems must have been. Say for example a tidal wave in the Yangzte Delta forced them to adopt a new and radical business model, how could they be sure they could immediately put their hands on an application from a fat, underachieving, cynical and depressed loser? Well I just kept faith in them and hoped one day I would get an unexpected call from Dai Ichi Kangyo International. I did receive one positive letter though. Well. It was from someone I had never heard of and it invited me to "drop in for a chat." I took them up on it and I was due to drop in on the day of the Talk About It! Awards so I would easily be able to go missing for a few hours. That was the Tuesday before Christmas.

Otherwise my life outside Martins Fleet was not fantastic. We still did not have a proper bank account and for the fourth consecutive month my wages had gone missing somewhere in the ether. Unfortunately having got away with it once I'd had a few more losing bets on my debit account and I was coming to realise that there would be a price to be paid when the day of reckoning finally came. I had also promised to spend Christmas with Caroline in the countryside in a cottage. Just me and her. Great.

I had avoided Stacey Arnold on two fronts but coming up to the end of term I was in debt to the tune of two overdue meetings. One was that I had never been to one of her Employment Law updates and as a Divisional Director it was my duty apparently, the other was that I was to give her a de-brief on the progress of sacking of Patrick, which I avoided on the basis that I wanted nothing to do with it. I had left my last meeting with Moiraigh under the obligation to come up with loads of evidence against him but since it was them that wanted to sack him and not me I didn't do anything. I made a little bit of effort at first but any information I wanted I had to go to Moiraigh's department to get it. What the fuck. Stacey had now escalated it to a summit meeting with me, her and Declan. Declan had insisted that Franck attend too, since he was still officially Patrick's boss too. Not that he got in the fucking neck all the time like me.

I hadn't got a meeting with anyone at European Match but I had written a brilliant business plan and New Media had done loads of great illustrations for me. I had everything I needed now and that was going to be my major personal project in the New Year.

24.

I was pleased with myself. I'd taken the suit that had spent so long on my bed to the cleaners and got it back in time for my interview on Tuesday morning. I had also been out and bought a new shirt and tie on the Monday and for the first time for a long time I managed to come out with a shirt that was the right size. I invented a dentist's appointment not a pretend client like I usually did so that saved me the pressure of reporting back on a non-existent meeting. As I set out for my little chat with the private bank in Finsbury Circus that bright December morning I felt good about things.

It turned out to be more than a little chat, it seemed that I had been in the right place at the right time because they were going through a formal recruitment process for several new positions and there was an established routine to go through. First I was to have a session with the Head of Human Resources "to dot the i's and cross the t's," she smiled, but it seemed more likely to me that I was going to get a grilling. She introduced herself as Miss Prudence and I didn't know whether it was a joke, or a formal way of saying her first name or whether she was very cold and just plain formal. Or a dyke. Then she said I was to meet the Head of Trading for a short chat and then I was to spend the last half hour or so with the person in charge of the Options Desk, I got the idea that he was going to be much younger than me.

"So if you'd like to follow me,"

I don't whether it was me or her. She was one of those people who had practised at being serene. She asked simple questions, slowly and clearly, slightly sotto voce, without fear or favour and then gave me the floor. There was something about the silence she left after her question that obliged me to fill it. Had I been confident I would have answered in the same simple tones that I had been asked. Instead I felt obliged to talk. She had a very slight nod of the head as I finished each point which was to sympathise and to say, please, do go on, this is your only chance, tell me everything, make sure that you leave nothing unsaid, I am being very fair with you and I want you to fully exploit the opportunity.

For me that was a disaster. I did what footballers do when they are interviewed I started myself on sentences that were officially finished before the point was made or before I had used a verb so I ended up dragging them out into long waffley circular nonsense.

At one stage she threw me an open question about my attitude to training and discipline, and as much as I wanted to say to her, that I was convinced that strict training and discipline was the only system that worked, especially with new recruits, that I wholeheartedly believed in a system based on rank and experience, respect and merit, that I would respond well to working in conditions like that and that I relished the opportunity to be given some real workplace skills. That it had been the great regret of my working life that I had never been taken in hand in that way and that what I had to offer would go to waste without finding an employer to take that approach with me. Well I said something a bit like the last part but it didn't come out like that.

In the end I heard myself saying, "if it wasn't for my age I'd join the Army, I wish I'd done it when I was younger, that discipline would have served me well then and kept me on the tracks, although I feel I've got myself back together again now."

To which she nodded and smiled serenely.

Later on I told her I had lots of friends. Although she seemed to respond more positively to that.

I had obviously blown it right at the start but I still had to go through the process with the others. And I did a bit better with them. Though not a lot.

The Head Trader, Peter Willow, was a proper bloke. He had no real interest in interviewing and we had a good chat. He gave the impression that he ended up in his job just as he might have ended up in any other and that he just got on with it and did it. He happened to be doing something and to be someone that I would have loved to have been. He didn't really have time to interview me because he was working continually and it was obvious that his job kept him fully occupied and stimulated. He said that there was really nothing to the job that anyone bright couldn't do and that it would have to be learned on the job and that he wished me well with my application. He picked up on horse racing as an interest on my CV and asked me what I thought would win the King George. I was too excited by the question so I overdid my answer. I was rather too forceful in saying that Looks Like Trouble couldn't be beaten.

"I'm not so sure," was his wiser response. He clearly knew the subject but unlike me he knew all about it and it wasn't the be all and end all of his life, he also held down a fantastic job and probably had an interest in all sorts of other subjects.

"The only downside is an obligatory six months training period in New York," he said, "would that bother you?"

"No not all," I replied. I was desperate to say something more enthusiastic but the words didn't come.

"I can't say I enjoyed my spell over there too much," he added, "New York would be a great place if it is wasn't for all the Americans."

I tried to laugh for him but I was glad he said something silly. It gave me the confidence to say a little more myself, so I came back with:

"each time I go to New York, the first thing I do is buy a great big apple." He didn't laugh. In fact he didn't say anything, apart from perhaps, "quite." I couldn't be sure. My interview with him was over.

I was only with him for five minutes yet in that time he imparted such an insouciant approach to work and life that I left his office devastated by jealousy.

My efforts had been extremely poor but at the time I hadn't finally given up when I went in to see Carl Smith. He was younger than me though not by much and he was clearly someone who had worked his way up. He totally lacked quality. He was a skinny twat with a crew cut with gel in it, he wore a cheap suit, a pasty complexion and smoked red label Marlboros all through our interview.

He spent about fifteen minutes telling me how he ended up where he was. I said absolutely nothing just nodded in appreciation. Well perhaps when he told me about one of his promotions I might have said, "very good," I can't be sure. Towards the end he was telling me that during office hours they had right barnies while the markets were live but that "down in Head Office," and he gestured with his head towards the window, "we're all mates and everything's equal."

"You do drink doncha?" he said. He wanted to know if I was one of the lads or not but I couldn't think of any words to reassure him so I said:

"Yes."

Then there was a silence, which he ended by saying:

"Good, good, that's good. You know it's very important, we all work hard here all day but when it's over it's over. Very important to me that is, for everyone in my team." And as he said 'everyone' he grimaced and made a head butting motion whilst drawing a small circle in the air with his index finger.

"Yeah, it's very important to unwind," I said and managed to sound less like one of the lads and more like a fucking ponce.

Then he had a long sigh and said, "what do you know about options?" I knew quite a lot since I'd done my bollocks punting options a few years ago, but I didn't want to let him know I was a loser yet so I didn't say that. I could have said almost anything to give him some confidence that I knew the subject but I just couldn't find the words to get going. Being a tiny little bit of an intellectual about it I thought that although my knowledge was probably a long way in advance of the typical new entry and would probably be much better than the person that ended up with the job, I didn't know what I didn't know as it were. So I found it difficult to assert that I had a good knowledge of the subject.

In the end I found myself saying something that someone that knew virtually nothing about options would say, I said: "well you can have a double option or a single option," and he said, "never mind you'll get all the training on the job."

I just don't know how people like him expected to interview you when they just threw out open questions like that. I suppose other people know how to answer open questions, it's called technique, training, education, breeding, parents that bring you properly so that you know how to have a conversation. My training had been given in front of the tele. Then he said:

"Have you got a good sense of humour?"

To which the only decent response was: "well I know you're a cunt," but instead I said, "yes."

In the silence that followed I filled it by telling him I had lots of friends again. Just in case the dyke didn't share her notes with him.

It was her that collected me to show me out and thank me for coming and her cold detached handshake told me that I wasn't one of them.

I was glad the end wasn't protracted because I'd received a short notice warning on the way to the lift and knew that I only had about three minutes to get to the bog. I reprimanded myself for my poor toilet management especially when I was playing away from home.

I sped off, knowing that that I could go to one of my favourite basement Corals round the corner and have an hour with the Racing Post before I surrendered to going back to the office. But when I got there it was closed for refurbishment, which meant that it was going to be changed from the dark, dingy, anonymous club in which we all felt at home to something with vending machines, and things to eat and fruit machines and bright lights and helpful staff - to open themselves to a wider younger audience. Karl Marx said one day capitalism will eat itself and I know exactly what he meant.

More importantly for me I had no time left on the clock and I didn't know a MacDonalds or for that matter anywhere else open with a functioning toilet in the area. In the end the only place I knew with absolute certainty and a degree of seclusion was a long back street behind Marks and Spencers. As I remembered it was a dead end back street with lots of large rubbish bins and things like that and was guaranteed not to have passing trade in its far recesses. I opted for that as the only reasonable place I could get to in time. I must admit to feeling slightly ridiculous as I hauled up my overcoat and dropped the strides of my smart suit to crouch and crap but in a way it had become slightly second nature to me and I was a little blasé about it. I was congratulating myself on keeping a midweek special coupon when I sensed I was not alone. I looked up and some distance away someone was making their way towards me but from the direction that I thought was a dead end. There must have been a small alleyway leading from Finsbury Circus. It was a female form walking with some purpose and she had to have seen me. Even if she hadn't she could see me now pulling up my pants and refastening my belt. She was reasonable close at that stage and I thought that if I rushed and tried to get out in front of her that I might only end up a few paces in front of her and that would prolong my embarrassment. In the end I decided that I would wait for her to pass and then go and find the alley that she had come down. That way I would have one short sharp excruciatingly embarrassing moment but it would be over quickly and I could put it behind me. As the figure approached I felt sure she knew me and me her. Long before I could make out her features there was something about her that I connected to. I don't know what it was but I knew I would know her. As she passed she said, "hello again Hector," and I said "hello again Miss Prudence," to her back. Even if she hadn't seen me shitting, which was unlikely, she found me hanging around in the depths of a back street shortly after being interviewed by her. What made matters worse was that when I went to look for the alley that I thought she had come down there wasn't one to be found. She had obviously just come out of the back door of their office. As I got there the twat with the crew cut came out. He had a double take at me and then he said, "you can't get the job by hanging out at the stage door you know." It was an opportunity to illustrate my great sense of humour but I was overwhelmed by embarrassment and so I just said "I got lost trying to find a cut through." Then I had to suffer the indignity of walking back the length of the street alongside him.

As we walked past the site of my relief he said:

"that sort of thing is disgusting," and in keeping with our conversational protocol I said:

"Yes."

"So where do you come from?" he said,

I thought he meant what part of the City, in that I had got myself lost. So I said, "just over there," pointing roughly to the top end of Moorgate. He looked at me like I was mad, so I said, "I've never been here before." Then he said "fair does mate, I've got to go down here now, see ya."

"Yeah see ya," I said as he disappeared.

I took myself off to lunch and with that, it being the period of the lunchtime yankee, I got to the bookies in time for the fourth of seven from Folkestone. I loved the 2.00 and 2.30 and resolved to stay for the half hour and have a quick in and out. They were both small fields with opposable favourites. In the 2.00 a five runner handicap chase Henderson had the favourite making its seasonable bow. My personal view was that his string wasn't fully firing and it was worth opposing first time out. Next in the betting was also first time out, trained by a bird and ridden by an amateur, next was Secret Bid, Folkestone specialist and won last time, the other two were crap. The 2.30

was an average novice, the favourite trained by Gardie Grissel was worthy enough but I liked the Sherwood dropping in class. The rest were rubbish. It felt very straightforward so I reached for the phone and had £300 win Secret Bid, £200 double.

The Henderson was soon beaten and I only had to shake off the amateur ridden on the flat. Only I didn't, Secret Bid never got there he just went up and down on the run in.

That left me £500 down and a decision to make. If I went in large chasing on Hopeful I could do myself serious damage. I looked again at the form and thought that the favourite was perhaps worthy after all. I had been out of work for about 3 hours by then as well so I decided to take it on the chin and walk back.

Walk was something of an exaggeration really I shuffled. As I walked I reflected on my morning: abysmal performance in interview; got caught shitting in public by my interviewer shortly afterwards; lost £500 betting on a useless race at Folkestone which normally I would not have given a second glance to and now I had several hours non attendance at work to explain. I was particularly troubled by my preparedness to shit in public places. It had become nearly normal behaviour for me and it suddenly hit me how abnormal it was. I started to breath deeply and I was saying "Oh God, Oh God." The shame took over and I stopped and leaned against a wall and I was saying, "not shitting for fuck's sake, not shitting," when two office girls walked passed me and started laughing. They snapped me back to life. Then I felt a new shame over that. In the end I sighed deeply and sure that no-one was looking I said out loud, "pull yourself together."

My arrival at the office coincided with my friend the Evening Standard seller arriving back into position.

"Y'alright mate."

"Oh I could be better," I replied.

"What you not backed all them good things that's gone in today?"

"Not exactly," I said, "I had a few quid on that thing of Alner's I thought it should have won."

"Mountain summink," he said,

"No that was the Henderson," I corrected him. I couldn't back a fucking winner but I knew my facts.

"Oh yeah, I'm a cunt me I done that Secret whatsiname there it let me down for a right few quid it did."

"Oh yeah what did you do?" I asked, prolonging my agony even further.

150

"I did that thing of Elsworth's then Silver whatsiname, that thing of Williams, it was you that put me on to him, he's a right good trainer him in'he? Then that fucking Secret thing and then I've just had that Sherwood go in."

When he said, "That Sherwood," it struck me like a dagger in the heart. If I had chased my money on it, it would have got turned over. I didn't bet it and it went in. My fucking life.

"Yeah I've had a 5p each way Super Canadian, if the Lady Herries horse goes in in the next I've copped for a right few quid."

"Good luck," I said, barely able to speak. He was getting just as much fun out of horse racing as me, in fact about 100 times more and he kept it simple and affordable and it didn't ruin his life. I had some sort of fucking death wish with it.

25.

I needn't have worried about being out of the office for so long, normal office routine had been suspended in contemplation of the Talk About It! Awards that were going to take place that evening.

I decided to have no part of it and resolved to read my emails and fuck off. I had one off Declan which simply said, "PLEASE COME AND SEE ME," and when I read it I shat my pants. My morale was low and I knew that I was incapable of investing enough energy in any lie to make it believable so I went straight to see him to confront my fate. He was on the phone but gestured for me to stay so I took a seat.

He was on what someone else might have called a business call. Normally I would have listened and allowed it to wind me up, but I had reached the stage where I couldn't give a shit about anything so I sat there empty headed waiting for him to finish and deliver the final verdict. I had decided to take a standing count then throw in the towel if there was any more to come.

He hung up and looked at me square in the face.

"How do you think your standing is in the business?" he opened.

"I don't know," I replied, hedging my bets. Not knowing whether I was heading for a bollocking or a sacking opportunity all I wanted to do was keep my ammo dry.

"I'll be honest with you Hector. In parts you are very well thought of but in other parts of the business your reputation is appalling."

"And."

"I want you to present an Award tonight. It's got Tim's backing and it will increase your status in this business. And you need to."

I was going to pretend to have a stomach ache and avoid the Talk About It! Awards altogether. In fact I had promised to go out to dinner with Caroline in the certain knowledge that I would be going straight home. Now I was being given a couldn't be refused offer. I would have rather brushed my teeth with dog shit.

"Jesus, what an honour, I'd love to," I heard myself saying, "which award did you have in mind?"

"The one everyone's talking about," he said and winked at me.

"Oh yeah," I said, not having a fucking clue, "there's been a lot of excited talk about the Awards, which one in particular is it?"

"Most Valuable Contribution." Then he just beamed at me. It was as if I'd won the Nobel Prize for Literature. He was proud for me. I had to be grateful.

"That is fantastic, I'm just so very, very grateful, thank you Declan," I lied, "what's the procedure?"

"Go and see Karen Mahoney, it's Organisational Learning's show,"

"Oh please not her, " I couldn't help it it just came out.

"Oh don't tell me you've upset her too Hector? Just go and do it. For me."

And then he said, "and another thing you can do for me in return. We are going to have that meeting with Stacey Arnold tomorrow. In fact I insist on it as your payment back to me. And you can make sure you go to her employment law seminars from now on too. It's obligatory."

"Yes I did," I said as I left him.

I went in search of Her Royal Lowness Knockers Mahoney straight away. There was no getting out of the obligation I had just accepted and I decided I needed as much time as possible to prepare and get myself in the right state of mind for taking the stage. An assumption that is too often made for those trained as barristers is that they are natural public speakers, whereas I gave up the profession because I was unutterably useless at it and terrified of speaking in public. It was my father that had decided that I would be a good barrister not me. Not least among his faults, which I remember mostly as a level of criticism that amounted to an unasked for competition, was that he was occasionally capable of seeing me as something far in excess of my abilities. Just as I wasn't a scientist nor was I a barrister. According to him though, all the world regarded barristers as "class" so I needn't worry even if I didn't take to it.

I remember when he had nothing better to criticise me for, he used to say things like, "look at the way he's cutting that caaayke." Then he wanted me to stand up in front of outstanding intellectuals and argue with them. Cunt. He didn't bring me up, he just competed with me to be the one that was right. I wonder if he's noticed that it all turned out wrong?

Into the world of Organisational Learning and it was like entering Santa's Grotto. Everyone involved, and there were many - and making a refreshing change for me the boundaries between personnel, recruitment, organisational learning and personal assistants were blurred in the maelstrom of activity that afternoon - were like pigs in shit. They were all working with fevered delight. The first night of the Talk About It!

Awards, it might as well have been the first ever night of the Oscars for them. And it was made all the better because, apparently, it had been dreamt up by someone at Martins Fleet.

I picked up the first compliant looking bird I came across and told her that I was there to be debriefed.

"Hear that girls. He wants debriefing."

And Scrubbers Haircut shouted out,

"Facking Hell you'll be lucky Hector."

I just quite didn't hit the mark with anyone I met. Posh people found me far too common and the plebs thought I was a ponce.

There was no-one available to tell me what to do. No stage manager.

"Facking typical. All that's been done ages ago. What are you like?" was Scrubber's signing off remark.

"I'm a bit scatological to tell you the truth," I said.

"Yeah, don't I know it," she replied.

"No, you don't actually," I thought.

I realised I was going to be on my own and took myself off to prepare.

I would have gone home to do it but when I rang Caroline to beg a little sympathy for my predicament I got a response which was totally unsympathetic so I decided to go to the venue itself. That way someone might tell me what the fuck was going on and at least I would be sure that I wouldn't be late.

I had picked up from one of the land girls that there was what was always referred to as a security alert at Liverpool Street so that made a cab the only choice. The other was walking which wasn't really an option and if the cab took a while I had that to spare and I could reflect a little.

I got a cab surprising quickly for it being Advent and when I settled in the back seat I told the driver that Liverpool Street and its environs were out of bounds.

"Another fucking security alert," he opened.

"Yes apparently," I said all chatty.

"I'll tell you what," he said, "they're a right fucking nuisance these fucking terrorists or whatever you call them."

"What gets me," he adds, "is that you can be going along, all innocent, and get your fucking arm blown off for nothing,"

"for nothing, or a leg, or an eye or something like that. I would fucking hate that, to lose a part of me like that. Don't you think? Fucking cunts."

He wasn't having a conversation with me just talking out loud really. I was his excuse for talking but I didn't have to talk back. He wasn't one of those opinionated cab drivers for all that, he talked with a weary resignation, beyond bitterness. He had just been hurt too often.

"I tell you what though," he started up again after a delay, "I'd rather be right in the middle of a fucking blast than on the edge of it. If I had to choose between losing me arm or something like that, I'd prefer to be right in there and get it all over with in one go. Better than living the rest of your life like that. I'd want it all over."

Then there was another long silence.

In the end he said, "Don't get me wrong. I don't want to get blown up or anything like that."

Then there was silence. Until he said, "not that there's anything much good about living."

We never said anything else until he dropped me off. When I paid I gave him a tenner on top.

155

26.

When I arrived at Vinopolis, this year's trendy corporate venue - once it was the Masonic Hall in Covent Garden - the gig was still being put together. I was about two hours in front of the official opening and I could only find people involved in logistics. There was no-one of any seniority or stature there to help me and I started to panic a little bit. At times like that I needed friends "in the business" who could put me wise to what was expected but I knew I had put myself beyond reach of most of those who could help me. I was well and truly on my own.

I tried to think about how other award ceremonies worked, since that was clearly what they were trying to emulate, and I convinced myself that I was to play a minor role in introducing the real hero, the award winner, and that it was not about me. In fact the less about me the better and given that I was capable of winding most of the people at Martins Fleet up the wrong way the least said the better I decided. But what was everyone else going to say? I had at least to match other speakers, Declan had told me it was about increasing my stock and it was obviously going to be people of a certain seniority that were presenting awards, so something was expected. This was the first year, so there was no history to call on or comply with it. That might be a good thing, in fact it was a good thing. I could make that one of my central themes, that the award winner was setting a high standard for other years to live up to. But everyone else would say that. And I didn't even know who they were. And those wankers had had several weeks to prepare. They had probably conferred all corporately and I was the sad urchin left on the side who didn't quite live up to their corporate way of behaving. I was the objectionable twat that nobody liked and everyone would love to see fall flat on his face. That was what this was all about. No it wasn't. I had to concentrate on the words. The only thing I knew was that it was an award for the Most Valuable Contribution, that was what was usually given to some twat who was owed something but couldn't be fitted into all the proper categories. Anyway who was it? Someone had said that Gordon was a certainty having bailed his client by going to a land fill site and finding loads of documents that had been thrown away by accident. I didn't even know if he had in fact won. Why hadn't I asked Declan? I was such a twat. Even if he had won I didn't know anything about the real facts behind it, I didn't know whether it was his fault that the documents were thrown away in the first place or not.

There was only one thing to be done and that was to ring the prize winner himself. I rang him. I rang him at his desk. I rang him on his mobile. I rang him at all of his client's offices. I rang him at home. I rang him on his girlfriend's mobile. I rang him on his girlfriend's office phone. I rang him at his girlfriend's office in general. Then I started with his friends. All the numbers were begged from the previous people I talked to and the person unlucky enough to pick up the phone. That must be what it's like trying to get hold of me.

After about half an hour I gave up and decided to play it by ear. And by that time people were beginning to arrive. At first organisers but increasingly just punters. They brought a happy mood with them. This was I suppose the Martins Fleet Christmas Party and everyone seemed to come with that spirit of wanting to enjoy a party about them.

Official Christmas Parties had been banned at Martins Fleet. That was because they were prejudicial to night shifts. Instead everybody was to get a box of handmade chocolates and a bottle of champagne, because you had to recognise Christmas. And all that added up to the general Martins Fleet work force coming out with a determination to have their Christmas Party on that night. I don't know why but things like this mattered enormously to most office workers. They looked forward to the Christmas party for months and talked about it for months afterwards. As December approached people would say you don't do any work next month it's great, you go to client parties, department parties, the works party (it was always called the works party) and you seem to spend everyday down the pub. The month of December was to be relished for the three weeks leading up to Christmas it was just fun and games.

Only it never was. In every office I'd ever worked, there seemed this desire to have fun but a reluctance to be the one to say, "lets go and have fun." And somehow the time just seemed to dwindle away into Christmas Eve then you looked around you and you saw that everyone had already gone to enjoy their private Christmases at home. True, occasionally you would hear tales of how the Accounts department had gone out and ended up in a Karaoke Bar and everyone got shit faced and someone who was previously considered a wallflower gave a fantastic rendition of Can't Take My Eyes Off You by Andy Williams. But mostly Advent just slipped away unnoticed. Everybody actually got some form of Christmas Party to go to, well except for this year at Martins Fleet, but as a rule they did, and when they did a tremendous effort was made to have a good laugh. I could never quite understand the sheer determination to enjoy. For me it was like the FA Cup. Once upon a time it was the only live match all year and the nation waited for it, a rare treat of a live football match from start to finish. Now you can watch Yeovil v. Doncaster live on Friday night if you've got nothing better to do and no-one cares about the FA Cup. And in the same way we don't care about the treat of a Christmas party as a rare and well deserved release from our labours. Most office workers go out and get pissed and take cocaine whenever they want. So what the fuck about Christmas? Well what the fuck but it still meant an awful lot to an awful lot of people. The only rationale that I could find was that most people that work in offices suppress their sexual ambitions towards their colleagues and see Christmas as an accepted venue to let the veil drop. Fucking hell. Have you ever seen the state of birds who desire a job in Personnel? For a photocopying company? Me I'd prefer to drop my kecks and have a dump in front of Miss Prudence.

And so the hall filled up and I found myself at the back of the hall leaning against the bar with John Goody. He worked at one of the banks and although I had only met him a few times we really hit it off together. He was one of those great people that can make the best of any situation, even working at Martins Fleet, he was engaged in life and he made it his business to know what was going on. He was up to date with everything in the business and within the clients and with current affairs. He just launched himself into life and loved it. I spent my entire time with him laughing and I just loved being with him. He was the obvious person to ask about Gordon and the Award but I just got carried away with the conversation with him and forgot to ask.

The difference between us came down to our jobs. He was happy in his job and had many years of solid employment behind him which formed a structure for his life. He could enjoy all the interesting little episodes that his life threw up. My life was just a series of pointless episodes while I waited for it to begin.

Seeing us enjoying ourselves Tim Hartley made straight for us when he arrived.

"How are you guys? OK by the look of you. Careful Hector you're on before me, I don't want you upstaging me."

"You needn't worry about that Tim." I reassured him.

"What's that then?" said John, but Tim was not one for listening as well as speaking so he said:

"You're looking smart Hector been for an interview?"

"No Tim, I shat my pants earlier and went home to change."

Then we all laughed our heads off for ages.

Then Tim said, "can I have a word Hector?" so I stepped aside with him about two paces.

"Sorry John, excuse us a moment," he said and I thought that I should have said that.

"Hector, it's Zurich Privatbank," which is where I had been for my interview that morning and when he said it I was terrified.

"Yes Tim, what is it?"

"Well there's a lot of changes going on there at the moment and I think something good is going to happen. I've been thinking that you might be right to head it up for us."

The bank where I'd been for an interview only that morning. I'd totally fucked it up and got caught shitting by my interviewers shortly afterwards.

158

"That sounds great. Yes I know something about them and I think they are recruiting. I'd be very interested." I was on automatic pilot so I just said the exact opposite of what I wanted to say, since that was the only thing I could do fluently.

"Great. Come and chat to me on Monday morning."

Monday was Boxing Day but what the fuck.

"Great Tim I will. Thanks."

"Good luck tonight. And no stealing the good jokes. Have a good night John."

Meanwhile John was small talking with one of the HR birds. I am sure, as I arrived back, he was saying, "my cock would look great in your mouth."

She just laughed and said, "don't be cheeky." I'd have been disciplined on the spot for the same thing.

She moved on and left me with my friend. I was so astounded by what he'd got away with I couldn't find the words to ask him if he'd really said it, instead I asked him what he thought of Tim.

"Why's that then. He wants you to be his Bag Man?"

"No. Something really weird, he just sounded me out about something, that I had a sort of private interest in really, if you know what I mean."

"No I don't know what you mean when you talk in fucking riddles Hector. Do you want to try again?"

"Ok but this is between me and you. I went for an interview today at Zurich Privatbank and Tim has just come and asked me if I want to lead the Martins Fleet effort in there. Do you think he knows?"

"No fucking chance. Don't you know what we say about him? He's a dumb blond. Good Chief Executive, I'll give you that but he's thick as shit. Don't worry old son. You want out do you?"

"Oh Jesus John I'm desperate."

"Listen I'll ring you with a name tomorrow. It's a mate of mine in recruitment at Morgan Stanley. Give her a ring and go and see her. But I'll tell you something, do yourself a favour and do it before Christmas."

"Are you serious?"

"I'm always serious now buy me a fucking drink. And you can give me a present when you get the job."

"You can bank on it John. What sort of large one are you having?"

"As it's you Hector I'll have a large Glen Grants." He was better at saying brand names than me so I gave him a twenty and asked him to get me the same while I went to the bog.

When I came back, there was Tim, John and Gordon talking together and John was saying, "they shaved its back and wrote FUCK OFF in magic marker."

They laughed like it was the last joke they were going to hear, then they all turned round and looked at me as if they'd been waiting for me to come back.

"So I've won then?" said Gordon. And Tim followed with:

"Well in Hector you fucking pillock."

"I wish I knew who'd fucking won. I am supposed to give the award in about an hour."

"Yeah and it's supposed to be secret until then." Tim added and I started to feel like I couldn't do anything properly. However being slightly pissed by then and feeling that somehow Tim knew about my interview and everything I'd confided in John I decided to take the bull by the horns.

"Look Tim, I've been dropped in this at the last minute and I can't find anyone who'll tell me anything about it, who's won, what I am supposed to do or what."

"And that's why you're standing at the bar getting pissed is it?" It didn't matter that I'd been trying to do the right thing for the last five hours.

"I was talking to John because he's the sort of person who might know," I said.

"Don't fucking bring me into it," and John threw his arms up and I started to feel very isolated.

"Look," said Tim, "it's an open secret that Gordy's won but don't go round telling everyone. Don't get pissed just have a word with Gordon and sort something out between you."

It was a semi-reprimand but that was my life. I was used to it.

When he'd gone I said to Gordon:

"Come on Gordon be a sport lets get together and sort something out."

Gordon was great. If he'd had an intellect he would have been a diplomat or something like that. He was like a posh version of John Goody just not quite as bright but he didn't have a bad word to say about anybody.

"Ok grab that table, I'll refresh these and we'll sort something out."

And with that I finally felt a little bit of confidence about what was to come.

When the event actually got underway I was astounded by how seriously they took themselves. Declan was MC and he treated it entirely as you would expect him to do for something important. He wore a dinner suit and he had a script and I shat my pants. He handed over professionally to those who were about to present an award and they in turn were given a round of applause as they came onto the stage, then they read a script appropriate to the award they were about to present.

No-one seemed to realise that the whole thing was a pathetic charade. Apart from me that is. As the short list for the "Team of the Year" was read out, I could hear excited whispers from the respective managers, "they've got it, they've got it," and then when the name was read out "The Night Shift Team at Plantation House" there were yelps and cries and cheers and even tears. Even seconds and thirds were met with great grunts of satisfaction, slaps on the back and heartfelt, "well done, you deserve it," and "thanks but it was all down to you really." If it wasn't so pathetic it would have been sickening.

My mouth dried and I knew my end was coming. I was too drunk to pull myself together, with the couple I'd had a lunchtime and the drinking while I waited in the early evening I was now beyond recall. I went into a sort of daze and thought of nothing at all. Just waiting like the condemned man to be lead to the noose. To shut everything out in the moments leading up to my moment on stage I shut my eyes. Then the next thing I knew my name was being called out and everyone around me was laughing.

As I walked up to the stage I had a sense of everyone in the audience doing no less than smirking and some more senior figures were laughing openly. I heard someone say: "Jesus look at the state of him."

I just concentrated on putting one foot in front of the other and I became very aware of my doing it so that in the end I was walking like I'd just learned to walk for the first time. It felt like it took twenty minutes to reach the front of the audience. As I got nearer and skirted the front seats to go up the stairs at the side I allowed myself a glance sideways looking for a friendly face, but came there none. I put my foot on the first step and I went cold and the blood drained out of my body. When I reached the last step my mouth was as dry as paper and I knew I wouldn't be able to speak more than two sentences. That meant that when I reached the microphone the first thing I said was: "can I have a drink?" and that brought the house down.

Instead of bringing the drink of water I thought I'd asked for someone brought me a large glass of red wine and just being glad of something liquid I had a large swig.

Suddenly I didn't remember any of mine and Gordon's preparation, so after a reasonably embarrassing silence I said: "It's an open secret who our Most Valuable Player is, so I won't embarrass him by any unnecessary flattery. Please be upstanding for Gordon Fern. Then because Gordon was so widely loved and because a certain atmosphere had taken hold the whole place went mad. They whooped and hollered like at a Presidential election drive. They got to their feet and they cheered and wolf whistled and clapped and clapped for fully five minutes. Gordon and I had our arms round each other's shoulders and raised our other arms in recognition of the applause. We started laughing half way through and by the end we were laughing our heads off.

When it all died down, I thought that as presenter I hadn't done enough, so I said: "Please Gordon share with us the experience that has brought you this great award."

"What do you mean?" he said.

And I didn't know what to say so I said,

"Well did you wear your suit to the tip?"

"Yes I did actually," he replied but he was so charming it sounded hilarious and everyone started laughing again. When it all subsided I said,

"Wellingtons or brogues?"

And for some reason Gordon and I started laughing and we couldn't stop. Then the audience joined in and we laughed and laughed a forbidden laugh that undermined the entire seriousness of the evening. As it finally subsided, spurred on by the support of the laughter of the whole audience I declared that Gordon was going to put his award up and he and I were going to have a swim-off across the Thames to decide the real Most Valuable Player in the company. With that we started taking our clothes off and down to our boxers we lead a procession off the stage, up the aisle, out onto the balcony and towards the Thames. Tim still had the biggest award to give in the supposed climax to the evening but the entire audience seemed to be following Gordon and me in our challenge. We climbed over the wall of the balcony and descended the old iron step ladder cemented into the wall about 20 or 30 feet to the shore of the Thames. Once there we found ourselves on a sort of pebble shore with the Thames itself about 30 feet away.

The idea was to have a race to the nearest bridge and back and we actually got as far as going in up to our knees. As drunk as I was I knew it was a bad idea. I could feel the currents rushing against my legs as I struggled to keep my footing yet I felt strangely compelled to go through with the stunt. As far as I could see so did Gordon. But just when it came to get serious about the race there were at least two or three other people with us who had followed us down and not being as pissed as us told us that what we were doing was idiotic and insisted we got out of the water and back up the ladder.

It was harder going up than coming down not least because the seriousness of my error was beginning to dawn on me as I went back up. Also I didn't remember the top step of the ladder being missing on the way down but I do remember being manhandled back up and over the balcony wall and once safe just being left to drop. I also had a sense of being left by everybody apart from Scrubber's Haircut appearing against the flow of bodies and throwing my suit and other clothes down towards me and saying:

"You're gonna need them you facking idiot."

I got dressed on my own. Staggered my way back to the main road and flagged a taxi down and went home to sleep. The only thing on my mind was how I was going to get into bed without being noticed.

27.

As a general rule I have always found that the extent to which you should regret the evening before is proportional to the rate at which realisation dawns on you the next day. Very bad behaviour often wasn't remembered until tea-time. With one exception. When you have been an absolute fucking dickhead you wake up knowing. I woke up with a start and shouted: "you stupid fucking cunt," at the top of my voice. I looked at the clock and it was only 7 a.m. but Caroline wasn't next to me. I was confused and frightened. All I knew was that something terrible had happened.

"So what happened then?" She'd appeared in the doorway and rather than throw any light on the matter she wanted questions answering.

"I don't know."

"So it wasn't quite as boring a night out as you thought it was going to be?"

"Yes it was it was worse. Well…." but I was still piecing it together in my mind. It was only when she demanded to know how come I smelled so much and why I was damp when I came home that it all started dropping into place.

"I think I'm in a lot of trouble. I've got to go to work."

"Hector. Do what you have to do today but do not come home late or drunk tonight. Our Christmas holidays start tomorrow and I don't want any cock-ups or last minute hitches."

For all of the hangover and my reluctance to face the music I set out with a purpose in my stride. I had never managed to convince myself about the most direct route in. I always went and came back by a shallow curve to the right of the object destination quite convinced that that route was always the fastest, wherever I was. I knew that couldn't be correct but it felt like it was. That day though despite telling myself that the only thing to do was to go straight to work and take it on the chin, I felt myself meandering off the instinctively right route. By the time I turned right into Gosworth Road by Ladbrokes I felt my stride shorten. I crossed the road to follow a little alleyway, my preferred off the beaten track route when I was coming home. Into the back street and the hotch potch of council flats that are hidden away behind the Barbican and I was virtually not going forward at all. I suddenly sensed myself commentating on my own walk to work. I had been saying, "this boy's a really good walker," all the way to Ladbrokes and as I crossed the road I was saying, "his stride is shortening noticeably." When I finally noticed that I was talking out loud, I was shouting, "he's dossing in front. He's running around on the spot." Then just before I became conscious of what I was doing I raised my right arm and I was going through the motions of whipping myself down the quarters to get myself going again. "He's completely downed tools," I was about to say when I snapped out of the trance. I shuddered, suddenly aware that I might not have been alone, and I regretted shuddering too, since it was too reminiscent of a horse. I dared to look round and saw someone walking towards me from behind and I couldn't say whether they had seen me or whether they had walked with their head down since they had turned the corner. I didn't have the nerve to confront the situation so I carried on as I was. I acted like I'd suddenly got myself going again and I ran off down the street like a horse. The way I figured it, dressed as I was, they wouldn't know whether I was being filmed for a commercial or something like that. Even so I galloped as fast as I could to the next corner and then turning right into the next road which was always busy with a street market, I couldn't suddenly change stride since the people I was running towards would notice the change. Instead as I turned right I dropped into a hack canter down the central aisle of the market until I turned left. Once there I went through the gears from trot to fast walk and eventually pulled myself up outside the dry cleaners.

I thought that I'd calmed down as I came towards the end of the street with the junction with Old Street about another 100 yards further on. I had definitely stopped breathing hard and the first flood of sweating had passed. I had assumed a normal stride and to all intents and purposes I was a regular person going to work. I realised later though that the adrenalin was still pumping a little too strong.

On the other side of the street two ten year old boys were on the way to school. They had stopped to stamp on a glass bottle which was wedged against the kerb to try and smash it. Such other pedestrians that there were just walked on by like it was perfectly normal. To me it was one of those wanton acts of hooliganism that contributed to our lives being yet more awful than they need be. So I shouted out. I just tried to sound adult and commanding but they ignored me and carried on with their mindless pursuit. So I crossed the road, picked up the bottle and I said, "don't do things like that you pair of fucking arseholes."

"Fuck you," the smaller one said.

Then they followed me at close quarters while I went off with the bottle. I carried on on the same route to work and only stopped to drop the bottle in a dustbin on the way.

They kept on at me trying to draw a reaction and I had decided on the silent approach. I thought that would make them more wary of me but instead it made them grow in confidence. The more I didn't speak the more they pushed.

"You're dead you fucking poof. Next time you come down here," the bigger one said. Then they started dancing around me trying to push me or land a sly kick. In the end the smaller one took a swing and I had to sway to avoid him. I'd had enough by then so while he was off balance with his back to me I cuffed the back of his head with the back of my hand and said "fuck off you little cunt." I figured I didn't have to make so much allowance for his childhood innocence at that stage.

I barely made contact with him but he lost his balance and went sprawling across the pavement. Then the pair of them immediately took a new tack with me. Without delay they both launched into a dialogue about abuse and going straight to the police and telling their teachers. It was well rehearsed, or at least well learned and I was not at all sure whether they were going through the motions to scare me or whether they knew how to get the agents of social care onto my case. I was out of my depth so I took the first right onto Old Street and walked away from them fast and reminded myself to take a different way home from then on.

28.

My preoccupations with child abuse and my inadequacies as an adult chastiser kept me occupied to the door of Martins Fleet. By rights I should have felt ashamed and hung around the outside door for ages instead I just found myself in reception. By then it was about quarter to nine but something about the atmosphere in reception told me I was one of the first people in the building. Not that there were ever many people in reception at that time of day but there was nevertheless a strong sense of nothing doing. I was encouraged by that and made straight for my desk from where I would go and see Declan immediately and iron out any problems resulting from the night before.

As quiet as it was you could bank on what people there were in the building all being there on my floor. As I opened the door from the lift lobby I suddenly became very frightened indeed. How did I have the nerve to confront everyone like this? So shamelessly. I was as rude as possible to most of them at all times and I had lost the friendship of most of them. I was there I told myself, I was half way through the plunge into icy water and there was no turning back. I opened the door with something of a flourish and presented myself to my critics.

I was immediately pleased to see that although it was busy enough it was nowhere near full and I had that sense of the morning after the night before reinforced again. I dwelt in the doorway because I didn't have the courage to go straight to my desk in case I had become the company pariah overnight.

The first to notice me was Helen Smith who smiled a little amused smile then bowed her head to allow her to laugh to herself. It caught on slowly but within a minute the whole office was laughing and cheering and calling me a bloody nutter. If I say it myself it was a warm reception. I glanced up to take in Declan's office knowing full well that proletariat adoration was no guarantee of the ruling classes being amused but it wasn't occupied and the lights were turned off. I caught Amanda's eye and she gave me a reassuring shake of the head to confirm that he wasn't in yet.

As I made my way to my seat the junior managers next door woke up to the commotion and came through to cheer me on. In the end there was a small round of applause as I sat down. Immediately I was surrounded by people wanting to know all the about the evening. It was them that saw it not me. And that was all I had to say. It was me that needed to have the blanks filled in. I wanted to know what had been the reaction afterwards? Had I upstaged Tim? Had the evening been a success or had I ruined it? Was I in trouble? There was something about their being amused that told me that I wasn't in much trouble. They were so compliant that I was quite confident that I hadn't been slagged off by Declan and he was in turn a slave to Tim and to Barrow. I couldn't ask directly whether I was in trouble or not but I managed to ask a couple of collateral questions based on bits and pieces of information that came out and these gave me some crumbs of comfort.

It was pretty obvious that there had been an executive and senior management sponsored night out until at least 5 a.m. which at least was evidence of a generally happy mood and good spirits. To which I added the good news I extracted from Amanda's statement that: "it just all seemed to get going after a while and turned into a great night." To me that meant that I had been the catalyst in getting the evening going. Never mind that I may have been the only blip on an otherwise perfect company evening, I was listening with hopeful ears.

When it finally subsided and I was left alone sitting next to Amanda I plucked up the courage to ask her if she thought that I had upset Tim. But for all my being pleased to have asked the direct question she gave me one of those non-answers that didn't help me at all.

"At first I thought that you had gone too far," she opened, but that was her opinion and not what I'd asked for, "but," and my spirits lifted, "Tim just carried on like nothing had happened," and they fell again, "he did make some reference to it but I can't remember what it was. It was all pretty funny actually but we had to keep serious for Angelica's award."

Tim would have had to make reference to my performance I knew that and I knew that it was a racing certainty that he probably said some bland platitude and moved on. What intrigued me was whether, as I would have said with certainty if I was there as an objective observer, he had immediately forgotten all about it, or whether he thought that I had ruined the evening. My instinct after hearing about the late night out and, as nobody had told me that I was in big trouble, was that I'd got away with it but I couldn't help but re-run all the snippets of conversation I had heard that morning interpreting them first one way then the other.

The only way I could guarantee myself a genuine reaction to the evening was to ask Franck. That was the sort of thing for which we were an unbreakable team, we each loved the civil disobedience of the other. He would tell me where I stood without fear or favour. And chances were if there had been a proper big late night out Franck would have been on it.

He wasn't in at his desk which meant he probably had been out late with everyone else. I knew him well enough to know that probably meant he wouldn't come in all day. Either that or he'd be in a hotel room in Kings Cross and it would be a while before he surfaced. Nevertheless I tried him on his mobile and I was encouraged when I got an engaged tone. That meant he was up and about. I kept trying and I kept on getting the engaged tone. I didn't understand telephones, I thought that all mobiles went straight to an ansaphone message as soon as they were occupied but suddenly for the first time I discovered that they can be engaged too. I'd never done anything like that with my phone. It was typical of Franck that he would find a feature like that and employ it. I couldn't understand why he would prefer it to work like that rather than let it go to the message but he would have his reasons. Something about not being forced into an obligation to do anything that you might not want to, he would have said. That would be right up his street: controlling who interacted with his phone and the terms on which they did it. Franck used technology to make it work for him and the funny little private world he lived in. He was the only person I knew that paid £5 a year to prevent 1471 from working on his home line.

After several minutes of ringing him I became very resentful of the engaged tone. I think I hated everything about the telephone. If I had to call someone and it was engaged for a long time I could become apoplectic with rage. What the fuck did they talk about? Using a telephone as a device for having casual conversations was for faggots. More than that though I hated being called. Whether it was for business or for pleasure the sound of the telephone ringing made my stomach turn over. It represented someone else's desire to speak to you at that moment, whether you wanted to or not.

Apparently there was a rule in our office that the phone wasn't allowed to ring more than three times. That meant that if you were doing something else or, god forbid ignoring the phone and letting it ring on to the ansaphone on purpose, someone else in the office was allowed to answer your phone on your behalf. When they had they would shout over, "I've got someone on hold for you Hector can I put them through?" They had no idea that it may not be appropriate to answer the phone at that moment, they didn't care less whether it put you on the spot.

You couldn't get away with having the phone switched to ansaphone all the time to avoid the attentions of the rabble, that was noticed to. What you had to do was leave your phone in normal working guise, then as soon as it rang, hit the divert to ansaphone button quick before some dickhead intercepted it. That kept the non-cooperation discrete. Only once, when Stacey Arnold had been on my trail and I was away from my desk by the fax machine did I break the unwritten rule. My phone started ringing and before it got onto the third ring I shouted out, "don't you fucking dare pick that up." I meant the 'you' in the plural sense meaning all the middle managers in the office but perhaps, thinking about it, that's what Sarah Chawdrey had complained to Declan about.

If we did answer the phone as instructed I didn't see how I wouldn't end up doing that all day and do no work at all. Perhaps that was what was called working, talking on the phone to other people that never did anything either.

And if it wasn't that you were prey via the mobile too. When you weren't talking on the phone at your desk you were expected to be available to talk all the time you were away from it on the mobile. In the old days in eight hours work you probably had some quiet time to yourself to do some proper work. Today you have to talk on the phone every minute that you are not in a meeting or not writing a document. Even coming to and from work and sitting in taxis. That is why the quality of work that most of my colleagues produced was appalling and why all of them worked over 10 hours a day.

Not me. I didn't even answer the phone at home. It was bad enough working but to get three hours liberty each night before bed and back to the same tomorrow I wasn't prepared to throw one of them away on a phone call. If two bores rang you on the same night that was the entire evening gone. If you picked up the phone it was "their" call and it was them that determined the length of it. And I just hated being part of a small-talk conversation, there were so many better things to do whether you actually did them or not. So I just never picked the phone up and never answered my mobile.

The real essence of what I hated about the instrument was that the caller was always purposeful, they were calling to say something. I felt always that their call demanded a proper response and I just didn't know how to say that I wasn't ready to talk about the subject and that I'd ring them back. I sort of felt that I was being too hard on them to say that and so I always tried to accommodate them with an answer. In doing so I created obligations for myself that I didn't want. And taking on these unwanted obligations made me feel under pressure and unhappy and terribly, terribly weak. Anyway, the problem in hand was that Franck would not answer my calls, I didn't call it a reasonable condition did I?

In fact, I hadn't managed to contact him when Declan breezed in. It was getting on for 10 o' clock and although it was perfectly normal to be carrying a brief case and wearing a coat when you returned from an early meeting there was something about him being like that at nearly ten o' clock that told you that he was coming in for the first time. En passant he called out for me to join him and my early confidence at having got away with it evaporated in an instant.

"How did it go?" I didn't have a clue what he was talking about. It could have been a cool rhetorical question to force me into an admission about my unacceptable behaviour the night before. He was horrible enough to talk to me like that but I didn't think he was classy enough to take that approach.

I really didn't know what to say. Eventually there was just an unbroken silence between us. Then he said:

"Well?"

"Jesus," I thought, I don't want to work here and I have got no respect for the prick, "what am I being so weak for?" I was letting him walk all over me.

"I having got a fucking clue what you're talking about. Why don't you ask me a normal question?"

I sounded aggressive and when he responded calmly I regretted rushing in.

"I am talking about the meeting you've just been to."

"Oh that. What?"

"The meeting with Stacey Arnold that we arranged for 9 a.m."

"Well I was waiting for you," I had forgotten entirely, if I had ever known that the meeting was set up for 9 a.m.

"Don't you ever listen to your messages?"

"Yes, always."

"Well if you did you would know that there were three from me this morning telling you to have the meeting without me because I was going to be in late."

It was one of those ironies of my life that the thing that had exclusively occupied my thoughts all morning was the thing that I didn't do and that it cost me on that particular day. I couldn't tell him that I had been thinking all morning about how important it was that I listened to my messages frequently. Nor did I think to say that perhaps, as he was late it wouldn't be out of the question that I was late too, although that was pushing it since he was in at about 7 a.m. every morning to my 9.30. He had obviously started off being aggressive because he was a little bit ashamed at being late and missing a meeting, the importance of which he had stressed and he wanted to push the blame my way a little bit.

"I'm sorry I didn't check them this morning I have been trying to get a call through to someone since I arrived."

"Who's that?"

"Err, John Goody," I lied, "He came up with some decent information for me last night and wanted me to call him this morning to go through it," I said unnecessarily.

"Why didn't he speak to Amanda about it?"

"I don't know,"

"Well who's it about?"

As usual I had put myself under pressure for no reason at all.

"Do you mind if I leave it until after I've talked to him so that I've got the full story?"

"OK. So I take it you haven't met with Stacey."

"Yes. I mean no. I haven't."

Then his phone rang and instead of finishing his conversation with me he picked it up. Then I suddenly felt really sorry for him. He was like the fat kid that wanted to be like all the others in the gang. He was a real tryer with an average intellect. He'd had his night out with the big lads and that would do for him. Now he was back at the grindstone. Fun over for another year.

Just like Mr Postlethwaite our newsagent when I was growing up, he only went out once a year to the Newspaper Vendors Annual Dinner. I remember Mrs Postlethwaite used to say to my mum just before Christmas each year, "He has one night out per year but by God he doesn't half enjoy it." Then she would raise her eyes skyward to indicate he was still in his bed. He died of cancer five weeks after he retired. Declan put his hand over the receiver and said to me that he had to take the call.

"Just set something up with Stacey for tomorrow," he said and went back to his conversation. I didn't get the chance to say that I was on holiday the next day I had no choice but to leave the room. That meant that when I didn't turn up the next day it would be "typical" of me and he would say, "why can't you just be straight with us Hector?" Other people got the opportunity to be straight, with me events just conspired against me.

As I was opening the door I heard him say, "just a minute," to the other person and he put his hand over the receiver again and called out to me, "by the way great stuff last night Hector. Just what we wanted."

I wasn't cut out for business.

29.

He had indeed left three messages, as had Stacey Arnold. I decided not to call her back, mainly because she was an insufferable bitch but also because I'd get into a terribly confused state about the meeting the next day. I knew myself well enough to not even start out on that route. I would let all of that fall until the New Year. I did have a message from John Goody and just to hear his voice cheered me up.

"Alright you bloody nutter? Do you ever pick your phone up? You missed a great night out last night where did you get to? Anyway I've got that number for you and I'll tell you all about it when you ring me back. Don't piss about though. Ring me before 10 and I'll set it all up."

It was after 10 by then but he forgave me. Apparently he had never laughed so much in his life as the night before. I wondered whether it had gone down badly with Tim or Giles or Julian. "They only wish they could do things like that," he said to me and with that I felt I was finally out of the shadow of the evening. If I managed to avoid Tim until after New Year everything would be forgotten about. If I was unlucky enough to bump into him today I still didn't count on my chances being great at avoiding a good going over and a black mark on the record. Such was the way of business it could go one way or the other for you on the basis of an avoidable accident.

The net result of the phone call was that I should present myself to Anne Sykes of Morgan Stanley at 2 o'clock, who would be expecting me and who was currently recruiting for people with a strong business background to work for them in emerging markets, whatever that was. Apparently she was a right good sort and I should enjoy myself in the interview. I was told to make sure I went looking smart, which I took to mean better than normal. John Goody was one of those people that you would have described as always being immaculate and that was not a label you could hang on me. I bought expensive things but I never quite had enough of them to stop them getting a hard wearing. With four hours to myself to get to Morgan Stanley I decided to go out and buy something decent to wear to the interview and to finish my Christmas shopping. For some reason it had become my job to get the turkey, smoked salmon and all that. I think it started because I worked somewhere near Leadenhall Market, then it just continued. Caroline had given me a float of £300 because of our bank account problems to make sure that I got the lot, no excuses, and I was happy to accept since that way I could have a sneaky cash bet on the King George with which, if successful, I could replenish the lost funds in my old account.

I really believed in Looks Like Trouble but I liked Fiddling the Facts a lot at 33/1 especially since it was close enough to the race to get no runner no bet. The only reason Fiddling wouldn't go to Kempton was if he went to Chepstow for the Welsh National instead. If he turned up at Kempton I thought he had a great chance of being in the three, so I had £35 each way, I needed to keep some back to make sure I wasn't short of anything for Christmas and she had told me to get some caviar, which would make a bit of a hole in the slush fund all on its own.

More to the point I had the time to get myself kitted out. As my only decent looking suit now smelled of the Thames I was wearing something that had hung on the back of the bathroom door for at least six weeks in the hope of breathing a new lease of life into it. It was now so shiny and hard and set into its creases that it only looked acceptable for the first day it was worn after the cleaners. It was too knackered to take to the cleaners often so instead I wore it over and over in the belief that I wasn't making it any worse. I would suddenly become embarrassed by the state of the thing and that's when I would leave it hanging on a hook in the bathroom. Just as suddenly I would decide that it wasn't too bad and I'd put it back in circulation again. One thing was for sure it didn't fit John Goody's idea of being well turned out.

It's hard work buying a new suit just before Christmas. All of the good winter stock has gone, there are no sales and you have virtually no choice. You either buy something that was made for men that own one suit from Marks and Spencers or you go to a proper shop and pay £500 for something and hope that you can get it tailored within the hour. The alternative is to search through every off the peg suit in every menswear shop and hope you turn something up. I'd been doing that for about an hour when I gave up the ghost. There was either no rhyme or reason to the styles and sizes or you had some old fucking queen on your shoulder trying to sell you something the whole time you were in the shop.

With all my various fuck ups and other problems I had no other choice but to use a credit card. I, personally, had not got round to abusing that yet. Caroline had made me frightened of doing that. But I couldn't help but think that with my luck as it was there would be some disaster or other on the horizon very shortly and I would need the credit card to bail me out of a more dire situation than the one I was in currently. I was terrified of facing the consequence of Caroline if I had spent the available balance on an unnecessarily expensive suit when that day came.

In the end I did something that I often did. I bought something at a reasonable price for next season, or perhaps left over from the old one, from Marks & Spencers for cash counting it as something of an investment, or at least a bargain. If I felt confident that I got the job I would keep it and if I didn't I could bring it back and get my money back. That would leave me a bit short on the Christmas fund but only temporarily. It was only a way of managing cash. I had to buy the shoes to go with the new outfit and that was an excuse to buy myself a decent pair of loafers for the first time in my life. I always admired them on other people but I had never quite pulled them off. I had made a couple of injudicious purchases earlier in my life but I always put that down to not having spent enough on them. Those loafers had not been the nice comfortable wide looking shoes that I admired so much on others, mine had looked like pointy slip-ons. This time would be different I told myself. I would buy a bit of quality. It was only Marks & Spencers in a bit of an end of year clear out but they looked just like the ones that I always admired on others.

I'd forgotten what it was like to buy things in M&S. No different from when I was pre-school and went with my mum to get the shopping. The men's section till was shut down. That meant that I was directed to the tills in the food hall to pay for my new gear. I did what always happens to me in Marks & Spencers. I stood behind a middle aged woman who on having her two items passed through the bar code machine by the girl on the till decided to ask if they had a choice in tomatoes. You see she had picked up the vine tomatoes but she didn't really like them. She preferred plain, round, English tomatoes, "like normal." The one-celled outreach worker on the till didn't really know so she made a phone call to her supervisor, who instead of lying to the pair of imbeciles and saying that was what there was, take it or leave it, went to do a thorough inventory of stock. She was trained in customer service. She could have been stood by the fucking till in the menswear department but that wasn't the service she was interested in giving. When it had been decided that it was the vine tomatoes or nothing. Then. At that point. She got her purse out. She owed £1.85 and I saw her with two £1 coins in her hand but something stopped her from giving those over. She couldn't make up the 85p in change, despite trying about three or four times. In the end she settled for making up the 35p part of it in change which she gave with the two £1 coins. It didn't help the girl on the till. She just sat and stared at the open till draw for about a millennium. Then the woman said, "do you know if the 22 comes down here?" to which the girl said it didn't but proceeded to tell her everywhere it stopped between The Strand and Bethnal Green. At the end of that she still hadn't rendered the change and had forgotten where they had got to so she said that she was going to call her supervisor again.

At that point I said that I would be paying for the lady's tomatoes and I gave her £2. Then she said to the woman, "what did you give me in the first place?" and the woman didn't remember so I said, "it was £2.35," to which the woman said, "you can't be right love, they only cost £1.85." I started trying to explain to the woman that she had given the extra money to make the change easier but that made the pair of them look at me like I'd lost my senses. The thing on the till actually started laughing. In the end I gave the woman another £2 back out of my own pocket to which she said, "but what about my change." In the end the woman decided I was "trying to diddle her," despite going home with her original £2.35 intact. As she left I heard her saying, "I don't know why I bovvered he won't eat 'em."

I went back into the menswear department after I'd paid and put my new outfit on straight away and carried the old clobber in my shopping bags. For a few strides I felt OK but suddenly the good judgment that always deserts me in the changing room was there in twenty-twenty clarity by the time I reached the first corner. A sharp gust of wind blew the trousers of my new linen suit against my legs and I was struck by the overwhelming sense that I was wearing slippers and that everyone else knew, like those dreams where you are the only one naked. It was the middle of winter and I was the only one unseasonably dressed. Everybody else had grey wool suits and overcoats, whereas I was dressed as proper person might dress for a weekend in the middle of summer. The linen suit was not chic as I supposed and in the wind it displayed too readily the poor cut of the trousers. They ballooned at the hips and went to drainpipes at the ankle. What my mother would have called harem pants. The jacket looked ostensibly like a suit jacket in the shop but outside I realised that it didn't have any pockets and had a distinctly casual look. I caught a look at my reflection in a shop window and I saw someone I didn't recognise. I suddenly saw what everyone else saw. When you looked like me you should use all your efforts to blend in not to be noticeable.

There was no hiding it from Anne Sykes, "you look ready for the holidays," she said as she arrived to collect me in reception.

"Yes, I'm sorry I'm a bit casual but I'm ready for an early exit tonight."

"That's no problem we dress down nearly all the time here now, where are you off to?"

"Brazil."

"How exotic. You sure want to come and work here there won't be many of us jetting off to Brazil for Christmas."

"It would be a small thing to give up believe me."

And then because I'd got into it nice and fluently and because Anne was one of those wonderfully warm people it just went from strength to strength. I had a great open conversation with her. I managed to tell her how dreadful it was for a self respecting person to end up working at Martins Fleet without sounding like a loser and she agreed with me without sounding patronising. I explained to her that a relative success with my little company was all very well but not fulfilling and she understood what I meant whilst still being very complementary about my achievements and I think I got over to her my ambitions to work in a proper place like her bank without sounding like a useless dreamer.

Then it happened. There hadn't been a normal pattern to my day and I hadn't thought of toilet management. It was too late now and when I got a warning in the middle of my interview I knew it had to finish quickly or I was in trouble. I don't know why but I just couldn't find the words to bring the interview to a temporary halt. For some reason I felt that would have made me look ridiculous. At one stage, after had I grimaced and breathed in deeply, she asked me if I was alright.

"Yeah I'm alright," I squeezed out on my breath as I exhaled, barely audible.

Our conversation had been smart and enjoyable, between two people on level terms but now only she was speaking. I looked at her intently and prayed for her to finish.

The more I didn't speak the more she felt obliged to fill the gaps. In the end I was looking at her with pure venom, willing her to shut up. Internally I was pleading for her to finish. I stopped listening to what she was saying, I couldn't, it was just a noise washing over me. For an instant the pain and longing ceased and in the temporary calm I found the courage to say:

"Thanks very much for giving up your time at short notice to see me but I really must let you get back to your work," and as I was doing so I started to raise myself up out of my chair. I prayed again, this time that she would show me to the door and it would be all over. She half looked like she'd taken the cue but then she asked for my CV, which I hadn't brought over and that set her off talking about what I was to do next, if I was interested of course, and the timing of events and who I should meet next and all that bullshit. It was too late anyway. The movement in raising myself up from the chair caused a fundamental breach of the final resistance. It had happened. I sat and listened to her while I filled my pants. Completely. Emptied the tanks. The bodily pressure was over and there was some relief in that but it was short lived. Next I was terrified about smells and stains and lumps and leaving a trail. I went onto automatic pilot for a while. While she continued to whitter on about something else I tucked the bottom of my trousers into my socks. I realise now that she would have expected an explanation of that but I didn't think of it at the time. Then I loosened the back of my shirt so that it could flap down to cover any embarrassing stains and lumps while I walked away from her out of the office. Then I realised that the shirt was just as likely to be stained and I started to put it in again. After a while she realised that I wasn't listening and brought the interview to an end. Then the hard work started. I had never previously had to think about how I exited a room after an interview before, things like that came reasonably naturally. Now all of a sudden I had to learn. I had to think about how I would normally do it and how I would have to vary that today and how I could keep that natural looking. In the end I shuffled along to the door sideways instead of walking to it with her and then as she held it open for me I walked out backwards. As we walked back to the lifts I tried to walk a half a pace behind her so that she wouldn't stop but so that she couldn't smell me or see any evidence. When we got to the lifts I absolutely insisted that I should see myself out. Rather too forcefully I realise now but I had to get some space between me and her. She didn't leave me there she waited for the lift to come and when it did I shuffled sideways into it again. I thought it was significant that she didn't shake hands as we parted.

The lift was crowded which short of being empty was the second best. Not that I was confident of my position. At one stage some London Cunt trader whispered to another next to him, "facking hell Darren was that you?" and they both giggled til they got out. I figured that I should go all the way to reception so that I would be guaranteed a toilet. I didn't want to be found wandering around some forbidden area with soiled trousers.

When I reached reception I had to go back through the security turnstiles only to be told that the toilets were on the other side and I didn't have the right sort of temporary pass to get me back across. I was forced to join a queue of people that had forgotten their pass and other temporary visitors to explain to the security guard why I needed to go back in. They all went through slowly but steadily but when it came to me he said that going to the toilet was not a valid reason for someone of my status. There was a big queue behind me which compounded my agony, I was stood there with my trousers in my socks and ridiculous slippers sticking out wearing stupid clothes for the season probably stinking of shit and begging to go to the toilet with seemingly no right to go. In the end I swallowed my last drop of pride and pleaded and he let me through.

The luxuriously appointed, spacious and hardly used ground floor toilets were a haven and I finally drew a breath and felt safe. It is unsavoury to remember all the details but the cleaning process took over half an hour and wasn't entirely thorough. I prayed to be alone when I exited so that I had an opportunity to dry my clothes under the hand dryer. I got a good ten minutes out of that before anyone else came in for which I was thankful. Then I had to face the public with what I had. I was as good as I was going to be.

As I crossed the security barrier again I was delighted to see that the guard that let me pass was off duty although I was sure I was under surveillance. Then I knew I was because as I passed through somebody shouted to me to "come here now." I would have got out of the building anonymously were it not for that. Because of it though Anne Sykes who was on her way out too noticed me again.

"Still here Hector?"

"Yes, I had something to do."

"And your trousers aren't in your socks anymore?"

"Err no."

"Anyway I think he's waiting for you. Have a nice holiday."

"Yes I will thanks Anne. Happy Christmas."

I had to suffer the indignity of explaining to the ape from South Africa that I had a poorly tummy which was why I had spent so long in the toilet. Otherwise I was delighted to leave the building as soon as possible.

"How many bags do you have?" he said and I didn't know. Quite a few really.

"Well did I know what was in them?"

For the large part I did. But I forgot to mention my old suit and that failure dragged my second interview of the day out far longer than it need have done.

"It would have gone a lot better if you had been more honest," he concluded, so I said: "it would have gone a lot better if you weren't a fucking baboon," and I hoped it was him that found the boxers I had hidden round the U-bend. Once in the open I found the best looking pub I could in the area and went straight to the gents to finish the clean up process. I changed into my old suit and threw away the trousers of the new one. In the circumstances I didn't think I could really get away with taking them back to Marks & Spencers.

I went home and straight to bed.

30.

We were officially on holiday on Thursday morning. Nevertheless, we started at 7.00 a.m. and I felt like I was sneaking away. Particularly because I hadn't actually booked the time off. Had anyone asked me they would have known that I had planned to be on holiday from Thursday but nobody had and I hadn't got round to telling anyone. I worked in a kind of limbo and I didn't have anyone to tell those things to and nobody ever gave me forms to fill in. It wouldn't have preyed on my mind so much were it not that I really had intended to tell Declan that I wouldn't be available for his rescheduled meeting. The only reason I hadn't done it was because of my small disaster the day before. I'd meant to say something every day for about a week so that it wouldn't be a surprise when I finally said it but, just like usual, it got put off for lots of good reasons until finally it was the day itself and I hadn't done it.

Franck and I were the only people in Martins Fleet to have a company car. It wasn't company policy to have one, ours were left over from our Gilligan Somes days and they were a forgotten part of the deal that was hardly mentioned. Mine probably had no book value any more. A five year old Renault. That was my prudence. You got a tax break if you had a car over four years old so that's what I bought when I finally got one. Franck of course had a new one. I'd suggested that we flogged the cars and kept the cash or at least most of it because every now and then Martins Fleet remembered and reminded us that they were company assets that needed liquidating. Franck said he needed a car, "it was one less thing in his life to worry about."

In all the previous incantations of our business it somehow worked out that he was the only one that ended up with the car. Once, he promised to lend it to me for my holidays but it turned out that I could only pick it up a day after I'd left and I had to get it back for him to go shopping the following Saturday, so it didn't really work out.

"What are you doing?"

"Nothing I'm driving,"

"No you're not you're miles away and you're talking to yourself."

"No I'm not. If you don't like how I am driving you can always drive yourself."

"Fuck off Hector. Just drive. You're speaking to yourself and getting yourself worked up like a madman. If you don't calm down we'll have an accident."

Then boomh, a loud bang and the car started skidding.

"Hector. For FUCKS SAKE," she was screaming.

I got it under control and came to a halt on the hard shoulder. Is was only a tyre that had blown.

"I thought you had it serviced last month?" She had a way of asking perfectly normal questions as an accusation.

"I did but we probably just drove over something."

"On a motorway?"

"I don't know. Yes they probably do look at the tyres in a service, in fact they do. Look we can apportion blame later let's just get on with it."

I'd had plenty of experience in changing tyres in my life but there was something about doing it in the pitch black and freezing cold that made it the worst of all the DIYs. In the dark I had to line up the nuts by touch whilst still keeping the new wheel suspended in the right position. At first I daren't ask Caroline to help because she thought it was all my fault for having a faulty service. In the end out of desperation I did and we still didn't manage it. Finally I gave in to ringing for the AA. We were to wait about an hour or so apparently, so I continued trying and after about forty minutes I fixed it. We cancelled the AA, and set off again only about an hour behind schedule no damage done. Within half a mile the other front wheel blew. This time there was no spare so we recalled the AA and sat and waited.

"Yeah really nice service you got there Hector, this motorway just seems full sharp objects on the road," she said, arms folded, bitter.

After an hour the AA hadn't arrived. I persuaded Caroline to call them again and they told her that we had already cancelled the order. "That was the previous one," I heard her say and I interrupted her and begged her not to win the argument but to make sure that they came this time.

Half an hour later they arrived. The diagnosis was that the suspension was shot and it was the suspension springs that had burst the tyres.

"You really should keep cars of this age up to date with services." the AA man said.

I wouldn't have minded but the only specific thing I mentioned to them at the garage was to look at the suspension. Not that I knew anything about cars but the service had followed quickly on the back of my log and tractor incident at Windsor a month or so ago. It was all stiff and solid I'd told them, then added 'not bouncy' so that they'd know I wasn't just any old mug that they could rip off. "Don't worry we'll have a look at it, it's easy enough replacing the suspension," they'd said.

"That'll be £630 please." That's another thing they said.

The car wasn't fit to drive so we had to wait for his colleague to come with a pick-up truck. After an hour he hadn't arrived and when we called the AA to ask where he was they told us that we had cancelled the order. Caroline started sobbing a little bit then.

Half an hour later we were on the road and luckily for us, the driver told us, he knew a very good garage close by where we could leave the car to get repaired.

In the garage his friend told us how complicated it was to repair the suspension and that he would have to send away for parts. We should give him a ring in about a week's time and he would tell us how much longer we would have to wait before we came and picked it up. Caroline told him he was miles from anywhere and that we were going back to London on the 28th but apparently that wasn't his fault.

We decanted our pathetic little Christmas from the boot of our car into the pick up truck and the friendly AA man drove us on to the nearest place to hire a car. £300 and five hours later we were back on our holidays.

Declan rang shortly afterwards and when I told him that I was on holiday he sighed a despairing sort of sigh and said, "well it'll have to be New Year now then." I started to tell him that I had tried to tell him the day before when he had been on the phone but he'd already hung up. As events had unfolded I could have gone to the meeting and set off after it and lost no time.

It wasn't quite the early get away that Caroline had banked on so I made it my business to put all my efforts into cheering her up and forgetting about work. It was easy and enjoyable and I wished that I did it more often.

31.

Our cottage was actually semi-detached but none the worse for that. We were on the main street of the village opposite the church, close to two of the three pubs and not far from the newsagents, post office and general store in a village that didn't have an estate agent or a building society. I didn't think that villages like that existed anymore. True the village store was actually a Spar mini-mart and nobody went in any of the pubs but it was a living breathing English village a tiny bit too far to commute to London and all the better for it. We felt at peace. I actually spent the first 48 hours day dreaming about living somewhere proper like that for the rest of our lives. I managed to convince myself that the two hours train journey to commute to London was do-able and that my life would be so much the richer for doing it. All I needed to do was fall into the groove. I needed a regular office job with not too many ambitions, just to turn up and knock it out each day. I even convinced myself that I could carry on working at Martins Fleet and just toe the line. I did that wherever I went on holiday, it would have been the same had we gone to Brazil. I'd have been running the local bar or hiring out boats after two days of day dreaming. Poor Caroline, if I wasn't inconsolably distressed I was untouchable in reverie. She was one of those people who could just enjoy what she had. Me, I'd be searching for ever.

We were quickly introduced to village life when our semi-detached neighbours paid us a visit during Christmas Eve. Apparently Christmas was a very big thing for Carole Huntley, all the family came to her but not this year because they were going to see their daughter who lived in America on the day after Boxing Day and their son would be working the day shift as Head Waiter at The Royal in Sandwich all day for ·Christmas, which wasn't exactly fair, she said, because he needed his Christmas too, but then again he was perfectly happy to do it because he was alone, not that he wouldn't come straight to his mum if he did get the time off, and she would be happy to have him and still would despite the need to get organised next day, they would just have to make sure they didn't drink too much, which was easy enough because they weren't big drinkers, although she did like to take a brandy and coke, especially at Christmas but tomorrow they would just be curling up in front of the tele, although she didn't allow that for normal Christmases, during normal Christmases tele was banned from the 23rd until the 28th, or until the last guest went home, instead of tele everyone was forced to play games. And so it went, our introduction to village life. She stayed for two hours and ended up insisting that we went for a drink after church that night and for lunch on Boxing Day. We were so completely overwhelmed by her that we said yes just to stop her talking.

"I'll give you a knock later on, on the way to church," was her parting shot and we just said, "yes, OK," I may have even thanked her.

I didn't really mind a friendly drink after church although I was more inclined to search out a bit of village life in one of the local pubs. We did mind that we had been robbed of our Christmas Eve afternoon of buying a tree and fresh food and wandering round Sandwich, that was always the best part of Christmas, the preparing. Going through the motions the following day, especially as a couple, revealed it for the non-event that it really was. I say that from the perspective of being part of a couple. Christmas was only good for one thing as far as I was concerned, the Christmas meetings at Kempton and Chepstow, the King George and the Welsh National. Once that kicked in on Boxing Day with a full fixture list you were kept in the warm glow of fireside punting all the way to the New Year meeting at Cheltenham. And I did resent the invitation to be talked at again on Boxing Day.

In the end I allowed Caroline to talk me into going to be polite rather than pretending to forget, which was my preferred option, but I had to promise to get up and leave and be firm about it when the time came. She knew I was a sucker for the extended invitation and one more drink. Not because I wanted one, more because I felt I was being too harsh on my hosts when I had to be firm about the refusal. I inclined to the view that I tried to time my leaving so that I didn't get up in the middle of a sentence or the middle of a point being made and that Caroline was insensitive to that. Sure I understood all the signals she gave off but I didn't always respond until I had given myself the chance to make a rounding up and signing off statement. That wasn't so easy with people like Carole who never came to the end of a sentence.

We went in early to ensure a post-lunch get away of no later than 1.30. I knew by then that Fiddling the Facts was a non-runner in the King George and the field had cut up nicely to leave Looks Like Trouble as a very compelling 7/2 second favourite. At that stage my plans were to get into Sandwich reasonably soon after lunch to take in the two novices in the bookies, pick up my non-runner and re-stake on Looks Like Trouble which I would be able to watch from the comfort of my own armchair. You had time to do things like that when you didn't live in London. In that plan I was going to have a decent little bet on Gloria Victis who looked like the business against a load of rubbish in the novice chase and I really liked the look of a long shot in the opener, Afrostar, who had really only travelled over to keep Doran's Pride company but who I had noted ran a really game race at Cheltenham a month earlier. They'd been repeating the video when I had my Dines experience and it had struck me that he was a reasonably classy animal and that he was really only beaten by the course at Cheltenham and would have a much better chance at an easier course like Kempton. Often horses would find Kempton so much kinder than their previous racecourse experience and keep on going when the form book says that they should pack up. The only real dilemma I had was how to combine them in a reasonable bet. I hated to put 25/1 shots in with a 2/1 favourite and a 7/2 joint. It felt wrong, they didn't really belong together. It seemed ridiculous to have the straight win double or treble, because 25/1 was so out of proportion to 2/1, but an each way acca made no more sense for it having a 2/1 shot in it. That's why really I wanted to be there live in the bookies to bet race by race at an appropriate level. I would always kick myself if all three went in but doing it that way I was likely to come out in front even if I only backed one short priced winner.

As things turned out I needn't have worried, Carole broke out the turkey sandwiches at quarter to two. I'd already missed the first two races and I knew that my chances of seeing the big race, let alone getting a bet on, were diminishing fast. I started to detest the moronic bitch. Her stories went round and round without a pause, changing subject each time she couldn't think of an end for the sentence she was on. She was talking about seasonal vegetables when I finally plucked up the courage to interrupt her. There was nothing else that could stop her apart from sleep or death. She must have been used to it I suppose but I felt like I was being inexcusably rude as I butted in to stop her. I couldn't think of a good excuse to take us away permanently for the entire afternoon, all I could find was, "I must just pop next door to check the fire." It's funny how if I'd had a proper appointment to keep that afternoon it would have been easy to come out with it and leave but as I had to make one up my own knowledge of its falsity would have meant that I would have put it over in a completely different unbelievable way. It wasn't as if we could have stayed indoors next to them once we had made our killer excuse. We would have been obliged to go out and wander about all day. I comforted myself with that thought as I left but I knew that in taking that little break I had sort of implied that I'd be back for a longer session.

I got in next door and put the tele on and I saw that Gloria Victis had gone in at 2/1. That was a blow but it was no more than a good solid favourite winning, such things didn't make you rich. I didn't have much time to fuck about, just enough to ring a bet through and get back, so whilst phoning, I flicked on Ceefax simultaneously and as I got through, Afrostar 20/1 popped up as the winner of the first. I swallowed and shivered and on heavy breaths I was saying, "oh please God, no, no, not me, please,"

"Are you alright sir?" said the Yorkshire accent on the other end of the phone.

"Sorry I've just had a bit of a fright." Only another gambler knows how much an avoidable missed winner hurts. Winners don't come up too often and you need all of them to keep the percentages right. I was doing a quick mental calculation of what I would have had going on for even a small each way treble and I decided that I had not yet missed the boat.

"I'm not sure how much I've got in this account but would you try a £1,000 for me?"

"That's £1,000, Looks Like Trouble, at 7/2. I'll just get that authorised for you .... And that's been accepted. Thank you for betting with William Hill."

I was on and the normal morphine comfort of being on wasn't there. I felt cold and frightened. I knew that my chance had already been and gone for the day and I had missed it. And I knew for all my wanting it and all the feeling of injustice about the harsh way it was taken from me that I couldn't make up lost ground with a large bet.

When I re-entered the neighbours, the first reaction from the Moron was that I looked like I'd seen a ghost. Even Caroline asked me if I was feeling OK. I blamed it on the cold weather, accepted a large brandy and knew when she opened with "did I tell you about the ghost we had in our old house?" that I wasn't going to be watching the King George that year. She'd just got on to telling us how her second daughter died of cot death but that she would never do anything different and that young babies need to be kept warm, when I decided I couldn't take anymore. Mind you it was midnight by then and I was drunk enough by that stage to be reasonably direct about my preference to go to bed and to sleep. I was so drunk and tired that I didn't even check Ceefax for the results when I got in. I ignored it in the full knowledge that by avoiding Ceefax I would be able to squeeze the result the next day which gave me more chance of having had a winning bet. It had no chance if I went in cold at midnight.

As I went to get the newspaper the next morning I talked myself into the possibility of it having won. It was a poor renewal and there was really only Seymour Business that was up to beating Looks Like, and I was in the fortunate position of never having rated Seymour.

I still look at the Form Book today. It was a really poor renewal of the great race and in the commentary next to Looks Like Trouble it says: "was a massive disappointment and Williamson never looked happy on him. Connections blamed the testing ground. He is much better than this and well worth another chance." The connections needn't have blamed the testing ground. If there was a sign in the Form Book which indicates that Hector Somes has had a large bet, the uncharacteristic form would be easily understood and placed aside by the disappointed connections.

And it wasn't the loss on Looks Like Trouble that bothered me. The thing that went round and round in my head was missing two winners because we happened to rent a cottage next door to a moron.

32.

Twelve days holiday between the old year and the new one might as well be twelve weeks. The bright new ways of the new one throw the tired old, easy going ones of last year into such sharp relief that it could be a different age altogether when you return to work. It's not that everyone picked up where they left off, it's more that they start with the zest and enthusiasm of their most productive months of last year. I never quite knew how it was that there were new ideas in circulation that weren't there at the end of the last. "God Hector where've you been?" It's as if a coterie of company intelligence convenes on Christmas Eve and works on a new plan which reaches maturity during the holidays and is old news by the time the ordinary workers come back to work.

I re-drafted my own personal timetable for the New Year and it amounted to two things to keep Martins Fleet happy. I revisited Declan's seven point/eight point plan and knew now that it amounted to no more than to create a PowerPoint presentation that I should show to Tim Hartley when he had the time to spare. His reaction determined what happened next. The other thing was to pretend to make or to make genuine light hearted efforts to sell Martins Fleet contracts to law firms. I could fulfil most of the last requirement by "engaging" with a current client to work with them to decide what a "quality product" looked like. That would cost me nothing and buy me time.

I felt so confident that it was easy to carry these things off that I went in straight away to see Declan, acting like I was pushing the case. It was all very well to be chased and bollocked continually about everything I hadn't done but I figured that Declan only got round to thinking about me when he had nothing else to do. I thought that if I switched roles a little with him he really wouldn't have the time to devote to me and the pressure thus exerted would mean that it was him that avoided the meetings not me. Since it all depended on Tim Hartley being prepared to give up half an hour or so one day to hear me out I could count on him not being bothered to do that for a reasonably long time. The more I pushed, I thought, the more that I would be a pain in the arse that everyone wanted to avoid.

"Tim will see us on Friday 28th, we've reserved the Presentation Room for the afternoon. All the Executives will be there." and then he looked up from his glasses like Eric Morecambe might and looked at me straight in the eye without talking. I said nothing and after about thirty seconds or so there was still a silence. After a while he started nodding his head really slowly, then little by little a smile broke out on his face until in the end he was virtually laughing.

"It's exactly what we've been waiting for Hector," he said and I think that I was supposed to start cheering and jumping up and down. For him we had pulled off a coup worthy of Barney Curley, it was clear that I wasn't quite as delighted but I had to say something so I said, "great."

I should have said, "what the fuck am I going to present? You haven't put any effort into working with me. We are no nearer now to understanding what our Legal Solution is now than you were before I came here," just like proper people would have done, as Franck would have done. Me, I just said, "great."

"We've got three weeks to modify your good work to date to bring it in line with the new corporate information channel model." Even I was aware enough to ask what that meant. Apparently it was widely known and Declan looked at me in disbelief when I asked for an explanation.

Marketing had always been a challenge to Martins Fleet. The essence of the problem was that they were a photocopying company that wanted to float on the Stock Exchange and needed to pretend to be more sophisticated than that. Even during the short period that I had worked there I had been through about three or four new marketing initiatives. That was because Tim knew that a proper approach to marketing was long overdue but each time he reached a conclusion about the new way forward with his new Marketing Director he would become embarrassed by the new branding at the last moment and pulled the plug on the whole scheme. The Marketing Director would be fired and all marketing initiatives had to be personally endorsed by Tim in the interim, until he hired a new visionary who was great until Tim next felt embarrassed. It had been a terrible time for me, since all we did at Gilligan Somes was to mail shot and follow up the best looking responses. I was probably the only person at Martins Fleet that had ever bothered to think about marketing and as a consequence I was prey to every new marketing bird that Tim introduced to the company.

I had to justify myself to people who would say to me, "before I endorse this plan I want you to show me the response rate per 1,000 and the conversion rate per response." It wasn't valid to say, "I've been doing the same thing for ten years and it works, just trust me." It was like that business, because I knew something about something I was subject to 100% scrutiny. Someone else who didn't have a clue could do whatever the fuck they wanted.

At that time we were without a Marketing Director and so one had to assume that Tim had either invented the corporate information channel for himself or got it from his current favoured guru, which to Tim meant someone English who had gone to America and made a load of money. It was a concept borne of shame. But the bad news for the likes of me was that Tim had finally settled on the idea so firmly and finally that a brochure had been commissioned. That was as far as he had ever gone and that meant that the no-one was going back on the idea. What always amazed me at moments in corporate history like that was that fucking cynical arseholes like Barrow suddenly became totally compliant. His razor sharp perceptions deserted him, his constant reversion to saying "no" stopped, his objectivity and sense of shame disappeared.

Tim did not have the nerve to say that his company did all the photocopying for big companies that had better things to do. It was common currency for them to use terms like "document distribution", to describe the act of taking the photocopying back to the desk of the person that asked for it, but "corporate information channel," that was a fiction too far.

It wasn't that Martins Fleet was employed in the area of business activity which all the world knew was called the corporate information channel, it was that Tim made it up and claimed that Martins Fleet not only worked in that arena but that they managed it. Managed it! By photocopying, faxing, opening mail and delivering it he had the audacity to claim that Martins Fleet managed the 'corporate information channel'. It made me cringe to think about it. And suddenly apparently I had to stand up in front of people and talk about it. It was bad enough trying to win photocopying contracts.

I tried to ask Declan what it meant but he couldn't really find the words to explain and told me to read a mock up brochure that he handed me and an early draft PowerPoint presentation that he would send to me.

I should have waited and reflected but I demanded a meeting with Tim before the big day so that I could talk to him about how my thinking, which I had been told had been endorsed by the Executive, would fit with his new ideas. Declan said he would do what he could. It was a stupid thing to do because it elevated the status of what I was doing and made it look like I really cared. I should have just let it fall and acted like it had nothing to do with me and carried on doing my own thing, as Franck would have done. For all my not caring I couldn't help but rise to the bait.

And it was true I didn't care but I was really struck by the injustice of this new game. It suddenly imposed a completely new set of criteria on the work that I had to do and nobody had given me any sort of warning about it. Had I been doing any work at all it would all have been wasted.

I slumped back down at my desk with the draft brochure and resigned myself to the fate of the corporate information channel and tried to learn what it meant.

"Exciting times, eh?" It was unusual for Amanda to be the one that started up a conversation, especially with me.

"I can't make head nor tail of it," I wasn't in the mood to make the best of the awful situation I found myself in.

"You are such a cheery soul Hector. Come on it's the New Year loads of great new opportunities," she was the sort of person that was capable of describing a business opportunity as exciting. I looked up and she was tanned which struck me as strangely exotic for someone that worked at Martins Fleet.

"How come you know all about these things when you've been away for the holidays?"

"Away? I've been working."

"What?"

"Martins Fleet Sub-Continental, I've been in India, do keep up Hector."

"So that's where we're doing it is it?"

"Yes I suppose so, I'd like to think I didn't go there for nothing."

"How does it work?"

"It works very well. Very impressive set up. Joe Mancini is a very credible businessman."

"And we channel work out to India?" If she said yes to that I only had to work out what corporate information meant.

"That's the idea."

"Photocopying? Is that what Nexus is about?"

"In a way I suppose it could work like that."

"Oh Jesus Amanda, please just take five minutes and tell me what it's all about, I can't understand any of it."

"Oh you poor love, does your brain hurt today? What don't you know?"

"I don't know anything. I mean I don't know. How do I know what I don't know? Start at the beginning tell me why you went to India."

She had been to see a factory run by an American called Joe Mancini but that was all she was prepared to tell me. She clammed up in the name of having a professional attitude but it was really so that she could have a few more days belonging to an exclusive club that the rest of us didn't. The most I extracted from her by inference was that there were lots of high level meetings taking place at the moment that were all about Martins Fleet Sub-Continental and apparently it was especially suited to law firms. The place, as I was soon to find out, and as far as it was possible at a place so determinedly dreary as Martins Fleet, was buzzing about the new India stuff. I had no idea whether that was the same thing as the corporate information channel, or whether it facilitated it or if it was related at all.

I knew it was only me that those things happened to. Who else but me would be asked to perform the seemingly innocuous task of putting a presentation together that it met with the confluence of major re-branding exercise and a brand new way of doing business. If that's what was going on. The early signs seemed to say so. At companies like Martins Fleet errors in communication were jumped on. You had to be painstaking about arranging a review for a recalcitrant employee, even the announcements about somebody leaving took weeks to receive approval and subsequently be sent out. I had even been in meetings where the timing of the distribution of such announcements were talked about at length and still left undecided at the end of it. Yet momentous decisions just floated in without a word of debate. Martins Fleet was now expanding into Asia, or partnering with someone in Asia, or partnering and re-branding in Asia or some other such incomprehensible arrangement with a lack of explanation that wouldn't be tolerated on a stationery requisition form. I was confused and I felt a little bit that the sky might start falling in on me soon and if I was truthful I felt a tiny pang of jealousy that I had been excluded from all those big things going on. I decided to take my first illicit break of the New Year and have a think about where I stood. I went out to pick up my non-runner and have a decent breakfast.

I rang Franck from the Nelson and I couldn't even tempt him into a greasy on the first morning back. But he did do one thing for me, he could tell me what Martins Fleet Sub-Continental was about. Some place in India run by Joe Mancini, ex-major consultancy, in Chicago, did all the things that Martins Fleet said they did but in India, for about hundredth of the price. Joe was somehow known to Tim or vice versa and they had somehow done a deal to re-name the operation Martins Fleet Sub-Continental instead of Monsoon Trades or whatever dotcommy name they'd had to date. He didn't know any details but he knew it was a definite goer and that the word was we had to sell their services like mad to all our existing UK clients and lead with it to bring in new ones.

"How come you're so close to the action?" I asked him idly as our conversation was petering out.

"Get this," he says, "I'm part of sales." He'd been part of a major re-organisation over Christmas which saw the sales force multiply from Andy Scott into a force of about ten people. Franck was in there and Chamberpot and basically anyone who had any talent in the business. Except me. I suddenly felt very neglected. I even sensed that Franck was a little bit more one of them as he told me. He even sounded happy. I wanted to know everything, when and how and why and by who but he had to ring off to take a call. Suddenly something had happened at Martins Fleet that was a little bit better than normal and there was I, not only not part of it, not only still stuck in the boiler room but totally neglected and even kept in the dark by my old partner until it was too late. Well that's how I saw it, they probably hadn't thought about me at all.

It should have made me pleased, my disposability played to the exit strategy but yet the news demoralised me further. Suddenly I was thinking of the daily commute from the cottage in Kent and doing a regular sales job, selling an easy product for big figures and big margins and big bonuses and I wanted it.

I went to cheer myself up by picking up the non-runner and I arrived at the bookies as they opened up, a social faux pas only topped by waiting outside a pub for the morning opening. I didn't think anyone had spotted me and I slipped in.

"No, love it was beat."

"I know but it's a non-runner."

"Not if it ran in the race love it can't be."

"It ran in a different race."

"No love it can't have."

"What do you mean it can't have?"

"Look there's no reason to raise your voice, I'm not paying you out on a loser."

"Look at the slip it says 33/1," I hadn't wrote the name of the race but there was only one race for which the horse had been that price, "the horse wasn't anything like that price at Chepstow," I wished I'd done my homework, it would have been much more convincing to have quoted the right SP.

"That means nothing love, on the day of the race anything can happen," the patronising bitch told me.

"But the horse was never 33/1 for Chepstow."

"it might have been you that wrote the price on the slip, how do I know?"

"I didn't, I mean I don't know, no, you wrote it, I probably said it and you wrote it," I was useless at being definite at moments like that. I never knew whether perhaps I had done something different to normal and I always tried to remember properly rather than just assert that I was correct.

"Well that doesn't mean anything."

"So if the horse won at Chepstow would you have paid me 33/1?"

"Not necessarily if it was a mistake."

"So it's meaningless then, you can accept any sort of bet you like and then decide whether you pay after the race?"

"We have to have rules to protect ourselves from cheats."

"So I'm a cheat now?"

"I've been in the business 25 years and I don't need any lessons from a young thug like you."

"It doesn't sound like you've had any lessons from anybody you stupid, thick, bitch."

"Get out of this shop."

"Fuck off."

I was steaming as I left the shop and intent on revenge. She had been a strange hybrid between the non-sequitor and too thick to argue.

I went straight to the print room and begged a piece of A1 paper and went with it to the Presentation Room where I would have enough space to open it out. As usual it was taken by Organisational Learning so I had to make do with the lobby space that was often used for parties outside the lifts. The cupboards there were always good for a marker pen and I set to work on my poster. It was to read, "BEWARE THIS SHOP IS MANAGED BY A PRICKESS," and I was making reasonable headway when Tim walked by and asked what I was doing. I could normally count on myself for some sort of response that was at least slightly plausible but at that time, kneeling on the floor with my poster half written, looking up at my Chief Executive, I felt very stupid indeed and I couldn't find anything to say. It was as if my father had stumbled across me playing with a Barbie doll.

When I didn't answer he eventually said, "well I'll leave you to it then," and strode off down the corridor. I was all upset at being excluded from the new developments and yet this was how I presented myself to the boss. I clung to the hope that his inability to concentrate for more than five seconds would mean that our meeting was soon forgotten and I continued with the task in the hand.

Within fifteen minutes I had it taped up in place on the front window of the bookies. I was so pleased with the poster particularly at the level of a piece of art that I decided to make a smaller one to hang off a nearby lamppost to reinforce the campaign. I'd be back with that after lunch I told myself.

33.

If I came back to work with anything like a New Year's Resolution it was that I would not allow myself to be put under pressure by other people and I recognised that required a bit of effort from me. I was tired of feeling sick, nervous and scared all of the time. I was frightened of the future and depressed about the past and I just wanted it to end. One day not very long ago I had been playing Subbuteo and listening to the Beach Boys and I was very happy. I tried Punk Rock and pints of beer just to see what it was like and I'd felt terrified ever since.

I set aside the afternoon to try and understand the corporate information channel and just that. To enable me to do that in my own little cocoon it meant that I had to listen to all my phone messages and deal with them properly and quickly and the same with my emails.

The first thing I dealt with was Stacey Arnold. She had cc'd Declan on a final demand for a meeting with me the following morning. I decided that I could either let her stalk me for the rest of the time I spent at Martins Fleet or I could have the meeting with her and get her out of my life. That was how other people dealt with their shit jobs, they just went with the flow. I would do that. Similarly with all my telephone messages I methodically went through them all and removed them from my in-tray. There was one from New Media with the latest set of artwork for Social-Lites which I didn't think I'd commissioned. It made me realise that I hadn't done anything to take my great new idea forward since November so I wrote it in my notebook and put an asterisk by it. I also had another from the same woman that had left a few messages before Christmas. I recognised her voice from those messages but I'd always erased her straight away since she just gave a number without saying where she was phoning from. This time though she stressed how urgent it was to respond. I always had her down as one of the Martins Fleet losers that wanted me to give a presentation to someone who looked after the toilets at Mega Bank but today in my mood of clearing the decks and her slightly compelling message I thought I should give her a ring.

Sally turned out to be the accountant at SpreadBets.com, with whom I used to have an account until I bit off more than I could chew one Sunday night. My extravagance had been on touchdown shirt numbers. I didn't know anything about American Football and I didn't really realise that they had shirt numbers like 89. The match hadn't even been on television, I had the bet out of desperation on a bad day, chasing the earlier debts I ran up watching the soccer. For me it was just like tossing a coin, a red or black call and I thought it would be a good idea to have a large stakes even money bet on the basis that I was due a win after five or six losing bets during the day. I went blind and sold shirts, then realised the match wasn't on the tele and so I spent the night lying in bed pretending to be asleep while I secretly watched the numbers on Ceefax clicking ever upwards in a state of total fear. At the end of the match I owed

SpreadBet.com £3,000, which I didn't have at the time. They let me off with a standing order for £150 a month which I thought was very fair. The only problem was that it was soon forgotten about and that lead to my problem that day with Sally.

I still owed £1,200 and the standing order had not been paid since August. Between the problems on the new bank account, my fear of letting Caroline know about the debt and my lack of attention to detail I ended up in what lawyers call an invidious position. One thing was for certain I wasn't going to own up to Caroline about it now. That would be worse at this stage than owning up to it at the beginning since there had been two years or so of deceit going on since it was first incurred. It would also mean that she would scrutinise the statement from my old bank a bit more closely when those funds were finally transferred. Sally told me that she was perfectly within her rights to issue proceedings against me now but she was open to begging and she seemed to have a genuine sympathy for my predicament with the bank. She was however, loath to let me go off the phone without making some sort of financial gesture and I wasn't in the position to give one. I begged more than I ever thought that someone with a university education would have to and she let me off with an immediate fax recognising the debt, promising to pay it within the month and confirming all my contact details. In the circumstances I was delighted.

I had no idea how to raise the debt discretely from Caroline and given my recent run of losers it wasn't something that I could lose in the transfer of funds from my old bank account. That was going to be a disaster in its own right. Given that that problem was going to surface at any moment I decided to confront it so that I could prepare for my fate. It filled me with dread just to start the process of talking to the bank's call centre. I still didn't have a bank card or anything that showed that I belonged to the bank, and so I had no means of knowing what my new account number was and I didn't feel that I could ring Caroline to ask what it was. I didn't have the stomach to start all over again explaining the story afresh to someone new and I had no idea how to get hold of the last person I talked to that was vaguely helpful - I'd written her direct number on my notebook which I'd left next to the tele at home. That would mean that if she had done any decent work on my behalf I would probably set someone new off on the same course who might unravel it all. Utterly trepidatious I picked up the phone and set off on a journey and about one hour later I was put through to the woman that had been helpful a month or so ago. She was just about to call me actually.

In the end she asked me if I could spare her one more day. She would call me in the morning with everything buttoned up ready to go. In the circumstances I was delighted.

34.

I spent a sleepless night and I was in the office for 8.00. I phoned my contact at the bank but I just fell into the call centre system. All I wanted to do was leave a voice message so that she knew to contact me as soon as possible but I wasn't allowed -they had re-engineered their business with the customer in mind, after all-. I needed to know the real detail of the mess I'd got myself into and my rough estimation was that my gambling errors accounted for about £2,500, which added to my spread betting error meant that I would have a £3,000 to £4,000 shortfall to find.

One thing the sleepless night had given was a solution, of sorts. I had one asset that Caroline knew belonged to Martins Fleet but that Martins Fleet didn't know that they owned. Me car. With that one asset I had a chink of light to get out of trouble unscathed. I went to work on Exchange & Mart and Auto Trader until the working day began. That was 9.30 in my book, I was a trained lawyer when all was said and done.

According to my messages my friend at the bank called me just after 9.30 when I was officially due in my HR meeting with Stacey Arnold. I called her back and we got down to it straight away. The funds were there and ready to be transferred.

"All I need is your go ahead and the nightmare is over."

"Don't transfer anything," and she started laughing.

"How much is there?" I was nervous.

"By my records I am to transfer, £15,309.80."

"What?" I was expecting much more but that was only a very rough guess, I never had a clue how much money was actually lost to tax and national insurance and pensions and that sort of thing. There was going to be a hole alright.

"Is there a problem with that?"

"Well there may be yes," I said. I asked her if she was planning to send me a statement for the interregnum and she assured me she was. "Well then," I thought, "could she send me an advance copy by fax today?" and she certainly could. And if it could come absolutely immediately and if she would do me the great favour of not transferring the funds just yet. I needed the chance to put some cash back into the account to replenish it before it was transferred. And that was no problem, I was just to go and stand by the fax and wait.

Stacey came before the fax. She wondered out loud whether I was planning not to turn up to another scheduled meeting and instead of searching for the right words I told her to shut up and mind her own business and that I would come in a minute.

"The problem is, Hector," she said in a very loud voice, "it is my business and I have absolutely no confidence in you to come in a minute or any time after. In fact I am certain that unless you are escorted to the meeting personally you will go missing just like usual," to me and anyone else that could be bothered to listen.

"Davina," I shouted across the office, "my syphilis tests are due through in a moment, will you put them on my desk discretely so that no-one knows about them?" Then I limped out behind Stacey as if I had a tender cock. It got a few laughs which encouraged me more than it should because I started whistling loudly and shouting, "come by Glen, come by." At the lift she lightened her mood a little and said:

"I don't know, what are you like?" I didn't feel like sympathising so I said, "why don't you go and look on your files?"

The meeting was me, her and Moiragh and it was about our plan to sack Patrick.

"He's still here then?" I ventured, which was a mistake judging by the voracity of Moiragh's response. It so happened that they'd been waiting two months for my report on his poor accounting and in the meantime they'd had to get on with things by themselves. Moiragh had apparently thought up some question and answer scheme in the guise of an asset audit to prove his incompetence.

"Why don't you just put it to him that you think he's incompetent?" I suggested. Stacey told me that we'd been through that before and for all the reasons that she told me before it was a non-runner.

"You never know he might just agree with you,"

"Hector I wish you'd take this process seriously, this is getting ridiculous," and I suppose really it was a too casual comment but I wasn't prepared to be talked down to by a haughty bitch like that so I said, "he probably hates working here as much as everyone else and he would bite your hand off if you asked him to go."

I was told that that was not how HR works and if I couldn't take it seriously there was no point in continuing with the meeting.

"But I am being serious," I protested. I should have just told her to fuck off, but I actually believed I was.

"We have given a commitment to have Patrick out of the business by the end of January," Moiragh told me, "and without your co-operation we have had to take matters into our own hands to accelerate the process. The original plan has had to be let go by your inactivity. Instead of handling this matter correctly we are now going to direct negotiation with Patrick regarding the terms of his release."

"And what commitment have you given Patrick?" I asked.

"That he will be given a fair hearing,"

"How can you give him a fair hearing when you've already decided to sack him?"

"So you want him to stay now?"

"No, I'm just saying that you have given two contradictory undertakings,"

"What exactly is it that you want Hector?"

"I am trying to ask you why you are pretending to give Patrick a fair hearing instead of just sacking him,"

"So now you're an expert in everything,"

"I didn't say that,"

"And now he's in denial. What is it you want Hector?"

"I only asked you a civil question,"

"This is the most ridiculous conversation I've ever had. Is it because we're women you won't co-operate?"

"I not not co-operating,"

"Oh no you're being perfectly co-operative excuse me. That's why Patrick's still here and we've made no progress in two months."

"That's my point,"

"What?"

"That you've already made your minds up,"

"Now I've heard it all," and she sighed very deeply.

"You're dying to tell me what you've decided already so why don't you go ahead?"

She was a prime example of the non-sequitor but I wasn't sure whether she qualified as a female or a psychopath.

"It means that we will be paying him more than we necessarily would under the original plan."

"But you're paying him with my money," I told her. It was only money that would have counted towards my bonus which I had long since given up on but she didn't know anything about that. I was sure that she didn't know any details about my deal so I laboured the point. In the end I made her feel a little bit like she was making free with my private money and I also made her acknowledge that she was encroaching on forbidden ground and it was decided that we would adjourn and reconvene around Declan's desk the next day in his weekly catch-up with Stacey.

"Right, thanks, see you tomorrow," I said getting up.

"Where are you going?" Stacey said.

"Well, nowhere, to my desk, you know …."

"You're staying here for my employment law seminar, as agreed," and she sniggered like it was a fucking game. Anyone else of my rank would have been able to say that they had some compelling reason not to be there and to thank her for her effort but that they really had to be going. Me, it was taken that I'd have nothing better to do and I could be trapped like that. We were all supposed to laugh then, the sniggering little tramp. If I'd have told her I was off and not to take liberties with me like that it would become some major personnel issue, typical of my insolence. If I accepted and stayed it was a great little joke that we all shared in. I decided that if I was to stay I should try and make her suffer.

35.

What was formerly known as the training room until it became just another office, filled up quickly with the detritus of Martins Fleet middle management. Stacey's ego required that she continued to claim it on Wednesday mornings to give her employment law seminars. She evidently needed access to all of its visual and audio aids to learning. I was mystified as to why a shameless personnel tart like her was allowed to give the rest of the company an update on the law. God knows there were plenty of people who were actually allowed to call themselves lawyers that weren't up to it. For Martins Fleet she'd do, any one with any authority in the business probably didn't even know what she was up to.

Today's subject was European updates to the Data Protection Act. Riveting. The stupid cunt just relished giving the class.

I had come across the Data Protection Act earlier in my so called career at other shit companies and I can honestly say that I had never understood it. True I'd never actually bothered to read it all but I'd read enough of it and I had never come to terms with it on any level at all. It was obvious that it was meant to prohibit the exploitation or abuse of personal information that you held about private individuals but in actual fact it was so convoluted that it added up to anything but that. And as usual with moralistic legislation like that, companies that would have never been in breach of the original aims of the legislation took it all on board and in doing so made a misery of the lives of all their employees in complying with it, whereas those that would have always been in breach carried on and ignored it. I say that but I didn't really know what I was talking about. For me it always seemed to be a breach of the Act to keep a mail shot list but I knew that hundreds of other companies did, so I never said anything.

She had no fucking clue about it. She just stated things as established fact that had to be complied with and everyone else in the room was so dense that they just wrote down everything she said. She was too thick to realise that there may have been a subtlety of interpretation or a vagueness about it that wasn't yet settled by practice or by litigation.

"So," she said, "anything of that nature must not be kept on file,"

"Where do we keep it then?" I said,

"Nowhere,"

"What, we're supposed to forget it are we?"

"Thank you Hector, if we can continue."

"No, I want to know. If you know something prejudicial about someone, do we have to expunge it from our memories our note pads our email messages?"

"Well yes."

"How do we know it was prejudicial?"

"Hector don't try to wind me up."

"No, if we have some information on someone that may or may not be prejudicial what do we do with it?"

"You can talk to your HR adviser."

"And when we do, will you be taking notes?"

"Normally yes."

"Well do we destroy those notes when we've finished?"

"If it is prejudicial yes."

"But that isn't the file?"

"Is this leading to something Hector?"

"Earlier you said we can't keep things on their file that are prejudicial. Did you mean that we can't keep any information at all?"

"Not on their files."

"Well what do you mean by files?"

"Their record."

"What does that mean? Is it any information about them in the entire building or is it a physical file in a filing cabinet?"

"Their personnel files, I think we all know what that means."

"I don't. Is it a file somewhere made of paper?"

"Hector, we all want to get on."

"So do I but I don't understand what you're trying to tell us. Where is this mythical file. You haven't made it clear."

"Hector you know very well I am talking about their personnel files."

"And they're specific special files are they?"

"Yes they are."

"Where are they kept?"

"They are confidential files kept in Human Resources."

"So how the fuck do we make sure that we delete information from them?"

"Hector we know you don't want to be here but please don't be abusive."

"I want to know. How do I access these important files if they're under lock and key in Human Resources."

Someone else said: "you send an email to HR, with the information."

"What? This crucial personal information, I have to tell any old person in HR what it is?"

"That's right Hector, it's called trust."

"What if it's none of your business?"

"Hector this isn't doing any of us any good."

"Alright then, if you're not up to answering that, what if it's not prejudicial?"

"What if what isn't?"

"To remind you we were having a conversation about whether information that we learn about one of our employees might be kept on some mythical file or other, if it was prejudicial to them."

"If it's not prejudicial it's a different matter altogether."

"What sort of different matter?"

"What? You're not making any sense Hector."

"I can always speak more slowly if that helps. But, for example, you might want to tell me who decides whether the information we have is prejudicial or not."

It turned out that it was her. I was pleased to say that I ruined the class. I kept those questions going for fully forty minutes almost from start to finish. In the end people were just getting up and going. And finally there was just me and her. As soon as the audience was down to me alone, I got up mid sentence and left. That would fucking teach her I thought.

When I got back to my desk the statement was there. I had a £2,500 gambling short fall to make up. That meant I was £3,700 in the hole altogether, so I rang up Auto Trader.

36.

Seconds out round two, Declan's office Thursday morning. Me, Big Dog Moiragh, Cunt Stacey and Declan.

"What we've decided," the little cunt says, "is that we are going to offer Patrick a settlement of £19,000 to leave."

"But he would have left for half that six months ago or whenever you started this fucking process," I said. Then she just bounced up and started shouting, "I can't work like this, he's just so rude, I can't be expected to work like this," and stormed out of his office, followed shortly by Big Dog Moiragh, shrugging her shoulders.

When she'd gone Declan looked at me for an explanation. I just said, "you do employ the most fragile people Declan."

He was up for a fight and told me that I should try harder with everyone. I wasn't in the mood for tolerating arseholes anymore, so I said, "just in case you didn't notice it was me that suffered the indignity of unjustified outburst which I thought I took very well in the circumstances. Why the fuck didn't you back me up? If they were any good at their jobs you'd have had a fucking wanker like Patrick out of the business for a month's wages a long time ago. We all have to go at the fucking speed of the worst in the class in this fucking shit hole and if anybody is brave enough to speak up, which seems only ever to be me, they get crucified for it. And by the way it's my money that they're paying his settlement with." And the adrenalin was up and I was in the groove for the exit plan so I added: "And if it does come out of my deal to make a settlement with him you can consider it a resignation issue." That would mean that he would have to tell Barrow about the whole episode and that had to help my cause.

I thought I had him but as usual I had gone one step too far, even when I was playing a blinder, and so he started saying, "ooher keep yer hair on," mocking my accent and making it look like I got all aeriated for nothing.

"Lets have a conversation about the corporate information channel instead," I said.

"What about it?"

"Well this famous presentation that now needs completely re-writing to be compliant with it, is due in two weeks and I can't make head nor tail of it."

"What the presentation?"

"No this corporate information channel. Can't I just be left to do what I was going to do?"

"Hector, Hector. There is nothing but the corporate information channel. It's what we do, it's what we say we do, it is a unifying across the board once and for all marketing policy. We are going to do everything on that basis from now on. No negotiation."

"Well I don't get it."

"What is it you don't get?"

"Everything. It just sounds like a collection of words that don't mean anything, I'm lost Declan."

"I don't think Tim would like to hear you talking like that. I mean it, he is very serious about this."

"Well tell me this for example, the first thing the brochure does is to give our definition of what it means.

"Yes."

"Well it's hardly self-evident, is it?"

He didn't say anything. He just looked at me like I was wasting his time.

"Alright, and the definition is something like: the data and information that is crucial to the efficient provision of your company's core products and services."

"Yes."

"What does that mean?"

"What it says."

"But Declan, it seems to me to be a very inelegant way of saying something too ambitious."

"Yes I would agree with you it is ambitious."

"Do we really want to say that we manage all that?"

"Don't we?"

"We do the photocopying."

"Hector, I'm going to arrange for you to see Tim to talk him through all your objections. Then you'll be clear."

"OK," I said, "thanks." Why didn't I learn to keep my fucking mouth shut?

37.

"I hear you're the man to talk to about the law," it was a big American accent behind my back. I turned round to see the distinctly unimpressive figure of Joe Mancini,

"Hi, I'm Joe, how are you?"

He thrust out a stubby little arm from his short fat body and prodded his sweaty fingers round mine. He was no more than five foot seven and he smiled a big gap toothed agricultural smile. He sported a close cropped haircut flat to his spud shaped head and my first impression was of one of those children's games where you make up a human being by sticking bits of plastic together. And for all his unfortunate shape by far the worst aspect of his appearance was his clothes. His suit looked cheaper than one of Declan's and fitted him worse. The sleeves came right down to half way across his palms and the trousers crumpled over his rubber shoes, His nylon white shirt was as good as grey and the top button was missing. His tie hung down to cover his fly. Normally an ensemble like that would have drawn me to the man but there was something aggressive about his style that made me hate him from the start.

"We're putting together a team of people to talk about taking the India proposition to law firms, do you want to come along?"

"Yes, I'd love to," I said, "why have you chosen law firms?"

"We're taking it to all the clients, but most of the success we've had in the States has been with law firms."

"So you're up and running already?"

"We've been going three years. You bet. And let me tell you, what we're doing is made for law firms. Do you know all the big ones?"

"Yes I suppose so,"

"Good contacts?"

"Yes some," and I reluctantly went into a conversation with him at my desk which meant that he had heard all I had to say that was of any use to him about law firms in England. Desk meetings are always like that. Ours was supposed to be a little hors d'ouevre before the feast and I served him all four courses in trying to prove to him that I knew what I was talking about. He'd probably go away and say, "that Hector's not a bad sort," then I would become progressively disappointing at each subsequent exchange.

I was at first reluctant to ask while we were talking together, about which of his great services, was particularly attractive to law firms but he wasn't getting round to telling me. He just assumed I knew what he did because he thought Martins Fleet was a proper company, and I didn't want to show my ignorance. In the end I plucked up the courage and it turned out to be typing, he didn't say it like that, but it involved lawyers dictating their documents into dictation machines and someone in India, in Joe's factory, typing it up for about one hundredth of the wages of the secretaries in England. That put me a step further down the route but what that had to do with the corporate information channel was still anybody's guess.

I could understand why somebody wanted to get their routine work done somewhere cheap and I could understand why someone in India might want to do the work when they had nothing else to do. But for the life of me I couldn't understand why Martins Fleet would want to make a virtue of sending all that work overseas. There were virtually no skills in Martins Fleet and if they sold themselves on anything it was that they were there on hand to manage the work, they managed what nobody else could be bothered to manage, or the corporate information channel, depending on your perspective. Yet they proposed to send as much of it as they could to India. Wasn't it obvious that one day someone in India would pick up the phone to the client and cut Martins Fleet out? All they did was stand in the middle and put the price up. That must have been why they were so keen to put their name on the operation and assert a bit of control and ownership. But charlatans like Joe were everywhere, he could start up new factories whenever he wanted and call centres were ten a penny now. Their clients could go anywhere. I obviously didn't know the whole story and I had to remind myself that the current scenario was only good to me if I used it to get out. Beyond that it could remain a mystery. "I have no interest in the operation," I heard myself saying.

"You don't eh?" said Scottish Robin, who looked like he'd been standing by my desk for half an hour.

"I hear you're the man to talk to about law firms?"

"What?" I was terrified of a strange conspiracy set up by Tim to undermine me.

"I didn't mean to frighten you, you don't have to say yes you know."

"No, no carry on Scottish," I said, although I wasn't sure that he knew his nickname and if he didn't Scottish was a bit harsh from a semi-stranger, "someone else has just said that to me and it gave me a bit of a shock."

"A man in demand, exciting times," he came over as a bit of a lad, albeit that he was the nearest thing in dress to John Goody in Martins Fleet but he was utterly sober when he spoke. He was younger than me but he was quite prepared to trade in non-jokes then back them up with a hearty laugh like someone twice his age would do.

For his ills, apparently, he'd been given the Scottish account. That meant the whole of Scotland for everything. Whereas everything else was divided up into stupid names and divisions and sub-classes of services, because we had one Scottish client, his division was called Scotland and he was supposed to sell as much as he could there. That was his job. I seized on the opportunity with another junior salesman like me and asked him how he was getting on with the corporate information channel.

"Ah they've put a channel between England and Scotland have they? About time to, a-ha, a-ha, a-ha, a-ha, a-ha,"

I joined in on a couple of a-ha's to keep him company but I checked no-one else was listening first.

"No can't help you there, what's all this about?"

And so I told him everything I knew about it so far, as much for sympathy as for anything else. And at the end I surprised myself with my directness by saying that in the current circumstances I would not really be able to assist on any sales calls.

"No matter, Hec," he said comradely, "I'm no going on the tour til the start of March, you'll have it settled by then I doubt? If you turn around and tell me that it's still not on in March, I'll be turning around myself and telling Tim it's up to him to turn round and tell the clients directly himself," he said that a lot too.

"Oh yes, definitely," I said for no reason at all, "did you say tour?"

"Hector, Scotland is a gold mine for our services and I am fixing up a promotional tour for the Spring to go and see as many targets as possible. I believe, but you'll have to confirm it for me, that we have some of the major law firms up there and I'd like to incorporate them in the tour."

"Sounds great," I said without any conviction at all and I wondered why I didn't have the knack like him of staying largely in the background and organising my own little world. Everything I did seemed to be in full public view.

I couldn't think of anything to say at first so I ended up being far more enthusiastic for his tour than I should have been and I gave a slightly firmer than my intended equivocal response to his invitation to take part. At the time I thought in terms of a legitimate week off work with hardly any work and a few games of golf and a day at the races.

"So I just need you to tell me how we sell Martins Fleet services to law firms. The easy part, a-ha, a-ha, a-ha," he quipped. And then I had exactly the same conversation with him for the next hour and a half that I'd just had with Joe Mancini.

38.

It took a little while before the meeting that Joe Mancini had invited me to materialised and that played into my hands because Tim had said that there was no point in going to see him until I was up to date with MFS, as it was now being referred to. And that in turn made it pretty sure that the seminal Legal Solutions presentation that I was to give to the board was odds on to be put back too.

When it came it was about as smart as a Martins Fleet meeting could be. Tim wasn't there but only because he was known to be too thick to make a telling contribution at the level of detail that the meeting demanded and neither was Fulsome-Wank on the basis that he was more operational, i.e. he swept up the shit once everything got started. For meetings of this sort it was only Barrow on the board that was of the required calibre. In addition there was Joe 'Spud-Head' Mancini, Chamberpot, me, Franck and a bright new thing called William Attenborough. It turned out he wasn't too bright at all but at that time he cut a dashing figure. Straight out of the army he had gone in and made his reputation in turning round a large bad client. He looked the part and spoke like a businessman and in the musical chairs over the holidays he had ended up as Franck's boss. I pitied him that and for me that would be his acid test, not turning round the big client. At present Franck loved him mainly because he wasn't me whilst at the same time being a little bit like Franck thought I should be. In the meeting he pushed far too strongly for the response he wanted to get, more so than I would have done at the height of my depravity at Gilligan Somes and I made a mental note to check out the Franck William relationship in six months time, if I hadn't got parole by then.

As much as I hated each of the individuals around the table there was a comfortable feeling of being back in the big time, albeit at Martins Fleet. It was the highest quality set of brains that could be assembled and it was nice just indulging in the pre-meeting small talk - such a massive hike in quality from the Monday morning fodder - that I thought for a few moments that I should make a go of it and try and enjoy my job. Everybody had genuine leisure interests and spoke in an informed way about them. It was so rare for me to find myself in such company I absolutely relished it. It turned out that we all thought someone else was coming and the pre-meeting small talk went on for much longer than it should have done. There is something about the company of men, that men need, that could never be explained let alone replaced by a woman.

The cultural low point of the conversation belonged to Joe who was going on a Dickens Walk that evening but in his favour he pushed the point and he turned out to be an avid reader of classic works. I'd read them all too. A fact which was well known to Franck, so as usual, not content with taking part in an enjoyable conversation, he tried to turn the conversation into a competition with me. He was as rude as he could be without completely undermining Joe, who he wanted to impress, about people that needed to live in the past. In fact I think he said something about the weakness of English people to live in the past. He was very proud of the fact that he was up to date and knew what was in the charts and read new novels when they came out and went to new restaurants. He didn't just do it all cool, like he wanted to be, he shoved it down your throat. He would have loved to have been one of those people that when a conversation comes up about something current and it comes round to his turn to speak he could say," yeah, I know about that actually," but he was too worried that he might not get the opportunity to say his piece so he would always dive in and let everyone know that he was informed and up to date, whether they wanted to know or not. He read Time Out that meant.

"You strike me as a bit of a reader," Chamberpot ventured to me.

"Oh yes, I'm with Joe really I've read all the classics."

"I had you down to be at the forefront of culture like Franck."

"No I don't like modern novels really," suddenly the conversation seemed all about me and I didn't want it to be, I always went over the top instead of just batting the ball back. It was like Chamberpot knew I was good for a punch line and he was pushing for it. He took his entertainment vicariously that cunt.

"They're the only things worth reading," he said, "I get through one a week on my train journey."

"They all seem the same to me. It's like they're all re-workings of Catcher in the Rye, just that the main character is a bit older each time."

"You're too high brow for me Hector," Chamberpot said laughing, he had just as much interest as Franck in reducing my stock.

And God love him, Joe said, "yeah I know what you mean there Heccy."

At that point Barrow called the meeting to order. Just when all the attention had been on me. Just when the meeting had lost its levity. Just when I had been the one to make a serious point that went against the spirit of the chat we were having. I felt like the only one that nobody wanted there.

So we were there to talk about how to sell Martins Fleet Sub-Continental services to law firms. Had I exited the prologue with a bit more confidence I would have kicked off the meeting by asking to be brought up to date with the MFS experience, instead I winged it and pretended that I was as much in the know as the rest of them. The rest of the team, actually.

As the meeting progressed Franck and I moved towards centre stage. Before long it was obvious that we were the only ones that knew what we were talking about, more so even than Joe who boasted of major law firm clients already signed up and working in India. Attenborough was off the bridle after about fifteen minutes, Chamberpot cried enough after taking the water and Barrow was totally in awe of us. He finally realised the talent he had bought. Too fucking late I told myself. Franck and I were turning them on and it put me in mind of the best of our performances at Gilligan Somes.

Then after a while Franck started doing something that I knew well from our Gilligan Somes days. It wasn't enough for him that we'd impressed our audience and achieved all we set out to do. He had to beat me and to press the audience into recognising that he was the talented one. He always forgot that all he had to do was close the deal, instead he allowed himself to be taken over by a massive ego and it swept him along out of reach.

Each point I made he was there behind me to damn me with faint praise and take the point on to the real issue. He condemned me by my implied omissions and he showed no shame in preening himself in public. The pity was, had he shown some humility in showing off he could have taken his audience with him, instead he was so palpably proud of himself and the more he pressed the point the more he detached himself from the good sense he had been talking. When he made cute little academic niceties he grunted like a little pig in self-congratulation. He was so carried away with his own brilliance that he didn't realise that he was occasionally talking nonsense or, more particularly, that no-one cared. Towards the end he said, "Recently I've been genuflecting on the state of the market," and Barrow smirked and Chamberpot giggled a little bit, Attenborough and Mancini didn't have a fucking clue, although to be fair Mancini had one eye in Wigan at that stage. Me, my face was blank, my normal hatred for Franck had turned into undiluted detestation. Franck was proud of his vocabulary, he was the sort of cunt that would go home and learn a new word out of the dictionary each night so that he could use it casually the next day. He thought that because he knew how to use antediluvian in context that it was a mark of his superior intellect. Whenever I used a malapropism in his company he jumped on it like a ton of bricks. Once I was trying to give our staff a good bollocking over their under achievement on a bit of work we'd done and I described it as atypical instead of typical, not meaning to say the opposite. He was in like Flynn and absolutely agreed with me to say the exact opposite of what he and everyone else knew I wanted to say. Me, I just let his idiot conceit go. I didn't tell him what genuflect really meant. He could find that out in Time Out next time going to church was back in fashion.

At the end of the meeting there was one thing certain: that the best prospect for Martins Fleet Sub-Continental was to go full steam ahead into the legal market. Franck tried to make it an issue of selling the technical solution so that he was the hero rather than me but Barrow said, "I don't see this as a technical sale, this speaks much more to engaging with the client which makes it Hector's territory. Joe can add technical and operational credibility to the sale. For the only time in my life I liked him.

Then everyone agreed that it was a great pity that I hadn't been there over the Christmas holidays when Chamberpot went with Attenborough and Mancini to try and sell a contract to out-source the word processing department at Derek & Mammery. That contract would be worth £5 million a year to Martins Fleet and I had been overlooked for it. Nobody said that I should pick up from thereon, Chamberpot didn't offer to give it up as he should since it was nothing to do with him and Barrow didn't insist on changing the sales team as he should have done and as we all expected him to, it was just let go. The best opportunity we had was already lost as far as I was concerned. Probably the only decent lead we'd come up with quickly. The meeting finished by Joe promising to come and see me to fill in the gaps in my knowledge and I was to be forwarded the proposal document for the Derek & Mammery bid to edit it into shape. And yet they still didn't swap me in for Chamberpot. Being a cunt I promised to do it. Just like Chamberpot would have done for me for a promise of no reward.

39.

For the first time in twelve months I was working properly again and I was surprised how fulfilling it felt, despite the employers. I now had a thorough working knowledge of Martins Fleet Sub-Continental and what we were trying to sell. It wasn't photocopying and for those few weeks I was a lot less ashamed of my job. Barrow had obviously had a word with Tim and our big meeting for 28th January became me having a chat with Tim about how to put together our legal solution. I still did not have a clue what the corporate information channel meant and how that related to the stuff in India but I assumed that Tim would put me right on all that. I decided that my tack with him would be to talk about the original proposition based on my original business plan, then bring in the India stuff and then to ask him to tell me about the corporate information channel and to seek his advice in pulling it all together.

The meeting scheduled for a 4 p.m. start actually started at 6.30. It was Friday night and Tim was tired and had no interest in being there.

"I understand that you're targeting law firms with my Indian set up," he opened and I said yes and told him how fantastically well suited to a legal sale it was and how excited we all were about it.

"That's great," he said, "just what I was hoping to hear, tell me all about it," so I told him again about how excited we all were about it.

"And Derek & Mammery is already near closure?"

"Tim, that would be a dream start. The boys have done a great job there." What I should have said was that I didn't know anything about it, that nevertheless I wrote the proposal and that it would have been much better if I was involved. Instead I praised Chamberpot for my work.

"How do you get on with all that technical stuff?"

"Well it's quite straight forward really, no real barrier to selling, and all pretty well established. You must have been very impressed with them?"

"Don't ask me I don't know anything about it," he said then laughed his head off.

We went on about India and MFS as he referred to it and what a super bloke Joe was. Did I know he had a weakness for casinos and shagging? Which I didn't.

Then he said, "What's all that got to do with the corporate information channel?" Which was my question. So instead of saying, "that's my question," or saying, "what is that all about because nobody has been able to explain it to me?" I said, "I think we can tie it in very well because, for example, out-sourcing a word processing function is key to managing core corporate information for law firms," and I went on, telling him why MFS was so brilliantly suited to the aims of his new marketing initiative. It became more and more absurd because he didn't understand all my references and circular arguments so I made him promise to wait for my presentation to him which would make it all clear.

"We're all depending on you Hector," he said while yawning, and then he said, "do you want a pint?" And I felt obliged to say yes, even though I promised to meet Caroline and her friends for dinner at 8 p.m.

As we left his office he said, "Seriously though Hector, I need to see this legal proposition soon. I want it signed off by the end of next month. Agreed?"

And I said, "that suits me. Agreed."

On the way to the pub he said, "oh by the way Hector, what's this Social-Lite business you've been working on with New Media?"

"Aah you know about that already do you? It's a decent little opportunity through a friend of mine at the company. I'll bring you up to date with it next week."

"OK but don't fuck about, we've already spent a lot of money on the account. I want to pull the plug if it's going nowhere."

"Yeah, no problem Tim. I'll give you all the detail in the week."

I felt flush in the pub since I'd sold the car during the week. It seemed to be worth about £7,000 so I sold it for £5,500 cash. My intention was to replenish the short fall on my account and buy some postal orders to pay off my SpreadBet.com liability then to give the balance to Martins Fleet and tell them that's all I could get for the car. They wouldn't know any better. Anyway that night I had the money on me so I thought I would stand a few drinks for the Friday night crowd. It was their money after all. When it got to 10 p.m. it was just after too late to make it up with Caroline so I left a oner behind the bar and went to redeem myself with her.

To make it up to her and her friends for arriving late I settled the bill in cash. They thought I'd had a winner and I didn't put them right about the misapprehension. It did me good with Caroline to make her think that I picked up every now and again. It's funny when you gamble but everyone thinks you always carry a large wedge yet it's the hardest thing in the world to manage one properly. When I had my first ever job as a runner in a proper West End hotel the lobby boy who was about seventy and a proper gambler told me this one day from the side of his mouth, absolutely sincere, "Son, son come here," I went up to him sideways and he said, "never lose your wedge. Never." I said, "thanks," and carried on. I didn't realise what he meant until

215

about fifteen years later. Money doesn't attract money. The number of wedges I've had where I thought that I would never have to go to the bank again.

They all go eventually but those that are nurtured, topped up and gambled and lent with prudence stay a while. At first they just disappeared on me and with those early ones towards the end, when there hasn't been a winner for a while, they run out like the sands going down in an egg timer. Suddenly you can't even stand a round of drinks and it's no use recalling casual loans then.

That's why it's always best to gamble from a wedge, when it's gone it's gone and you can disappear for a while with it until you are recovered enough to come back. It makes you realise that a lot of money is not a lot of money. You become a little more fearless and you learn to take it in your stride. And losing two hundred pounds cash is much better than losing two hundred pounds on credit. At first it stings but that helps you get your levels right. You soon come to know where your personal limits lie, it keeps you in charge and you get used to the big figures eventually. After a while a big number doesn't sting. There are no nasty surprises. Cash is cash and cash is king. There's no arguing, you've got it or you ain't.

Get a good wedge together and it feels like you'll never have to draw a salary again. A good well managed £5,000 could, in theory, be the same £5,000 they bury you with. Not a lot of people know that.

40.

February was spent at my desk. I batted my presentation backwards and forwards with Declan to try and include what my instinct told me was correct and what I knew of Martins Fleet Sub-Continental and what I could make out about the corporate information channel. I didn't enjoy the job but at that stage I was recognised as having but one role and I stuck to it. Other than that I was interrupted frequently by Joe Spud Head and infrequently by Big Dog Moiragh who had taken over responsibility for sacking Patrick. One day Patrick caught me on the telephone and he said, "I think something very fishy is going on and I thought you should know,"

"Go on," I said, "what is it Patrick?"

"Well," he whispered, "they are doing an asset audit and they are going into the finest detail."

I thanked him and felt bad that he was watching his own execution and I also realised that of all the times to sell my car and casually give them fuck all for it on the quiet this wasn't the right one, so I kept all my ill gotten gains and had a few hundred to myself to support the wedge for Cheltenham. It was only a few weeks away.

Scottish Robin also became a feature of my life. "Tell me again what are the names of the main departments of a law firm. And litigation means when you go to court right? And would you mind looking up the Top Five law firms for me, it's for my report see, and where does that information come from?" And so on and so on. Usually the same questions, he couldn't exactly turn around and present his report without knowing that sort of information.

The worst by far though was Joe Spud Head. He'd got in the habit of coming straight to my desk when he was free and making free with me. Who did I know here, who did I know there? Did I know he had a great contact at Linkearlers? He used to say to me, "come on lets do it, do you have his number, lets call him," and I used to have to say, "no, I am not allowed."

"What do you mean, lets do it," he would say, "Tim's behind it, we're selling," then I would say we've got this thing called the corporate information channel we've got to sell our services behind that I can't just go and ring up who I want."

As the month went on he lost more and more faith in me until in the end he treated me like a clerk and called me to his office if there was a specific piece of information he needed about something. Finally at the end of the month a great lead came in from a contact of his to out source a big word processing department from a mid-size firm and by then he'd lost so much faith in me that he took William Attenborough and Chamberpot off to close it.

On the day they went to do the sale I went in to see Declan to do a bit of straight talking with him. I wish I could say that being a pain in the arse like that was part of the grand strategy but the truth was that I felt that I was being treated badly. A genuine grievance.

"Why was it," I wondered, "that I was hidebound by the corporate information channel and people like Joe and Pisspot could go out and sell what ever they wanted however they wanted. Would Tim criticise them for a non-compliant sale if they came back with the deal? I was supposed to be the one that added credibility to legal sales not Pisspot, who as far as I could see was just hanging in there for commission. And why was I still excluded from the Derek & Mammery sale?"

He chose to pick up on the last point rather than any of the others and I kicked myself for not using the Prime Minister's Question Time technique: one clear question at a time, each one demanding its own response. The power of a diatribe is all very well in its place but it often serves no purpose and I should have only said Pisspot once.

"Hasn't he handed that over yet?" I'll have a word with him."

"But I seem to be the only one that has to follow the strictures of this new marketing regime I can't find anyone else that knows about it, let alone uses it to sell anything."

"That's not true," he said.

"What?"

"Go and ask one of the girls in marketing if you're having difficulty with it."

"It's not that I'm having difficulty with the concept."

"You're not now? That's good."

"Well it is, but that's not the point."

"Hector, you're saying you don't want to do it but I'm telling you, you do. Forget about these sales calls that are going on at the moment, I'll have a word with Joe and make sure that you go on them from now on."

"Thanks Declan," what a weak, prick I was.

"I really do want to stress, Hector, getting it right for Tim is the only thing that matters. Just concentrate on that. Have you got the latest draft of the PowerPoint presentation?"

"Yes, I have."

"Good, Tim has kept his and Gerald's best personal contacts for you as soon as the presentation is OK'd," Gerald was our esteemed chairman and when he said that I felt like a sulky teenager.

"Thanks again," I said and I left.

41.

After I read Declan's email to say that the final non-negotiable date for my presentation to the board would be Friday 10th March, I opened the next from Scottish Robin to see that the tour of Scotland was confirmed for the week, Monday 6th to Friday 10th of March and it sort of implied that I was going to be there with him all week. Apparently there were twelve appointments. And so I hadn't done any work for about ten months and suddenly I was committed to two things in the same week. I decided the lesser of two evils was Scottish and I rang him to tell him that I couldn't be there. You couldn't say that he was pleased but he was very nice about it and said he'd have another go at turning around and saying something to the clients so that it would be set up for the following week.

 Declan called a progress meeting with me a week before the big day and I lied and said that it was going very well. All I'd done at that stage was to give myself a crash course in PowerPoint so that I could edit the standard company presentation into something that made sense to me. I hadn't actually started any of the editing at that stage and the truth was I hadn't really started trying to properly understand what the presentation I'd been given was all about.

"I've got a couple of dates for you to pencil in your diary," he said and he looked up like he was about to tell me I had cancer.

"Tuesday 14th March, Managing Partner Linkearlers, Thursday 16th March Managing Partner Maxwell Chest," I was supposed to say, "wow."

"I can't."

"For God's sake you can't be taking more holidays Hector you're never here, you'll just have to cancel them."

"No I'm going to Scotland with Robin."

"What? Scotland, what the fuck's that? We haven't got a strategy for Scotland. You'll have to cancel, it's just not important enough."

While he was going on I realised that we were talking about Cheltenham week. That was far more important to me than anything else, I hadn't missed a Cheltenham for ten years and this year I had big plans to construct an exit strategy bet. I'd just got caught up in corporate bullshit and I had forgotten my priorities and hadn't even thought about Cheltenham, well I had but I'd just put it casually down in my mind as the third week in March, which meant some time in the future. I knew now that there was no way I was going to Scotland but it seemed that there was no way I could get away with another holiday and pretending to be sick at a time when I was right in the spotlight would be very noticeable.

"Please Declan I can't I've put him off about three times already because this presentation with Tim has been postponed so often. I can't let him down anymore he has given firm commitments to everyone and it would be terrible for him to have to withdraw them again."

"But the whole thing is pointless and we're supposed to be opening up a new market here. This is very bad timing Hector. What the fuck does he think he's doing? Leave it with me I'll talk to him."

I prayed that he wouldn't take him to task and cancel the tour, that would be the only way I'd legitimately get to Cheltenham now. At the same time I couldn't, as I wanted to, call Scottish and tell him that I was only available for Monday since he would turn around and tell Declan if he confronted him about it. I had to leave Robin to fight my corner for the tour to go ahead and to turn around and tell him that I was only going to be there on Monday nearer the time. I didn't hold out much hope for Robin against Declan I just had to hope that he turned round so often he bored him into submission.

I'd just trust to luck and make sure that I went to see Scottish in a few days time to see if it was still on. Or better still I'd ring him up and get him prepared for Declan so that he would be ready for him and also so that I could overstate his anger so that later on when I withdrew my labour down to just the Monday he would understand. Then I had to hope that he didn't cross paths with Declan again before we left, or turned around and saw him if they were on the same path..

What I would do would be to overstate the importance of my presentation to Tim on the Friday before the tour and then say that we had presentations dependent on it the following week if it went well, then I could confirm to him that I was indeed required by Tim just before the trip. I'd ring him after the presentation the following Friday night.

42.

Truth be told I didn't think about Scottish Robin again until I was getting on the train with him at King's Cross the Sunday before Cheltenham week. I'd spent the entire time in the run up to the presentation pre-occupied by it and the entire time since in a state of shock at my behaviour while I was giving it. I was still in something of a trance when I ran into him. Normally it would have caused me a massive amount of stress to tell him some bad news at the last minute but it didn't bother me that day. I delivered it with an air of resignation. When I told him that I would only be there for the day on Monday, I simply tagged on that I had to return to the office because I was in serious trouble and had some important meetings to attend. In a very real sense I was in serious trouble in that I was about to lose my job although that had been my aim and it should have been a liberating experience. It was just the utter shame of how it had come about that haunted me. That and a constant nagging worry that I would be sacked and lose my deal meant that I couldn't get it out of my head.

I didn't really remember much of the meeting in word for word detail, just an all pervading sense of shame that I'd carried with me since. I remembered the odd thing and as time went on certain other specific things I had said came back to me. As a result the train journey to Edinburgh was interspersed with my cries of despair. I had to pretend to be asleep to excuse the more voluminous cries but when I shouted out, "no innki-pinninkis," as we left Newcastle I had no excuses left. Scottish asked me if I was alright and he told me that I didn't have to come if I didn't want to but I assured him that I was OK. I was going to have to make out I'd been in Scotland for the week when I got back and I needed at least one day there around which I could build the lie. We didn't go out to eat together when we arrived. I went to bed early and I got the idea that he was happier spending some time on his own too.

By Monday morning I was feeling a little better although by no means out of the woods and I thought that I did a reasonable job of convincing Scottish that he was looking at a new man over the breakfast table but when he disappeared to "make a few confirming calls," as soon as we'd finished, I couldn't help but think that he was making last minute alterations to make allowance for my condition.

"There'll be no need for the computer," he said on the way to the first of our two appointments that day, "we'll just talk with him." Perhaps he knew something about my presentations by then or perhaps he knew that the recipient wouldn't understand it.

Our meeting was with the Director of Corporate Services and it turned out that he was the one that ordered the stationery and made sure that the central heating worked. He wasn't exactly my market but I was glad of that as all we did was to sit about and chat for an hour or so. Then Scottish and I went for lunch. By then I was coming down and I was thankful to him for setting up such a soft meeting for starters. Over lunch I was finding my feet again and I started to talk to Scottish in nearly normal human terms again. We should have only had one pint but I persuaded him into having three and as we started the last one I finally sensed that I was fully grounded again. A little bit of beer euphoria and I plucked up the courage to be frank with him. I wasn't sure whether he'd already checked in with the office on the state of my behaviour, as it happened he had, but I confided in him that I'd lost the plot on Friday and I needed a few days on my own to recover and begged him not to turn me in while I took a few days off. He promised he wouldn't.

The second meeting was even worse. Whereas David Crosby had been a Director of Corporate Services, Dougal MacTaggart was a Practice Manager. That meant that besides the central heating and the toilet paper Dougal sat in on partners' meetings to take notes or something and that made him think that he was twenty times our intellectual superior. We were the photocopying people and he was a Practice Manager at a law firm. He was thick and proud of it.

We had decided on the way over that it was probably not necessary for me to show him the new presentation. We fell back on an old one that Scottish knew well and my role was to elaborate and draw out the explanations of the general into specific legal applications. From the outset he had a false view of his superior intellect and he sneered his way through the presentation.

"You're speaking very much about electronic aids for lazy lawyers and that won't go down very well here," he said as soon as we mentioned the word technology.

I told him that we had implemented a system similar to the one described at Maxwell Chest, to which he said: "we don't throw money at gimmicks and we don't fall for flashy salesmen."

I tried to find some common ground with him and I asked him what was the computer system they used.

"We have some computers of varied marks, we don't show any particular allegiance to any supplier," he assured me.

"But no system as such?" I asked him gently.

"System?"

"A computer network."

"Computers networked together. That sort of system?"

"Yes, that's what I mean."

"One word Mr. Somes. Bugs."

"Bugs?"

"We take a realistic stance on the danger of bugs and we refuse to be prey to them."

I didn't say that he refused to be part of the real world too like I might have done had the meeting taken place a week before. Instead I just looked at Scottish and made a gesture with my eyes like, "let's get out of here." He was smart enough not to delay in taking the bait and within fifteen minutes my Scottish tour was over.

My train wasn't for a while so I took myself off for a pint at a couple of pubs in Edinburgh and I was glad to have a few of hours to myself to reflect. It was cold and after a while I realised that I was drinking my eighth pint of the day. After the beer supported come down of the day suddenly I'd tipped the scales a little bit the other way. I decided to set off for the station and put the Scottish tour behind me.

43.

When I got to Edinburgh train station it was getting on for 7.00 p.m. and I was cold to my very bones but I could put up with the hour or so until the train arrived. I was tired and cold and hungry and I was delighted with my decision to go first class so that I could have a proper meal a bit of comfort and a sleep. I'd be home late but not too late that setting off for Cheltenham the next day would be compromised in any way.

The train arrived after about twenty minutes and there was something about the way it limped and spluttered in that meant all was not right. It certainly wasn't. There was no first class, that had been cancelled because the adverse conditions had put the scheduled train out of service. About the only fucking time in my life I could afford to and had the desire to go first class and it was cancelled. How unusual for me. I got into the cold unlit carriage that had been re-commissioned for one night only. There was going to be no buffet that much was obvious, so the only thing to do was to go to sleep and hope that I woke up in King's Cross five hours later. I didn't take my coat off, it was so cold and I had the feeling that this might be one of those trains that never warm up. I was right. I dug my hands into my coat pocket and wrapped it round me as a blanket.

There was no way I could go to sleep. For a kick off who the fuck is it that invented head rests? What the fucking hell are they but a nuisance? They don't rest your head, they make you sit with your head leaning forward at the most uncomfortable, unsustainable angle. Who the fuck commissions them? They are in every car, every train, often found in lounge furniture, they are in every office, every aeroplane, every public waiting area. And they are all exactly the fucking same. THEY LEAN FORWARD. They do not work. The people that design those things must have never, ever had to use them. It is transparently obvious the first time your head ever comes into contact with one of those things that they are absolutely unfit for purpose, they do not do what they are supposed to do. They don't work. They do not rest your head, they get on your fucking nerves, they drive you mad, they make you feel like breaking everything that is breakable in sight. They make you hate the Twentieth Century and for that matter the Twenty First too, they are completely fucking useless contemptible items. They are neither use nor ornament. They were probably invented by some fucking cunt that conducted some customer research first and put his trust in the answers giving to him by the fucking useless wankers that can be bothered to respond seriously to things like that. Either that or some fucking public body run by arseholes that neither have a clue about nor do they belong to the world that we live in, invented them for health and safety reasons and have insisted on making us all suffer for our health ever since. I can imagine that the first version of headrests were perhaps acceptable but they were expensive to produce so institutions like British Rail were allowed to make cheap versions of them "because the safety element was so important", so that today we end up with something that is ridiculous, uncomfortable, of no safety value whatsoever and would be rejected by everyone if they had anything like a choice. I tried to go to sleep with my head jammed between the seat (the headrest) and the window and I woke up about every 30 seconds.

Well actually I was first jolted out of my semi sleep sooner than that by the public address announcement. It came in at about 400 decibels. I didn't have a fucking clue about any word that was said. Maybe I heard "Attention please" but I couldn't be sure. It was absolutely indecipherable, just a load of metallic noises. But not something that could be ignored. It was a violent noise that forced you to listen. It went on and on, not a recorded message, an ad lib one from the guard, or perhaps he was our customer service representative, I forget. It was a foul and abusive and unnecessary intrusion into my life. It gave me no information whatsoever. I was simply assaulted by the noise. He clicked the microphone off and relief descended on the carriage. We had collectively responded like we were having our wisdom teeth extracted and we all noticed the sigh of relief as the message switched off as it ended. Within no more than 45 seconds he started again. It was like being tortured. I think I shouted out "please stop," but I can't be sure. It was as if someone was drilling into my ear. What the fucking hell was he trying to achieve? What was he saying? If it was important enough to say it twice why didn't he make sure that the PA system worked? So that we could hear what he said? In the old days he would have walked through the train and told us all face to face nowadays he was forced to deliver the message efficiently, which meant telling everyone at the same time through a PA system that didn't work. The fucking pedants that managed him would have insisted on him delivering the message that way. That the PA system was like inflicting torture on the recipients was unimportant, that would be a surmountable hurdle in the matter of delivering information efficiently to the customer base. That was just an Information Systems department issue and they would get that right eventually. As for them in Customer Communication or Health and Safety or wherever the fuck their stupid made up career resided, they had discharged their duties by distributing an inaudible PA message. They would probably call that service.

"Part of our enhanced, all class service, includes immediate communication on all matters of importance to our valued customers."

We weren't passengers we were customers, we knew that – we'd be told so often already. We chose to travel from Edinburgh to London by train with this service provider because all the fucking hot air balloons and tug boats were fully booked on that particular night.

How could anyone that had actually bothered to listen to that absurd and violent assault on our senses not want to stop it? When he next put the microphone down he didn't switch it off. Feedback built up and within a few seconds an excruciating high pitched whine was delivering undiluted misery to every one of us. I put my hands over my ears and cried out for mercy. Sometime later we were back to silence. I imagine one of my fellow customers, nearer to the guard, and with a little more will to continue living than me had gone and told him to switch the microphone off. I think that they must have also told him about the volume of his previous messages because within ten minutes he was back on again and this time, despite being unbearably loud and the last thing you wanted to hear in a semi-slumber, it was actually discernible. He said: "thank you for your patience ladies and gentlemen, we are very sorry that you have had to suffer these conditions at the present time. The weather has upset a great deal of our planning and we have had to substitute the current train in at short notice. That does, unfortunately mean that we will be without a buffet car, unless we can pick one up in Berwick-Upon-Tweed and we are doing all we can about that at this moment and if we can provide you with a buffet at that point we will of course do all that we can to make that possible at this time. If we do we will be able to provide you with hot and cold drinks and a limited range of sandwiches, crisps, cakes and biscuits, and we hope that we will be able to do this by the time we reach Berwick and we are doing all we can to do this at the moment. We are sorry to report also that the heating is not working and we are doing all we can to bring this into operation as soon as possible but we regret that we will not be able to do this before we reach Leeds. So please rest assured that we are doing all we can to get you to your destinations as soon as possible in as much comfort as we can. As I say we expect to be able to offer you a buffet on reaching Berwick which should be within a short time now, where we will be able to offer you hot and cold drinks, sandwiches, crisps, cakes and biscuits. Thank you and have a safe journey, the next station will be Berwick-upon-Tweed."

Within no more than 15 seconds he came on again "The next station will be Berwick-Upon-Tweed, we thank customers for their patience while we try to pick up a buffet car" and on he went. He probably said a variation of the message about 4 times. In the end I was shouting out "Shut the fuck up," it wasn't one of those where I wondered whether I was speaking out loud. I was conscious of shouting out. I was being driven mad and I could stand no more and I didn't care who heard.

Eventually he shut up and after about half an hour of bumping and grinding and shunting and forwards and backwards we set off.

As soon as we set off he was on again.

"Welcome to all those customers that joined us at Berwick-Upon-Tweed." There weren't any. "We would like to announce that the buffet car is now in operation, serving hot and cold drinks, sandwiches ....."

What was wrong with him? I knew that he had to follow company rules but didn't a little bit of personal pride or common sense or something tell him that what he was doing was entirely inappropriate? Didn't he know that his barely audible high volume announcements only served to further alienate an already pissed off clientele? Didn't he know that we didn't give a fuck about a buffet car and would have preferred to have been left in peace to go to sleep? Didn't he know that his announcements would have been better delivered in person where he could have seen if someone was asleep and ignored them?

The truth was he probably did. I knew that from my job. He was probably a normal bloke who wanted to do a normal job and he was turned into an arsehole by being forced to observe the terms of a service level contract that meant nothing to him or his passengers. It only meant something to his manager and the pricks that ran his business. Just like I was supposed to preside over contracts that said things like there will be a fax run to all floors every twenty minutes, so he had to read out idiotic statements that he would have preferred not to and we would have preferred not to hear. Although I classified him as a twat I started to feel sorry for him, and I decided against bollocking him when he came round to check my ticket.

Within ten minutes he was on again, "I regret to announce that your driver has been taken ill and will be changed when we reach our next destination which is Newcastle station."

We were in that fucking station for an hour. The driver taken ill? How often does that happen? How often am I travelling home, desperate to be at home on nights like this? Answer: as often as the driver is taken ill. It was worse than misery. It was worse than anything. It was an endless, unendurable, solitude. It was like being in prison in Siberia. At that time then it felt the same as forever.

It was well past 9.30 when we finally set off again. The train was fuller for having stopped at Newcastle and I was glad of the warmth they brought to the train. Not that I was pleased while they got on and off the train wondering whether it was going to set off or not. If anything the mood lifted slightly with the near drunkenness of the majority of people that got on there. It was early enough for them not to be pissed but there was a definite mood of having just slipped another in before the train. One bloke was pissed. As we pulled out of the station he was shouting: "we all agree Arsenal are cunts," he'd changed the lyrics from the well known, "we all agree Arsenal are bastards," or wankers, which scanned and could be said to be something of a self-mocking re-working of the original. His didn't and he rejoiced in the irony of the unexpected ending. He loved it so much he could hardly sing it for laughing. The only problem was he couldn't understand why nobody else found it funny too. In the end he was shouting out, "laugh you boring wankers, you're frightened of laughing, laugh." Finally he said, "Mebbies this'll make you laugh you fucking arseholes," and he pulled the communication cord.

We were about twenty minutes out of Newcastle station and god knows how long until the next one. We just sat and waited. Those of us that had been on the train since the beginning sat there in silence. Me I just locked into a vacant trance. Unhappiness felt like this. Someone who was slightly bolder or perhaps hadn't quite given up on the notion that life was worth living confronted the drunk. They said, "you fucking twat," and the drunk said, "go and fuck yourself." Really we should have just slit his throat. That's how it would have been done once. It wasn't so much that we live in days where anti-social behaviour was tolerated out of fear and apathy. It was more that it was let go out of despair.

It was too cold to go to sleep and the carriage had been brightly lit since we came to a stop. All I wanted to do was go home. I wanted to be in my bed. I wanted to be alone. I didn't want to share my miserable solitude with all those miserable bastards. The human race. It was such a fucking ugly disagreeable thing. The way to think about the human race is this: imagine all the new clothes for sale in all the clothes shops in all the world. Then try to think if you have ever seen a member of the general public that looked well turned out. Take my point? I knew from my own experience. Brand spanking new outfits looked tired and shabby after one wear or one wash. New clothes that promised so much turned out to be ill-fitting and didn't go with other new clothes. Expensive things looked cheap. Cheap things looked Third World. We all looked so utterly down trodden, cheap, awful, undistinguished, same, grey, ill, unhappy. Drones. Everybody just accepted the misery of their real lives. And most people got on with it. I didn't. I detested the ugly fuckers and I hated being one of them.

The Police arrived after about forty five minutes or so. Something like that, I had ceased to care. I'd been in an alarm pulling situation before. What happens is someone, previously the driver in my case, goes through all the carriages until they find the illegally pulled communication cord and then they re-set it and then the train sets off again. Perhaps proper trains were different but we had to wait for the police to arrive and for all six of them to walk through the carriages looking at us all. Then some massive technical issue arose and for a while there was a lot of serious talk about having to send for an engine to pull us into the next station. I nearly started crying then. The train set off again after about an hour and a half of delay.

We went at about 10 miles hour when we finally set off and it seemed to take several hours to get to Doncaster where we waited while the carriages were decoupled and re-joined endlessly. Eventually our friend came onto the PA to say thank you for our patience, I don't know why I certainly didn't have any, and that now we would be pleased to know that everything was in order and we would be making all due haste to Leeds from where we would change trains so that we could finish the journey in warmth.

After about twenty minutes the train stopped again. Our friend came on to tell us that there had been an incident. Not that it hadn't been incident packed to date. I interpreted it as the first suicide. With all due respect to the driver he went reasonably quickly to our next stop after the announcement. It was an unscheduled back water station when we eventually pulled in but the police were waiting for us. Just before they boarded two girls came running through the carriage. One of them sat next to me and tried to look all nonchalant while the other carried on. A few minutes later the police came through with, as it turned out, the steward from the buffet car. The steward? I was so desperately unhappy I couldn't even be bothered to angry about that.

"That's one of them," he said pointing to the girl next me. He was a bit one-eye-in-Wigan and at first he seemed to be pointing at me. The girl just ignored them like they weren't there and so it was me that felt obliged to answer.

"What have I done?"

"I think you know, sir," said the first policeman obviously mistaking his cross-eyed pointing too.

"Well I don't fucking know," I shouted at the top of my voice.

"You'll find yourself in even more trouble if you carry on in that tone," says policeman two.

"So it's an offence to shout at a policeman now is it, you poor sensitive fucking wanker?" I said that too loud too.

"Right that's enough, get off the train," says policeman two and the third policeman started to make towards me to assist me off the train.

"If you touch me I'll burn the fucking train down," I said, which I shouldn't have done really because at that stage I was in trouble and I was only really saved by the timely intervention of the steward.

"It's the girl that committed the offence," he said and I was secretly very relieved that he piped up when he did.

"I ain't done nowt," she said,

"Sir," says the steward, "I can positively identify this as one of the two girls that robbed me bar," warming to his task as an upstanding member of the community.

"No I didn't," said the girl, threading her arm through mine, "I've been with my boyfriend all the time, apart from when we were fucking in the toilet."

I think because I had been obnoxious she thought she had a chance if she weighed her lot in with me, especially with the implied term of an after-incident shag for not turning her in.

I looked round to find a sympathetic face in the carriage but that had seemingly evaporated after my outburst. I thought that I was expressing anger on behalf of all of us but really I just looked like another dickhead contributing to the continued torture.

"Is that right?" said policeman one.

"No," I said, "it is not right."

"OK love off you come with us" and as she got up to leave she put her head about two inches from mine and I thought that she was going to kiss me to reinforce her false alibi but instead she just hissed at me:

"You fucking tosser."

The sad part of the incident was that I had puckered up for the kiss.

Then before she'd gone she reached down and squeezed by balls really hard.   I convulsed in pain. And she shouted back to me,

"see what you missed you fucking yuppie,"

Then the third policeman says to me,

"you too, you'll need to answer a few questions too."

I could hardly walk because of the pain in my bollocks.

"Come on, we haven't got all night, this train's late enough," he said it to me but it was designed for everyone to hear.

I felt sick and ill and I couldn't walk properly and I felt wronged because if anything it was his fault that I was in the condition I was. I couldn't think of a decent response, all I managed to say was, "Rue de Balzac."

Getting me of the train was a pure act of revenge, he made me stand out on the platform in the freezing cold while they dealt with the two girls and finally when they had been all buttoned up and put in the van he turned to me and told me to grow up. He did it to make me feel like a cunt, which I did, but also so that it was me that had held the train up for another ten minutes when it could have been on its way. I tried not to look at anyone when I got back on board but I did catch some glances and they made me feel like it was me that had been responsible for the entire disastrous night.

I tucked in between head rest and window and tried to sleep until Leeds.

We were immediately ejected from the train when we arrived at Leeds station but there was no new train to get onto. Our friend the guard, our fine upstanding steward and driver just vanished into the night and none of us had any idea what to do. As a mob we hunted down anyone in a uniform and eventually found someone locking up a waiting room.

"Do you know where the London train is please?" said a determined little old man.

"You've had it pal, long since gone."

"No the replacement train for the one just gone out of service."

"Listen my friend, there's no more London trains going from here tonight."

"No but …" I started, prepared to tell the whole story, but the little determined man just took my arm and said, "lets try somewhere else." I knew then he knew that I was volatile and mad. He had suffered the same nightmare as me but with a silent steadfastness. I on the other hand had shouted out and nearly got myself arrested and we were only at Leeds. I swallowed hard and went cold inside as well as out. It's a price I had to pay, this realisation of the real me. Like I woke up a little more each day.

There being no instructions, no staff, no trains, no notice boards and when you could finally actually do with one, no PA announcements. And many platforms. For all we knew the last train that had been put on for us had come and gone again without us. As a result we just stood there on the platform waiting for something to happen. It was snowing heavily and freezing cold. I wasn't angry anymore. Just empty. Incapable of feeling or thinking. But too tired and cold to sleep. I tucked my hands under my armpits put my chin in my chest and tried to hang on. I had a sense of very cold air coming up my trouser legs and thought that I should do something about it but that it would involve moving and surrendering too much heat from my current position. I thought of Physics class when we were studying specific heat capacity and I imagined a great burst of hot dry air being released from my body as I opened my arms. That thought prevented me from moving for what seemed like twenty minutes or so. Eventually I broke the spell and I bent down and tucked my trousers into my socks, then resumed my robin redbreast position. I was reciting that rhyme to keep me going, like my gran used to do when we were walking home in deathly cold weather.

The North wind doth blow
And we shall have snow
And what will the robin do then poor thing?
He'll go to his barn
And keep himself warm
And tuck his head under his wing,

And sometimes you said poor thing again at the end. I loved that little rhyme, it warmed me inside. I loved the half rhyme with barn and warm that you could only get away with if you had a broad Up-Cumberland accent like my gran and granddad. I said it to myself about half a dozen times. Then I started crying.

Sometime later a train pulled in on our platform and as we were the only sign of life around we presumed it was for us so we got on. Nobody checked who we were or explained to us what the train was we just got on and it set off straight away.

It was warm, the lights were dimmed and I settled into a sleep. I wasn't looking forward to waking up again shortly afterwards in the middle of the night in Kings Cross but I just accepted any offer on the table at that stage and was glad of the most meagre of comforts. Needless to say I was woken by a PA announcement just as I was losing consciousness. It said:

"I am sorry that you have had to suffer a very difficult journey this evening. This replacement train will take you without stopping to Milton Keynes and Stevenage. We hope to have you there as soon as possible. And once again we are very sorry that you have had to suffer considerable delays this evening."

He didn't say Kings Cross. That was for a good reason, the train wasn't going to Kings Cross. Apparently it was too late by then to go that far and we should have thought ourselves lucky that they had found a train that would go as far as Stevenage. That meant that we would arrive at Stevenage at something like 1.30 a.m. with nowhere to go and nowhere near home. There were probably about seventy of us and there would be some competition for the only cab still in service.

As it was it was actually worse when we arrived. It wasn't so much that it was Stevenage, it was more that on this particular night, as we left the station we were met by the police and blizzard. Not only were there no taxis, the whole area had been designated a 'disaster area,' well I could have told them that, and what this meant was that nothing was going in or out, no hotels were accessible, nothing. The policeman told us that they had opened the Leisure Centre for shelter and just presumed to start taking us there.

I couldn't take any more. I just said no and started walking. I didn't know where I was going and I didn't care. I sort of half hoped I would perish before I came back to my senses. At one stage I decided to walk to Cheltenham during the night. Then I thought better of it and decided merely to walk to London. Then I had a brainwave to walk to the M1, that would probably only have been a day or two away. For all I knew I was walking in the opposite direction but I didn't really care if I had to walk the wrong way round the globe to get there.

I trudged and trudged. I knew it was the wrong choice but the station was soon long behind me and I wouldn't have been able to find it again if I had wanted to and it would have been deserted anyway, everyone would have long since been shuttled off to the Leisure Centre. I had done this so many times in my life, just set off without any idea where I was going. I knew I should've thought about it first, but something just compelled me to get going and work it out for myself. Just to get away from the rest of them really. And there I was alone, cold, lost, late and regretting not taking the safe option. I walked for a long time before I saw any sort of road sign at all and when I did it pointed one way to a name that sounded like a suburb. A suburb of Stevenage? Jesus. And the other sounded a bit like there may have been a bit of commerce at the end of the road. Then I realised I could have had a nice lift to the Leisure Centre off the police and gone on my search for taxis and other life forms then. What an arsehole I was. I had ended up in the middle of a housing estate and I had no clue where to go and what to do. Then, too late, I had a proper think about the options.

I was re-buckling after taking a dump behind a privet when a car stopped next to me. I was too old and fat to be interesting to paedophiles and if he'd seen me shitting surely he didn't have sex on his mind, even if he was weird enough to have me on his radar, so when he said do you want a lift I just said yes and got in. I didn't tell him that I wanted to go to Islington until he'd pulled off and when I did he said he was not interested and started to slow down. It was only a ruse to get more money because as he slowed he said that he would have to charge at least £50 to go that far. To make sure I said "If you promise not to talk I will give you £80." And with that I was home by 4.00 a.m. I put my head on the pillow at 4.15. Bliss. When I woke up it would be Cheltenham and reality would be suspended for a while.

44.

I was perfectly capable of sleeping in until mid morning, fully justified on the back of a late night, particularly where I was a innocent victim in suffering the late night. But Caroline put paid to that. I don't know one other man who having got to bed late wouldn't sneak into bed without disturbing the bitch, or getting up unusually early and be happy to get changed in the dark for fear of waking her up. And I didn't know one woman that wasn't prepared, in the same circumstances, to make as much noise as possible. The routine for her was to put on the central light as soon as she came back from her shower and thirty seconds later to put the hairdryer on for about ten minutes. I don't know whether she puts it on at full blast or whether those fucking machines only go at full blast all I know is that sleeping is over once they start. It's like the harshest alarm clock and it can't be turned off. I was at that stage where I couldn't wake up but it was impossible to sleep. By rights I could have been indignant, not to say allowed to shout out, without redress, something like, "shut the fuck up you ignorant selfish bitch," but I had the feeling that I was being given the cold shoulder treatment, there was just something about the way she was stomping around a decibel or so louder than normal for 6 a.m. and I was sure she had the hairdryer on turbo charger. There was something aggressive about her silence so I felt obliged to say something neutral.

"What's the time?" I knew perfectly well what time it was.

She turned round to talk to me revealing her Bay City Roller fluffy bob – why the fuck do people use those stupid machines to dry their hair?

"I thought we were going to Cheltenham?"

"When?" I said, deliberately misunderstanding her.

"What was all that bullshit about getting in early and being prepared?"

"It was bullshit."

"I know it was. Well I haven't done it for you. And you've got about ten minutes according to your great forward planning or was that bullshit too?"

"Give me a break my life is hard."

"Yes we never stop hearing about hard it is Hector. It's hard for everybody around you too if you ever stopped to consider them."

"Look I had about the worst day of my life yesterday."

"What again? And so soon after the last one."

"Jesus, just be nice I haven't done anything to harm you."

She went silent then and went back to the turbo charged wind machine. I shouted out, "It makes you look ugly you know, you nasty cunt," confident she couldn't hear me.

"What was that?" she said clicking it off. So I said,

"We're supposed to be having a few days off together don't let it get off to a bad start."

"Look you've got five minutes left, get ready and I'll reconsider."

"You're too kind to me sweetheart."

"Where exactly were you?"

"Stevenage for a large part of the night."

"Oh," she said, sending her features into sharp relief again. She knew that Franck's horrible wife came from Stevenage and she thought we'd all been out on an impromptu beano, but she didn't have the nerve quite to accuse me.

"It's a long story," I said, "I'll tell you in the car."

That didn't please her and I resolved to live in horrible conditions until she knew the actual story, which by that time was bound to sound made up.

"Fuck it." I thought.

I hadn't packed and my careful pre-planning of rig outs for the three days suddenly became three bundles of the bare minimums, four days worth of underwear, two pairs of shoes, a suit, a casual outfit, consisting of trousers, pullover and three shirts, and a car coat for all purposes, smart, formal and casual, weatherproof and not too ponce to go to the pub in. I was quite glad I had to rush because dressing for Cheltenham was always an ordeal for me. I would never know whether I was dressing for warmth, to look stylishly country, to look urban and cool. I tended to take down the clothes that would serve for all these aims but somehow managed to wear a bit of all of them at once. I set off in moleskins, Paul Smith wool polo neck, which had bobbled since I first owned it and looked like it came from a jumble sale, suede shoes, cuffed and dirty and a suede jacket. In theory it fulfilled a few Cheltenham requirements: reasonably stylish in an urban gambling sort of way; could be warm to a point, although I new it would let me down when I needed it most; plenty of pockets for kit and money. And although in my rush I forgot to bring a scarf or sunglasses so that I could top off the outfit I was reasonably pleased that I was properly kitted for the first day. Until I caught a reflection of myself in the gents when we got to the Little Chef. Then I realised that my jacket, trousers and shoes were old and shiny; I was far too fat to carry off the look, and could even have got away with the slightly distressed look if it had all been hanging off a slighter frame. As it was I was hot, red, greasy, unkempt and very puffy through lack of sleep. I looked like a cross between Frank Worthington and Elvis in the Vegas years.

We stopped at the Little Chef because we had been making good time and as long as we were in the small village 15 miles outside Cheltenham where we usually stayed, by ten o'clock all was well. As that was more likely than not we decided to have a refuel at the Little Chef near Junction 14. I liked Little Chef's because they were old and naff, and well, little, and so utterly different from a motorway services station. I needed a stop to get a look at the Racing Post and have a little reflect. In the last 36 hours the ample studying time that I had set aside just hadn't happened and now I was behind the clock. I had less than 5 hours to go and I needed every spare few seconds I could soak up.

As we walked in we were stopped by "our Manager" David.

"Good Morning ....." he lisped, his Little Chef baseball cap sitting on his ears, leaving the tiniest, glimpses of forehead between his brown plastic glasses and the peak of the cap.

"...... my name is David, and I am your Manager at Little Chef. We hope that you enjoy your time with us, we have a large range of breakfasts and lunches available and can I show you to seats, are you smoking or non-smoking?"

We were slightly bewildered at our greeting, it being delivered about three times as fast as normal conversation and being completely unexpected. Especially such a pure form of American service industry speak in the heart of England. At a Little Chef! It broke my heart.

"Thank you, would you like to see the menu, please don't hesitate to ask me for anything you might need, would you like a daily newspaper?" David rattled off as he showed us to our seats. In truth he was one of those people that my gran would have described as having just missed being backward, and it was nothing less than cruel to force him to behave a little more like a vacuous imbecile.

What hope people like him had in building some sort of a life around a shit job had to be lost in being trained to behave like an automaton. There would have been a time when David would have been a cook in a Little Chef. Now he was a Manager and he was living in false hope. He was more enslaved than he would ever otherwise be and what I could not understand on any terms at all was that me, his customer, the person he was serving, the object of his off by heart welcome messages was supposed to feel better to be told all that rubbish. What sort of fucking useless dickheads decided that it is a good idea to do that? Who decides that it improves businesses to talk to people like that? Do they make more money? Do people go back because a half wit has talked to them like a child? Not me. I said:

"Thank you David. I know that you have to say all that crap but what I want is this: I want two cups of coffee, the Racing Post, any other daily newspaper that you are giving away free and I don't want you to speak to me anymore, until I leave. If you do I will give you a £5 tip. Do you understand?"
David said:

"Thank you we have a wide range of coffee products, would you like a cappuccino, filter, espresso, mocha?"

Me: "filter."

David: "would you like milk with that?"

Me: "yes."

David: "would you like skimmed milk, semi-skimmed or full fat milk?"

Me: "Oh Jesus David, just bring me a cup of coffee, just like you would make for yourself. Please don't ask me anymore questions."

David: "Sugar?"

Me: "Please David, I am going to start crying."

David just looked at me.

Me: "No sugar."

He came back no sooner than five minutes later with two luke warm cups of coffee and a Daily Mail.

"David," I said, "Yes sir?"

"this coffee is disgusting and I have been waiting for the Racing Post for over five minutes."

David: "Would you like another sort of coffee sir?"

Me: "Oh Jesus please don't start that again, no I will stick with this horrible coffee. But please give me a Racing Post."

David: "Yes sir, Racing Post, what is that?"

"David please stop talking to me, get me the bill, I want to get out of here as soon as you can manage it."

David: "Yes sir, I hope you enjoyed your meal with us, are you sure there is nothing else you would like today?"

"Yes David I want to go back to earth now. You've had your fun with me, please let me go, I want to leave."

"Very well, I will bring you your bill or you can pay at the till on the way out."

There was no one else in, so rather than wait for David to go and come back again I opted for the till, where one of the girls managed by David served me. I said a little prayer for her.

45.

Within half an hour we were in Bourton-on-the-Water and within fifteen minutes of that, having met Jim and Liz and changed cars, we were in Cheltenham.

Jim wasn't strictly, legally in the true sense of asserting ownership, my friend. He was my dad's. Well my dad's brother's actually, who also double up as my uncle. The way it went was that aged about 24 I tended to meet Jim at the races more often than either my dad or my uncle so that in the end he was more my friend than theirs. Jim didn't stop going to the races like them. In fact he would never stop doing anything good like that as long as he lived. He'd only just given up playing cricket and rugby, he was one of those. He had come to earn a living by ending up with a few market stalls and that gave him the opportunity to carry on a dual career as a nearly pro-gambler. When I first met him he had an old dog of a wife that everyone was frightened of and who Jim had met while her real husband was doing a bit of bird. Now, in my era, he went out with his ex next door neighbour, the exact opposite to the original harridan, a gentle creature called Liz, that had fallen into his lap by her husband not returning after a particularly enjoyable golf tour in Spain.

It had all come about a bit quickly. Not long ago it had been the beginning of winter and I was drafting my non cooperation lists. Then I foresaw at least once a week trips to the provincial courses to hone my personal formbook. It was to be a six month project called 'Preparation Cheltenham' where my job was to be no more than a vehicle to provide funds for my real and alternative life. Before I knew it we'd slid into Christmas, then I'd become accidentally central to life at Martins Fleet. Then one way or another I moved inexorably towards the most humiliating moment of my humble life to the exclusion of just about anything else.

I hadn't been racing round the gaffs, I hadn't spent every lunchtime in the bookies doing my homework, I hadn't videoed the racing on the weekends. I hadn't even kept up to date with the formbook. Jesus I had the worst job in the world, if it was nothing else it was easy. All I had to was to work at half pace and that was more than enough to do everything that could reasonably have been asked of me. Instead I let everybody wind me up and turned the whole thing into a back me or sack me issue. The only contact I had kept with racing was the odd disastrous trip into the bookies to lose a few hundred quid. God I should have had a fistful of ante post vouchers by then, not have been on the losing end of a few grand.

As the weeks rolled by into Cheltenham it came to be that I didn't have the time to devote to horse racing homework. Even though I didn't really work and I didn't really have a proper job I always seemed to have the spectre of some horrible work based obligation hanging over me that occupied my time and my thoughts. Eventually I'd said to myself that I would have a really intensive swotting session prior to the Scotland trip. That was put paid to by the shame of the presentation that rendered me immobile in the 48 hours in its wake. Then even on the way to and back from Scotland itself it still didn't happen. Now, here I was on the very day Cheltenham began with about 2 hours sleep, no studying done and the first race a few hours away. I was a fucking shambles.

When I had first pulled my non-cooperation project together it was based on a negotiated exit from Martins Fleet and the prospect of a boost of funds from Cheltenham to make the decision easier. Now, a sacking on the least possible favourable terms to me was all but an inevitability and I needed to win and big. I dared not think about the desolate wastelands that lie after Cheltenham as a consequence of losing.

It had become something of a tradition to go to Li Due Scale for brunch. Why I don't know. I think I probably went there with somebody once and took it that it was the sort of thing that they did, when in fact they had probably wandered into it randomly. It wasn't called Li Due Scale every year, the current owners had once been to Italy or something. It was only by counting the spiral staircase down to the toilets that you could in truth get two staircases out of the place and only that if you counted the five steps up from the outside as the first one.

Caroline wanted to eat because she'd missed out on breakfast in the Little Chef. I refused because she chose to describe it as 'brunch'. That was the essence of aspirant middleclass to me. Aspirant anything was bad enough. But someone who desired to be middleclass? Oh dear. And anyway you didn't go there for eating. You went there for a livener before racing. All racing people knew that.

My custom was to have an Irish Coffee because that was what I had the first time I went there about ten years before. I had probably been there with about twenty-five different people since and it was in fact nothing of a tradition at all. I knew that there was a lie about the Cheltenham Festival that there is a craic. I knew there to be no such thing. As Franck once famously replied to a New York cab driver many years earlier "we've been all over the Upper Backside but we couldn't find the craic." Well in my time I had been all over Cheltenham and there is no craic. Journalists invent it to get an annual commission. But for some reason that didn't stop me looking and trying so Li Due Scale it was.

As we made our way there I had one of those shooting embarrassment pains when I thought about all the people I had dragged there over the years. It was only a sad little café done in a reasonably contemporary style. It claimed to be a wine bar in the evening but I had never had the courage to go. I was thinking about what a pitiful evening out it must offer as I walked through the door accepting the first flood of disappointment at being there again. There had to be tons of places in Cheltenham, what with the plenty craic, where you could soak up the pre-Festival atmosphere but the only other place I'd ever found was Bella Pasta, and, well, Due Scale kind of beat it. Suddenly a familiar feeling came upon me, I regretted being the one who took responsibility for knowing "somewhere". We'd been wandering around Cheltenham a little longer than we should have because it is a place that I nearly but don't quite know. I sensed the other three getting a little bit fed up with me. Rather than it feeling like I was accommodating the other three, giving an element of leadership to an uninspired team, now it felt like they were somehow indulging me. Like they would put up with it for a while but wanted to get it over as quickly as possible. I started to feel ridiculous. There was no one else in. The bloke behind the bar - the temporary waiter in the franchised café - didn't shout out, "oh no, not you again. We had enough of you last year." Instead he looked like what he was; an agency worker suffering the acid pleasure of the hourly clock running and the misery of an early start.

My heart that had sunk on coming in, warmed slightly at the prospect of an Irish Coffee, a fortifying brew as good for the constitution as a half time cup of Bovril. Me and Jim would have one, Caroline a Bloody Mary and Liz said "will you ask if I can have a very weak tea please" in her pathetic, soppy, girly voice that is her attempt to apologise for being awful company.

"That will probably depend on how quickly you take the tea bag out," I said trying to make a joke out of it so that she wouldn't feel so bad about being useless and instead I sounded like a pompous prick and alienated her a little bit more.

We had our drinks. Then, because it was early, and there was nothing else to do, we had another. Half way down my next drink I was getting impatient. If we had been talking about horse racing at least at semi-pro level I would have been fine but because there were two birds with us there was no horse talk other than at an utterly superficial level. On the opening day of Cheltenham! With no form banked.

I wanted out. I needed to get to the bookies to put on life changing bets and needed time for at least last minute re-reading the form book in there and I wanted to get to the races early to minimise last minute problems, as there always were, when you didn't have proper racing people with you. The drinking dragged and instead of feeling fortified I felt light headed and a little nauseous. I knew that I would have a four o'clock hangover and I'd feel sick, cold and full of piss all day. Then the waiter came over.

"Not having another are you?"

"No thanks," I said without thinking of the others.

"You up for the races are you?" he said with the faintest West Country burr. I was momentarily encouraged thinking that he represented local interest and information.

"Yes, are you interested in racing?"

"I should say, I have bet every day of me life."

"Oh Jesus Christ," I thought. "Oh really what do you fancy today?" I said.

"I should say McCoy will ride a few winners. He's riding out of his skin."

My initial joy had completely evaporated, he was just a loser that hung around in betting shops.

"I think he could ride the winner of the opener," I said drawing out the conversation far longer than I needed to.

"What's he riding in that?" asked the waiter.

243

"Rodock."

"Bloody good horse that, bloody good," said the waiter struggling to find anything more constructive to say but trying to sound like a proper form student.

"I think he needs a bit further," I said knowing that he didn't know what I was talking about.

Liz caught my eye and nodded her head slightly as if to say how impressed she was with my knowledge and it made me feel absurd. It made me think of myself as Franck when I sat next to him in one of those meetings, where he reeled off easy answers to simple questions, his chest bursting with pride, making those little snorting noises because he was so proud of himself. I pitied him when he behaved like that, utterly ignorant of the fact that he was the only one that was impressed, but only a little, I still managed to detest him for his transparent self adoration. Now I was Franck and Lynne was my fawning audience. I responded with a look which I thought showed how embarrassed I was to have got myself into this situation but when I gave it I only managed to feel like I was being modest about my acknowledged brilliance.

"That he might but he'll take some beating," the waiter said.

I went for a lie to round off the conversation, being incapable of discouraging losers any other way.

"I'll come back and buy you a drink if Rodock wins."

"No need," he said, smiling a big moustachioed vacant smile to each of us in turn round the table, "I'll be pissed off me head long before you ever get back here, if that happens."

I suddenly felt responsible for that twat. I had brought the gentile Liz here when she didn't want to come, made her sit and watch while me and Jim got drunk at 11 a.m., indulged a tramp in front of her when everyone was desperate to go and made her listen to things like "I'll be pissed off me head long before you ever get back." I felt low. We made an excuse and left.

The next stop was Ladbrokes. Everyone had been in favour of going there on the way to the races. We'd agreed on our way into Cheltenham in the car that it was a good idea but really it was just to indulge me and Jim. All that I could think of though was that Liz and Caroline were going to be subjected to the same discomfort while they waited for twenty minutes or more in a betting shop full of people like the waiter. I tried to focus. I had cobbled together a two grand wedge and I was determined to act like a pro for once.

"I can take a reverse out of that and bounce back," I was saying to myself as we walked the long road to Ladbrokes.

"I haven't got any ante post vouchers," I thought.

"Why not? What's the excuse? If it wasn't that I had my time taken up all day with a job I hated I would be on top of my game."
"Bullshit,"

"How can I not find time out of a job I hate to follow my interest in racing? Jim would. In fact a dozen people I could name could. Instead of spending all day thinking how unfortunate they were, they would use the opportunity of working in a shitty useless job to fund their fun, which they would do in working hours".

"I just don't know how to be cool about things."

"What's that?" said Caroline.

"What's what?"

"I thought you said something."

"No. I was day dreaming."

"Please stop," I told myself.

We walked into the bookmakers and Jim and I said to the women to write down what they wanted to bet with the time next to it on a betting slip and that we would come back shortly to turn it into a bet. That was to buy some time.

I went into the heart of the shop and faced what was for me a normal Cheltenham conundrum. I knew well the idiocy of having multiple bets but I could not get the thought out of my mind that if I connected with a winner early in a multiple bet it saved re-staking on the horses after that. I wanted to cover the good things for the week and have a decent bet for the day too but I knew to do this to a level worth winning anything would set me back £300 which meant that when the first two races went against you, you were on the back foot at a very early stage. To do anything less there was little point, I might as well bet in singles and play up any winnings.

I regretted not taking a professional interest through the year and having a fistful of ante post vouchers already. Me, I preferred losing £500 on a seller at Folkestone. However, there were only three good things that week: Bacchanal currently trading at about 5/1 for the Stayers; Istrabaq - that wasn't a betting proposition at my level; Edredon Bleue perhaps and Monsignor which in the way that only gamblers knew I wanted to oppose. And I suppose, in a way, Florida Pearl was sort of a Gold Cup horse in waiting. In the end, despite the doubts, I decided to combine them all minus Istrabaq in a tenner yankee, £110 all in, covered just in case.

I also allowed myself a tiny indulgence of £80 at 25/1 Paul Carberry to be leading jockey for the meeting. That bet would keep me company when my others were going astray.

We arrived at the course and a horrible recurring nightmare began. Instead of meeting with the usual crowd of bohemians, drunks, journalists, ex-jockeys and old friends like I was brought up to think that Cheltenham was all about, we started by waiting for Jim to sell his spare tickets, wondering where we were going to watch from, where we were going to find something to eat and whether we would find a bar where you could buy a drink in less than the time it took between races, and if we could where we would drink it. Just like I did every year and just like I said I would never do again every year.

This year Jim had organised seats and although that without doubt would put us outside the ambit of any craic whatsoever it would make the whole experience, short of being comfortable, endurable. Although for some reason, what that amounted to actually was two too many tickets and one too few seats. So rather than get in and soaking up the atmosphere and enjoy it for once, I ended up doing what I always ended up doing; waiting for Jim by the turnstiles for him to buy or sell tickets.

The truth was I had long since lost the joy of the hustle and bustle and sense of anticipation in the crowd, these days I saw them as coach loads of pissed obnoxious peasants who knew no more about racing than I knew about bingo. I looked around the Ring and saw all shapes and sizes, young and old from coach trips who had set off from their local pubs at 6 o'clock that morning and cracked their first beer at the end of the street. Smarter ones wore leather jackets from catalogues and smarter still had thought to tear the racing page from the Daily Mirror to bring with them. Others had come on the trip in shirt sleeves, drunk by lunchtime. I looked at them then, hands in pockets, bent forward against the chill wind blowing up the course. The end of the world would look a little bit like that.

I was hoping for a final hours study and composure before battle commenced. With fifteen minutes to go I heard Jim's voice behind me, "there you are, come on Hect,"

"Jim, at last, come on there's hardly time for a bet,"

"oh," says Jim, "I've had mine on the way back."

"Go on," he says, "be quick."

I said, "don't hang around for me Jim, just give me the badge for the seat."

"I couldn't get another," he says, he wasn't sorry or anything like that. "you're a big lad, just sneak in for this race and we'll sort it out after."

"Righto Jim, see you later."

At ten minutes to the off before the first race on the first day of Cheltenham the ring is an impenetrable wall of ignorance. I went to the first board I could find and had £50 each way on Silence Reigns without bothering to search for a better price and set about fighting my way back to a seat. I sneaked in through the security cordon and edged onto a seat with someone's bag on it.

Silence Reigns qualified for the bet on the basis that it had a similar profile to my last winner of the race, Tartan Tailor, it didn't matter to me that the profile hadn't thrown up a winner since. I was a man of principle after all.

I waved to the girls and Jim, six or so rows behind. "Look at those fucking bitches," I thought to myself, "they haven't got a fucking clue about what's going on why the fuck do they come with us? What do they get out of it? Why do they have to be involved? Why don't they have their own interests? Why don't they fuck off and leave us alone for one moment, one tiny moment of unadulterated fun on our own?"

"Cheer up mate you haven't lost anything yet," said the little bantam weight sitting next to me. Had I spoken out loud? I gave him a grinning shrug and looked down the course with my binoculars.

Then when they came into line a feeling of complete satisfaction washed through my body. Joy. I knew then that I had adopted this singular method of going to ruination for life.

My horse didn't win but Paul Carberry's did, which was an entirely satisfactory alternative outcome. Besides my bet on him, he was riding Frozen Groom in the next and that was my nap of the day. If that went in I was off to a flyer. He might not stay the minimum trip in top class but that was a risk I was prepared to take at 12/1.

I decided that this was one of the bets I was committed to at the meeting and I made an adrenalin inspired decision to increase the stake to £200. I decided to act quickly to get some time to myself so I told the others that I was going into the ring early as it had been so difficult for the first race.

"I'll see you here after the race," I shouted over my shoulder. By which I meant the overcrowded bar-cum-betting shop behind the stands, which was made all the more unbearable by the hundreds of people who were prepared, not to say delighted to stay in there throughout the day without leaving their seats. I could not come to terms with that. What difference these people found between sitting in a betting shop within Cheltenham racecourse and one outside it, I had never been able to understand. Unless it was just the thrill of a an outing on a charabanc that brought them out.

I went into the ring alone and felt momentarily liberated. My own man. The ring was no less impenetrable for the race being twenty-five minutes away. To get a bet on you had to push and shove your way through a human barrier six people thick. Some had put their bet on and were coming back, others like me were on their way in, large numbers of them were just standing watching the prices vary and others were dedicated pickpockets. There was a total lack of dignity in the way you were forced to behave at Cheltenham. Nevertheless I looked earnestly to beat 12's and it couldn't be done, it was even trading at 8's in places. I took the 12's and started to fight my way back out to the fresh air again. As I shouldered and shoved my way through a sea of uselessness I heard a PA announcement. Paul Carberry had given up his rides for the day. I reassembled myself, straightened my hair, brushed myself down, took a deep breath, put the bet in the right inside pocket where betting slips lived, that had a button to close it and put the extra money I had taken out by mistake back into the inside left pocket, that had a zip fastener. It would be safe in there but in live conditions it was hard to put the wedge back together so after a while that pocket would just be a jumble of notes and later on it would become impossible to take the right amount out without grabbing a fistful of random notes and try to sort them out in plain view of the public in the wind and rain.

But Paul Carberry? He'd just ridden the winner in the first. It couldn't be right. I didn't know what was going on. Was it because of the horse? Was that pulled out too? Everything was run of the mill normal, there was no sense of intrigue, scandal or of a sudden and unexpected big news story. Although 90% of the people within a 50 yards radius of where I was standing would have no clue and no interest even if it was. I was free for thirty minutes so I set about finding out. I headed for the nearest haven of horse racing intellect in the racecourse which I decided was the Press Box end of the paddock. As I arrived I could see the declared runners and riders displayed on the old mechanical apparatus that was common to all racecourses. The way it had been done since there had been racing. I loved the way that even at a meeting as prestigious as this the names of the jockeys were painted in black onto the white steel nameplates in a variety of typefaces and point sizes. Against number 11 it said BJ Geraghty. I looked around for somebody to ask but nobody looked likely either to know or prepared to give the information if they did know. I stood there mute, angry and confused hoping that the expression on my face would draw in a nearby sage to explain everything. None came. After 10 minutes of looking up at the jockey's names down at my race card, waiting for more PA announcements to add further clarification to this breaking story and coming to realise that I was the only person in the race course that cared about the story, I realised that I was alone in knowing that Frozen Groom should win on form. Eventually I just asked the first person that looked like he might know.

"Has Paul Carberry given up his rides?" I tried to sound like I was a big grown up punter, a Face, one that they had just happened not to have run into yet.

"Yes, the back injury."

"The back injury. THE back injury? The one that everyone was talking about? The one that was declared in bold print next to the prices for Champion Jockey for the meeting?"

I berated myself for being so useless and uninformed. My security bet, the punt that would keep me company when all the others had gone wrong, was already down. My single crumb of comfort was gone after one race.

I started "Why me-ing". Then wandered away from the paddock when a country-set lady with a posh court jester's hat looked at me as if I was mad.

"I must have externalised," I thought as I dragged myself off.

"I could stop a fucking train if I backed it to arrive at the next station," I thought that too or perhaps I said it. I don't know I was rambling.

I shuffled about looking for a place to watch the next race and headed towards the lawns in front of the main stands.

"I'm a loser and I've started losing," I was saying to myself. I knew Frozen Groom couldn't win.

I settled for a place about 100 yards on from the winning post, just as the lawns started to slope and stood there alone to watch in crowded isolation.

Did my bet directly cause the fall of Frozen Groom?

Yes.

Would he have won if he stayed up?

Yes.

Did he lose because his regular jockey Paul Carberry wasn't on him?

Yes.

Did I cause Paul Carberry's injury by backing him to be the champion jockey at the meeting?

Yes.

Therefore, would Frozen Groom have won if I didn't exist?

Of course he fucking would you cunt.

I had one more short-listed proper bet that day, Take Five in the last. I had £200 at 15/2. Produced perfectly at the last by Norman Williamson, I sat and waited for the "at least I'm straight for the day" moment and instead I watched him run out of gas up the hill and finish a gallant second. I suddenly felt cold and lonely. Hungry, desolate, desperate. £700 down for the day. A feeling I knew well settled on me, a strange mixture of self loathing and feeling like the victim of the worst sort of bad luck. I wanted desperately to get my money back and if I was offered a black or red spin for the rest of my wedge at that moment I would have taken it. I walked like an automaton to the main gate thinking what awful company I was at moments like that. A proper person would have put his losses behind him and taken a real interest in his wife's view of the day out. "Had she backed any winners? What were her high points of the day?" I should have been indulging her with the sort of questions I was asking myself.

"Be big about it Hector," I told myself.

What did she think? My poor long suffering wife, she was as much punished by my gambling as I was myself.

I made an effort to talk to her and she seemed to be surprised to be talked to. I had created a miserable mood that would be hard to lift with a few superficial questions. The conversation was proceeding staccato and she knew that it wasn't a genuine conversation as much as I did. We were heading towards the newspaper seller at that main gate. I bought two copies, one for Jim, and I couldn't help but to turn straight to tomorrow's runners. I carried on the staccato conversation but I wasn't concentrating on it at all after thirty seconds. As I walked, head down, occasionally glancing upwards to correct my direction a warm, comfortable, confident feeling came over me. I couldn't wait until the next day.

46.

The sport over, we adjourned for the craic. Bourton-in-the-Water was about 15 miles from the racecourse. We stayed there having long since learned that such little craic as there is, it is not found in Cheltenham itself. As a younger man I would have ended the day at the course with a couple of pints at the Queen's Hotel, which is always packed to the gunnels for about two hours when it suddenly empties as fast as it filled up. Nowadays, we travel as a unisex group and things like that just aren't done. The birds pretend to like racing but they haven't got a clue. They don't even know what's won as the winner passes the post, even when they've backed it. The truth was they're bored by it and put up with racing as an indulgence of their male friends.

As we walked through the first car park, I suggested going for a pint at The Queens but it fell on deaf ears. Liz, who daren't directly say no said:

"How far is it? It isn't a long way from the car is it? It's a bit cold."

and Caroline said, "I was hoping we could have some dinner soon."

It was their turn. We had been indulged all day. They didn't realise that they had no business being here, turning our craic into a Cotswolds outing. Jesus next time we could skip the Gold Cup and go to Blenheim Palace instead.

The fifteen minutes drive back I spent with my nose in the next day's card, occasionally checking a point of information on form with Jim who drove. We arrived at the cottage and then waited for about an hour for the girls to get changed.

"That is why we have time to drink pints of beer," I whispered conspiratorially to Jim.

He just rolled his eyes. He knew. He hated it more than I did, but he could stand it because unlike me he spent his life as a single man. He had the lads, the golf club, the rugby club, never missed an important race. He had his own time and space. He knew how to manage his woman, to make her feel appreciated while he did absolutely what he wanted. He had what I would never have: balance and judgment. With me it was the exact opposite, if I manufactured a few moments away during a weekend it always felt like I'd been sneaky and deceitful. It's a little bit to do with the way you fall in love. If you make people idolise you, you create a dependant. I just didn't have the judgment to train my girls to expect me to disappear at weekends to do my own thing. I always owed them me. I was bound to give myself up to the relationship when I had any free time because I was the only thing both of us loved.

We wandered as a four into the village about ten minutes stroll away. At the first pub restaurant, Liz said:

"this looks nice," by which she meant it had a sign saying home cooking and had an open fire.

To me it looked like a nationally franchised operation in an old building. It had laminated menu cards and it stank of saturated cooking fat. However all I wanted to do was eat pie and chips and go back to read the form book, so I said:

"looks great to me."

I knew that talking about horse racing would be absolutely verboten that evening, after all "we've spent all day talking about horses, can't we change the subject for a little while?" To which the honest answer was "why don't you stay at home or go on your own fucking holidays." Nevertheless I knew that it wasn't on to spend the evening as I wanted to, as it should have been, so I was all for getting it over and getting home as soon as possible. It wouldn't be so easy, Caroline who is about 30,000 leagues more sophisticated than Liz was not prepared to go in. However, instead of saying "I don't want to go in there, it's cheap and nasty," she chose simply to look at me with a certain look, a concentrated look which conveyed upon me the obligation to politely refuse on behalf of both of us. I understood the look well enough and threw a deaf ear on it. Eventually Jim decided to be gallant and broke the silence with a:

"lets see what else there is,"

A sort of half hearted agreement to go into the next pub with meals was made. It turned out to be a proper pub that was managed by its owners, which pleased me, it had a range of meals from scampi and chips to chicken kiev, which pleased Liz and it also had a restaurant area with people eating steaks which pleased Caroline. The clientele of the pub were instantly recognisable as the ticket touts that operated at Cheltenham. They were having a whale of a time, "just like we used to," I thought.

After dinner of deep fried something I was at the bar. I was alongside a drunk tout, one I recognised as having once bought a ticket from him. I fought the temptation to tell him how I knew him because I remembered clearly how he had taken the piss while I was buying the ticket. That day the conversation had gone something like:

"I'll buy and sell tickets."

"What are club tickets?"

"What are what mate? They get you in the ground."

"How much?"

"To buy or to sell?"

253

Silence.

"I take it you're buying Sir?"

"I want six club badges."

"Fifty-five quid."

"So how much for six."

"How much? You work it out. One costs fifty-five. You want six. Multiply fifty-five by six. It's easy you work it out."

"Well I mean …."

"I mean you're wasting my time. It's three thirty for six."

I gave him three hundred and thirty pounds.

The tout was youthful, say early thirties, long hair, leather jacket, sufficiently worn to look stylish, jeans, smart suede boots and everything assembled over a lean body. And he looked like he enjoyed life, he accepted what he had and what he was and was making a good job of living with it, I was insanely jealous of him. Until we had a conversation.

"You alright cocker?" he said.

"Yeah thanks."

"Going tomorrow?"

"Yeah are you?" I thought I'd pretend I didn't know he was a tout.

"Sort of mate.

"What do you fancy for the Queen Mum?" I thought I'd try and speak like my new friend.

The tout had to re-focus to look at me, then did one of those involuntary dips of his head, like when you are falling asleep on a seat with a headrest.

"Flagship Thingy," I realised then he was very pissed.

"Oh why's that?"

"He's the favourite inni?"

254

"Oh…."

"Can't be beat according to that bloke on the telly……. you know that bloke on the telly….."

"John McCricrick?"

"Yeah, yeah. No, not him." He kept dipping, talking at me through his fringe.

"John Francome?"

"No the poof, you know."

"Oh yeah."

"I loved the Queen Mum you know."

"Oh yeah, it's a great race."

"No the Queen Mum."

I ordered my round.

"Hey Henry, do you agree?" He was talking to me.

"With what?"

"Queen Mum. It's important to love your country. You know? Do you love your country?"

"Yes," I couldn't think of a longer answer. I could only think of "yes" or "no" and I thought it would be better to say "yes."

"Hey Stuey, this poof doesn't love his country. Fucking Yuppie."

"I do actually."

"Oh I do actually," he said mimicking me.

"I've got to take these drinks …."

Stuey looked at me and signalled with his eyes to get going while his friend was distracted trying to get the weight of his head balanced in the middle of his shoulders.

It's not just that I was denied the craic but it was an evening spent with fucking birds in mid-Cheltenham, looking over my shoulder in case I got a good hiding from a ticket tout, £700 down on the day. That had to be over-punishment. I started to think that the wheel of fortune was starting to turn my way again.

47.

The Wednesday promised better, for a start it would be just me and Jim, the girls were to spend the day shopping. But it didn't start well. Me, in the way that only people who bet too much know, had taken against Monsignor, the good thing in the Sun Alliance, the good thing for the meeting. It had come to Cheltenham with seven career runs, seven wins and not often by less than 10 lengths. But I thought I had detected a chink. Had I been a bookmaker rather than a hapless punter, I would have laid even money for as long as there was money in my satchel. As I wasn't I simply had £50 each way on something else so it didn't hurt too much when Monsignor dismissed the opposition with impunity. Besides he was 1 out 1 in the £10 yankee.

In the Queen Mother I felt I had to stay loyal to Edredon Bleue. The loyalty had cost me dear last year and I did not want to sit and watch him make amends this year without being on. Truth be told, Edredon had not acquitted himself well during the wet winter but the ground had come right now and in any event with a regular winning winter behind him he might have come to the race as favourite. At 7/2 with his favoured ground he felt like value to me. He was, in that he won, but he won because Tony McCoy put his head in front on the line. I thought of the waiter in Li Due Scales perhaps he wasn't such a bad judge after all.

I was off and running - and had two out of two in the yankee – but more importantly I was on the first stages of the upward sloping graph like sales charts that you see in business plans, the "hockey stick" as we'd learned to call it when we were selling up. I found my next winner in the Form Book – I didn't have to waste time on the convoluted procedure for saving seats, or queue up for drinks, I just sat and read the Form Book. What's Up Boys had been paid a nice complement in the first. I went into the ring to have £50 each way at 40/1 and the bookmaker said to me, "I hope you come back". I did. The horse had half the field in front of him at the last then sprouted wings to win in the shadow of the post. I thought it was churlish to complain about a 40/1 winner but I had no idea I had won until the red and black silks flashed by the post in the dying strides. I missed the entire process of hopelessness, turning into untenable optimism, into just a little bit of hope, of confidence, of a massive surge of adrenalin of euphoria, of doubt, did he win after the post?, of "I've won" of the wonderful opium velvety warmth of victory of £50 each way at 40s. But I was happy to accept that life was on the up.

Next I went Lord Noellie, the horse I fancied, without the favourite at 11/4 rather than 9/2 that was available generally. Lord Noellie won which made the insurance pointless but betting him like that I was tempted to have more on, £500 rather than £200. It was time to buy a bottle of champagne.

At that stage I stood about £3,500 up for the meeting, which whilst being a welcome advance from the previous day's position, was only the very beginning of the exit strategy punting I had to bring off and that thought brought with it a sudden cold shiver of reality. Nevertheless I was going in the right direction and I told myself to stay positive. A positive attitude would bring its own opportunities.

"Have you noticed?" I said to Jim, "there's no birds here today, there's no problem with seats, no running for drinks, no putting £5 each way on the Tote, no going to the paddock. And we're a few grand up. You work it out."

I got talking to the bloke next to me, a Scottish man that I recognised from the Hotel I stayed in last year. He was staying there again that year too and I was a tiny bit jealous as I talked to him, he came as one of a group of about ten mates and they stayed up late getting drunk and talking about horses just like I used to do. But when he talked horses he knew what he was talking about. He was just that little bit more connected with the game than me and he talked openly about what he knew.

The last race on the card that day was a bumper which Willie Mullins had a habit of winning. He had a few runners one of which, Tuesday was high in the betting, "but the news is", said my new friend, "that Mullins thinks more of the other horse, Joe Cullen." That was the one being ridden by Charlie Swan. The conversation had taken place before the second race but I had banked it. I had been given many tips before and they rarely won but there was something about the earnestness with which this information was imparted that stayed with me. The race came and I went into the ring to find 14/1 and had a go with £200 each way. Coming up the hill Charlie Swan sat swinging on the bridle behind the favourite and you could have heard a pin drop. Well you could if it weren't for me and a few Scottish men who nearly lifted the roof off on our own. He went away up the hill and as he did there were enough Irishmen on too to make a big noise.

The day was over and I was £7,000 in front with tomorrow still to come. I didn't have enough room in my trousers to take all the money home so I resolved to leave the Joe Cullen money with the bookies overnight. I decided to wear my car coat with deep zip pockets the next day in case it went well.

48.

As we were flush it was appropriate to take the girls out. I suggested the hotel in Stow where I had stayed with Caroline the year before, it was only a couple of miles up the road and I thought that we might meet up with my new Scottish friends.

It just didn't work the same with female company so instead of getting pissed up with the lads we had a quiet meal as a four. They couldn't even enjoy the fact that it had been a winning day. The women were cold, uninterested, tolerating at best and we were in the mood for a night out. We nodded and gave a thumbs up to our Scottish friends who were having a whale of a time at the other end of the bar. As time went on it was obvious that we weren't going to meet up socially with them so I sent a bottle of champagne over. I was £7,000 up and nearly half of that was down to Joe Cullen and yet this act of largesse drew disapproving glances from Caroline. She said nothing but I took her look to mean that she considered it to be a far too excessive gesture.

As the meal ended our new friends came over to say hello on their way out to a pub in the village. There was all the banter and bonhomie of a group of people that have shared the same good fortune, albeit tinged slightly on their part by their not knowing whether we had made more money than them. The group broke up into small conversations and I drew someone I took to be a new addition to the Scottish group, a Londoner if his accent was anything to go by. We talked about what had been and moved onto what was to come.

"What do you fancy tomorrow?"

"My banker for the week is running tomorrow," he hadn't asked me what my banker was but I thought I should tell him. Just like my dad would have done. Too much information, too open, not answering the question I was asked.

"What's that?"

"Bacchanal in the Stayers"

"In this ground?" he said, and in doing so he made me feel stupid.

I had decided to back Bacchanal come what may when I watched him finish second over two miles five furlongs at Cheltenham in January. He failed by the shortest of margins to pull back the good thing Lady Rebecca that day. I knew that he had to improve for the race. It was the three star nap for Cheltenham in my notebook.

"Have you backed him yet?" he said.

"No, but he's leg 3 in a yankee with the first two in. Besides that, no."

"Well just be careful," he said as he moved away.

"What did that mean though, *in this ground?*"

I'd soon find out.

We got there are a reasonable time which gave us an invaluable hour on the Racing Post and the Form Book. I knew that the seat charade was going to begin all over again and I accepted that it was going to be as generally un-enjoyable as Tuesday had been. Still I was up and it was time to kick on. Bachannal Day. I had him in my yankee too. Then a horrible thought hit me. Yesterday's winners. I'd had four: Edredon Bleue, 7/2; Lord Noellie, 11/2; What's Up Boys, 40/1; Joe Cullen, 14/1. A £5 each way yankee on those four would have netter in the region of £150,000. I'd already done enough. That was my chance. God had delivered. I took no notice. Realisation. You rarely did things like that once, twice on consecutive days didn't happen. I swallowed hard and wondered what Fate had in store for me next.

I ignored the Triumph hurdle as a betting proposition, as I did every year, yet by putting everyone else's bet on I found myself watching the race from the lawns in front of the stands a long way from our seats.

As a consequence I couldn't find my party after the race and I wanted to press on to get the Bacchanal situation managed properly. The bar behind the seats was just a scrum of people.

"Why did they let so many people in, the greedy fucking cunts? £100 per day to be treated like fucking cattle." I was probably externalising but I didn't care, I was surrounded by fucking gyppo's who were somehow given access to the bars behind my seats that I had paid a fucking fortune for in the expectation of a little bit of comfort and the tiniest crumb of exclusivity. Every thing, every fucking thing that is ever sold to you in England is somehow flawed. Not so much flawed as just plainly absolute fucking diabolical rubbish. It doesn't matter whether it's buying a daily newspaper or finding a doctor to fix your back, or go to the dentist or getting your car repaired. Anything. Everything. And Cheltenham Festival tickets are as good as example as anything else.

On my third lap of the balcony, the long back corridor and the crowded bar I saw them at the edge of the balcony, I couldn't be sure whether I was in such a bad temper that I hadn't noticed them the first two times or whether they had just wandered out from their seats without a second's thought about me. I tried to stay even tempered but I was on the edge.

"Any good?" said Caroline.

"No," I was looking at my feet.

"Look do want me to bet something for you in this race?" It was meant to be direct but it sounded more aggressive than I meant.

"Oh err well if you're….. it doesn't really matter."

"Just say."

"Err Mmmhh Mmmaahh, what's he called?" she was searching through her pockets looking for the racecard. Then she didn't know what race it was she was looking for. I just stood there and said nothing. I knew she meant Mister Morose, but even though I was desperate to go I punished her by punishing myself. I just stood there mute.

"Mister Morose."

"OK."

"What are you betting?"

"It's Bacchanal's race."

"Oh is this his race?"

"Yeah."

"Anyone else want a bet putting on?" I asked out loud. There were no takers so I made to set off.

"Should I meet you here with the tickets before the race?"

"Don't bother, it's alright".

"Oh err £5 each way," she shouted after me. Like it would be anything different.

I set off towards the ring and came to it from the outside of the stands and found it virtually impassable. I stood on the outside at the top of three small steps down and hesitated. "What was I going to do?" I made to go and stopped myself again. I decided to stand the bet for Caroline, that was one thing less on my mind. I just couldn't quite get it right about Bacchanal. I was between two stools. I sensed the clock ticking, the horses were already out on the course, it was a small field and the three mile start was in front of the stands, time was running out. The official going was good to firm and I just couldn't get those words out of my head. Someone who knew more than me had said that. I had a few quid going on to it from my yankee. 'Be careful' he'd said. 'Be prudent' I told myself. £5 Large at 5's gave me a £30k pick up in 5 minutes time. I could face Monday with a bank like that behind me. No. Yes. I was hesitating and I knew I had gone off it. Definitely Not. It doesn't fell right. I would have a few quid on a fast ground specialist, Silver Wedge. Yes I would do that. Would I? Yes, yes that's what I would do. Is it? Yes. I think. I shuffled into the ring decision made. The PA commentary system announced they were off. I rushed up to the first bookie that hadn't rubbed his prices off and had £50 each way Silver Wedge.

262

There was no point in trying to see the race at that stage, I decided I would just stand in the ring, see a bit on the large screen, see what I could and listen to the commentary and then I suddenly felt very unenthusiastic. I knew I had done the wrong thing. The result was inevitable. As I stood with head bowed in the heart of the ring a cacophony went up around me to urge Bacchanal up the hill. My Bacchanal, my banker for the meeting. Since January. Eleven to two. The horse I came to back, the horse I believed in. My three star nap. I needed to start making life changing bets. I had the horse and the stake and the will and I still didn't do it. I had backed Silver Wedge. That was even worse, I had never believed in the horse. I backed that rather than my banker. What sort of an arsehole was I? Why?

"That fucking London cunt, '*on this ground*?'"

"Why did I listen to other people? Why did I give their views any validity?"

I thought for a moment that my luck was balanced since I was put off backing Bacchanal from the same source that gave me Joe Cullen.

"Bollocks."

"Why do I listen to arseholes?"

When the Form Book came out later it would say "All surfaces come alike to him."

"On this ground?"

There was a steward's enquiry announced and I wished for him to be thrown out so that my vacillation might yet be vindicated.

"I have got £7,000, I have fancied the horse since January and I have £100 on Silver Wedge. What sort of cunt am I?"

I was shaking my bowed head as I wandered back to my seat, drawing deep breaths of despair. I had a pained expression on my face, not of anger more of deep dissatisfaction. I was frustrated and wanted to tell everyone about it. I wanted to wind the clock back. I wanted to have done what I set out to do. It felt unreal, it felt like I could do it all again properly tomorrow, all I had to do was find the right person to ask. I felt empty, pathetic, useless, lacking balls, lacking commitment, lacking courage. I didn't believe in myself. I hadn't believed in myself. I had taken a stranger's view as a better one than my own.

It was over and I had lost. Not just lost a bet, lost a fantastic opportunity.

"Oh Jesus," I must have said it out loud.

I sulked my way back to the balcony.

"He won!" they said when they saw me.

I couldn't bring myself to say that I hadn't backed him.

"Yeah," I said, trying a smile. "I didn't really have much on in the end. Because of the ground."

I felt dreadful and wanted to go home. My enthusiasm for horse racing, betting and Cheltenham had disappeared altogether.

I went and sat down on my own for a while and still in a state of shock I went to watch the Gold Cup at least I had three out of three in the yankee rolling onto Florida Pearl. I lacked the will to work out what it was going on exactly. All I knew was that it was bound to be less than £5 grand at 5's.

I sat and watched Florida Pearl do what he normally did in the Gold Cup, come to the last fence as the best horse in the race and then patently not stay up the hill. I didn't even raise myself up out of my seat as he came swinging down the hill. Looks Like Trouble won. He had been inexplicably bad when I had had a £1,000 on him at Christmas in a worse race. I shrugged my shoulders.

"When you've gone you've gone," I thought.

I had never had a bet in the Foxhunters on the basis that I didn't know the names of any of the horses participating but opting out of the race gave me time for reflection. I took myself off to a remote bar far from the busiest of the crowds with the Form Book. I decided that there were still three races left and that I shouldn't give up.

Aghawadda Gold never ran a bad race. He was top weight for a competitive handicap but his credentials were rock solid. He ran excellently, right up to his form and came third. Minus £1,000.

The Cathcart should be a race of status, the middle distance version of the Gold Cup and the Queen Mum. It isn't and as such it doesn't attract an outstanding field. Novices can win it. There was only one horse in the race, Castle Sweep. The more I looked into it, the more I was struck that there could be no other result. It was a tremendous bet at 3/1. By the time I got to the ring, the 3's had gone, the 5/2 had gone and I just missed the last 9/4 because the philistine's that go racing these days don't understand betting etiquette. You don't queue. I got my £2,000 on at 2/1.

As soon as I did I knew that I had made a mistake. Everyone can't be right. It felt too easy.

The Form Book eventually said "Castle Sweep has been a model of consistency in all his completed outings for quite some time now and this looked tailor-made for him.

However, for whatever reason, he downed tools approaching the third last and his jockey soon accepted the situation."

"It was me." I thought, "I could stop a fucking train."

The last race of the meeting is an impossible two mile handicap, maybe the hardest race of the meeting to find a winner. I was punch drunk and delirious by then. I knew that I didn't have a clue but wanted my money back. I knew a little form and had a cursory dive into the Form Book and came up with something that couldn't win, that had decent form, that wasn't a rag, it just wouldn't win. Nevertheless I had £500 each way on it. It started going backwards three out.

That was it. Cheltenham over. Instead of going home with a wheelbarrow full of money, I had given £4,000 back. I felt hollow. It would take me a long time to come to terms with that day's work.

Over and over I rehearsed my errors walking back to the car park.

"I came to back Bacchanal, I didn't, I had £4,000 on horses I didn't care about." I kept saying that to myself. I couldn't understand how I had let it go so badly how I had let a golden opportunity go begging.

I berated myself for being such awful company for Caroline. Why hadn't she seen me yesterday when I was unbeatable? She only knew me as a sulky loser. Knowing this I couldn't lift my mood, I couldn't pretend to be happy when I wasn't. They all knew, the people with me. They knew I had lost badly and they walked beside me in silence. I knew that they knew a loser when they met one.

49.

I woke up on the Friday morning and it took a few moments for realisation to dawn that Cheltenham was over for another year. When it did I felt cold at the contemplation of what lay ahead. Four hours down the M4 my new life beckoned and as I thought about it for the first time it made me scared. I'd gone into freefall the day before and that made me swallow hard as I recalled the damage I'd done. Even going back to London with 7 or 8 grand was no bad thing. Liquidity was going to be important to me. I'd managed to act like a cunt and give a large chunk of it back.

Jim shouted upstairs, "get that Jackpot sorted out Hector while I get the bacon on."

The Jackpot, the Tote Jackpot was what nearly everyone that went racing had a go at. It meant trying to predict all six winners on the card and although you could have as many choices as you wanted in each race, provided you paid for them, it was hard to win. At a meeting like Cheltenham it was virtually impossible to win. That meant that the day after Cheltenham when the circus moved on to some Gaff track with small fields and rubbish horses there was invariably a massive Jackpot to play for.

The beauty of that for dedicated losers like me was that it provided the perfect come down. A chance of landing an important bet without the full on race by race absorption of Cheltenham. It also meant another throw of the dice and the prospect of that took away the gnawing anxiety that I had woken with.

I persuaded Caroline to enjoy one more day 'en repos' in the Cotswolds – to which her response was simply to raise her eyebrows.

By rights you have no business spending all day in a bookies the day after Cheltenham, particularly in the aftermath of meltdown and loss of control. I was made of different stuff though.

"So you fancy having a proper crack at the Jackpot Jim?"

"If it's worth winning sure, how much is it?"

All that Jim fancied was spending all day in the bookies. He couldn't get enough of it. It was his life's work.

"There's about a quarter of a million carried over, plus today whatever goes in today."

"Could be nearly a million quid. That sounds worth the effort, don't you think?"

I didn't need any convincing. It meant that I still had a chance of not having to turn up at work on Monday and that was enough for me.

"How shall we do it?" Which was always the question when you were going to have a serious pop at the Jackpot. How many selections. It was important because Jackpots could be expensive. We settled on two or three in each race so that we could have a reasonable stake. That meant somewhere between 64 and 144 bets at £10 a line. Good, a plan.

I dived into the form and one hour later I had a short list of two horses per race and I knew that the winners had to come from them. Nevertheless I had to endure the agony of watching Jim go through the exact same process as me as soon as I had finished. I wished with all my heart that Jim wouldn't repeat the same exercise that I had just completed. I daren't usurp him in his task and rather than say anything I just sat and waited. Eventually I thought that Jim was just reading articles and not form any more.

"Are you ready, it's getting close to the off?"

"What already," he said all surprised. Then he said, "right what've you got?"

That meant another twenty minutes we didn't have going through the why's and wherefore's of our selections. I had to trust him, he had to trust me, we would marry our two ideas together and put the bet on. Simple.

Instead the process of justifying why we had arrived at our selections began. Jesus, I thought I liked Jim because he was a man of action.

"The first race is simple. Only x and y can win," and he said the name of two horses that I didn't have on mine. It was going to be a long process and he didn't have the faintest notion of being behind the clock about him. I was so anxious about the time that I was minded to give in to his choices on every race. It was a pity that I had taken a strong and contrary view in that race and I felt like I had to argue my ground. According to me the obvious chance of the first two in the betting had to be overlooked for Loganlea. I couldn't believe that Jim couldn't see it. It was a typical reading between the lines observation that Jim was much more experienced and better at making than me. In fact it was very typical of the sort of job that Jim had pulled off in the past. It was a selling hurdle and Loganlea had shown some little bit of ability. It had been run in going it didn't like and had been made to look like a non-stayer. But in this company over the minimum at an easy track like Fakenham on good drying ground, it looked to me like this was the day.

In the end I won the day with Loganlea and one of his but I couldn't stand another 6 times through that process. It had already cost us 10 minutes to get that far and he still didn't have any sense of urgency about him.

In the end I insisted and made him agree to go through the rest of the selections in the car en route. We set off at five past two with the first race less than twenty minutes away.

"where exactly is the bookies Jim?" I said in an interval between analysis.
"Oh you'll love it, it's one of those old ones in a back street in Stow."

"Stow? We've got no chance of getting there on time."

"You just rely on your Uncle Jim," he said, winking as he pulled out round a tractor.

Within five minutes of the off we settled our joint selections. The process had gone reasonably quickly because, the first race excepted, there was a large amount of common ground. I could see where Jim was coming from then, he knew that we'd be largely in agreement and could have got an agreed bet out of the way, straight away.

We were still more than three miles away from Stow on country roads, so I told him he might as well slow down because it was a lost cause.

"Aye," he said, "it's probably not one of those bookies that could take a Jackpot anyhow," now he tells me.

"Why don't you ring it though then?" he said, all full of good ideas if someone else was going to do them. I had no chance with my bank account under scrutiny from Caroline and all previous misdemeanours. I had actually closed most of my accounts and deliberately forgotten the numbers on some others.

"I haven't got any telephone accounts," I said, "what about you?"

"Me either," he said, all casual, "least not, one of them sort" by which I think he meant one that would take a Jackpot bet. All of Jim's accounts were held with little independents and blokes that had pitches on the Gaff tracks. We pulled up outside the bookies getting on for 10 minutes after the first was off.

The bookies belonged to another time. It was no more than a converted garden shed, what I had learned to call jerry-built without really knowing why. I imagined my dead grandfather taking me step by step through the construction, breezeblocks, which would be described as the best building material you can buy, probably because they represented the height of technology to him in the 1960's. He would list their attributes: affordable; large; uniform; lightweight and then stress flexibility, good for insulation, easy to pack with cement to make a denser brick. He would round off by saying that they were endorsed by professional builders comparing two imaginary builders one who was ahead of the game using flexible breeze blocks and one who was an outdated old plodder using bricks; "Matey with the cement blocks would have you a house up in six weeks, the other bugger wouldn't have the foundations in then and he'd give you a better a house for it at the end than he ever could."

268

If the example was long or complicated I often became muddled about which "he" was Matey and which "he" was the other bugger. When that happened I just said yes at every pause and hoped I wouldn't be asked any questions.

Then the whitewash cover, why it was better than paint as long as you were prepared to renew it each year, then the corrugated iron roof, which were always called zincs whether they were employed as roofs or fences, or whatever they were made from. Zincs never had a great deal going for them except the price - it was always better to have a proper roof where you could. Zincs were more the roof material for hen huts. Then inside the lino floor, which was really called oil cloth. The oil cloth down in Gibson's corner shop had been there for over twenty-five years and showed no sign of giving up. That's why it was chosen for hallways and kitchens, it took a lot of traffic and it was used where most mess was created.

The counter was open, no glass partition, just as they once were in shops with an access hatch. The top was worn formica, and the front aspect was vertical strips about an inch wide slightly convex and heavily painted such that it couldn't be said whether they were plastic or wood. It reminded me of the larder cupboard in my grandfather's house, I used to drag my hand along making a frrrrrrrp sound as I passed over the curved struts, I recalled its smell, a warm smell of tea, eggs, butter and bread. There was a kettle on the counter and it looked as if the regulars in the shop were a little bit more than clients. I felt like Jim and me were intruding into their snug little private fiefdom. I thought momentarily that they might not have enough money in the till to meet our winnings but I needn't have bothered.

Loganlea had gone in at 14/1 and it rooted me to the spot when I looked up at the screen and saw the news. Jim I knew was less sentimental than me but I still did not feel that I got enough recognition for finding a 14/1 winner, nor enough sympathy for the loss of it, nor enough what-iffing for the Jackpot bet that we didn't get on. A 14/1 winner that would throw a lot of people out of the Jackpot. We would have been one of the few still running. So we may not win a share of a million quid, but the fun it denied us. Just a squeeze God. That's all I want really.

I knew that the luck was agin me, that part of the wheel of fortune that favoured me was just spinning away out of sight and my instinct was to leave the shop but I was with Jim and we had negotiated two to three hours of solitude before we were to next meet the women. Had the afternoon gone to plan I would just have sat in front of the television and watched each leg of the jackpot as it dropped in. As it was because fate had conspired to make us five minutes late, well more Jim than fate really, the exact same analysis on the same races with the same horses took me from enjoying a pleasant afternoon with a fun Jackpot bet into financial meltdown.

I decided to follow the selections made for the Jackpot: that would prevent me being distracted off course to Folkestone and elsewhere and it would mean not re-reading the form over and over.

Unfortunately it didn't quite work out like that. Where there was a fifty fifty, I took the other one. Where there was a good thing that couldn't be backed at odds on I tried to find another to make the forecast. Where I'd been strong on one horse and Jim on another I changed my mind to back his because he was in better form than me, then watched mine win with him on it. Then I went off to the other meetings to try and organise short-priced across the card doubles.

Suddenly it was the last race at Fakenham. I had watched all my selections win in the Jackpot and I was about £400 down. And now suddenly the event that I would in only slightly different circumstances, have been desperate to happen, I now hoped with every fibre of my being that it wouldn't.

I looked at the two final Jackpot selections and couldn't see beyond them. I also needed my £400 back so I chose one over the other and had £300 the second favourite at 7/4 and was pleased to see it come again to 13/8.

In the race he was there but faded like a loser in the straight and finished third. The other one won. I should have backed it. It was the horse I wanted to back. It was the horse I had selected in the morning.

We would have won the Jackpot. It was my idea and I'd organised it. My original shortlist that I did all on my own was enough to win. I'd lost because I included Jim and relied on his contributions and relied on him to get us to the bookies in time.

It was strange how in a distinctly personal pastime like gambling something like the Tote Jackpot always felt that it was to be participated in communally. Someone like Jim did not let anybody else get in the way of what he wanted to do. He didn't give a flying fuck for them. But me, trying to include him and alert him to the possibilities of a great opportunity had fucked myself. In fact it hurt more because I had allowed him to fuck me. Just like that time I'd let Franck give me a lift to a job interview against my better instincts of getting the tube and we got lost and I ended up fifteen minutes late.

"Oh Jesus. Why me?" My breath drew shorter and for a few seconds I thought I had been shot. I staggered out of the shop and said, "No I'm not," simultaneously with the old boy asking me if I was alright.

I got outside and leaned against a wall and started to try and breath more regularly.

"Oh Please God, no more," I was saying that as Jim came out of the shop looking for me.

"Are you alright?"

"Yeah I just came out to look for a newsagents."

"Do you want to watch the last?"

"It's only a bumper isn't it?

"Yeah, there's not a lot of point."

"I don't mind."

"Well we might as well stay for ten minutes we're here now."

"Yeah OK," I said.

I knew that Jim had been winning. I saw him collecting for one thing and he had that air about him like a winner.

"Who wouldn't win in conditions like this?" I thought, "It's easy for any self respecting pro. It's only cunts like me that fuck it up."

The last race was a maiden bumper. There were only really two horses in it and Right to Reply at evens had beaten Native Emperor, 9/4 last time at Sandown, fourth versus fifth, three lengths.

"That was Sandown, this is Fakenham," I reasoned looking for an excuse to back the larger price. "Plus Native needed the race." I had £500 to clear the afternoon's errors. Right to Reply won unchallenged.

Jackpot in. Financial meltdown for Hector.

I couldn't swallow for fear of being sick. I went cold, trembled slightly even, nearly started crying. I couldn't speak.

"You ready?" said Jim all chipper.

I said nothing I just walked towards the door.

"No good?" said Jim.

"Not really," I replied but I hardly got the words out. Just the shaking of the head told him all he needed to know, "did you?"

"No not in a race like that. I just had a fiver on something."

"A fiver," I thought, "this is Jim speaking a big professional punter. A fiver. Why don't I have such restraint? I have nothing on the horses I fancy and £500 on a fucking bumper. Jesus I had nothing on Bacchanal. Oh God I'm ill,. I'm dying."

I was almost too reticent to look up the Tote returns in the next day's newspapers. In the end I forced myself and saw that the Jackpot paid £21,000 to a pound. Our £10.00 stake would have made 36 winning tickets instead of 26 but nevertheless a shared dividend of about £200,000 had been lost. Not a life changing bet but a way down the road towards it. As it was I had lost about £6,000 in two days.

Caroline and I drove home in silence. All I could do was to re-live the last two days over and over in my mind. I found myself repeating that I "had lost control so badly on Thursday and I knew it. Then I went and did it all over again on Friday. I went into freefall." I was suffering from gambling incontinence and that was the last thing I needed with all my other problems. It wasn't just losing my shirt that I needed to worry about.

50.

I didn't have the nerve to go to work on Monday. I knew that my time was up but I was just too fragile having lost the plot so badly at Cheltenham and knowing what I had to face when I got there. I needed a day of recuperation before I could face what was coming. Normally I accepted the slide into reality reasonably easily in the aftermath of Cheltenham via the Midlands Grand National and a few pints on Sunday. It wasn't so easy this time around and I was still in a stake of shock at my gambling free-fall when I woke up on Monday morning. I tried hard to switch my thoughts to the coming problem rather than the one behind me but it was like one of those dreams as you're waking up when you try to cling on to the old good dream rather than the new uncontrolled bad one. Mine was more a matter of switching my thoughts from one disaster to another. An invidious choice they say. By tea-time I was fit enough to eat mash potato, beetroot and grated cheese, which was always a barometer for my morale. I'd unplugged the phone, not listened to my mobile and not looked at our home emails so that I could guarantee some solitude in which to recuperate. That meant that I had no new information to stew on, I had enough with what I already knew.

A couple of glasses of wine later and I was really coming round. For the first time for four days I laughed when I recalled one of the several faux pas I'd made at the presentation a week earlier. And for the first time I told myself that I might be close to my goal of getting out free with my money. A little surge of confidence went through my body and I suddenly felt engaged again and moved out of self indulgent reverie and back into life. "Bring them on, bring them on," But I really did have to train myself out of speaking out loud.

The week leading up to the presentation had passed like the week leading up to my maths A' level, I knew that there were some basic simple things to learn but I just couldn't get round to doing it. There was something about the phrase, "Delivering advantage and business value by managing and improving our clients' corporate information channel," which opened the presentation that I found insurmountable. I found it too long and cumbersome and essentially meaningless. I would have managed better if it was the concluding sentence of the presentation. I could have just said, "therefore ….." as I finished and brought it up at the end. But the idea of talking over it as the phrase built on the opening screen to set the scene and the atmosphere of the presentation, it was just a pretension too far for me and I never really got anywhere near to getting down and working with it. I could usually count on myself to be slightly creative, even with something I didn't care about. A little bit of bullshit got the juices flowing and thereafter an ego charged assault on the work usually happened. This time the spark to start the process never happened. It meant that I went into my make or break meeting with the board unprepared at any level to give a presentation. I was, in a way, quite proud of that as a strategy even up to half an hour before I went in, but as those first screens rolled into action and I had nothing to say, it became the regret of my life. The recurring nightmare of sitting an exam without preparation had now become an actual living, breathing, reality for me. Sure I cared about many other things much more than I cared in any way at all for Martins Fleet but I had never looked so squarely in the face of shame.

The bad start added to my problems in that what micro-specs of confidence I had to call on disappeared, my mouth dried, my voice went up an octave and I became beetroot red. That meant that my intended casual walk through the pro-forma presentation, pointing out its idiocies, inappropriateness, contradictions and plain clumsiness became absurdly inappropriate. But since it had been the only thing that I had put any effort into preparing I had to do it anyway. It was either that or complete silence. I was forced into it too because I had slightly edited their presentation to support my own funnier one. I had reached the stage on that Monday night when I could see the joke in my having changed the headings "Review, Re-engineer and Manage", into "Piss-up, Cock-up and Fuck-Up," and even the point of having done so, not that I managed to make the point at the time. I was going to say that what bullshit consultancies called Review was actually no more than a period of client engagement, getting them to believe in you, making friends; that re-engineering a business was a gazillion light years too ambitious for Martins Fleet and that Fuck-up was the inevitable result. However my killer point was that we had a vested interest in managing their fuck-ups not to say encouraging them. That would reflect well on us. In its simplest form my point was that each person at Martins Fleet should be engaged at each appropriate level in the client company so that we were involved but not responsible for all the client initiatives. It didn't come out like that though and when I recalled the slide that said, "A cat can't kill a dog but could a cow kill a horse?" which I wrote to make the summing up point, I winced again. And the sour taste of a nasty moment came back to me again and stayed. I held my stomach like I'd been shot and I groaned a deep and long, "no," In the end I'd cupped my face in my hands and I was making breathy dry sobbing noises until I eventually stopped because of the smell of cheese. I got up onto my feet but then froze in awestruck terror as I recalled, "The Power of Innki-Pinninkies," to describe Martins Fleet Sub-Continental.

I remembered then that in the early part of the presentation they had been slightly more forgiving before they knew how bad it was going to be. Barrow had asked one of those brilliant questions that demand a brilliant response but where the implication of the question is that there isn't a good answer. It was just a wonderfully observed truism that ruthlessly exposed the inherent contradiction in the premise of the whole presentation. That really was the final crushing blow that meant that I was going to die in front of them. I couldn't think of anything to say at all, so after an excruciating silence I found myself saying, "Vorch sprung der technic," then I just carried on.

The shame of the afternoon would stay with me a long time but of all the hardship that I brought upon myself that day nothing would ever damage me more than the awful silence at the end of presentation. Usually if something was very, very bad you could count on someone to laugh. Or at least one of them to pity you a little bit and to say something about everyone having an off day. But not then, not for me. Nobody said a word. No-one said a single thing, not even to leave them alone while they talked amongst themselves. I just packed up and left in silence. And not a stunned silence either. It was a silent fuming anger. Anger at my gross impertinence and incompetence. That they had paid their hard earned money to me and that was what they had got for it.

51.

My fate was inevitable on Tuesday when I returned to work but I still had to turn up in person and take what was coming on the chin. I made no pretence of it being anything other than my last day and I started packing up my personal effects straight away. I phoned Franck during the morning to confirm what I already knew but he seemed genuinely not to know that I was on the way out. I suppose they didn't know quite how close we were or weren't and they left Franck out of the loop as they would have called it. We agreed to adjourn in Best Pub half an hour before kick-off so that I could bring him up to date. If I hadn't been sacked we could talk about Cheltenham and have a bet on the football.

I went out for a pint at lunchtime and sure enough on my return I was called to a meeting at 6.00 p.m. with Declan and Julian Barrow.

Barrow, the arsehole, actually bothered to go through the motions of a normal sacking, Declan was mute throughout.

"We have been conducting a certain internal debate," he started and I started laughing.

"Aah you can see what's coming then?"

"Yes," I said.

"It's our view that it is not working out. We will both have our own reasons as to why it has not worked out and both sides may feel that they have something to say on that subject but I don't propose that we do it here or that there is any benefit in doing that now. We feel that we have a worsening situation and we want to act now before it gets much worse and our relationship wholly breaks down. I am sure that you are not enjoying your time at work and the relationship we have is not working for us, so we believe it is in everyone's best interest to end it now," he hadn't mentioned "bad leaver" or gross breach of contract or anything like that.

"That's all very well but I have contractual expectations that I need to be assured about," it was the only thing that mattered to me.

"Your contractual rights remain unaffected by this. We have always known that it would be an expensive decision for us to make but we are prepared to make it knowing the cost to us. I acknowledge what you are owed under contract and that there is no way out of that for me and I assure you that I do not intend to seek a way out of it," I couldn't believe it. He went on:

"There are some important documents that I'll get prepared for you that you'll have to go through with your lawyers. I don't suggest that we have a conversation about that now. I'll prepare them then let you or your lawyers come back to me when you've considered them. You can just pick up the phone or perhaps get your lawyers to call me directly. I haven't finalised the documents yet but I expect to do so very soon."

"Please don't keep me waiting for it. You've said that before."

"No, I won't delay. In fact what's your address, we will have that in the records won't we?"

"Yes," and with that I was as good as free.

"You're entitled to stay here to work for the period of your notice or you can go. I take it that you prefer to make a clean break?" He could see the broad smile on my face.

"As I've already packed I might as well go," those little victories still meant so much to me.

"I would just like to say how sorry I am that it hasn't worked out. I have after all been in from the beginning and it is a great pity. I do believe it could have worked but we all have our opinions as to why it hasn't,"

"Yeah fascinating. Have you finished?"

"Yes. I was going to wish you good luck but in the circumstances perhaps,"

"Goodbye. And goodbye Declan,"

Silence

"I said goodbye Declan,"

Then there was a barely audible grunt.

"Fuck off you peasant."

For a moment it looked like he was going to get up and have a swing but he must have thought better of it.

I had them behind me two minutes later.

52.

Franck was waiting for me in Best Pub when I arrived with my box of possessions. I had that, I still had £2,500 from Cheltenham week and I had my deal intact. He couldn't believe the conversation I'd had with Barrow when I repeated it back to him. I still had to wait for the documents I reminded him but insofar as Barrow could be relied upon I had nothing much to worry about.

"A great plan well executed. A total success," he said to me. It didn't feel like that to me but the ends justified the means. He was only flattering me after all. He knew I had a tendency towards the ridiculous.

"What was the clincher, do you think?" And I told him that I had to have finally won through with my presentation of the previous week. He claimed he hadn't heard about it so I told him and as I did then, it seemed absolutely hilarious. He especially loved the bit where I had brought up a slide that said, "Henri Paul wasn't a drunk," Franck liked things like that because he still had a bit of the student lefty about him and he liked an inappropriate dig at the establishment. I didn't find it that funny at all, just shameful, when I'd written it to be slightly shocking, I think, something about not trusting initial perceptions. I couldn't really remember by then, it was as if it had happened to someone else. I knew it would come back to get me some time in the future but then for the first time and perhaps the last I could enjoy the moment. We had both long since harboured the ambition of knowing the job was over and making one more sales tour round the old targets taking the piss and being ridiculous and getting our own back on the pompous and down right disagreeable. My presentation was probably the closest either of us would ever come to achieving the goal. I didn't tell him what cost it came with I just let him admire my bravery in being prepared to put myself out there like that.

"So what now?" He wanted to know. All I knew was that I didn't want him in my life anymore and I didn't want him to cast a light judgment on any ideas I had so I said I had no clue. "Perhaps find a job I like," I told him.

Then we had a normal night in the pub. I said I had to get home and tell Caroline the momentous news that she had no clue about. She was a worrier and she would need reassuring but instead as I'd done so many times before with Franck we kept having one more until the match was due to come on and he said should we have a little bet to give us an interest, so I rang Caroline and told her something reasonably serious was going down at work and that I had to have an important debrief with Franck and I might be a little while yet.

"What do you fancy then?" I said hanging up.

It was only one leg of the League Cup semi-finals, whatever it was called these days. I stopped paying attention after it was renamed the Milk Cup. The home team were 4/9 and it was hard to see them getting beat. When that was extrapolated out into all the other bets available we couldn't find any value in any bet, even stupid ones. Once the appetite was whetted Franck and I weren't the types to give up so in the end we resorted to having a bet on his semi-dormant spread betting account. We'd both been hurt in the spread betting markets before so we proceeded with caution. We had a safe little bet on the favourites going long of their performance. We might not get it right, we reasoned but the damage wouldn't be too great either and if they gave the away side a good hammering there was always the chance of making a few quid. Good. Back in the comfort zone.

The match never got going really and by half time we were bored with it. We'd have probably given up on it but for the enduring financial interest and the desire to know our fate. We started talking and only had half an eye on the match as they neared half time. Then when half time arrived Franck said:

"Oh did I tell you I might have some bad news for you?"

"What's that?"

"You told me you sold your car didn't you?"

"Yes,"

"and did you ever tell them about it?"

"No and it's a bit late now. Why?"

"Well mine basically just blew up the other day and it's going to cost a lot to repair it."

"Your insurance will cover it won't it?"

"No it's too much and I don't want to ruin my insurance by making a big claim,"

"How much is it going to be?"

"I've had a quote for £5,000 or so."

Then there was a long pause. Then he said,

"I'm sorry but I'm going to have to be a cunt about it. It's their asset and I'm just going to give them the bill to pay."

"That could be dangerous for both us," I said. I wanted to say "what the fuck do you think you're doing you stupid selfish cunt." If it wasn't for him and his stupid selfish short-sightedness there wouldn't be any cars to get worried about. If that lead them to the fate of my car, that could ruin my deal, it should by rights ruin his too because he would be a bad leaver too. Except he'd be free to make a new secret deal with them if he was still there. Perhaps he already had. Perhaps they'd asked him for evidence to renege on my deal and promised him a cut of it.

"I'm sorry mate," he said. And like a fucking wanker I said, "well try and keep me informed."

Shortly afterwards I was feeling drunk so instead of going home and leaving Franck behind me forever I stayed out with him. As the match progressed the favourites refused to get on top and it started to draw out into a nil-nil. In cup ties like that you know when both teams decide to shut up shop with about twenty minutes to go to take the gamble on extra time and penalties. As realisation dawned on us we came to calculate the complacency of our safe bet. If it stayed nil-nil, we were losing £2,500 between us, more if one of ours got sent off or conceded a goal. Jesus. Another great decision.

And that is what happened. Then we tried to get a bit back on the favourites at 8/11 for extra-time and that was nil-nil too. We were £3,500 down at the end of the match so there was really only one thing left to do and that was to get our money back on penalties. The outsiders, who had ridden their luck all night were 7/4 to win the penalty shoot-out which looked like tremendous value for an even money shot so we had one last fling of the dice at a £1,000 each. The home side won comfortably, in fact I don't think our side scored one at all. I handed Franck most of the £2,500 I had left and parted never to see him again.

I was too far gone as a hopeless useless gambler to reprimand myself. In fact I laughed most of the way home. In fact I was so relaxed about the situation, when I stopped for a shit in the churchyard I cleaned up with a couple of twenties. The only thing that hurt was that I could have given him the money towards his car repairs so that I didn't have to live with the threat to my deal.

53.

"Come on Hector, you'll be late,"

"I'm not going,"

"Don't be stupid, get up,"

"I'm not allowed,"

"What are you talking about?"

"I've been dismissed,"

"Oh God no Hector, tell me you're joking,"

"No I've lost my job. And with any luck nobody will find it,"

"I don't believe it, what are you playing at? What are we going to do?"

"Don't worry the deal's intact everything's going to be alright,"

"What you've got a cheque have you?"

"Don't be stupid, it doesn't work like that,"

"Well how does it work Hector? How do you know that this famous deal is going to be honoured, because I don't trust Martins Fleet and I don't trust Justin or Julian or whatever his name his and I thought you didn't either, or so you told me the other day. How come you're so confident?"

"I've been assured by Barrow,"

"The man that you told me you wouldn't trust as far as you can spit. And I'm the one that's stupid?"

"He's got no intention of stitching me up, he admitted that he owes the money, on the record,"

"On the record? What were there a team of journalists in the room too?"

"Don't be facetious,"

"Lets see it then,"

"What?"

"Lets see this assurance you've been given,"

"I don't know what you're talking about,"

"The letter or document or whatever it is that says he owes you the money,"

"That's not what on the record means,"

"Oh thanks big lawyer Hector. You'd rather have the word of known liar while he's sacking you, than a signed document would you?"

I had to admit she had a point and her arguing style was faultless.

As she left for work she shouted out:

"Have this fucking disaster sorted out when I get back."

It wasn't sorted out when she got back, nor the next day, or the day after that for that matter. I finally received the letter from Barrow the following Tuesday and it was something less than I had imagined. It said nothing about my deal or the guaranteed payments, it only said that we had agreed to terminate my employment and told me what money I would receive as notice payments and holidays not taken, although that didn't amount to much. Shit. It wasn't going to be plain sailing.

I picked up the phone and dialled Barrow's direct line straight away and he was there and he was prepared to talk to me. There was nothing about the deal, as he'd promised I told him.

"No, no, you misunderstand, we've got a deal, that's going to rest in place."

"What, over three years?"

"Well yes," oh fuck.

"But you told me the other day that you knew it would be expensive to sack me and that you were prepared to pay,"

"Yes and I am. Look mate, I think it's something you should talk to your lawyers about." Mate? The miserable, dishonest twat tried to buy me off by calling me mate. Like I was supposed to react well to that. Like I couldn't see through the transparency of his false counsel. How did he have the nerve to say something like that? The cunt had fucked me and I'd bought the sucker punch. No wonder I was his mate.

There was a terrible paradox to using lawyers to resolve disputes. Even with two unreasonable parties like me and Barrow, if we honestly assessed the value of our claim and our liability we would arrive at a similar figure and be able to make a bargain. He owed me about £400,000 and I would have taken £250,000 and he would have been happy to pay it. The deal could be done in about thirty seconds. But lawyers first tell their clients to be cautious in case they made any accidental mistakes that only another lawyer would know was a mistake. Once the communication is limited to the lawyers you're in a proper dispute and when that happens each side squeezes the case. Nobody takes a reasonable view anymore and an unreasonable demand is met with an unreasonable general denial of everything. Three years later the judge imposes a reasonable solution on the parties. The one that they could have made without the lawyers at the beginning. It often happens at the door of the court. Each side suddenly realises that they're going to get their arses kicked for being ridiculously obstinate for three years and make a deal. Just like they should have done right at the beginning. That's why they're always trying to reform the law. They've got no chance. Not while lawyers are still greedy, ambitious, middle class wankers who can be bothered to argue the toss they won't.

I was given the first opening in the diary which meant I had a meeting set up for ten days hence. Caroline softened her position slightly and gave me the ten days to prepare and to make a good job of getting my money. And I didn't make a bad job of it, although I regretted not emailing all the important documents home on my last day in the office, instead of being all clever about packing up my bags in advance of my sacking. That meant that I had a few holes in my story but I was basically prepared.

Unfortunately for me I had City lawyers. I used them when I was flush when I first struck the deal and now I was sorted of wedded to them for anything relating to it. That meant that I paid big prices for everything. Suddenly I realised what an act of capricious excess it was. The other thing that I regretted about this firm was that their offices were about four hundred yards from Martins Fleet and I could easily cross paths with one of the enemy on the way there. I put a suit on for the first time in a few weeks and set off on my old walk to work.

It was always a strange sensation walking into a lawyers office for me. I had trained as one and it would have taken but a simple twist of fate for me to have been someone working in an office like that. And until recently they had been my clients so I was used to being there but I was also used to being treated like a bog brush salesman. That wasn't entirely unfair either when you looked at all the people in sales careers selling products to lawyers. Yet there I was, their client, the man who paid their fees, a businessman. The irony being that I had been sacked from one of the worst jobs it was possible to find, I was unemployed and I didn't have a single skill in the world with which to find another job. I had to play the businessman role a little longer not for the good it did my ego, I was thoroughly ashamed of my wafer veneer of respectability, but for my interest in getting my money out of Barrow without any delay. If the dispute dragged and I didn't get the money I wouldn't be able to meet the lawyers fees. So right from the outset it became a game of brinkmanship about how well to do I was. I had to act sufficiently cool about money in general and play out the role of how successful, at least financially, I'd been whilst giving the whole process a touch of urgency. I was terrified of getting dragged into a proper dispute with proceedings and general delay but at the same time I had to be prepared to take a reasonable fight to them. It's fair to say I was nervous and unsure of my ground as I sat there waiting.

I was collected by a well turned out young man in his middle twenties. Once upon a time clerks would have been ten years younger. I was thinking that to myself as I was shown into the ground floor meeting room. What a nation of pussies we had become.

The lawyer was the usual one I dealt with, he was about my age, a junior partner. Unusually for me I wasn't at all envious of him. I never was with lawyers. If anything I felt sorry for them. They were all part of the City phenomenon it was true but they were the least glamorous part of it by miles. Some of them, like Simon, my corporate man, made up for it by having a brightly coloured lining in his suits. Others made a point of snatching up the best looking chocolate biscuit with a reckless abandon as if they did crazy things like that all the time. Franck and I had a pretty reliable league table of law firms based on their biscuits and I was ashamed to say that mine had those horrible sweet creamy ones that came in variety packs from Marks & Spencer where the star attraction was wrapped in gold foil. Simon was stuffing an entire one of those into his mouth as I explained my predicament. The sad thing for people like Simon was that they bought into a system that never had a pay off. Right from the beginning as an articled clerk they start working twelve to fourteen hours a day and weekends. They don't say no then because they want to be kept on, then they keep on doing it because they want to move from Associate to Junior Partner and get the good clients with whom they can make their name, then they work their way up the partnership, then when they're higher up the partnership they're playing with their own money and they don't want to jeopardise everything they've worked for and then it's time to cash their chips and they realise that life has passed them by. Maybe it doesn't feel like that to them but it definitely looked a lot like that from the outside looking in.

Immediately Simon decided that we needed his equivalent in employment law to come in, which meant that the meter was immediately running twice as fast. He told me that he hadn't re-read the agreement in advance of the meeting in case that was a waste of costs for me. It really meant he hadn't been bothered. As a consequence we weren't going to achieve much, he told me. That would be another meeting another day that I'd be paying for. He did tell me that, off the cuff, and he would revisit the agreement before saying for certain, his instinct was that Julian was right, there was nothing in the agreement to compel him to pay me otherwise than in the schedule agreed, i.e. over three years.

We talked around the possibilities using that premise as an assumption and it seemed that apart from demanding a bonus payment that I had been denied earning by my dismissal the only pressure I could bring to bear on them was by bringing an unfair dismissal claim. That meant a dispute and time and bills and I was reluctant but I didn't say so. It amazed me the way the law worked. Martins Fleet wanted me out and I was delighted to agree and yet I still had a solid unfair dismissal case. Whereas Barrow lied by implying he was going to pay up straight away and there was nothing I could do about that.

They told me that they would talk to each other, so that I was running up bills while they ate chocolate biscuits when I wasn't there, and that they would give me a call to come back for another meeting when they had done that. I thanked them for their time, which I had paid for, reflected that we could have achieved exactly the same outcome with a thirty second phone call and set off to go home.

There was a commotion outside on the steps as I went out. High pitched shouting and I noticed a policeman too. It felt like it had something to do with me somehow but I didn't see how it could. I carried on down the steps and turned left to set off towards home.

"I won't ask you again," it was a voice behind me and I was sure it was directed at me. I turned round and the policeman was shouting angrily at me.

"Come here now. You," he said pointing at my face. The street was busy and people were slowing down to look.

"What do you want?" I wanted to be angry but I was a bit worried and I couldn't get the right words out.

"These boys," and he gestured with his head to his left to two grinning ten year olds, "have got a serious complaint against you."

It had been them that had been making most of the noise and I realised then that they had been shouting something like, "that's him, that's him," amongst other things.

"Yes?"

"I'm going to have to ask you to come to the station with me to talk about it."

"It's a joke right?"

"It would be better if you just came with me."

"Well I'm not. I've got nothing to explain to anyone. I don't know who these boys are," but as I said it I realised I did. It was the two boys that I had stopped trying to break a milk bottle on the day I'd ran down the street like a horse.

"I am prepared to put you under arrest here and now if I have to."

"Fair enough," I said, "take me away."

As we made our way to the police station I thought of all the people I knew that might have passed by unnoticed and witnessed the incident. I thought that the scene perhaps more resembled my helping the policeman in a citizenly way than actually being arrested. To add an air of verisimilitude I thought that I should engage the policeman in conversation on the route but I couldn't really think of any small talk that might be appropriate to say to him. You can hardly ask them if business is brisk when you're being taken in for questioning. In the end I settled on asking him where the police station was exactly and I could tell in the way he responded that I shouldn't say anything else.

I used the time to reflect on the incident itself and how best to explain it. It had been innocent enough on my part but I was conscious of using the right words to describe it. It could easily sound much worse than it was if I wasn't careful.

I was handed over to two new people for questioning, one of whom seemed quite senior to me. They asked me if I knew the two boys and I said I did, which got proceedings off on the wrong foot since they reminded me that five minutes earlier I had denied knowing who they were to their colleague. It made it look like I knew I'd done something wrong and I was in general denial, which went right against my strategy of being as constructive, open and honest as possible and trying to appeal to them as reasonable people. If only I'd been more like my father I could have just told them that I was a reasonable person and that would have been it. Job done.

Once I'd admitted knowing them I was asked to repeat the story of the broken milk bottle and my good citizen behaviour. The evidence in chief always sounds convincing and I was pleased with my account. So much so that I ended with, "that's all there is to it. Can I go now please?"

"All there is to it?" the senior looking one said.

"Yeah."

"I don't call a fractured skull, a broken arm and four weeks in hospital, all there is to it," he said.

"I call it nothing to do with me," I said and raised myself up out of the seat.

First he yelled, "sit down," at me with such ferocity that I was sitting before he reached the n of down, then he said, "listen to the fucking brave child batterer. How'd you like it if I did that to you? You wouldn't be so fucking smug then would you?"

I didn't think that policemen were allowed to talk like that anymore and it made me frightened. I knew that I should shut up shop and ask for my solicitors but I was too embarrassed for them to see that I was accused of something like this. So instead I just sat there and went through the questioning. I didn't make a good job of it either, in fact I became so morose at my predicament that I could hardly speak at all. It all added up to coming over as someone who's been rumbled and knows it. I simply mumbled a few general denials and that was as convincing as I could manage.

In the end they told me that they were minded to charge me but that they would let me know within a day or so. And the senior one told me that I was lucky that I hadn't been charged there and then and put on bail. Being a cunt I thanked them for that.

It wasn't that I didn't want to tell Caroline, it's just that she was so frustrated with me over the minimal progress I'd made with the lawyers that the timing was never quite right. And she was so furious at the contemplation of unfair dismissal proceedings that I daren't add another woe to the pile. There was also something about my demeanour that infuriated her. Apparently if I had such a transparent lack of willingness for a fight it was no wonder that everyone walked all over me all the time. I just couldn't bring myself to tell her the real reason for my new depression.

Two weeks later when I was asked to attend my next meeting at the lawyers I still hadn't told her. There was something about having not told her straight away that meant telling her later looked dishonest, or at least like I had something to hide. Also I had another problem, I didn't have any spare money to pay for new lawyers secretly on my own, so I decided to seek some representation from the lawyers I was using and get all the fees put on the one bill.

This time it was just a meeting with Mike Bennet the employment lawyer, I'd already been dropped by Simon who merely sent word that they were entitled to rely on the three year payment scheme and there was no real way round it. Being downgraded from a corporate matter to a personnel case like that was humiliating. I was no longer the businessman client, just another loser that got sacked.

"So that means we have two things to discuss," said Mike, "let's start with the unfair dismissal."

I told him that I didn't really have the stomach for litigation and he 'knew what I meant,' he said, but he did tell me that it was the only means to exert real pressure on them. And apparently I had a good case. The pressure exerted was supposed to make them start negotiating about how much of the next three years payments they were prepared to pay now to get rid of me once and for all. Then we had to make a case for being denied my right to make a bonus, which was like pissing in the wind as far as I was concerned but Mike told me it was all pressure that would help our case.

I was to go away and come up with my side of the story and send it to him from which he would produce a strong letter to send to Martins Fleet to get the whole thing going.

".. but think about it carefully," he counselled me, "I don't want to threaten unfair dismissal proceedings if we aren't going to go through with them."

I thanked him, although I had already translated those next two stages into a least another month's delay, then I asked him if I could have a word with someone who could help me with a little criminal matter. In the same way that certain people know how to say, "it's a little misunderstanding," and sound quite convincing about it, I sounded like I had something to hide and that I'd been up to no good. He'd find out soon enough by asking his colleague what I'd said but I didn't have the nerve to tell him to his face.

I spent the next few weeks getting my case together and by then it had become my full time occupation and it was recognised as that by Caroline as well as me. I also spent a lot of the time worrying about my court case which I didn't share with Caroline. I knew that I hadn't done anything wrong but I didn't seem to have the means to prove it. I comforted myself with the thought that in cases like that the CPS often dropped them for lack of evidence. That and a good lawyer behind me made me feel better occasionally but in truth those confident moments really only punctuated long periods of utter despair.

After sending in my thoughts to Mike Bennet, I had to give him time to put his letter together. A week later I'd heard nothing and I was about to call him when I received a message from him. It was only to check a part of my story which meant that he had only just picked up the file. That went on over a period of about two weeks while he got my case together, then he produced the letter, which wasn't half bad. He was much better at writing than speaking.

I was impatient for a response and I started ringing to find out a week later. I needn't have bothered, time was on their side and they strung me out. Eventually the response came a month after our letter and I was summoned to the office to go through it. I thought it was significant that I didn't get any highlights over the phone.

"It's pretty serious," Mike told me as I was sitting down. He sucked in his lips tight to his teeth to pause before reading so that I would know that something bad was coming.

In the way that only lawyers can, the points against me were neatly lined up under particular headings and in doing it that way it never sounded quite as bad as it could have done, say if someone was just putting the boot in, in general. Under the unfairly denied bonus point, they asked me for an explanation of the Social-Lites project and why I had spent £10,000 of unauthorised budget and I was to respond to the point that I had deliberately not cooperated at any level during the last six months of my employment, that would also be relevant to the unfair dismissal point Mike said. Then there was a heading of gross breach of contract and I was asked to confirm that I sold a company asset for personal profit, to whit, a car, which was followed by the most serious allegation, Mike said. He paused again before telling me that they were prepared to make a case of sexual harassment against me.

"Who am I supposed to have harassed?" I was indignant and immediate but the effect was lost when Mike said, "it's more than one person," actually.

"They allege," he said, clearing his throat, "that you have an aggressive, bullying and uncooperative approach to all female colleagues,"

"What?"

"but specifically they mention two cases, one against a Sophie Chawdray, who you were supposed to have humiliated in an open plan office in front of her colleagues, then showed prejudicial behaviour towards her because she complained about the behaviour,"

I was starting to say, "that's absolute bullshit," but he talked over me and told me that the second specific case would be brought by Stacey Arnold for intimidating and bullying behaviour.

"That is definitely not true," I said, as if what had gone before perhaps was, but as I did Mike put in front of me the email that I had written to Stacey Arnold, where I'd written PISS OFF NOW on the bottom of it.

I told him that I wrote it but I didn't think I sent it and he just shrugged as if to say that I probably did and I'd just forgotten.

Oh crumbs.

Mike said that it would be better if I took a copy of the letter away with me and had a good think about the allegations and what my response might be to them and perhaps, he added, have a proper think about the case altogether, because he had to tell me, that it might be expensive to continue to fight them.

"I'll walk out with you I'm on the way to a meeting," he said.

But I had to refuse because I was going to get an update on my other legal problem. Just in case he forget that I was subject to criminal proceedings too.

The bad news was that the CPS were not dropping the case and I now had a date for the trial. Trial? Suddenly the gravity of my predicament hit me. That word sounded so serious, so much the last recourse against wrongdoers when all else has failed. They are put on trail. We are put on trial. I was going to stand trial. The good news was that the hospital still had not responded with the necessary reports which meant that it wasn't proven that my assault was directly linked in time to the boy's severe injuries. How fantastic. I managed to restrain myself from doing a lap of honour round the meeting room. She reminded me about the need to produce a good convincing character witness and told me that she would call whenever there was any news.

I went full time into coming up with convincing answers to the allegations. The car and the Social-Lites points were actually true. I should have been banged to rights on them but I found it pretty easy to come up with credible and reasonably irrefutable responses. True they were only "my word against theirs," type of responses but I could lie as well as them, all I had to do was stick to my guns. For the car I pretended that I thought that it was part of the deal and that Barrow had confirmed that to me in a meeting one day. As for Social-Lites I just stuck to the story that it was a genuine opportunity. They would have to go into some detail with European Match Co. to find out that it wasn't and I didn't think that they'd do that. I found most difficulty in finding something to say about the sexual harassment cases. Neither were true but when something isn't true there aren't any other supporting facts on which to build a response because the event didn't happen. All I could do was come up with general denials that didn't even convince me when I wrote them.

The hardest part though was Caroline, she had given up on any chance of getting any money out of the deal and was terrified that I would actually end up owing more money than we could afford pursuing fruitless court cases. She practically begged me to give the job up but I couldn't without having one more crack. I was sure that Martins Fleet were just trying to frighten me off as a tactic and that I had to stand firm. Her point was, that if I just let it lie, they wouldn't be goaded into responding and in time I'd get my money. It wasn't ideal to wait she said, but it was better than nothing at this stage. I already knew that it was too late for that. They knew about the car now and if I didn't respond they'd pursue that to its natural end and get out of the deal altogether. I couldn't tell her that though. The court case was in six weeks too and I still couldn't find the words to tell her about that either.

The next meeting with Mike was a hard one. I felt like he was more on their side than mine but I suppose he had to check the robustness of my responses. Eventually I satisfied him, with a few re-writes about the sort of response I wanted to give. He said that taking a fight to them like that was a serious matter and I had to be prepared to go all the way through with it. I assured him that I was. It was also a question of having the funds to do it too, he told me.

"Yes," I said, "no problem."

"Hector," he said, "this is a slightly sensitive issue but I must raise it."

"Yes, yes, go ahead."

"It's not just a matter of you assuring me that you have the funds. I've got to ask you to settle our bill to date and to make a payment on account to underwrite the litigation fees to support the litigation that we are going to say that we are prepared to enter into."

"That's fine," I said, trying to be nonchalant.

"You should know," he said, pushing an envelope across the table, "the bill's for about £10,000 and we're asking for £15,000 on account."

I had based my plans on paying the lawyers out of the settlement when it came and I had never contemplated having to come up with money ourselves. I just didn't know what to do, I was terrified of the situation I'd got myself into and absolutely terrified about telling Caroline the bad news. I couldn't just go bad on the debt because I still had the criminal case hanging over me and I needed them to see me through that. I was fucked.

I spent the next week not sleeping, hardly eating, just wracking my brains night and day to find a way out. I couldn't afford to go back to the lawyers but I couldn't blow them out completely, I couldn't tell Caroline because all that she had laid down as conditions before I started had been breached and we just didn't have a spare £10,000 knocking about in the current account. I didn't want to contact Martins Fleet directly myself because that would show them that they had me on the ropes. I didn't have a job and so I wouldn't be able to get a loan. I really didn't know where to turn. At one stage I sneaked a couple of hundred out of the bank, even though I'd been placed on a strict budget by Caroline and tried to find a little accumulator to come up with the cash but it lasted about as far as the second furlong of the first leg.

That sunny early September day as I trudged home, slouching in my track suit trousers, unshaven and unkempt, I realised that I'd become something that I'd always been terrified of becoming. I'd been there before but I felt shocked to the core. From having a reasonably prosperous life I'd quickly put myself beyond the safety net. Where was there to go from here? One thing was for certain, the deal was probably lost anyway but definitely would be if I left it to whither. I decided to pick up the phone to Barrow and get to the bottom of it once and for all. My only option I decided was to try and make a deal with him, get enough money to pay off the lawyers and get on with my life before I fell any further.

He was more open to discussion than I thought he would be. For a time I would say that he was reasonably constructive but it boiled down to a couple of points where he said one thing and I said another. I knew where he was lying and he knew where I was doing the same but we both said that we were prepared to stick by our respective versions of the lie, there was nobody else who could gainsay either of us. It came to the end and he just said, "I'll tell you frankly Hector, I'm not paying and I have no intention of paying you anything under the agreement."

Like an idiot I said, "what if I drop the unfair dismissal case?" and he just laughed. He knew I'd fired all my ammo. I felt too ridiculous to tell him that he was a dishonourable miserable cunt, I just hung up the phone. I didn't cry I just froze, like a statue, for about an hour.

54.

As summer turned to Autumn it was time to talk. I hadn't worked for several months and I had lost the major contribution I was supposed to make to our family finances and with that I'd lost an additional £10,000 cash which we didn't have. True I'd received about six months pay and I was still within the terms of that. I'd actually lived largely frugally during the summer but that didn't make for any better a home life. We hadn't taken a holiday and we'd essentially spent a glorious summer in our Islington flat. It was about three weeks to my trial and I still hadn't told her about it.

I knew that Caroline merited more than the life I gave her. She had merited more than the life I gave her when I worked and earned plenty of money, she definitely didn't deserve the situation that I'd dragged her down to now. For me I was waking up out of a dream. I had to get realistic about my life, make the best out of what I had and try and extract some joy out of my existence. I had decided that I would get a job, regardless of what it was and if I was good at it and enjoyed it I would rise up the ladder fast enough. If I didn't I would change it. I also decided to own up to my lawyers. I would ring them and tell them to drop everything. I would tell them that I could only pay out of a settlement and that I would have to owe it til then or make an arrangement with them when I got a new job. As for the deal, I would cling to the vestige of hope that with time they'd forget about me and without further action on either side I still might just qualify for the payments.

But whatever I did I decided I would put my heart and soul into it and be happy to be earning a living and be thankful that someone was happy to employ me. More importantly than ever I would work hard and play hard I told myself. I would devote myself to having a happy home life with Caroline. I knew now that was my only salvation.

The day she asked me to talk to her I'd been though all the broadsheets and the Evening Standard and I'd organised about half a dozen or so job interviews. Mostly they were only temp jobs but that didn't bother me. Not even for law firms where I used to send people to work for me as temps. I'd lost too much through being proud. Those days were over.

Caroline told me she had become very unhappy at the rut she saw us in. I agreed but she shushed me when I started to talk. "You see, Hector," she said, "I don't think you'll ever find what you're looking for. And I don't know if I can wait with you anymore," I tried to say something but she shushed me again. She had it all worked out. I'd done nothing since I'd lost my job she told me. It wouldn't have mattered what I'd have done, whether it was well paid or not, she would have supported me. But she couldn't support me moping around feeling sorry for myself. There was a life going on, she told me, which was just going to pass me by if I didn't do something about it soon. Just get out there and do something, she told me, I was talented but I let it all go to waste in my bitterness.

I kept trying to but in and tell her that I agreed and that I'd come round to the same conclusion and that I'd turned over a new leaf as of today, but either the words didn't come out or they sounded too much like they'd been made up to appease her on the spot. The only words that I actually managed to say were:

"I bought the Guardian today,"

"It's too late Hector. It's too late for us."

When we examined the bare facts we didn't produce enough income to cover the mortgage. We decided, well she told me, we had to sell up, pay off the credit cards, pay my legal fees and divide the small spoils between us if there were spoils to share. It was a newly built flat with lots of problems and we'd be lucky to break even after expenses.

"Maybe not," I said, "because the legal fees are £10,000."

"Jesus Christ Hector you fucking arsehole," she had a point.

But that was only the prologue because then she said: "then we should spend some time apart."

She'd been hinting that that was what was coming but it still stung when it did. Rejection. There's no clearer judgment. I agreed with her that it was the right thing for her to do. She started crying then and we didn't really say anymore. I comforted her and I told her I'd be out by the weekend so that she could get on and sell the place.

55.

Secretly I was quite pleased to be single. There was something about living in a private snug little burrow that had always appealed to me. I was answerable to no-one now and those things that to me were sacred and a precious part of the life I really craved, could be indulged in 100% of the time without any worries about letting down somebody else. I could read every racing paper and watch every race and re-run and analyse every race over and over. My little rented flat would be a study devoted to the science of horse racing. When I didn't work I would go to the races. I had to see some good out of what I had been through and for me that would be to realise a life long ambition of turning myself into a racing pro. I even liked the idea of having a rubbish little office job. One with no ambitions and no future just one that was well within my capabilities that I turned up and did everyday then went home again. It didn't matter if it wasn't really well paid, in fact it would be better if it wasn't because then there would be no distractions and hard choices. I would have a simple, enjoyable and fulfilled life.

With two weeks to go to my trial I found a job. It wasn't exactly a job, in that it didn't have a contract or any guaranteed hours of work but it was a job in that I turned up, did something, received £9.00 per hour for doing it and went home again. I was paid cash in a pay roll envelope each Friday lunch time. Officially I was supposed to ring in each morning before I went in to make sure that there was something for me to do but the way it worked was that there tended to be a little bit left the next day from the day before so it was always assumed that I would have to come back.

I was only a clerk in a law firm somewhere I used to send clerks to work for me. I'd spent a large part of my marketing money on recruitment departments for law firms, lunching them and buttering them up and acting like a big shot and it should have been a slightly shameful experience to turn up and ask for a job. It's not that it wasn't exactly, it was definitely chastening but after the initial shame of the application and the interview I found I could handle it well by keeping my head down and clerking away.

The hardest part really was fighting off the competition from the first jobbers that were my new colleagues. I worked with people that had been to average universities, not managed to find careers in the top class firms and were CV building by clerking for them instead. Secretly they hoped they would get noticed and get in the back door. It was awful working with them because they were nakedly ambitious and didn't have an ounce of cooperation in them. They seemed to think that they occupied a morally superior position for being like that too. At least when I was their age and those things became fashionable for the first time people were slightly ashamed to behave that way, or else it was obvious they were acting. One of my colleagues actually said to me, "firms like this are looking for ruthless ambition it's well known."

I tried to put myself out as the older wiser man who'd been round the block a few times but because of my stupid young face they thought I was one of them, just a slightly bigger loser than them. The girl that told me about ruthless ambition had been to Loughborough which she thought was significant, I must admit she didn't much look like an athlete to me and I was trying to tell her that the only way to do the job properly that we'd been given was to do it in a certain order. It so happened that we had to do the part I was charged with first and if she helped me with that I would help her with her part afterwards. She said to me, "do you think I'm stupid Hector? I'm not sharing any of my work with you." As soon as she'd finished the partner came into our document room and she said, "if you really can't manage I suppose I could help you out for an hour or so, I can go home later tonight." So despite it being my idea I said, "I'm not saying that. I'd prefer it if we both stick to what we're doing."

"You're being ridiculous," she said, which made the partner take an interest, "getting very heated in here," she said. Then she had a look at the little project we were doing and she decided that it would be best if we adopted an approach where we shared the work and did it in the right order rather than each do our own little project.

"Come on, open up a little bit, don't you want to go home early?" my little colleague said, "you're usually the first out on the dot of five."

I didn't say anything. I was like the injured animal that everyone keeps on kicking because it's too weak to respond.

That was the worst of the job really. Keeping it. There wasn't enough work to go round all of us, and work kept running out and starting again as cases and projects came and went. That's why I didn't take time off and why I managed my little bits and pieces to straddle days into the next morning. And it was why, where possible, I tried to work on my own so that I wasn't thrown into open competition with the new bucks.

With a week to go to my case I still hadn't come up with a good character witness. It was so late in the day that I had to ask Caroline really. She was estranged from me so I figured that her views about me would be considered reasonably objective. Not that I had anyone else to call on.

It was a fault of mine that I all too readily recognised that I was too open and too friendly and too eager to please, I always let everyone get the better of me because I was unable to imagine the worst of them. I always said yes, yet for all of my being like that, I didn't have a single person to ask to be a character witness for me. At first people seemed to like me. I gathered friends, but yet as I left each period of history behind me I didn't leave any one person on terms that I could go back to them. Friends, employers, teachers and now a wife.

I was just going to have to appeal to a higher sense of honour in her to do the right thing. It would take some preparing and I thought that I would build up to the phone call after I'd prepared, cooked, ate and cleaned up after, dinner. I was supposed to go to the launderette too but that would have to wait until another day.

It was like that living alone. It wasn't quite the haven I imagined where all your leisure hours free to be squandered on personal indulgences. Just making meals eating them and washing up accounted for hours, let alone the shopping and ironing and in my straightened circumstances I found myself going to the launderette, something I hadn't done since I was about nineteen. A phone call or a night in the pub spent a whole evening and then you were behind with the weekly rotor. The idea of reading newspapers and watching racing videos was absurdly ambitious.

I'd never been great at getting up and the routine of the night before made it especially difficult so I always woke up tired and behind the clock. I had but one thing to do and that was to hang on to my job, so little luxuries like setting the video, or washing up last night's dinner went by the board and waited for me to get in the next night. My slender grasp on employment also meant that I couldn't refuse any reasonable request to work late either. Not that we were paid overtime rates for it. The young bucks were quite pleased to accept neo-slavery if it helped them on the road to their career goal. We didn't exactly have a collective negotiating voice.

So I gave up one night as the trial approached to persuade Caroline to be a witness for me. It didn't start very well, especially giving her a week's notice when I'd known for a while longer. But she did have genuine sympathy for me. She was the only person besides me who knew that I just wasn't capable of assaulting children and fracturing their skull, however mad I was.

I didn't tell any of my colleagues that I was going to have to take the day off work the following Thursday for fear of the damage that would do to my long term prospects. And I was only planning on telling the recruitment birds on the day before so that they couldn't line up a replacement for me. If I did that and had a nice bit of work that wasn't quite finished all would be well.

On the Wednesday the day before my big day, the main girl that I dealt with came down into the office and said to me, "Hector, you're a barrister aren't you?"

"Yes," I told her, "by training anyway," I said.

"Good," she said, "I was wondering if you'd like to go down to court for us to take a note of evidence.

That was fantastic, just what I wanted, something that marked me out as bit higher quality than the rest and assured my position for a little bit longer. I saw the look of jealousy in my savage young colleagues' faces and I was even more delighted. I also knew how long a criminal case could go when it got going.

"I'd be delighted, what's it all about?"

She told me that she'd send me to the partner for a full debrief but that we perhaps had an interest in a civil matter on behalf of another client depending on what came out in evidence and I was to take a discrete note of evidence at the back of the court.

"Great, when does it all start?"

"Tomorrow." Shit.

"I can't," I said, "I need to take a day off tomorrow."

"And when were you planning to tell me about that Hector?"

"On the way home tonight," I said with my head hung. I'd made myself look ridiculous into the bargain. Normally that would have been alright, in fact there was a good chance that she wouldn't have noticed my absence at all, but circumstances had fallen so that it was one of those days when she was doing her job all thoroughly and correct. My ruthlessly ambitious colleague ended up with the job.

I was simply too unhappy to prepare myself on the night before the trial. During the week I had let the unwashed dishes build up to such an extent that my micro-kitchen space couldn't take them any more so I had transferred them to the bath to do one big wash. I did go into the bathroom at one stage to look at them but I couldn't bring myself to do it. I went to bed early and told myself I would attack the job with a bit more gusto in the morning.

The trial was to start at 10.30 a.m. and I got up too late to be able to wash the dishes before I went. I made do with a swill and I used the little time I had left to iron a shirt. The pile of semi-dried washing on the bottom of the bed failed to yield the shirt I was banking on so I revived the previous day's with the iron and set off to face my fate.

I should have been terrified. Either that or furious at the prospect of being labelled a criminal when I hadn't done anything. I walked every step of the journey in slow motion all the way to Southwark Court and thought about precisely nothing for the entire time it took me.

"Good news," the lawyer said, "they're withdrawing."

"What?"

"There's no case Hector, you're free to go."

"And that's supposed to be good is it?"

"Well, yes."

"I'm not sure I agree," I said.

Then standing next to me I noticed the ruthlessly ambitious young buck from work.

"What was I doing here?" She wanted to know, "it was her that had been selected to do the job not me."

I just said, "fuck off you poisonous little cunt."

Then my lawyer said, "I think I'd better go."

I started to walk towards the exit myself but stopped when I saw Caroline walking towards me. She had a bloke with her.

"Hector, Hector, where are you going?"

"It's off, it's not going ahead."

"So you were just going to wander off without waiting for me were you?"

"Yes, no, sorry. I've just heard the news."

"Right," she sounded annoyed.

"I'm sorry. Thank you, I appreciate it. Just a pity you didn't get the opportunity to tell everyone what you thought of me."

"You might not realise it Hector but it has been extremely stressful and upsetting preparing for today."

Then the bloke with her said, "I'm quite glad it's all over for us actually."

"Yes you must feel very relieved," I said. Then I said, "thanks I'll see you," and I started to walk off on my way home.

"Hector," she said all indignant.

I turned round, "yes?"

"Hector, God what are you like?"

I didn't know what she meant so I just carried on walking. Then she came trotting after me tugging on my sleeve.

"Aren't you going to say anything?"

"I have. Thanks."

"No that's not what I'm talking about and you know it."

"Isn't it?"

"God Hector, I brought Alistair with me because I need support too."

"Definitely non-sequitor," I thought. "Well done," I said, "what does he want a bone?"

"Well at least if you're insulting him it shows you're a little bit bothered."

She was upset with me because I hadn't been upset when I saw her with another man.

"I don't give a flying fuck. Thanks for coming. Best of luck with your new man I hope he turns out better than the old model."

"Oh god Hector, you're so frustrating. You might at least act like you loved me once."

"I did," I said.

By then she was crying and Alistair was at her side.

"She came here to help you," he said, "and this is the thanks she gets?"

Then he started comforting her and telling her it was all over and that soon I'd be gone for ever. I just kept walking.

56.

When I rang in to the office the following day they told me that there was little point in coming in just for a Friday. That gave me a nice long weekend to get right back on top of my game again. I got organised had a couple of early nights and I was ready to go full tilt at the job. Perhaps even try and work it up into a permanent position. I thought that should be my goal, to be achieved before Christmas. On the Monday they said that there wasn't much doing and to ring the next day instead and when I did they said it really was pretty quiet and to give it a couple of days. I didn't want to ring on the Thursday because that meant that they'd say there was no point in coming in for just one day and I wanted to keep my ammo dry and not waste another call on a rejection. I waited until Monday and they told me that they had all the personnel they needed for the week thanks. I did try again on the Friday but I knew by then I'd been dropped.

If only they'd been straight with me straight away I could have got something else sorted out. Instead I'd thrown two weeks away waiting for them to call me. Two weeks without money was significant to me now. Monday was the start of the new month, when my rent was due, that was £600 and I had £350 cash on me and absolutely nothing else and no access to anything else. Suddenly I was well and truly stuck and it had just sneaked up on me without my noticing. If I did nothing I was fucked anyway so I decided to have one last throw of the dice at Ascot on Saturday. There was a Group 1 Mile and a couple of other high quality races and I reasoned that if I kept my focus on them and did some real homework before Saturday I had a chance of pulling myself out of the mire.

By the time I was on the train I'd narrowed the races of interest down to two, the two Group 1's. One was the Miler's Championship and the other was the two year old fillies' mile, for what decided the championship in that division too. I loved the purity of those competitions. The races were framed so that the best horse had to win.

I was convinced about Gossamer for the fillies and I was just hoping that I might get 5/4, the only credible opposition to her was trained by a trainer out of form. The mile had to go to Noverre really, it had top class Group 1 form in the book and the others were nowhere near. I got talking to a fellow turfiste on the way and when I realised that he knew his stuff I wanted to check out my view of the form with him to confirm my opinions but, at the same time, I daren't because I knew a talked about bet will always lose. I knew that if I said that I was there to back two horses and what they were, that he wouldn't be going home later that day thinking that the bloke he'd met on the way up had been exactly right. Two out of two. It didn't happen. If I kept it to myself there was every chance that it would happen. We spent most of the time talking about the two year old colt's Group 2, for which I had done a lot of homework but dismissed as being too open an event altogether. He was actually very convincing about Tholijannah, which had been my view too but there were about four 4/1 joints and it wasn't the place to start looking for a life saving bet. We managed not to talk about the fillies race but couldn't help but touch on the mile. I managed to steer clear of saying that I was certain about the invincibility of Noverre and we had a conversation about his stable mate, the second string Summoner. It started by my telling him that it was a race that always through up an outsider. I knew because a few years earlier I had let go un-backed a 66/1 winner that I had given a chance to. Summoner should not be 33/1 I told him and he wasn't easily persuaded but told me I should have a decent saver on him if I thought like that. 33/1 imagine that. To have been able to have banked a 33/1 shot then would have turned everything round for me. A life changing bet. Breathing space and no pressure for a while. I deserved it I thought and I felt that my chance meeting with the stranger had pushed me towards the opportunity. If I had a good day with Gossamer and Noverre that would only yield a few hundred quid - enough to pay the rent and keep going for a while but that was it. Summoner would get me right out of the shit. I allowed myself to dream until the train clunked to a halt at Ascot. They're off.

I walked into the course with a betting bank of about £300. I loved Ascot. When I first went I in I always stood still and drank it all in. I'd been going to Ascot since I was about twelve years old. A great institution that was there before me and would be there after I'd gone. A place of stories and dreams and adventures. It was so much the essence of the life that I was supposed to have had.

I was stewing over the calculation which told me that a successful afternoon only allowed me to pay the rent and I didn't like it. I decided to vary the plan a little bit and have a little £20 on Tholijannah in the first. I liked it and my form student friend liked it. Twenty wasn't much but if it won I could stake higher on the next two and make something better out of the afternoon's work.

He ran really well but could never quite get to the horse that got an early lead on him. He beat the rest easily. The reading of the form was correct but the pace making 16/1 shot beat him. Close but not close enough.

Next it was Gossamer's race and that was what I was there for. I went into the ring and started looking for a price. Not only was there no 5/4 available there wasn't a trace of evens, she was 8/11 everywhere. I couldn't bet her at that price she wasn't any good to me. I stood and waited and hoped that the market went my way. In places I saw 6/4 on. A few minutes of waiting and I realised that she was solid at that price and I knew that I couldn't bet her. I thought I should keep my ammo dry for the next race, perhaps back the two horses I liked there rather than one at a bad price here. The ground was obviously soft judging by the result of the first race and the colts did seem to have difficulty in going through it. Perhaps Gossamer might not be able to show her real class in those conditions? Especially from the worst of the draw. The only other horse that had the class to win the race was drawn 1. She'd be able to pick the best ground under the trees if she wanted.

I went in £100 Half Glance at 5/2. Gossamer fucking murdered them.

I was shit or bust on Noverre by then. £150 win at 9/4. He ran really well. Gave a good beating to some good horses but he never quite pegged back his pacemaker, Summoner, who won at 33/1.

I drew my last £20 out of my pocket and had £10 each way My Lucy Locket in the last. I only really realised the idiocy of leaving myself without a single penny as the horses came into the last half of the race. It was OK though because she looked booked for a place and I'd get my money back. Even as they passed the post I'd have said that. But the replay revealed that a rag had come and short headed her out of third in the shadow of the post.

I walked out of the racecourse in a trance. All I had of any liquid value on me was my return train ticket. People were laughing and joking all around me. Some had won others had lost. None of them had precisely nothing in their pockets. Some were going back to their cars and driving home to their nice lives with their family, others were going to stop for a drink at the pub opposite the station, others were organising their nights out. Me, I just shuffled along, alone, silent in my only little, private, miserable world. The long walk down the path to the train station added poignancy. I'd known that road for so long now. I had memories of walking back down it after losing days and winning days. I remembered most those early days when I first came to Ascot, walking along the road with my parents, the beginning of another English summer, great races and great hopes before us. I knew then that Ascot would always be part of my life, as an older man I would come back here as a trainer or at least a big owner having made a fortune elsewhere. I would have a classic car and park in Car Park Number 7 which ran alongside the path from the station and have a champagne picnic out of the boot on the grass before racing started. It was just what was going to happen.

Today I needed Car Park Number 7 for a different reason. I received a short notice warning and went to do what I'd become so used to doing. It was quite well fenced and I made a bit of a job climbing into it. A noise in the distance told me that I'd drawn attention to myself doing it but I didn't bother. My needs were more pressing as I went off in search of a secluded spot. I didn't really find the ideal place but time was such that I had to make do with it. I was glad I did because the moment was suddenly a lot closer than I had realised. No spare twenties to clean up on today but I had kept my Racing Post and it seemed an appropriate gesture. I had reached that stage when suddenly I heard a violent sounding voice.

"Pull your fucking pants up now!"

I looked up and a policeman was approaching me at a fast march.

"What do you think you're doing?"

"Shitting."

"It may strike you as bizarre but round here we don't do that sort of thing in the open air."

It didn't actually but I didn't think it was worth trying to come up with some story about an embarrassing bodily problem I just said:

"You should try it, it's very liberating."

He said, "there's a pub less than two minutes walk away and a station after that, what the fuck's the matter with you?"

I should have tried to explain that I didn't really have that sort of time at my disposal and anyway I couldn't go into a pub with literally no money in case I was embarrassed into buying a drink for using the facilities or worse still having to pay to go in the toilet. Instead I just said, "have you seen the facilities in there?"

"Normally when people are caught in the act they show some contrition."

"Normally when I need to take a shit, I do."

"Come with me I'm taking you in."

So I went to another police station. After a bit of a dressing down, which I received in silence, I thought I was going to be let go but I wasn't. I was told to report to someone or other where I had to give all my personal details and empty my pockets while he made an inventory of what I had. They actually didn't believe that I didn't have any money and it took a little while to convince them how big a loser I really was. He said to me, "how would it be if your employers find about this?" And when I told him that I didn't have a job he said, "you're in a pretty sorry state aren't you?"

I didn't tell him that I had about one week's grace left on my flat too. I just gave him my address like I was a proper person.

Then they locked me up. I overheard one of them say something to the other as I was being lead away that implied they thought I was pissed. That meant I was being locked up to sober up and to teach me a lesson. I tried to go to sleep but the odour of urine was too harsh, even for me. Eventually they opened the cell and gave me my few pathetic possessions back at about midnight.

"You're free to go," he told me and when I asked he confirmed that there was no chance of a lift back to London. As the only asset I owned was a now out of date return ticket and the last train had long since gone I started walking.

I arrived back at my flat at 8.00 a.m. I slept for most of the rest of Sunday 30th September. On Monday morning I packed a couple of bags and prepared for the rest of my life.

57.

Three Saturdays later I woke up on the benches at the corner of Farringdon Road and Rosebery Avenue, it was a beautiful Autumn day and I'd been glad of the balmy night. I was dressed reasonably well for the weather. Warm and rain proof. It was the day after I collected my giro and about that time of year that the National Hunt programme got going again. I thought if I could spare a little of the giro cheque on trying to find a small double that would kick me off on the route towards a deposit on a flat and put me on the way again.

I refused a swig of larger from one of the lads for breakfast and set off for Islington High Street. As I made my way along it towards Upper Street I saw a familiar shape in the distance. As it drew near I realised that I was walking towards Caroline. I was slightly ashamed of my dishevelled appearance and I didn't want her to see me. I had a go at not recognising her and sliding past unnoticed but it didn't work. Just as I reached the opposite kerb she arrived, I'd tried so hard to time my crossing to be syncopated with hers that I couldn't have contrived a perfectly coincidental meeting any better.

"Hector," she said, "I didn't expect to see you today. "I'll see you in there," she said to her friends who went ahead into the Dome. I could see that she noticed how dirty I was but I told myself that I often looked like that when I lived with her and she wouldn't think anything abnormal about it.

She felt awkward I could see and she was searching for something to say that was a little more than small talk but nothing happened. She was the only person I knew well enough to ask so I thought I'd skip the small talk and go straight to a question that had been on my mind for the last few days.

"Am I living in hell?" I asked.

"Hector," she said, "we're all living in hell but some of us are good enough not to say anything about it."

I wasn't going to let her have the last word like that so I didn't respond and just carried on towards the bookies. I turned to look back at her after about twenty yards. She wasn't looking but I shouted anyway:

"Viva Las Vegas." It drew some strange looks but I was used to that by then.